I0822324

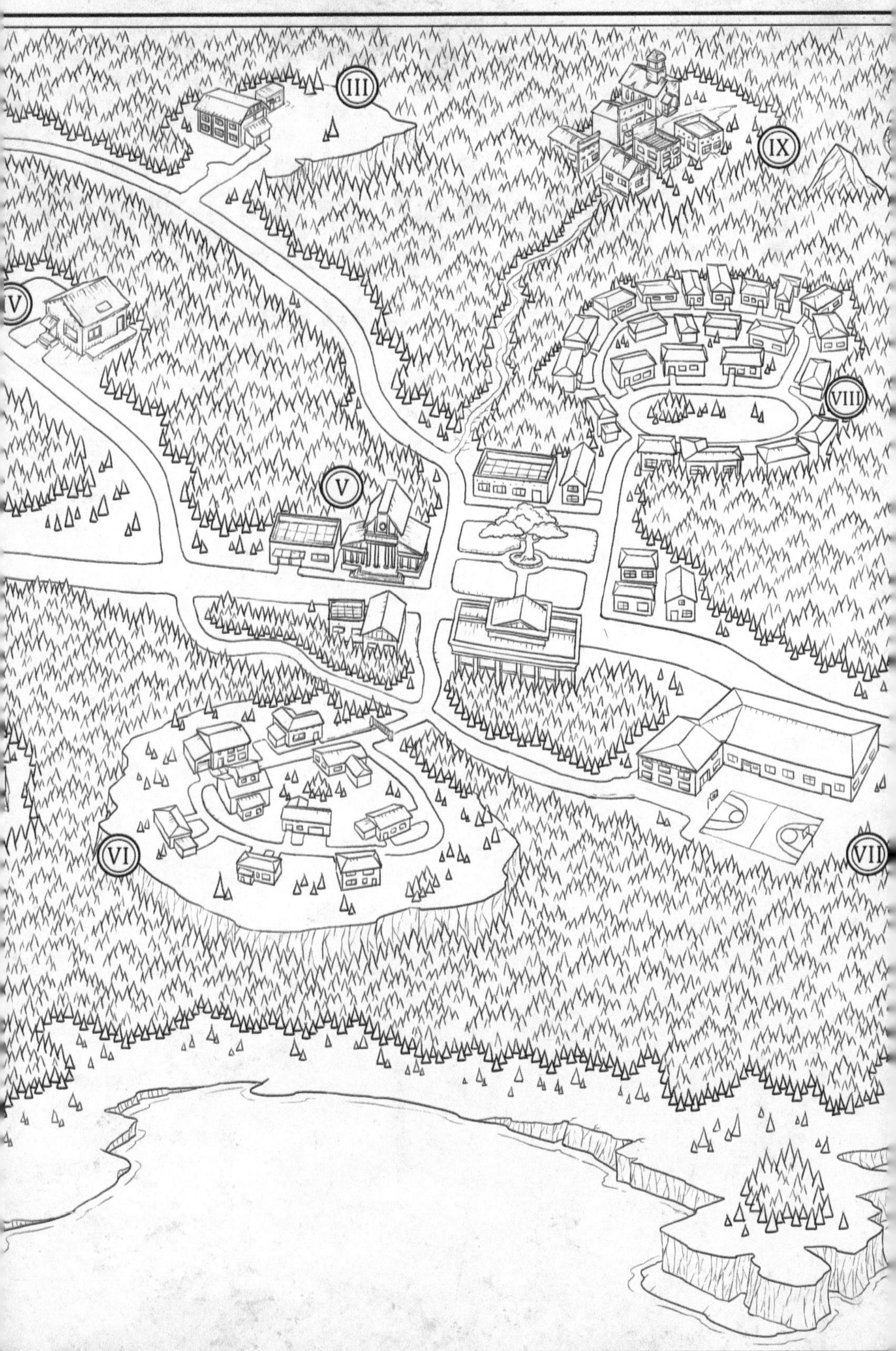
III
IX
IV
VIII
V
VI
VII

Wonderland

DREAMS OF NIGHTMARES

Immersed in the eerie tendrils of horror since 1997, courtesy of a haunting childhood encounter, Shamoot Kishore set forth on an enduring journey fueled by an unyielding fascination with the ominous. This sinister initiation marked the genesis of a captivating exploration, spanning the realms of films, shorts, poems, and novels.

Wonderland stands as a testament to SK's unparalleled passion for crafting stories that immerse readers in their darkest fears. Thriving on pushing the boundaries of horror, SK invites readers into a world where nightmares materialize through meticulous detail, immersive storytelling, and the evocation of profound fear. Wonderland beckons readers to confront their deepest fears and explore the twisted corridors of the human psyche, promising an unforgettable journey into the heart of terror.

Influenced by a myriad of literary and cinematic genius, SK draws inspiration from the classic era of '80s slasher horror, infusing a touch of humor reminiscent of the self-awareness prevalent in the '90s. The narrative tone takes cues from psychological twists observed in notable works, prompting a shift in storytelling approaches. As the 2010s unfolded, a resurgence of supernatural and folk horror influences played a pivotal role in shaping SK's craft. Within the symphony of horror, SK emerges as a maestro, skillfully orchestrating tales that resonate with the deepest recesses of the human imagination. Wonderland transcends the realm of a mere novel; it extends an evocative invitation, urging readers to explore the intricate balance between wonder and terror—a realm where nightmares are conceived, and fear is elevated to an art form.

Published in the United States by Diamond Standard Company LLC.

ISBN: 979-8-218-57065-1
Second Edition

15529 Seventh St, Unit 773,
Lathrop, CA 95330, United States
shamoot.kishore@gmail.com
www.talesbysk.com

Printed in the United States of America

www.talesbysk.com
@sham00t

To my unwavering pillars of strength—my mother, father, and brother—whose support has brought me to where I stand today.

For the incredible woman by my side, my wife—the beacon of light who continually reassures me that the world isn't as haunting as it seems.

May the Kishore legacy live on, and may our descendants lead purposeful lives, even more extraordinary than those who came before.

"The oldest and strongest emotion of mankind is fear, and the oldest and strongest kind of fear is fear of the unknown."

H.P. Lovecraft

Wonderland

DREAMS OF NIGHTMARES

I

OCTOBER 24, 1986

The fall breeze wafted through the classroom, carrying with it the scent of the ocean, a sign that the seasons were shifting. Mrs. Davis struggled to control the excitement of two dozen seventh graders, knowing that Halloween was just around the corner. The whiteboard reflected the afternoon sun's orange glow as the day gradually faded into evening. The noise from the students gradually ebbed away with the wind.

Jacob—his unruly brown hair tickling his eyelashes—adjusted his denim coat. As he glanced out of the window, he spotted a lone figure under a nearby awning. The boy looked familiar, but Jacob couldn't get a clear view. Breathing heavily, the boy's shoulders rose and fell rapidly. His brown eyes narrowed as Jacob squinted to see clearly, trying to discern if he needed help.

Moments passed, and as if compelled by an unseen force, the boy's head snapped up, locking eyes with Jacob. A shiver ran down Jacob's spine; it was as if he was staring at his own reflection in the classroom. He watched in horror as the boy smiled, revealing decaying teeth and a thick, black substance oozing from his mouth. The boy's eyes were hollow, consumed by darkness, and his pale, bluish skin made the sight even more unsettling.

The boy waved his hand gently, acknowledging Jacob's presence, before pressing a scabbed finger to his lips, signaling for silence. Despite the crowds of oblivious children passing by, the boy's grip tightened on a clump of his own hair, all the while maintaining his eerie grin. He then produced a rusty blade and brought it to his neck, the smile fading into a vacant stare. He began to cut his own throat, blood and bits of flesh spewing out. Jacob was paralyzed, unable to tear his gaze away from the gruesome scene unfolding before him.

It took a hand on his shoulder and a pull to bring Jacob back into the classroom.

Mrs. Davis spoke gently, "This time of year can be difficult for some, Jacob."

His mind was in disarray, and he couldn't fathom why she was offering comfort. He hadn't even been able to breathe during the disturbing vision, resorting to short, quick breaths to avoid alarming her. At first, Jacob couldn't respond.

Mrs. Davis continued, "I just want you to know that you can always come to me if you need anything, sweetie."

He glanced outside once more, still haunted by the ghastly image of the boy. But the boy had vanished.

Jacob finally found his voice, "Thanks, Mrs. Davis, I will."

His ivory skin was dotted with droplets of sweat. Mrs. Davis turned to the other side of the classroom and addressed another student, "Timmy, honey, I'm so sorry. Did you need something from me?"

Jacob looked over and saw Timmy, the last student remaining in the class. Timmy's weary eyes suggested a sleepless night—as if he had been daydreaming. An unsettling silence settled in the room. Wrinkles marred the surface of his worn checkered flannel.

"No, ma'am, sorry. I was just collecting my things. I'll see you tomorrow. Bye, Jacob," Timmy said.

Seaside was a small town nestled near the vast Pacific Ocean. The families here had deep roots, stretching back for generations. They all knew about Isaac, Jacob's older brother, who had passed away just before Halloween thirteen years ago. Isaac's death cast a shadow over the family every year, and the arrival of colder months made the atmosphere even more somber. Jacob's parents, burdened with guilt over Isaac's untimely demise, often engaged in pointless arguments during Seaside's chilly seasons.

As Jacob walked through the school's corridors, he couldn't help but feel the eyes of his classmates on him. October brought with it the same hushed whispers and curious looks from everyone in town. Weston's frustration boiled over.

"How many times did we go through this, Liam? We spent hours on that shit!" Liam, baffled by his math test, stared at his paper. Liam was the eldest of the bunch and could be easily picked amongst the crowd—his tall and lanky build was topped with poorly gelled blonde strands overlaying his darker roots.

"How the hell can you solve for a letter? This is math, not English!" He said.

"Come on, Liam!" Weston replied, exasperated, "You solve it by isolating the goddamn variable. You can't use shapes to answer these questions!"

Despite his smaller stature, Weston exuded an intellect beyond his years—his keen emerald eyes were framed by round tortoiseshell glasses. His clothes were that of darker hues, allowing Weston to effortlessly blend into the ebb and flow of a bustling crowd. Liam let out a frustrated bark,

"I still don't get it. This is like a foreign language."

"We've gone through every step a hundred times," Weston said.

He couldn't help but point out Liam's late-night obsession with a photo book. The book, "One Hundred Locations," contained photographs taken by Jacob's great-grandfather decades ago when Seaside was just beginning as a town. Some of the photos were used as historical references in the town hall.

"These aren't just any old photos, Weston." Liam defended himself,

"They're our town's history—a glimpse of what it was like before nerds like you showed up. It's like seeing our town's DNA. If I had never looked through it, would I have passed Algebra the first time? Maybe. But then again, we'd never know about Impossible City—now, where would you get your fix in then, huh?"

"Hard to argue with that," Jacob interjected, joining the conversation. Jacob, Liam, and Weston met in their usual spot, away from the bustling crowds of students. They gathered by the bike racks.

"By the way, Jacob," Weston inquired,

“Have you found your dad’s Freddy mask yet? I’ve got my grandpa’s old sweater to look creepy with my ax. Luckily, Kubrick’s style matches modern serial killers, or ‘The Shining’ had the worst wardrobe team in film history.”

Jacob sighed, “Not yet. I’m waiting for my dad to leave town on his business trip before I dig through his old stuff. He doesn’t like me snooping around his personal things.”

Jacob’s father worked as a salesperson, and his schedule was unpredictable. Some days, he worked just a few hours before coming home, while others kept him away late into the night. Those were the days Jacob dared not cross his father, who sometimes returned home angry after those trips. Occasionally, his father attended business seminars and training sessions in the city, trips that lasted the entire weekend.

During the week leading up to Isaac’s death anniversary, Jacob’s father would do his usual disappearing act. He claimed he needed some personal time, but Jacob knew better. When he returned, there was always the smell of booze, and his suitcase seemed like it hadn’t been touched during the trip. It was his strange way of dealing with the pain, and Jacob never pried further.

Jacob needed his father’s mask for his Halloween costume, but he didn’t want to risk getting caught and adding to his parents’ already somber mood. He pushed his bike out of the rack.

Liam chimed in, “I’m borrowing my dad’s machete. My hockey mask’s seen better days, but it’s better than looking like a balding weirdo.”

He gave Weston a playful shove, causing Weston to stumble.

"Don't worry, Liam. Not everyone needs to be a math genius in the seventh grade. The world will always need more garbage collectors and fast-food workers," Weston said, throwing an arm around Liam, "I'll catch up with you guys tomorrow."

With their goodbyes said, Jacob and Liam set out on their bikes. As they rode along the main road, the usual banter between them was oddly subdued.

"So, what's the Halloween plan this year?" Liam finally broke the silence.

"The same as every year: dress up, raid the mansions with the best candy, prank old man Vern, and then head back to my place," Jacob replied, a smirk playing on his lips as he thought about their tradition of teasing Veritas.

He was the local drunk, and he managed to find reasons to blow his disability aid money on alcohol and get into slurred arguments with anyone who crossed his path. Veritas was no better when he was sober; he'd been living in Seaside for as long as anyone could remember, his leg having been blown off by a Hawkins grenade during the war. He received an honorable discharge, which meant he got a decent pension and free medical care, although it was doubtful he'd seen a doctor in years. Laden with layers of dirt and discarded skin cells, it was difficult to discern whether his deeper skin tone was the result of infrequent showers. His clumped coal-colored hair seemed more like a potential sanctuary for wildlife, and his sun-faded, ripped clothes hinted at the harshness of the grounds where he found repose.

Feeling sympathy or understanding for Veritas was challenging, given his habit of accusing the townsfolk of moral decay. Most people just ignored him, treating him as though he didn't exist. Jacob could still hear his words echoing in his mind, a constant reminder of Veritas's bitterness.

"You all look at me with disgust for what I've become, but I was once a great man! I know who I am. I know who I am. And who are you all to judge? You wash your own hands from this filth that you brought upon yourselves. Understand me; I know who I am! And when I die, God will know I had no part in this twisted cesspool of a town!"

Liam brought Jacob back to the present,

"Do you think Nancy's actually going through with it? Her parents only seem to approve of her hanging out with those rich, uptight yuppies." Jacob thought as they pedaled past Seaside's grand estates within Crestwood Heights.

"It wouldn't be the first time she's snuck out without permission. Besides, she still believes she's adopted and that Hank and Violet are just a couple trying to save their marriage with a child."

As they rolled past the opulent homes, Jacob couldn't help but notice the extravagant houses, most flaunting large windows devoid of curtains or blinds. It was a curious blend of exclusivity and transparency within this community. Stringent entry requirements defined the neighborhood, yet intimate moments within homes were far from private. Rows of swaying palm trees held Jacob's attention until they approached Nancy's residence.

Violet, her mother, watered the garden on their porch, her gaze locking onto the passing duo. Her unwavering stare sent a shiver down Jacob's spine, his legs momentarily frozen in response. He wanted to confide in Liam about the unsettling classroom incident, but this was the first extended conversation he'd had since the arrival of October. The season would soon end, and he assured himself that the strange occurrences at school were nothing more than his imagination.

"It's fucked up, is what it is. They don't care about her, their own daughter. She lives in a prison, man." Liam muttered.

Jacob continued to survey the luxurious mansions and pristine walls separating them from the wilds beyond. His legs churned once more as he remarked, "It's funny, isn't it? All that money they have just to hide and be miserable."

They pedaled toward the forest's entrance, the sun casting a blood-orange hue as the day aged. Light seeped through the trees, and the blue sky faded to a cherry-red afternoon. After 3 PM, the winds grew stronger, carrying bone-chilling cold. As they ventured adjacent to the woods, the oakwood trees opened up, revealing more of the forest's expanse. Riding side by side on the narrow road, Jacob and Liam ignored the potential of oncoming traffic. The fresh air carried the scent of the nearby water, momentarily captivating them. Their daydreams shattered when a loud motor roared behind them.

A speeding pickup truck honked aggressively, signaling Jacob and Liam to move aside or face danger.

"Watch out!" Liam yelled.

Jacob hesitated for a moment before quickly following Liam, pulling to the side of the road. The truck was occupied by a family, their faces familiar to Jacob. He had seen their son, Timmy, not long ago.

"What was that all about?" Liam asked as he got back on his feet.

"I think it was the Andersons," Jacob replied.

"I wonder why they were in such a hurry to leave. There's no traffic out here."

"Or anywhere to go," Liam added.

Jacob was about to respond when his attention was drawn to the neon lights glowing in the distance. The branches rustled in the ocean's draft, creating a momentary pause as his eyes fixated on the sight. A flat field with dead grass and patches of dirt spread out before them. Pointed tepees and wooden booths dotted the area, leading to a massive tent in the background. The vintage arch letters of the tent pulsed with bright red and then dark blue-green hues. Jacob whispered its name.

"Wonderland."

II

WONDERLAND

The carnival grounds sprawled with red and white tents as the day transitioned into evening. The blue sky darkened as the scarlet hues faded. An array of tents and stalls surrounded the colossal main tent, their artificial lights buzzing.

"I've never seen a carnival in person," Liam remarked.

"Yeah, me neither," Jacob replied, their attention fixed on the empty carnival.

"I don't see anyone. Let's go in!" Liam suggested eagerly.

"I don't know, man," Jacob hesitated.

"Don't be a pussy, come on!" Liam parked his bike and started walking, captivated by the glow. Jacob scanned the surroundings for any signs of onlookers but saw no one.

As they descended from the roadside into the field, it felt like the deserted carnival grounds expanded. Movement in the distance caught their attention as if someone was following them. They slowed down when they reached the carnival's entrance. Wonderland seemed to have grown in size as they walked beneath the arched entrance. Inside, they found dozens of empty circus games and posters advertising incredible freak shows. Smoke wafted from some tents, hinting at occupancy, but each one they passed seemed eerily silent. They discovered an unusual symbol painted on the dry grass, and Liam noticed, "It's still wet," as he smeared the black dye with his shoe.

The winds that sang through the woods were muted inside Wonderland. The framework supporting the structures appeared charred, and the smell of ashes hung in the air as Jacob and Liam ventured further. Stuffed animal prizes on high shelves creaked on rusty hinges.

"Where the hell is everyone?" Liam whispered, his gaze fixed on the decrepit zoo animal rides with their rusty edges.

Unbeknownst to each other, they drifted apart, captivated by Wonderland's peculiarities. Their senses and the laws of nature seemed out of place here. Jacob's attention was drawn to a teddy bear that bore a striking resemblance to the one that once belonged to his brother. It wasn't a rare item, but what puzzled him was that it appeared torn and worn, much like the one they had at home. As he examined other prizes, he noticed they all shared the same raggedy features, as if the carnival had raided a thrift shop for its gifts.

Out of the corner of his eye, Jacob saw a stuffed animal tumble from its perch onto the employee-only section behind the wooden frame. The cloth curtain covering the back of the table seemed to stir strangely from within. His heart began to race. He glanced around but still saw no one, including Liam.

Climbing over the stationary bench, Jacob's breath quickened as the shivers down his spine made him more cautious, inching toward the peculiar occurrence. Reaching the bottom end, he lifted the fabric. In an instant, the darkness was dispelled. Jacob crouched into the space, his eyes adjusting to the sudden daylight. He gasped at the silhouette of a young girl just beyond the reach of the sun.

Her eyes were entirely black, devoid of discernible eyebrows. The sliver of light revealed only vague contours of her face. The setting sun made it just possible to recognize the same strange symbol on her forehead. She wore a retro outfit, something from his parents' era. She sat cross-legged, gazing at Jacob, as if awaiting his words. The emptiness of Wonderland still echoed around them.

"What are you doing down there?" Jacob asked, his voice trembling.

Her piercing gaze remained fixed, her pupils unresponsive, not even blinking.

"Jacob!" Liam's distant shout startled him.

Jacob backed out from behind the bench and called back to Liam, unaware of how deep he had ventured.

"Over here!" Jacob exclaimed, shifting his focus away from the girl. "There's a girl here!"

He bent down to resume his one-sided conversation with the girl when he was met with a dozen eyes gleaming back at him. His knees gave way, bringing him to the ground. The eyes belonged to children of roughly the same age as the girl, all wearing attire that was both unique and perplexing, yet all shared the same mysterious mark. Before he could break free from this trance, the girl spoke.

"Come play with me, Jacob," she whispered, her face devoid of emotion.

His legs refused to move, and the sensation of paralysis swept over him. Beside the girl's head, a pair of yellow eyes revealed itself, much larger and wider than the children's. The dim light from the broken wood exposed a mouth stained with blood. The creature's mouth moved in harmony with the little girl's, and her body began to sway as if weightless, like a ventriloquist's puppet.

"Come play with us, Jacob. Please, come play, come play, come play!"

The voice, once a girl's, began to deteriorate into a raspy, hoarse sound. Jacob regained control of his muscles and crawled backward, refusing to look away. As soon as he managed to grab a piece of the cloth, the creature slithered over the girl and effortlessly pushed the other children aside, swaying them like marionettes.

This creature had bleached, rotting skin, a bony frame adorned in tattered black clothing, and patches of dead hair. Her movements were fluid, and her shrieks were a horrifying blend of blood and despair. With all the speed he could muster, Jacob leaped, throwing the cloth back over the hidden entity and sprinting away. Her fingertips grazed him as her arm slowly retreated inside the concealing fabric.

Jacob sprinted around a corner on the dirt pathway, repeatedly glancing over his shoulder to ensure he wasn't being pursued. As he put more distance between himself and the abomination, he collided with Liam.

"What the hell, man!" Liam shouted as they both stumbled to the ground.

The acrid scent of burning wood enveloped them, stronger than ever.

"We need to get out of here, now. Something's seriously wrong," Jacob said.

"What do you mean? I haven't seen a single person!" Liam grumbled in frustration.

The breeze began to murmur once more as Jacob hurried toward the exit, with Liam following a few steps behind, scanning his surroundings.

"Still no one!" Liam exclaimed.

They found their bikes resting on the pavement with their wheels turned to the side. Liam's expression grew more serious.

"Did you see anyone there?" He asked as he picked up his bike.

Jacob hesitated before responding. Just then, he noticed that the skies had darkened significantly, far too quickly for the short time they had spent inside Wonderland.

"Damn it! I need to get home before my parents flip!" Jacob yelled as they both mounted their bikes and pedaled away.

Jacob stole a final glance back at Wonderland, but once again, there was nothing but an eerie emptiness.

III

THE WATCHED

Jacob's home stood down Crestwood Street, near Liam's house. It was isolated from the other tight-knit suburban neighborhoods, perched on the edge of the vast, dark green forest and the boundless, deep blue ocean. For generations, Jacob's family had called this place home. Originally purchased by his great-grandfather, the land had seen many changes over the years. When they first arrived in Seaside, they had built a decent-sized house. Connection to the outdoors and the environment ran deep in Jacob's family. His grandfather, Abraham Sr. was not only an avid photographer but also an author of books that detailed the various species of trees, plants, and fruits that thrived in Seaside.

As the sun completely faded, the gentle breeze turned into gusts. The creak of the front door announced Jacob's arrival. In the kitchen, his parents abruptly silenced their hushed conversation. An awkward stillness hung in the air. His mother stood there, holding a mug that emitted the fragrant scent of coffee and something stronger. Her face seemed pained, hidden behind a strained smile when Jacob approached.

"Hey, sweetie. How was school? You're back a bit late," she inquired.

"Where were you?" his father interjected sternly before Jacob could respond.

Jacob advanced further into the kitchen, pondering whether he should mention Wonderland. Nevertheless, he reckoned it might serve as a welcome distraction from the topic of Isaac.

"There's a carnival setting up at the Fairgrounds. I went with Liam after school to check it out. We've never had one here before," he hesitantly explained. Martha took another sip of her concoction, her smile faltering briefly, while Abraham's gaze remained fixed on Jacob.

"How did it look?" he asked.

"No one was there. I think they might have gone to town or something," Jacob replied.

"They usually stay for the week. You'll get your chance to see them live," Abraham assured him. Jacob nodded and began to leave the kitchen when his mother's voice stopped him.

"Jacob, honey, wait," she called out, her voice trembling slightly.

"Sit down. We need to talk."

A sense of unease washed over Jacob, and he couldn't help but feel overwhelmed. The interior of the house was dimly lit outside the kitchen, with corners shrouded in darkness. Jacob walked to the dining table and took a seat, waiting in silence for someone to begin.

"We've got some great news, dear," Martha began with a facade of happiness.

"Year after year, your father and I endure the sorrow of our lost baby, your brother, Isaac." She paused for a moment, whispering to herself, "Our poor baby, taken so suddenly."

Jacob's gaze drifted away from his mother's as she teared up. Abraham placed a comforting hand on her shoulder.

"It can be hard to understand at your age why these things happen. But we do what we can and must to survive for this family," his father continued.

"We're having another baby, and you're going to be an older brother, Jacob."

Jacob's parents fell silent once more.

"We decided this would be the best time to tell you, to shift our focus to something more thrilling and delightful. Isn't that wonderful?" his mother said.

Jacob tried to find words to respond, something that would satisfy his parents, but he was at a loss.

"Well, aren't you going to say anything?" Abraham asked, his voice tinged with irritation.

"Our family needs this, hope," he added as he stood and walked toward the window. "We've sacrificed so much and worked tirelessly to have and maintain what we have, Jacob. It's fair for us to have the need to rebuild this family, to give us another chance to be normal again."

Jacob weakly replied, "I can't wait."

He crept toward the stairs, desperate to escape the kitchen as silence hung heavy in the air once more, this time long enough for Jacob to slip away. Martha's feeble voice followed him down the staircase with each step he took, "And so our family grows."

Several hours passed before Jacob emerged from the side entrance, pulling the kitchen trash to the bins by the road. Seaside's street lighting was feeble, but the low-hanging clouds made them glow faintly. The branches of towering trees creaked, and the ground whispered with fallen leaves.

You're going to be an older brother, Jacob.

He tried to picture what that would look like, the happiness it could bring. But no matter how hard he tried to fill his mind with excitement and enthusiasm, Wonderland's dark influence lingered in his thoughts. The agonizing sensation of dread and unhappiness lingered for hours. Jacob could still feel the woman's searing eyes vigilantly observing him. The bottom of the trash bag tore open before he could toss it.

"Shit," Jacob muttered under his breath.

As he picked up the scattered scraps, something in the middle of the street caught his eye. A man dressed in a black suit was staring at Jacob. His expressionless face was unevenly smeared with paint, but the same crescent cross marking he saw on the children from earlier was clearly visible on his forehead. Slender and lanky, the man's eyes were yellow, and his skin was pallid. He squatted, maintaining eye level with Jacob. The creaking of the woods ceased. The man didn't move; his arms were unnaturally long, knuckles nearly brushing the concrete. A carved smile adorned his face, teeth stained yellow with traces of red.

"Who... Who are you?" Jacob mumbled, his voice trembling.

The man's smile slowly faded as he reached into his coat pocket and placed Isaac's teddy bear in the middle of the road, causing drops of blood to splatter from his sleeve. Jacob's jaw dropped, and his breathing hitched as he witnessed something that couldn't possibly be real. Time seemed to stand still, and the duration of this encounter became unbearable. An ear-piercing shriek echoed from beyond the forest, reverberating throughout Seaside.

Jacob's head snapped around, but the man remained motionless. In an instant, the man's head jerked back, and cracks emanated from his body. His pupils locked onto Jacob's once more, but this time, they were consumed by an abyss of blackness. His body began to retreat haltingly into the forest. A sinister grin reappeared on his face as he inched closer and closer into the murky trees.

"I'll see you soon, Jacob," the man whispered.

And then, he was gone.

Nature seemed to exhale, and Jacob became acutely aware of his surroundings. He stood up from the gravel and surveyed the open street, the bear now staring at him from the road. The night sky was veiled by swiftly passing clouds, and he couldn't help but wonder how long he had been outside. With a rush of fear, Jacob dashed onto the street and seized the bear, hoping to get away before the man returned—or something worse.

The intermittent hum of arguing voices seeped through the walls, making it difficult for Liam to sleep. His room was bathed in dim shades of crimson, peach, and yellow from his lava lamp. During the colder months, John and Wendy rarely turned on the heater, adding to Liam's sleeplessness. His closet light flickered on after multiple attempts, its bulb loud and glaring enough to vex Liam from the brink of sleep. Just as the conversation ceased, a sudden burst of light shattered the room's lull. The room was plunged into eerie darkness as shards of glass tinkled to the wooden floor. An outline of a person stood facing Liam, unnoticeable in the corner of his room as his eyes adjusted to the dazzling burst.

Startled, he rose from bed rubbing his eyes. The vibrant blue of his irises, now enveloped in the darkness of the night. The usual creaking of mattress springs and weathered floorboards was strangely absent, and each step he took seemed to allow the shadows to consume more of the room. Moonlight fragments played on Liam's face as he approached the open closet, intending to reach for the light switch. Yet, it wasn't what was inside the closet that left Liam failed to sense; it was the figures that appeared behind him, casting their shapes against the opposite wall.

These figures, men and women, stood silently, faces obscured by blood-stained garments and the haunting mark of Wonderland on their foreheads. They appeared frozen, like eerie, lifeless props. But then, as if descending with the grace of a feather pulled by gravity, she appeared above the motionless figures, suspended as if by an invisible noose. The woman from Wonderland, aged and frail, drifted towards Liam's bed, her spindly legs hovering. Her translucent form contrasted with the vivid, shadowy figures below, all bearing witness to Liam unknowingly.

The room remained shrouded in darkness as Liam tried to flip the light switch, but it refused to illuminate. The shards of glass on the floor sparkled in the moonlight. As he turned to walk back to his bed, the room had returned to its normal, empty state. He slipped into his bed, finding his sleeping position effortlessly. One last glance at the closet and the window before sleep overtook Liam. The room continued to shift with the changing colors of the lava lamp, but one corner remained shrouded in an unnatural darkness. Unseen by the celestial and artificial lights, the woman from Wonderland clung to the ceiling and walls with her slender limbs and long fingers.

Half of her face was obscured by her hair, and her yellow eyes watched Liam as he breathed, blissfully unaware of her presence.

IV

IMPOSSIBLE CITY

Nancy took a long drag from the joint, savoring the inhale before the smoke began to irritate her lungs. As a cough threatened to emerge, she quickly passed the joint to Cheyenne, careful not to drop it.

"Oh my god!" Nancy squeaked.

"I told you to be careful," Cheyenne laughed as she took the joint, blowing off the ash remnants from the tip. With azure eyes reminiscent of a summer sky, Nancy's petite stature held a subtle advantage in height over Cheyenne. Cheyenne, with her broader build, sported black, flowing hair that gracefully framed her sun-kissed shoulders, while Nancy's wild blond curls swirled in rhythm with the ocean breeze.

The sun shone brilliantly, casting an oddly inviting glow even on the rundown buildings and deserted homes of this remote area of Seaside. Decades ago, this place had been abandoned as locals realized the steepness of the hill could trigger a rockslide at any moment. Now, it was known as Impossible City, where nature defiantly confronted the remnants of human habitation.

Hidden in this ghost town, far from the prying hands of Nancy's parents and Cheyenne's uncle, they felt free. Cheyenne took another toke and visually guided Nancy through the process of smoking marijuana, though Nancy still coughed intermittently. Cheyenne smiled.

“My parents would kill me if they saw this, you know. When did you first start?” Nancy said.

“A couple of years ago, back in Washington,” Cheyenne replied between puffs.

“Most of my family did it when I was younger, so it was always around me. The smell calms me.” Exhaling a plume of smoke, Cheyenne added, “We use this herb for a bunch of things, too. It can heal the body, like cuts or stomach pains, and it helps you connect with your spirituality.”

Cheyenne and Nancy had become close friends since Cheyenne and her uncle had moved to Seaside a year ago. The thought of Nancy befriending her in public would be social suicide, according to her parents. Cheyenne’s family didn’t come from a family of means, and the high society with which Nancy’s family was associated with wasn’t fully accepting of people of color. It was for this exact reason it gave Nancy joy to disobey them.

They sat in the garden of an old church, its structures marred by the ravages of time. A muffled sound, reminiscent of an owl’s call, echoed from inside the cathedral. Cheyenne and Nancy turned their attention toward the noise. Through the doorless doorway, Weston entered, his hands clasped together in an exaggerated, playful manner. Liam and Jacob followed closely behind.

“Ladies, ladies, ladies,” Weston began as he settled between Nancy and Cheyenne, “You started the party without me.” Weston plopped down between Nancy and Cheyenne with a theatrical complaint.

"We waited a whole half hour! Why can't you guys ever be on time?" Nancy playfully scolded, inching away from him and passing the joint.

"It's not our fault," Liam chimed in, "We would've been here sooner if Weston hadn't clogged his toilet."

Amidst chuckles, all eyes turned to Weston, who was just about to take his first hit from the joint.

"That's how we're starting this? Really?" Weston snarled.

The five often hung out together, sometimes as a group and sometimes as just those available at the moment. One common thread among them was the desire to escape, to find solace in Seaside's deep woods or secluded spots, away from the watchful eyes of their parents. Each harbored their own grievances with their guardians but kept them to themselves. There was a palpable generation gap, a lack of mutual understanding between them and their elders.

To bridge this gap, they needed to delve into the histories and backgrounds of their parents, but none felt confident enough to do so. Their shared freedom felt exhilarating, like birds soaring over the ocean, the relentless waves crashing onto the shore, or unbridled winds whipping over the open sea. Cheyenne handed the joint to Jacob, who accepted it timidly.

"Have you guys heard about a carnival coming to town?" Nancy asked.

"I overheard Violet talking about it on the phone. Is there really one here in Seaside?"

"Jacob and I saw it on our way home from school yesterday. We went in, but..." Liam paused, glancing at Jacob as he coughed from the smoke.

"There wasn't anyone around," he finished.

Nancy sighed wistfully.

"I'd die to be in the spotlight. Just die. Imagine being center-staged, all eyes on you, performing your craft, wooing the audience, and the roar of applause in the big city." She closed her eyes and let her imagination wander, swaying with the effects of the cannabis.

Weston playfully tapped Liam's elbow, "Yeah, I think that's enough for her."

Jacob turned to Cheyenne, whom he felt somewhat shy around, "Do you think you'll still be able to come with us on Halloween?"

"I'll find a way," Cheyenne replied.

"My uncle doesn't like the idea of this tradition, or any celebration during the fall, but he usually falls asleep early. So, I'll find a way to meet up with you guys."

"He doesn't like Halloween?" Weston exclaimed, standing up.

"It's the only day of the year we can prank people and not get in trouble, the only day of the year we can get a ton of free candy, the only day of the year we can stay out as late as we want, and the only day of the year Liam can hide his deformed face from society!"

He gestured dramatically toward Liam.

A loud snapping noise, like the breaking of wood, suddenly echoed from inside the church. They all jolted up from their seated positions, like soldiers called to attention. Subsequent clatters of lumber followed, suggesting there was someone walking over the demolition. Cheyenne tossed the roach behind them as far as she could.

"What do we do?" she whispered.

"Just relax," Jacob replied, "If anyone asks, we're just hanging out."

No one emerged from the church, but the commotion persisted. Liam took the lead and headed towards the entryway.

"Let's go see what's happening there." He said.

Weston glanced at Jacob, then shrugged and followed Liam. Nancy and Cheyenne hesitated for a moment before trailing after Weston.

Nancy whispered urgently, "What the hell are we doing?"

"Are you coming, Jacob?" Cheyenne asked.

Jacob hesitated but was eventually coaxed by her grip on his hand.

The interior of the hallway behind the altar was dim, even with the sun outside. Stained windows that once displayed holy archangels were now boarded up with pieces of plywood. Mold had taken hold due to the high humidity, filling the air with a rancid odor. An eerie sensation of being watched overcame Jacob as they ventured further in. He scanned their surroundings more vigilantly than the rest.

Each step they took into the main floor of the church echoed throughout its inner dome, but there was no one in sight. The only peculiar feature was an open basement entrance at the crossing, emitting low murmurs and faint, deep voices from below.

"This whole place is giving me the creeps," Nancy said.

They stood over the cellar entrance, peering down. Weston offered a counter argument.

"What's the worst that can happen? We don't have anything on us, and it's not like whoever's down there has permission to be here either. This whole place is a no-trespass zone." The indistinct voices from below had transformed into sorrowful weeping, growing louder by the moment. Liam looked at Nancy and then at the others.

"Someone needs help. I'm going down there."

Jacob immediately stopped him.

"Are you insane? We have no idea who's down there. It could be a trap."

"There's five of us. If we stick together, we'll be fine. Now come on!" Liam urged.

Cheyenne was the last one to descend the steps. A lingering glance around the church, fiddling with her arrow necklace, and then she, too, began her descent. About halfway down, they noticed a fire being used for illumination. Shadows danced with the flickering flames, briefly revealing the room's contents. Before reaching the bottom, they spotted a man sitting on the floor, draped in a long trench coat that concealed his backside.

The chill in the air here was far more biting than at ground level, and the room was filled with dusty artifacts stored by the church. Jacob's eyes locked onto something as he descended, shimmering as the flames reflected in his pupils. The concrete beneath the man displayed the same red Wonderland symbol.

The man appeared to be in distress, rocking back and forth while softly muttering in a strange language. His voice oscillated from resonant to gentle, like a haunting melody. Candles were arranged perfectly at each edge of the Wonderland logo on the floor, and scratch marks marred the circle's surface. An uneasy silence settled over the group.

"Hey, mister, are you okay?" Weston asked.

The man gasped for air, his body trembling. Bloodshot eyes met theirs—his irises carrying the deep hues of rich earth.

"Vern? What the hell are you doing down here?" Liam's voice quivered with recognition.

There was a moment of eerie silence, followed by hysterical laughter from Vern. He stared back at them, his face contorted in madness, "The blood of your ancestors will bleed from your veins," he intoned. His demeanor shifted, his breath visible in the basement's coldness.

Only half of his face was visible in the firelight, revealing the countenance of a deranged old man with widened eyes and an unnaturally elongated smirk. Before he could approach them, the candles were extinguished, and his face became a mere silhouette. He looked around in delirium, then began screaming at the children, "Leave! Get out of this place!"

He charged towards them. They sprinted up the stairs as fast as they could, with discolored arms reaching through the gaps, trying to grasp their legs. Liam was the last to reach the top, where a hand clamped onto his ankle, causing him to tumble onto the crossing carpet.

"Fuck!" he cried out.

Jacob and Weston grabbed his arm, desperately trying to free him from the vice-like grip.

"Come on!" Nancy yelled, yanking Liam's leg.

As they focused their energy on unbinding him, figures of men and women surrounded the shadows of the church, watching them, their eyes bleeding tar. Cheyenne looked at these strangers and held her necklace again. They finally freed Liam, who stumbled to the ground from the force of their pulling. Through the darkness, they ran away from Impossible City and into the light of the forest.

V

DILATE

As they ran farther into the woods, their usual paths became obscured by thickening vines and branches. Keeping a straight course was no longer practical. None of them dared to look back; their focus was on avoiding slips on the forest floor and tumbles into unseen trenches. After nearly ten minutes of relentless sprinting, they stumbled upon a river.

Physically and mentally drained, Jacob raised his arms above his head to gulp down more oxygen.

"What the hell was that back there?" he panted.

"I don't know, man, but whatever it was, we should steer clear of Vern for a while," Liam replied.

"But we have to tell someone about this. Did you guys not see what I saw? Hands were reaching out from the stairs. And Vern, he tried to kill us!" Weston exclaimed.

"Maybe we just imagined some of those things. I mean, we did just smoke and all," Nancy suggested.

Weston shot her an incredulous look. "Are you kidding me? We've smoked before, and nothing like that has ever happened."

Jacob lowered his arms and spoke, "He's always been the town drunk for as long as I can remember, yelling at people over stupid stuff.

But Vern was doing some kind of ritual—dark magic kind of shit. It felt different there, didn't it? Something's not right."

Jacob tried to continue, but he noticed Cheyenne staring off into space.

"Cheyenne, you okay?"

She stood there, breathing heavily, still clutching her arrow necklace. Nancy touched her arm.

"Cheyenne?"

Dusk descended upon Seaside as clouds slowly expanded across the skies. Shades of dark gray, tinged with a hint of salmon, draped the trees and the woodlands. The air grew cooler, and their skin took on a rosy hue as evening embraced them.

Finally, Cheyenne spoke up, breaking the heavy silence that hung over them.

"Did you guys realize we were in that church for nearly two hours? It should've only been like fifteen minutes. What happened there wasn't natural; it was something demonic. I've seen Vern before, and whatever that was in that basement wasn't him, not even close."

"What do you mean?"

Liam asked, his voice trembling slightly.

"I don't know, but it feels like something bad is going to happen," Cheyenne replied, her eyes filled with unease.

"What did he mean by 'The blood of your ancestors?'"

Nancy inquired, her voice a mere whisper. The question hung heavily in the air, thick with tension.

"There's an old Native American saying my uncle told me. I can't remember it exactly, but it's something like—"

Cheyenne paused before continuing on, "'Day and night cannot coexist unless we allow it. The spirit world is all around us, but we provide the gateway into our realm.'."

"So, you're saying Vern summoned a ghost or something? He's a war veteran; why would he be messing around with that kind of shit?" Weston's voice quivered.

"We have to find out what that symbol he was sitting on meant; it might explain all of this," Cheyenne suggested.

Jacob nodded in agreement, "I know where we can start looking. That symbol was inside Wonderland, too. All over. Let's see if we can find some clues there." He glanced at the darkening sky, "We should all get home before it gets too dark, or we might get into some real trouble."

Cheyenne resided just within the borders of Seaside, in a rural area. Living with her uncle Chaska meant it was more challenging to sneak in and out unnoticed. Chaska had taken over an abandoned house, a fixer-upper he'd purchased at a bargain. The strong scent of burning sage greeted her as she entered.

Chaska's back turned to the front entrance and faced the sliding door that overlooked the expansive land. No lights were on, just the dim glow of the setting sun reflecting off white walls and illuminating drifting smoke and various healing crystals on a side table. His scarred right eye opened from his meditation, sensing Cheyenne's presence as the front door creaked.

"It's not good to be out this close to nightfall, Cheyenne," he cautioned, maintaining his meditative pose.

"Sorry, uncle."

Chaska had tried diligently to instill their customs in her, but the generational gap often clashed with his intentions. One indifference they shared was the smell of sage when burnt; it gave Cheyenne headaches, while Chaska asserted it was just the bad spirits locked in her head. Observing the simmering stew on the stovetop, Cheyenne asked, "Have you eaten yet?"

"I was waiting for you," Chaska replied, opening his eyes and grunting as he rose from the floor.

"Let Maka in, too; she's been all over the field today." Making her way to the glass doors, Chaska continued, "It's been impossible to get her to calm down."

Maka, their German Shepherd, had the entire pasture to herself, which was perhaps too much freedom for any dog. As Cheyenne whistled for her, she noticed movement in the distance. The grasslands rustled, but instead of Maka, a woman crawled through the unruly turf on all fours.

Her hair trailed behind her, and her body contorted in an almost animalistic manner. Cheyenne watched in stunned silence. As the woman's golden eyes met hers, Cheyenne's senses were overwhelmed by a deafening buzzing sound. The woman, with dirt-stained skin and torn clothes, turned her head and stood upright. Her gaze pierced Cheyenne's soul. Amid the buzzing, she heard muted barks from Maka, but her senses remained fixated on the woman. Chaska's intervention pulled her back inside the house, causing the mirage to vanish and the humming to recede.

"What is wrong with you, Cheyenne?" Chaska yelled, letting Maka in.

Cheyenne gazed outside again, but all she saw was the grassy expanse.

"I—I thought I saw someone. Sorry, Uncle," she stammered.

Chaska studied her briefly before instructing her to sit at the table and eat dinner. He peered at the grounds, his eyes narrowing with a frown. After one last glance at the brightening moon, he drew the curtains to shut out the gathering dusk.

VI

LOST ONES

Festive Halloween decorations adorned the school, but Jacob couldn't muster any enthusiasm. His sleepless nights had etched dark bags under his eyes. His thoughts were haunted after Friday's encounter with the suited man. He'd hidden the teddy bear under his bed but was mesmerized by its missing eye and worn cotton that bore an uncanny resemblance to his brother's. A flashback came from years ago when Jacob helped Abraham and Martha with spring cleaning; he remembered seeing the bear in his father's hand as he packed it in a kraft storage box. Sealed away into the dark corners of the space. Jacob's gaze wandered outside the classroom windows; the awnings were empty.

Meanwhile, on the other side of the school, Weston delved into files of students in need of tutoring based on their last quarter's report cards. His volunteering often clashed with his schoolwork, so teachers allowed him to organize his responsibilities during class periods. Principal Matthew's office was spacious, with a large oak desk as its centerpiece, exuding an earthy scent.

Weston muttered to himself as he sifted through the papers, "How the hell are you all failing Algebra 1, man?"

Principal Matthew entered, surveying the messy papers.

"Well, I sure hope these aren't all the kids that need tutoring, or you'll never leave this school, Weston!" he chuckled.

Weston, adjusting his glasses, sighed at the failing report cards.

"Mr. Matthew, I'm trying as hard as I physically can to help these kids, but they're just…stupid." Principal Matthew, a grizzly bear of a man in his mid-fifties, put his hand on Weston's shoulder.

"You need to be more patient. You kids are still developing your little heads, and sometimes, some learn faster than others. You can't expect a perfect test score from someone with only a couple of tutor sessions! Let's take a look at this one."

He picked up a transcript.

"Oh dear," he exclaimed, his features dimming.

"Well, just make sure to give some of them your full attention, and we'll hope for the best." He smiled. The lunch bell rang, and Principal Matthew retrieved his brown paper bag.

"Best part of the day, huh? Ready to go?" He asked Weston.

"I had a late breakfast. I'm just going to get through these as fast as I can so I don't have to later," Weston replied.

Principal Matthew frowned.

"It's not a good idea to work on an empty stomach. Trust me, I'd know!" He patted his bulging belly. "But I admire your work ethic, and I'll leave you to it, young man!"

After Principal Matthew left, Weston glanced at the report card again.

He took off his glasses and rubbed his eyes, "Fucking idiots, man."

As the school day dragged on, Weston continued to sort through his tutoring schedule. The once-chirping birds outside now stood silently on power lines and empty tables, scavenging students' leftovers. The overcast skies added to the gloomy atmosphere. Weston's eyes drooped as he leaned on his palm. Suddenly, a scratching sound jolted him upright. He scanned the room, expecting the noise to return, but it didn't. Sighing, he resumed skimming transcripts.

Then, a deafening metal thud erupted from behind him from the metal filing cabinet, causing Weston to jump in his seat. His heart raced, and he held his breath. More scratching followed as if something was trying to escape the metal prison. Weston cautiously moved closer to investigate, his eyes darting around the room. Just as he was about to open the drawer from which the sounds emanated, the commotion ceased abruptly. A rush of confidence surged within him, and he yanked the three-foot drawer open, stepping back cautiously.

The dark abyss at the back of the filing cabinet swallowed any light that dared enter. Weston leaned forward, crushing the files within as he prepared to peer inside. But before he could, a raven burst forth from the cabinet's depths, its wings flapping wildly against the metal confines. The bird's raucous croaks and frenzied struggle sent papers flying onto the floor. Weston, startled, flung himself to the ground, desperately avoiding contact with the agitated creature.

"What the fuck!" he exclaimed.

The room resounded with the raven's harsh squawks, and a gust of wind stirred as it thrashed its feathers, causing the scattered papers to dance. Finally, the raven managed to free itself and perched on the table's edge, fixing its intense gaze on Weston. Its wings lay tucked, and it seemed to gulp in the air, its eyes locked onto the vulnerable twelve-year-old. Paralyzed with fear, Weston couldn't summon the courage to shoo the bird away or even move.

Then, in an instant, the raven turned and flew out the window, leaving Weston trembling in his cold sweat. An inexplicable fascination gripped him, and he found himself staring into the cabinet's abyss. Pushing the chair aside, he cautiously approached, crossing a rug that had been disturbed in his earlier retreat. Peering inside, he discovered a bulging compartment, hidden until the entire drawer had been pulled out. His outstretched arm felt a stack of files wedged within. He struggled to retrieve them without causing damage, but with some effort, he managed to slide a loose bolt, releasing the stuck papers. He arranged the stack of coffee-colored documents, which appeared to be dated decades ago, on Mr. Matthew's desk.

They were contained in a manila folder, but the sheer number of papers spilled beyond its capacity. The folder bore the label,

LOST ONES

The top page appeared to be a student's permanent record from Seaside but with additional details about their family. Information about parents' birthplaces, religious beliefs, blood types, and personality descriptions was included—details one wouldn't expect on an elementary school academic document.

Weston examined a file from 1947 belonging to Emily Gilda, who had passed away at the age of seven due to hemorrhaging. She was of the Catholic faith, blood type AB, and was described as quiet, resentful, and antisocial, with sporadic fits of rage toward other students. Both her parents were marked as deceased in the same month. Weston continued to scrutinize files, paying attention to causes of death and parental information. There were repeated cases of hemorrhaging, some students going missing, and even instances of young student suicides. Most parents were either deceased, or one parent passed away within three months of the child's death.

The oldest file, dated 1895, was barely legible due to the ink smudging against other papers. Azazel had an older-looking file, but Weston could discern his cause of death—written in old English was,

BY FIRE

His eyes widened as he read those words—as if glimpsing into a darker past of the school that had never been mentioned. So many children's deaths, yet none of them seemed familiar or had ever been discussed. Why were these tragedies hidden? He hurried through the remaining papers until one slipped onto the rug,

ISAAC ABRAHAM CLAY

Weston's jaw dropped, and his knees gave way as he stared at the file. It was Jacob's brother, and the answers to countless questions might lie within. He quickly scanned the documents, noting that Isaac's file was different from the rest. Since he had passed away before attending Woodland Crest Academy, there were no personality summaries or beliefs. Instead, there was a family tree of the Clays, showing their connections with other families in the area, including Liam's and Nancy's. The following pages contained drawings made by a child, perhaps Isaac himself. They depicted family portraits and simple scenes, typical of a five or six-year-old's artwork. Each page represented a different activity, like a day at the beach or a picnic, with figures in the background. The drawings were signed,

Jacob Clay

However, as Weston flipped through them, a disturbing pattern emerged. Some drawings featured grotesque alterations. In one, Jacob had drawn red slashes on both arms, with blood splatters on the sides. Weston couldn't help but shudder.

"What the hell are these?" he whispered.

Another drawing depicted Abraham and Martha being hanged by a noose, while a child, presumably Jacob, held Isaac while they watched their parents suffocate. The cartoons grew increasingly malevolent and cruel, but one thing became apparent as Weston delved deeper: a shadowy figure, initially a mere smudge, grew taller and more defined. It lurked in the background of most scenes, always watching them.

Sometimes, it hid behind trees; other times, it was beneath the sand, but it consistently moved closer. It was always watching. The final page of drawings featured the symbol he had seen in Impossible City. Chaotic and unstructured, it was drawn repeatedly, converging toward the center in dark charcoal shades. Weston's hand grazed the etchings.

His thoughts were interrupted by distant voices from outside the office. Weston grabbed his notebook, hastily scribbling down as many names as he could from each file. After organizing the disarrayed papers and files, Weston readied for the town's library for further research. As he closed the cabinet and gathered his belongings, he glanced at the open window where the raven had flown out of. A strange stillness gripped the school grounds. The entire patio lay before him, yet the expected sounds of the outdoors were eerily absent.

In the distance, a group of five adults stood, their posture eerily rigid and their arms seemingly glued to their sides. Weston felt his joints lock, an overwhelming sense of dread washing over him. These strangers had been silently observing him, their lifeless gazes sending an icy shiver down his spine. None of them bore visitor's pass stickers, and none displayed cheerful expressions; only blank, vacant stares greeted him. He couldn't help but wonder how long they had been silently watching until a voice suddenly pierced the tension.

"Where are you off to, all packed up, Mr. Smith?" Mrs. Peters, the head office administrator, inquired, her oval-shaped spectacles boring into Weston's visibly anxious state.

"Mrs. Peters, I, um, was just finishing my scheduling work here. I'm heading back to class now," he stammered, his eyes darting nervously towards the window. To his relief, the mysterious figures had vanished.

VII

THE COVE

The salty tang of the ocean lingered on their lips as they ventured toward the cove. Their secret hideout, accessible via irregular stepping stones, guaranteed solitude. Nancy and Cheyenne often met here after school, whether to confide in one another about family and friend troubles, to smoke, or quite often, both. Unspoken but understood, they felt compelled to share their personal demons with each other despite their relatively short friendship. To have someone who knew them inside and out was worth the vulnerability.

Nancy, however, felt the pressure of growing into a young woman. The expectations of how to behave, speak, dress, and fit into a particular societal mold bore down on her. Her parents believed that adhering to generational standards was the only way to shield oneself from the world's disease and unhappiness. Uncomfortable in her own skin, she considered herself too freethinking for the stifling confines of this prescribed lifestyle and too unattractive for high society. Yet, the further she strayed from these norms, the better she understood herself, motivating her to forge her unique path.

"Geeze, did we take the long route?" Nancy inquired, trailing Cheyenne as they navigated around a boulder.

"I'm starting to think you brought me out this way to brutally murder me." Cheyenne grinned.

"Relax. If I wanted to, I could have killed you at least four times in the past hour alone. It's not that bad. We've only been hiking for about twenty minutes. My uncle and I used to go for hours when we were in Washington."

Nancy stopped to catch her breath, "You're telling me you used to do this for fun?"

Cheyenne continued at her pace, sharing tales of her hiking adventures. Nancy looked around as though she heard someone call her name, but all that surrounded them were ancient trees.

She looked ahead at Cheyenne before jogging to catch up,

"Healthy bitch."

They reached a thicket of shrubs and low vegetation concealing the entrance to their sanctuary. Nancy followed Cheyenne, who parted the branches to reveal the secluded ends of Seaside Beach. In the absence of human interference, this hidden paradise had been crafted and preserved by nature. The aquamarine sea, encased within the cove's ancient barriers for millennia, had acquired a divine pink hue due to salt minerals. Shamrock-green moss covered everything untouched by the sun except for the sand and water. The ground teemed with diverse flowers: saffron, lavender, seafoam, and cardinal petals as pure as a newborn baby.

As the sun descended toward the horizon, casting its distorted rays upon the tranquil rose lagoon, the quietude transformed into a dance of light and shadow. They walked through this Eden, marveling at its magnificence. But as they explored, they came across a nearly obscured warning sign, its metal frame tarnished by dust. Nancy wiped it clean and read the cautions. The sign warned of treacherous tides that could surprise swimmers, potentially poisonous plants, and territorial animals that could become aggressive when confronted by humans. Cheyenne rolled her eyes and moved on, but Nancy wiped off the sign's bottom, revealing the initials,

LC

She traced the small engraving a couple of times before Cheyenne shouted, "I'm starting with or without you!"

The cove offered an abundance of hidden spots, from massive rocks forming natural barricades to caves harboring enigmatic creatures waiting to emerge at night. Redwoods, reaching nearly two hundred feet tall, crowned the rocky foundations. Nancy accepted the joint from Cheyenne, determined to inhale more slowly this time. They settled on the grass near the edge of a steep ledge, their gaze fixed on the shimmering lagoon.

"There you go, now you're smoking like a pro!" Cheyenne remarked, giving Nancy's arm a playful slap.

"This place is gorgeous, absolutely stunning. It's so quiet and serene. Do you see what happens when you don't force things to meet certain standards? Nature unfolds as it should. Just look at this view!"

Nancy paused, taking another hit.

"But no, everything has to fit a certain mold. Nature is considered wrong, and mankind must 'save the day' by altering, changing, and manipulating what existed before we did. How does that make any sense? Tell me!"

Cheyenne looked at the joint and said, “I think we’re going to need more weed.”

Nancy shot her an irritated look.

“Hey, I’m serious. Don’t you get angry with all these rules? Don’t you want the freedom to choose everything—your haircut, where to travel, who to talk to, who to love, even what you want to eat, for crying out loud?” Nancy exclaimed.

Cheyenne inhaled and exhaled before responding, “We’re raised to be like our parents because that’s all they know. We want to break free, be treated differently, but it’s like we’re speaking different languages. Maybe when we’re parents someday, it’ll all make sense.” As they rested on the soft grass, their eyelids grew heavy, and Nancy yawned.

“Yeah, maybe.” The sun’s warmth enveloped them, lulling them into a peaceful slumber.

An electric buzz reverberated in Nancy’s ears, jolting her awake as daylight waned. The sound of ocean waves crashing against the cove and leaves rustling in the forest’s breeze filled the surroundings. She glanced around momentarily before the piercing drone returned, causing her to grimace and cover her ears to block out the noise.

Beside her, Cheyenne remained sound asleep, undisturbed. It seemed that Nancy alone could hear this disconcerting sound. She stood up and walked toward the water, searching for the source of this unsettling frequency. The longer she was awake, the more everything seemed askew. Doubt crept in about her ability to discern the time, the temperature, their location, and even whether she was still trapped in a dream.

The buzzing returned, more intense this time, causing Nancy to drop to her knees, her French-tipped nails digging into the sand. She let out a soft cry, enduring the torment until the agonizing ringing finally subsided a few moments later. Nancy surveyed the empty hideaway, and even with Cheyenne beside her, she had never felt more isolated. Nancy made her way to the lagoon, its tranquil, dark blue tides providing some solace. The pink hue had faded with the vanishing sun, leaving behind a murky surface. She moved closer to the waves, seeing her reflection faintly mirrored on the water's surface. Though the water was icy cold, she could bear it enough to rinse the sand from her hands.

As she dipped her fingers into the water, a gleaming rockfish glided toward her in the shallows. It moved gracefully, almost drifting with the current. Its silvery-gray scales had a radiant jade hue that made them entrancing to behold. Nancy's eyes were captivated by its shimmer. She extended her arm slowly to avoid startling the fish, hovering her fingertips above it.

But in an instant, a surge of water splashed up from below, and a bony hand clamped onto her right forearm, trying to drag her into the murky depths. Nancy screamed, twisting her arm in a desperate bid to escape, but the creature's grip was like a vise, leaving painful welts on her skin. Her body was pulled thigh-deep into the lagoon, and the creature's head emerged from the water, revealing only the top half of her elongated, grinning face, her long, black hair obscuring the rest of her form. Nancy screamed in terror as loudly as she could, hoping to wake Cheyenne, who remained lifeless on the grass.

She used her legs to push her body onto her stomach, struggling to claw her way back to the safety of land. Her cries for help became gasps for air, and gulps of water seeped into her lungs. Her fingernails turned black from the sand she clung to desperately. With the last vestiges of her energy, Nancy reached her arm out as far as possible toward the forest, but another hand emerged from the water and grabbed the side of her face. The woman's long fingers and nails dug into the side of Nancy's mouth and eyes, silencing her wails and nearly breaking her neck as she pulled her beneath the water's surface. The lagoon's tranquility returned as Nancy was completely swallowed by its depths.

Water erupted onto the beach as if glass had been shattered from the dusking sky. Nancy's body convulsed from the icy water as she struggled towards the northern edge of the lagoon, coughing up saltwater that had invaded her lungs. She whimpered and collapsed, her gaze shifting towards Cheyenne at the opposite end, nearly a thousand yards away. Her arm was a gruesome sight, punctured by the woman's nails and now oozing blood at an alarming rate.

The severity of her injuries became painfully evident as she felt lacerations on her face, wounds that would require stitches and possibly antibiotics. The buzzing resumed but at a lower hum. Nancy's breaths were shallow, and her vision blurred due to the blood loss as she scanned her surroundings for help. In her periphery, she noticed smoke rising from one of the caves about fifty feet away.

"Hey!" she yelled as loudly as her weakened voice allowed. "Is someone there?"

She limped towards the concealed opening, clinging to the hope of a miracle that might see her through this nightmare. Every step she took left a bloody trail in the sand. Pain washed over her as adrenaline waned, and tears mixed with the blood streaming from her face, causing an agonizing, stinging sensation. Her head swiveled from side to side, ensuring the woman wasn't near, but anxiety tormented her, and death seemed a more welcome prospect than encountering her again. She called out once more, "Hello!" but her voice had grown too feeble, and only the sound of waves crashing could be heard. At this point, her only wish was to be back home. With sorrow welling up inside her, she knew that her odds of survival were diminishing by the minute. The smoke intensified, taking on a darker charcoal hue as Nancy reached the cave's entrance. It was as though oil was burning within. She paused, hoping someone would emerge to help her, but there was only the crackling of the fire.

"Help! Is someone there? I'm bleeding to death!" she cried out.

Still, there was no response. She hobbled closer to the darkness and could see flames flickering deeper inside. It was a cramped space with rough limestone and dolomite walls haphazardly joined, allowing fragments of light to filter through. Nancy leaned against the rocky surface, applying pressure to her hemorrhaging arm. She took deeper, steadier breaths. Despite the plummeting temperature, both from her body shutting down and the cooling evening air, the lagoon's beauty once again captivated her. She took in as much as she could with her eyes before closing them, accepting the inevitability of death.

Suddenly, an eerie, raspy voice echoed through the cave.

“Do you need some help, dear?”

Nancy jolted awake, her eyes darting around. From the shadows emerged an old woman clad in a tattered gray robe, moving effortlessly towards her. Each step seemed to hover above the ground, yet her shoulders remained eerily still, like a marching soldier. Her face was featureless, marked only by deep wrinkles that suggested she was around seventy years old. Nancy strained to focus on her as she drew nearer, but her critical condition made it nearly impossible.

“Please, can you help me?” Nancy whispered, her strength waning.

The woman stood just inches away, her gaze fixed on Nancy’s injuries.

“Oh, look at you, dear,” she responded, her hand gently brushing Nancy’s hair.

An awkward silence fell as the woman examined the blood trickling from Nancy’s wounds. Nancy grew agitated.

“Take me to the hospital. I need help!” she implored. The woman sighed, her fingers brushing against Nancy’s injured arm where the wounds had started to clot.

“Your blood is getting so cold, dear. Come with me, we’ll fix you right up,” she said, gripping Nancy’s arm firmly.

What wasn’t immediately apparent was how concerning this grip would become. Nancy flinched as the woman’s harsh squeeze caused more blood to seep from her wounds. Another pause followed. The old woman’s face remained devoid of any human emotion—no compassion, sadness, or concern, just an unforgiving and somewhat sinister demeanor.

Nausea welled up within Nancy as the woman's grip felt eerily similar to the being from the lagoon.

"What the hell are you doing?" Nancy shrieked, attempting once more to break free, but her energy was depleted.

The woman stared at her with cold, unfeeling eyes, laughing hysterically as she tightened her grip. Nancy screamed so violently that she tore her vocal cords, tears streaming down her face. The woman's gaze fell upon Nancy's for the last time; her black pupils consumed the diameter of her eyes, bringing Nancy to a standstill, squealing no more—nor was her body recoiling away.

A cloak of milky whiteness swelled over Nancy's eyeballs. The woman's hand caressed Nancy's face gently before focusing on her forehead. Curling her finger, she exposed her long, uncut nail against Nancy's bare skin. Without expression, the woman began to carve into Nancy's forehead with such ferocity that blood flowed immediately onto the ground. It was as though her central nervous system had shut down, preventing her from feeling the excruciating pain she should have been experiencing.

The only movement came from Nancy swaying back and forth as the woman continued her relentless cutting. After several agonizing minutes, they both stood in a pool of blood. The woman placed her hands on Nancy's cheeks, examining the gashes that had been meticulously crafted to reveal the symbol of Wonderland. Satisfied with her work, the woman used her thumbs to close Nancy's eyelids before gouging them out simultaneously. Nancy's lifeless body crumpled to the ground as the woman released her grip.

More blood poured from her empty eye sockets, staining her face. The woman's hands were now smeared with fluids, yet she remained still, gazing forward with an eerie calmness as if Nancy were still there. She grasped one of Nancy's legs and began to drag her into the cave just as the night's navy sky welcomed the setting sun. Nancy's necklace snagged on the rocky sand before she was consumed by the darkness—a charm in the shape of an owl with sapphire eyes began to glimmer beneath the emerging starry night.

Cheyenne's eyes finally flickered open. She lay still, seemingly unaffected by the harrowing events that had just unfolded. As her surroundings slowly came into focus, she rubbed her head, trying to alleviate a sudden headache.

"Nancy?" she called out.

There was no response. She gathered her belongings and made her way to the lagoon, hoping for a better vantage point to spot Nancy if she were somewhere out of view.

"Come on! I have to get home before Chaska kills me!" Her voice echoed through the cove, but an uneasy silence hung in the air.

Cheyenne's discomfort grew with each passing moment. "Nancy!"

Her voice was now filled with concern and urgency. She scoured the area until she ended up on the north end. A glimmer in the sand caught her attention a few feet away. She approached cautiously, fidgeting with her arrow necklace. As she knelt and scooped up the stainless steel rope chain from the shallow sand, she gasped. The precious blue gemstone that made up the owl's eyes stared back at her.

"Nancy! Nancy!" she screamed, the desperation evident in her tone. For a brief moment, Cheyenne thought she spotted Nancy inside one of the caves.

"Nancy, are you in there?"

Silence filled the void as she breathed heavily, clutching her arrow necklace tightly.

"Nanc—!"

A pair of glowing golden eyes materialized from the darkness, fixed on Cheyenne. Her body froze, panic seizing her as she tightened her grip on her necklace. She fell backward and started to push the sand in front of her, initiating a hasty retreat. A voice emerged from the blackness.

"I'm fine, dear. Come here, and we'll fix you right up." Nancy's body appeared just outside the cave, yet the eyes lingered behind her.

"You look cold, Cheyenne. Come inside, and we'll take care of you."

Nancy moved with an eerie weightlessness, and whispers emanated from her eyes as she spoke.

"Come here, dear," she said, her tone softening. Cheyenne leaned forward, picking herself up but never taking her eyes off Nancy.

"Come here, dear!"

Nancy's voice turned demonic and raspy, and the sound of her roar was so disturbingly loud that it jolted Cheyenne to turn in the opposite direction and run as fast as she could. Nancy's face contorted into a malevolent smile as she was pulled back into the cave, where she would spend all eternity in the cursed cove.

VIII

EVOCATION

The air grew increasingly heavy as Cheyenne dashed through the dense redwood forest. With every step, she snapped branches and crushed leaves underfoot, struggling to maintain a steady, straight sprint. The weight of the events she'd just witnessed bore down on her, making the task even more challenging.

She knew Nancy was dead, but she couldn't fathom how things would unfold once the town discovered the truth. Rational adults wouldn't easily accept a supernatural explanation for Nancy's death. Cheyenne worried that blame might fall on her or that her smoking habit would somehow implicate her. But most urgently, she wondered if Jacob was at home. Her path initially led away from Woodland Crest Academy, traversing rough terrain and uneven walking paths. Jacob's house was about ten minutes away, but regardless of the distance and time, he was the only person Cheyenne trusted enough to confide in. She knew he'd believe her; he always did.

Inside his room, Jacob gazed out the window, his eyes tracking the swaying forest. The day had been long, and he was behind on much-needed sleep. His father's departure for a four-day sales convention in the Bay Area loomed in the morning. Jacob's father entered his room, an awkward expression on his face.

"Everything OK?" Abraham inquired. Jacob glanced up from his bed, noting the discontent on his father's face.

"Yeah, I'm fine," he replied. Abraham settled down next to him, his arm resting on Jacob's shoulder.

"It'll all be over soon; it's just that time of year. You know that."

"I know," Jacob replied.

"Be good to your mother while I'm gone. Listen to what she says, always. I'll see you soon," Abraham said, his voice filled with paternal concern.

He rose to his feet, the clicking of his shoes echoing off the walls as he made his way to pull the creaking door shut. Jacob wriggled into his covers, eagerly awaiting unconsciousness to grant him respite from the tumultuous events of the day.

A pebble tapped at his window, but Jacob didn't hear it. He sighed deeply, hoping to succumb to slumber. A second tap, this time from a larger rock, caused a slight crack in the glass. He turned to look over instantly, then rushed to the moonlight. Cheyenne stood outside, waving her hand, urging Jacob to meet her at the kitchen door.

He grabbed his hoodie and silently made his way downstairs, careful not to wake anyone in the squeaky house. Every door had a knack for squeaking, no matter how gently he turned the knob. Cheyenne's silhouette waited just beyond. The door squealed open.

"What are you doing here? It's almost nine o'clock!" Jacob asked.

"Nancy's dead! I don't know what's happening, Jacob!" Cheyenne exclaimed, hugging him.

"Cheyenne, what are you talking about?" Jacob was puzzled.

“We were at the cove, and something took her. It was controlling her. When I saw her again, it wasn’t Nancy. Jacob, it was horrifying.” Cheyenne explained, wiping tears from her face.

They stood on Jacob’s porch, whispering and constantly looking around to ensure his parents didn’t catch them.

“I don’t understand. What took Nancy? Where is she?” Jacob was growing anxious.

“There was an old woman; she took her into a cave. Jacob, she took her eyes! There was blood all over her. Whatever happened with Vern is connected to this. Nancy had the same symbol cut into her forehead!”

Cheyenne said as loud as she could in a whisper. Jacob’s heart sank.

“We need to get to Wonderland tomorrow night,” he declared before going on, “I’ve been seeing these demonic things too, things that shouldn’t be real. It has to be part of this carnival that just arrived in town. The same symbols are there.”

Cheyenne’s anxiety surged.

“What are we supposed to do? We don’t even know what we’re up against!” She cried.

“Maybe the woman took Nancy there.” Jacob said. “We have to find her and figure out what is happening in Seaside or one of us could be next.”

They locked eyes for a moment before both heard someone descending the stairs.

“Jacob? Is that you?” Jacob’s mother called out.

Cheyenne retreated to the side of the door, concealed by the wood, and without a sound, she made her escape back home. Jacob turned just in time to act like he was leaving the kitchen.

"Yes?" he replied.

"Who were you talking to? I thought I heard someone else down here," Martha said, her eyes scanning the room's corners.

"I was just getting some water," Jacob answered. He walked past her and hurried upstairs as quickly as he could. Martha gazed over the kitchen and then opened the front door to inspect the deck, her eyebrows furrowed in suspicion.

As Cheyenne entered her house, she was surprised not to find Chaska waiting for her as usual. His door was shut, and an unpleasant odor wafted from inside. Deciding to skip investigating another mystery for now, she hurried to her room. The comfort of being in her familiar space brought her unexpected happiness.

But Nancy's image haunted her, the memory of her gouged eyes refusing to fade. She couldn't shake the feeling that everything might be her fault. Perhaps if Cheyenne hadn't smoked, Nancy would still be alive, attending school, seeing her friends, and dreaming of a normal life. Nancy had been Cheyenne's first and only true friend in Seaside. Their bond was unique, akin to the relationship sisters share. They confided all their issues and worries in each other, feeling truly heard for the first time.

Despite their different backgrounds – they made efforts to understand each other's cultures, try new foods, and explore spirituality together. What deepened their connection was the shared trauma they both carried. While it wasn't physical, the emotional and mental struggles they faced brought them closer. They realized how small the world could be when two people could relate so deeply to each other's problems.

Cheyenne tidied up her desk and bed, attempting to prepare for some much-needed sleep. A bright orb passed over her window, as though a fire truck's lights were flashing on and off. However, her room faced the dense forest, making such an unlikely scenario. Through the wide-set glass, she could see only her own reflection against a black backdrop. Her desk lamp's glare obstructed her view of the outside, so she approached it to turn it off.

As she locked eyes with the mysterious outside world, she clicked off the light. The towering trees stood motionless, locked in their nightly dance. She gazed through the darkness, wondering what had caused the flare. Her fingers traced the cool glass, hoping to find something out there that would validate her sanity. She drew the heavy cotton drapes closed and headed for bed. After a long day of running and hiking, her body ached, and it pulsed with exhaustion as she nestled herself into the mattress.

"Why did you leave me, Cheyenne?" Nancy's voice whispered.

Her eyeless figure lay beside Cheyenne beneath the covers. Cheyenne turned her head and met Nancy's empty gaze. Dried blood stained Nancy's skin, her lips blistered, and her hair carried the scent of burnt wood.

"You were supposed to be my best friend, but you let me die," Nancy accused, crawling onto Cheyenne's stomach.

Immobilized by terror, Cheyenne could only let her tears flow. Nancy continued softly, "Why did you let me die?" Blood oozed from her eye cavity onto Cheyenne's face.

Cheyenne's eyes remained fixed on the ceiling as Nancy whispered into her ear, "I want you to be free with me."

Nancy's hands forced Cheyenne's mouth open, pressing on her nose. A loud gag followed by a sickening crack echoed through the room as Nancy's back arched. A tar-like liquid gushed from her mouth into Cheyenne's, who whimpered, unable to breathe.

The substance filled her mouth, and she had to gulp it down continuously to find pockets of air. Glassfuls poured into Cheyenne before her eyes rolled back, and she lost consciousness while the dark goo continued to flow.

As the morning sun filtered through her curtains, Cheyenne stirred. She found herself on the floor of her room, lazily opening and closing her eyelids while fixating on the ceiling. A faint wisp of incense smoke hovered above her.

"Where were you last night?" Chaska's voice was stern, and he stood with his arms folded, observing her from her desk chair.

The house was eerily quiet, allowing the creaking of wooden floorboards to echo with the breeze. He pressed, "Cheyenne, where were you?"

Physically, she appeared cold, pallid, and ill, but her mental and emotional state was far more concerning. It felt like an inescapable nightmare where dark emotions consumed her sanity. She knew these had emerged overnight, born from the malevolent force settling within her. Amidst this turmoil, she couldn't divulge the truth to Chaska. Revealing her involvement in Nancy's death or the possibility of inviting sinister entities into their home would lead Chaska to exile Cheyenne to their distant relatives in Washington.

There were moments in time when Cheyenne tried to explain how she felt or why she did something to Chaska, but in every instance, he would find ways to scrutinize her. Their relationship was tumultuous behind closed doors, and discussing something of this magnitude would likely provoke his anger. Cheyenne felt trapped between a wall and her demons; her only option was to endure long enough to find a way to set things right.

"I was with Nancy," she replied before heading to the bathroom.

There were faint, watery black stains on the floor where her head had rested. Cheyenne turned away, ignoring them, as she opened her door, inadvertently flooding the room with intense sunlight, revealing Jacob inside her house. Her surprise was evident, and she met Jacob's tired, bloodshot eyes.

"Hey, are you okay?" Jacob inquired, glancing at Chaska.

"We're gonna be late for school." Cheyenne quickly said.

She nodded and rushed into the bathroom. In the mirror, Cheyenne saw the sorry state she was in. Her hair clung together with the same thick substance from last night; both eyelids were swollen, and when she lifted her shirt, she noticed a spot on her side where her veins seemed unnaturally black, spreading like a sinister ink stain.

More tears shed while she rubbed her face and then eyes. From the second she applied pressure on her eyes; however, a squirt of blood rushed down her cheek. She looked at her trembling, tainted hands and inched closer to the mirror. Her fingers gently pulled down on her skin to look at the dripping coming from her caruncle.

Cheyenne saw movement coming from the inside. She squinted, watching the displacement as a black worm pushed its head out, splashing more blood. Her back met the wall when she flinched, gasping and profusely scrubbing her eyes. She looked at her hands again to find that there was no blood anywhere. And as she inspected every part of her eye, there was only her reflection looking back at her.

Their bikes crunched hundreds of tiny rocks as they rolled through the gravel roads. Seaside's weather was embracing the hues of autumn, with looming dark gray clouds that cast the forest in a deep hunter green. Both Jacob and Cheyenne carried heavy thoughts in their minds, but Jacob felt an added weight knowing that Cheyenne was grappling with whatever it was that she saw at the cove, and he was powerless to help. They needed to be even more cautious now that the news would eventually spread; Jacob was determined to protect Cheyenne.

The school was only twenty feet away when they spotted several police cars parked outside the front office.

"Jacob, I have to tell you something," Cheyenne said, her voice trembling.

“She came to me last night. I don’t know how, but Nancy was there, in my room, in my bed, next to me.”

“What did she say?” Jacob asked, his concern evident.

“That I let her die at the cove,” Cheyenne replied, her voice quivering. “Over and over again. It was like a nightmare I couldn’t wake up from. I feel like I’m losing my mind; it’s getting harder to tell what’s real and what’s my imagination.”

Jacob paused, his gaze shifting to the woods behind them, “You didn’t let her die, Cheyenne, and you’re not going crazy. I’ve been seeing things, too. I don’t know what all this means, but one thing’s for sure—you’re not alone. It feels like I’m being watched every waking second by someone, or something.” he said.

“What are we supposed to do? We can’t just go to the police or our parents for help,” Cheyenne said.

“Let’s meet up with everyone after school at Impossible City and see what we can figure out. Maybe Weston and Liam are seeing things too,” Jacob suggested.

Cheyenne nodded and leaned in to hug him.

A rare smile crept onto Jacob’s face as he held her close, “I won’t let anything happen to you, Cheyenne. I promise.”

They moved closer to the school’s entrance, but Cheyenne suddenly stopped, unnoticed by Jacob. She lifted her shirt and found the black spot on her stomach had enlarged, with more prominent stained veins.

The hallways were cleared of the morning rush by the time the two had entered. Jacob spotted Timmy by the lockers, grabbing several textbooks for homeroom. He made his way to him.

"What was with the Mad Max scene last Friday, Timmy? You guys auditioning for the fourth movie or what?" Jacob asked.

He didn't answer Jacob's question but maintained an awkward silence that was odd, even for someone as timid as Timmy. He stared back at Jacob as though he spoke a foreign language.

"W—what are you talking about?" Timmy replied.

Cheyenne peeked inside Timmy's locker; all his belongings had been cleared, yet his backpack didn't appear the least bit heavy. Jacob went on.

"Your dad almost killed me and Liam last Friday, you don't remember?"

Timmy shook his head before the bell sounded off and jolted him in the opposite direction. Jacob grabbed his arm.

"Hey, Timmy, wait——do you at least remember seeing that carnival at the Fairgrounds?"

Timmy reluctantly told him that he didn't. His pupils wandered behind Jacob and Cheyenne towards the double doors they had come from.

"Timmy, what did you see?" Cheyenne asked.

His lips quivered, but his eyes remained fixated away from them as though someone had been watching what he would say next.

"We're going to be late for class!" Timmy mumbled and broke away from his hold.

By the time they got into their homeroom class, everyone was already seated and quiet. Mrs. Davis stood glaring at Jacob and Cheyenne alongside Mr. Matthew.

When they entered their homeroom class, it was already quiet, and everyone was seated. Mrs. Davis and Mr. Matthew stared at Jacob and Cheyenne with somber expressions.

"Please find your seats," Mr. Matthew said, indicating the empty chairs in the middle of the room.

Weston and Liam exchanged bewildered glances, unsure why there was such a solemn atmosphere this morning.

Mr. Matthew placed his hand on the empty desk where Nancy used to sit, saying, "It saddens me to inform you that your classmate Nancy Thompson passed away last night."

Cheyenne wondered how they already knew; Hank and Violet wouldn't have been able to organize a search party quickly enough to find Nancy's body by morning. Liam looked up in disbelief. Jacob felt sorrow instead of shock, realizing their time to find a solution had been drastically shortened, and Weston's eyebrows furrowed with the unfamiliar experience of losing a close friend. Their gaze eventually fell on the vacant desk in the room, where Nancy used to sit, patiently waiting for the final bell to set them free.

Mr. Matthew continued, "We must respect the family's request for privacy."

Silence pervaded the first ten minutes of lunch, amplifying the grim atmosphere lingering over the school. Unappetizing cafeteria food, including cold mashed potatoes, moldy-looking vegetables, and unidentifiable meat, awaited their consumption, but their minds were elsewhere.

"She can't be gone," Liam said, his eyes fixed on the table. "Why won't they tell us what happened?"

"Maybe they just don't know yet," Weston offered, trying to provide some solace.

"They know," Liam retorted, his frustration growing, "The school wouldn't just go about its day if a student had died. They'd want to know why. The hospital or something would be involved."

"She was killed at the cove," Cheyenne said, capturing their attention.

Weston and Liam turned to her, wide-eyed.

"What?" exclaimed Weston.

"Who killed her?" Liam asked.

Cheyenne glanced at Jacob before responding, "We went there to smoke, like usual. And we both fell asleep on the beach. When I woke up and found her, she was outside of a dark cave away from where we were laid. But she wasn't alone. There was this person behind her, a woman — controlling her, changing her voice. I couldn't recognize who I was talking to anymore. This thing, it took her eyes—there was nothing but dark circles the last time I saw Nancy. She had blood all over her. Something demonic had power over her."

"She had Wonderland's symbol scratched on her forehead, Liam," Jacob added.

Weston's stomach turned.

"The carnival? Are you serious? You think Nancy was killed by some clown or some shit?"

"I saw it with my own two eyes!" Cheyenne cried, tears glistening.

"Don't think you're the only one here who cared about her, Liam." Taking a deep breath to calm down, Liam asked, "Is there a way we can get her back?"

"We don't know, maybe," Jacob began, "That's why we have to get to Wonderland tonight."

"But why would we go there?" Weston asked.

"Because whatever this thing is, it came from that place. Something's been happening in this town, and everyone's been acting strangely since it showed up. Haven't you noticed we're the only ones talking about Wonderland? If we can find out how to get rid of the circus, maybe we can bring Nancy back, our Nancy. It's our only option," Jacob asserted.

The bell rang, and they hadn't touched their food.

Weston stood up, saying, "Before we go to Wonderland, meet at my house at 7 PM."

Liam rode home alone, the forest passing by in a blur as he sped along the gravel road. The canopy of trees overhead swayed gently, a stark contrast to the urgency in his mind. Memories of a similar rush through these woods about a year ago flooded back.

"Hurry up, Liam! We're going to miss it!" Nancy had called from ahead, disappearing into the woods and toward the craggy hillsides.

Liam remembered that day vividly, as if it had happened only yesterday, the first time they were out alone.

'You're sure this is how we get there?' Liam had asked.

'What's wrong, future cadet? Afraid of a little danger?' Nancy had teased, her laughter echoing.

By the time they reached the highest point in Seaside, the sun was nearly gone. From this vantage point, they could see the entire forest and the vast ocean beyond. Liam had let his bike fall to the ground as he gazed at the breathtaking panorama.

'It's amazing, isn't it?' Nancy had remarked, 'And just think, all those birds flying around get to see this every single day of their lives.'

'Nancy, it's... it's incredible! How did you find this place?' Liam had asked in awe. She sat at the edge of the cliff, her legs dangling above the hundreds of feet below, and waved him closer.

'I bet you could draw a masterpiece from this,' she said.

Nancy was the only one who had seen Liam's early landscape drawings and recognized the immense potential within him, even if he didn't realize it at the time.

'A masterpiece? You think so?' Liam laughed. She had smiled at him.

'Make-out Hill, that's what this place is called, by the way,' Nancy revealed.

Liam snapped back to the present, overwhelmed by nostalgia and the lingering sensation of their first kiss as they looked out over the town they hoped to escape one day. They had come from entirely different backgrounds; Liam's family struggled financially, with generations of military men, while Nancy was born into wealth. His family was fractured, with parents who seemed emotionally absent, and he had shouldered responsibilities far beyond his years, including caring for his younger brother, Dalton.

Liam's affection for Nancy had grown from a young infatuation to a deep and abiding love. She had provided the attention he had longed for, someone who listened without judgment and understood that differing perspectives were acceptable. He wanted to be an artist, captivated by the wonders of nature, but he had kept his passion hidden, fearing his family's disapproval. When he was eight, his father had discovered a dozen of Liam's ocean paintings and promptly burned them. Family honor and conformity were more important than self-expression. But with Nancy, he could talk about art for hours, and she shared her dreams of travel.

She felt like a bird trapped in a gilded cage, her family's wealth offering opportunities but also imposing restrictions. Her parents rarely ventured beyond Seaside, and she yearned for the freedom to do it herself. Liam listened to her problems and offered solutions, but mostly, he offered a listening ear. He knew that her situation wouldn't improve as long as she lived with her family, but she held onto the hope of a future with him. After high school, they planned to leave Seaside together, uncertain about their path but determined to figure it out side by side.

Tears welled in Liam's eyes, and he slowed to a stop as he reached the road that led to his house and the woods. The blades of grass were undulated like a green sea, a perfect painting that he wished he could show Nancy. Lost in his reverie, he heard a twig snap behind him, like the sound of a breaking bone. He turned abruptly.

"Who's there?" he called out, his heart pounding.

Only the rustling breeze answered. A tense silence hung in the air as he waited for a response. He took a deep breath and turned around to find himself face-to-face with a naked, elderly woman.

"Shit! Who are you?" Liam cried out, his voice trembling.

The woman began to laugh, her arms outstretched as she took slow, shuffling steps toward him. Her eyes were entirely white, her teeth crooked and rotting. Laughter bubbled from her lips, mixed with drool of a sickly brown hue. Liam scrambled backward until he was far enough from his bike to make an escape. He managed to pick himself up and sprint away from the cackling woman. Even as he ran and pedaled with all his might, her eerie laughter echoed in his ears as though she were next to him. He put enough distance between them to safely glance back, but she had vanished, leaving behind an unsettling void.

IX

REVERIE

His eyes scanned the cul-de-sac through his closed, eggshell-polished blinds. At any moment, one of them could be the next to die without warning. Weston's house was nestled in the suburban neighborhood complex between the Woodland Crest and downtown. His parents, Adam and Mary, had moved to Evergreen Grove in Seaside around twenty years ago. They had become especially close to Jacob's family following Isaac's death, which had also brought the community together in mourning.

He checked the clock on his nightstand, and it read 6:43 p.m. After one last glance outside, he walked over to his bed and retrieved a secondary backpack hidden in the far corner underneath. Inside, he found random papers from the "Lost Ones" file and Jacob's Wonderland drawing. A bright red car started its engine in his driveway; his parents were off to Nancy's to show support. Weston watched them reverse and pull away from his street, giving him a somewhat rejuvenating sensation. He breathed a little easier now.

About twenty minutes passed before the sound of bicycle clatter echoed from the parallel road. Riding cautiously were Jacob, Liam, and Cheyenne, with Cheyenne leading the way. Daylight was waning, casting darker shadows over their features. They rode into Weston's backyard and parked against the side of his house. Weston greeted them at the door, and they made their way upstairs to his room.

"Whoa, whoa, hey, take your shoes off, man!" Weston said, stopping Liam from ascending the stairs.

Liam sighed, "Right now is when you're going to be most concerned with dirt on your carpet?"

"Yeah, because if I survive this shit, that means I'll have to hear all about that shit afterward. And I don't think I'll have the energy for both. Take your damn shoes off!" Weston said, ascending the steps.

Weston's home had needed renovations many years ago due to its faulty infrastructure. Termites and other insects had been found tearing through the wooden framework. Because of the severity of the damage, workers had used the house's open interior blueprint to make repairs from the inside out. The walkways were just wide enough for kids to pass between the gaps. Weston had discovered a hollow point in his closet that he had accidentally broken into when he was younger. Once you were able to maneuver through the slim corridors, there was an open space next to the attic that was hidden from the whole layout of the house. Large enough for Weston to create his own lair.

"So why'd you call us all here?" Jacob asked.

"The other day, I was going through some student files in Mr. Matthew's office for tutoring," Weston began. He spread the papers from his backpack onto his bed. "There was this folder in the back of his drawer called the 'Lost Ones,' and it had a bunch of records of kids and students who were either lost or dead. It even said what happened to their parents, and a lot of them died shortly after their kids." No one said anything; they simply waited for Weston to continue as he showed them the files.

"There were at least fifteen kids who were dead, and I didn't even go through the entire pile of papers. But no one has ever told me about any kid tragically dying here in Seaside. Have you guys heard anything?" Weston asked.

Each of them thought about it and couldn't think of a single instance.

"I mean, it's a small town; we'd know pretty fast if someone were gone. Word gets around fast, right?" Liam said.

"That's exactly my point. This is such a small place. Why has no one mentioned anything about anyone disappearing or dying? Especially this many?" Weston questioned.

The room fell silent, save for the chirping of crickets. They huddled in a semi-circle around Weston's bed.

"And then there's this. This was in the same folder." Weston pulled out Jacob's Wonderland drawing.

Jacob took the paper and furrowed his brows. He ran his fingers over the graphic and the bottom where his name was signed.

"Holy shit, Jacob, you drew this?" Liam asked.

"No, I don't remember ever doing this," Jacob muttered. Cheyenne looked more worried than ever. Jacob turned to Weston, who was packing his backpack with essentials.

"How do we know this was really mine?" Jacob asked.

"That drawing was with Isaac's file," Weston revealed.

Jacob's eyes widened.

"There wasn't a lot of information on it, but I don't think his death was caused by SIDS, Jacob. Follow me; you'll understand after I show you what I found in the library."

Weston zipped up his backpack and headed to the closet door. The sides opened as if it were an entryway to a panic room.

"By the way, don't tell my parents about this," he warned.

Liam, Jacob, and Cheyenne exchanged glances before following him into the hidden space within the skeleton of his house. They tiptoed sideways through the splintered wood until they reached an open area with several lamps, blankets, towering stacks of books, and a large timeline diagram documenting the disappearances.

"Wow," Cheyenne said.

Liam was the next to enter.

"What is all this?" he asked.

"This is where I come to be alone, usually to read and stuff or look at my dad's Playboy magazines," Weston said.

"But more recently, to look at the details of the missing children," Weston continued.

For his age, Weston was remarkably brilliant. He learned on his own terms, finding unconventional ways to solve equations, riddles, and develop language skills. This room was his portal to another world, one where he could create his own reality and have the freedom to explore it. They spaced out, examining the various items scattered around the room. One of them was a book,

Seaside: Nature's Canvas, 1882

It detailed the town's founding and its early members. Jacob flipped through the pages, landing in a section that appeared to be a map of the local wilderness and certain points of the beach. A bolded point at the edge of the sea had the initials

LC

"What's this?" Cheyenne said, touching a diagram pinned to the board.

"This is what's going to change everything," Weston said, approaching with an old, dusty book whose cover was nearly torn off.

"I didn't have time to look at every record, but I had enough to find a pattern in the disappearances." He pointed to the first entry on the timeline.

"Seaside was founded in 1882, and the first recorded death came thirteen years later in 1895: Azazel, who died by fire. Another case, Emily Gilda, died from blood loss in 1947, fifty-two years later. Her parents were also pronounced dead around the same time as her."

"I don't see a pattern," Liam remarked.

"I didn't either until I looked closer at the years when these children were declared dead: 1895, 1908, 1921, 1934. It's going in increments of thirteen years," Weston explained, looking at Jacob.

"Isaac died in 1973, thirteen years ago today." Jacob felt a wave of sickness wash over him at the thought that his brother's death might have been part of something larger.

"My parents always told me it was just something that happened to some babies, and there wasn't anything we could do to save him. What would be the point of lying to me?" Jacob wondered aloud.

"Look at this," Weston said, opening the untitled textbook.

Inside were additional historical details about Seaside's early years. He flipped through pages filled with articles and stopped at old sepia photographs. Though blurry, the last names of individuals in the photos were still legible. The first photo showed ten men in front of the town's first sign, some of them having surnames that are familiar to Jacob and Liam.

"Anderson, Matthew, Davis. I didn't know they were here from the beginning," Liam remarked.

The second photo displayed the first church and four families standing outside. None of them recognized the families from the names listed. But these families were dressed formally, as though part of a ceremony. The men wore long robes that reached the floor, and the women donned red gowns, identical to what Cheyenne had seen those people wearing inside the church at Impossible City.

The third photo, however, was what Weston wanted to show them. It featured two dozen individuals outside the gates of Wonderland.

"That can't be—" Jacob started.

"Wonderland. This was taken in October of 1895, around the same time as the first recorded death," Weston said.

The last names in the photo included several they all knew. As they turned the pages, more townspeople and circus performers appeared together, including a tall man in a suit wearing a top hat, part of the freak shows. He towered over seven feet tall, his right hand touching the ground as he stood surrounded by people who appeared dwarfed next to him. He held his left hand up in a gesture of greeting.

With each passing decade, new photos were added to the album. More modern-looking townspeople were photographed behind the same carnival. The same surnames appeared. An eerie feeling settled into Weston's hideaway.

"They all look so..." Liam began.

"Happy." Cheyenne finished.

"There should have been at least a dozen children missing at the time." Weston said.

The gravity of the situation intensified, veering into a more sinister realm. In the latest discovered photograph, a woman stood roughly thirty feet from Wonderland's entrance. Clad in a dress as dark as raven feathers, appearing to be in her twenties, she clasped her rawboned knuckles together. Her delicate, caramel-skinned physique was entrapped by an expression, projecting a piercing stare that seemed to reach back through the observer. The image itself elicited a spine-tingling sensation, as though the woman in the photo possessed an awareness of being watched. Jacob, keen-eyed, discerned a distinctive set of initials delicately etched in pencil on the reverse side of the portrait.

"AC." He whispered to himself.

"They knew all along. Those motherfuckers have been hiding this shit from everyone since this town was built!" Liam exclaimed.

"We need to go tell the police or something," he continued.

Weston closed the book.

"All we know right now is that kids seem to either die or disappear when Wonderland comes to town. We don't have any real proof of a conspiracy happening here. Besides, do you think they'll actually believe a couple of middle-schoolers?" Weston reasoned.

"We need to find some evidence at Wonderland that can tie them to the killings," Jacob said.

Weston handed them each a pair of headphones with long antennae and extended mouthpieces, "Here, take these. Turn them on with the button under the right earpiece. They're touch-to-talk."

"What are these?" Cheyenne asked.

"I made them. It's not that hard, really. My dad has a bunch of old headphones from work, and if you can find a battery-powered transceiver, you can install them to send and receive radio messages with one another. If each headphone is tuned to the right station, they'll all be on the same frequency."

"We'll be able to communicate from anywhere inside Wonderland," Jacob realized.

Cheyenne and Liam exchanged glances.

"Weston, this is brilliant!" Cheyenne said, a newfound determination in her eyes.

"Long live the nerds, baby." Weston laughed.

Gusts of air pulverized the immature saplings emerging from the outer forest. They didn't know what to expect going into Wonderland by themselves. There was no plan, only the hope that they could find a way to bring Nancy back. With each pedal, Liam's excitement overtook his nervousness. He believed, with unwavering conviction, that she would return if they could break this pattern of missing children. The candy-painted heavens barely pierced the night, its darting clouds sometimes revealing themselves to the lower altitudes where the town's streetlights played their feeble tricks.

Jacob, constantly squinting at the dim road, finally switched on his bike light. The others quickly followed suit, almost forgetting they had their own headlights.

"Over here," Jacob said as they came to a halt at a dead-end, flanked by a massive boulder.

Beyond the dense trees lay a pathway leading into the depths of Wonderland. Silence accompanied them. They began to put on their headsets. Liam struggled to adjust his, attempting to lengthen it without breaking it. Weston stepped in to help.

"Dammit, man, it's just a click and tug," Weston said.

A low buzz emanated as Cheyenne activated her headset, followed by a more pronounced ringing as Jacob, Weston, and Liam did the same.

"Turn the knob until you can hear me," Weston instructed.

"We have to be on the same frequency for this to work. Try to stay close, too; we have a leeway of fifty feet before the radio signal starts acting up. You'll know you're too far when the antenna blinks red."

"Okay, got it," Liam said, and Jacob nodded in agreement.

Cheyenne signaled her understanding. The carnival had fallen into an eerie silence since they parked their bikes. Apart from their hushed whispers, the only sounds came from the creatures of the dusk as they ventured out onto the earth. Their four heads peeked over the hill, curious and apprehensive, gazing upon Wonderland and its vast expanse.

The numerous nylon tents stood still. The ground upon which Wonderland was built had lost its grass, now a withered, yellowed patch. In stark contrast, the world outside the carnival thrived with lush green meadows. They retreated behind the boulder.

“Okay, here’s what we’re going to do. We’ll split into pairs to cover more ground. Cheyenne and I will go inside, while Liam and Weston will stay outside. This place has to be bigger than fifty feet, so we’ll stay within the range by walking close to each other,” Jacob said.

“And if someone catches us?” Weston asked.

“Run to Impossible City. They won’t be able to find us there,” Jacob replied.

After a moment to rally their confidence, they uncovered themselves to Wonderland and walked towards the unknown.

Their shoes crunched with every step they took, and each antenna maintained a hushed ringing. Seaside’s briskness began to show its disdain for human flesh the deeper into the night they prowled; their breaths started to steam into the air. Liam and Weston watched as Jacob and Cheyenne made their way towards the inner realm. Moonlight polished what could not be seen in the darkness, and although the neighboring tepees were roped closed, the inert carny booths that hosted games were uncovered. They looked back, and Weston gave them a nod, acknowledging that the search had now commenced.

Cheyenne touched the worn-down wooden base of a countertop. It was jagged as she ran her hand down its length. She picked her hand up to find it covered with residue of black soot. Soundlessness plagued this field from the dirt to its towering tips. Although Wonderland had been in Seaside for only five days, dust and cobwebs that looked accumulated over the decades buried the attraction from the inside out.

“This place reeks of smoke.” Radioed in from Weston.

“I don’t like this. Why is no one here?” Cheyenne asked.

Jacob turned his head, thinking he had glimpsed someone walking inside a tent. The numerous blind spots around them, coupled with their large headphones that hindered their hearing, made them vulnerable. Cheyenne stopped at one of the games, where a sign displayed bold text against a vibrantly colored, child-like backdrop:

HANG THE INDIAN!

The letters were adorned with faded rose ink, outlining a lackluster image that time had nearly erased. The game featured seven individual slots, each with a piece of rope for the players to pull. The combined tension would then yank on a single noose at the center of the enclosure. An empty stool awaited the next unfortunate participant, whether willingly or unwillingly.

As Cheyenne examined the mural’s scenic depiction, she noticed similarities to her own home terrain. Painted beautifully was an open pasture with trees in every corner, while the sky shared its space with the sun’s lemonade-yellow rays. Her eyes scrutinized the image until she saw a German Shepherd with a gray coat and blue eyes, resembling Maka. Confused and startled by the connection, Cheyenne’s gaze shifted to the next portrait, where a girl hung from a tree with her wrists slit open. Her mouth covered in horror, she recognized the girl wearing the same clothes that Cheyenne was wearing. Several children stood behind the girl, pulling the rope with smiles of joy on their faces. The horrifying depiction of her own death stared back at her, causing Cheyenne’s stomach to clench.

She touched her side, where the black tendrils were spreading across her body, and felt an intense, ear-splitting buzzing. In pain, she searched for Jacob, her voice trembling as she spoke into the mouthpiece.

"Jacob, where are you?"

There was no response on the other end, only subtle static. She moved breathlessly through the tents until she discovered Jacob lying shirtless on the ground, with three men whose arms were inside his twelve-year-old chest. Jacob's ribs appeared to have been forcibly pushed forward, causing an irregular angle in each bone. Blood stained the men's cheeks as they chewed with a wickedness that suggested they hadn't eaten in months. They stared at Cheyenne without pause, continuing to devour Jacob's tender flesh. Cheyenne was paralyzed.

"Jacob," she whispered, tears streaming down her jawline as she slowly moved backward.

The static from the headset was distracting, so she removed it from her neck. In her panic, she found herself running in a completely different direction, wiping her face with every stride. When she turned to check if anyone was following her, her forehead collided with Jacob's chin, sending them both tumbling to the ground.

Her forehead began to drip blood, and Jacob's chin had a graze, "Cheyenne, what happened?"

Jacob held his chin.

"Oh fuck, you're bleeding!"

"What's going on? How are you here?" Cheyenne asked.

"What are you talking about? I was looking for you for the past twenty minutes!" He said.

She looked at him and his chest. "No, I saw you—you were—you were just laying there! There were these men; they had their arms in you——inside you! They were eating you alive!" She shrieked.

"What men? Cheyenne, where did you go?" Jacob asked.

A thundering, sonorous blend of carnival sounds soared over the tents as the once-dormant attractions banished the darkness with their vibrant, simulated colors. Mechanical grinding and screeching echoed through the air as a musical performance filled the night. Wonderland had awakened.

Their eyes reflected a multitude of vintage pastel hues, both frightened and awed by the spectacle. Breaking away from Wonderland's new found beauty in its facade animations seemed nearly impossible. Cheyenne's eyes met Jacob's, and she noticed his antenna.

"Jacob!" she urgently muttered, grabbing his arm.

He followed her gaze and saw her looking at his blinking antenna. He turned his head, trying to locate Liam and Weston, but the multitude of objects obstructed their view. Jacob and Cheyenne stood and paced in different directions, attempting to remain hidden from anyone else present.

"Should we go back?" Cheyenne asked.

"They can't be too far away. Come on, let's keep going in. We still need to find some kind of evidence here," Jacob replied.

They sprinted around the corner, entering the heart of the carnival.

The headset expelled a surge of high pitch squeals as Weston fiddled with his frequency knob, "Fuck man, I think it's broken."

"It's so quiet in there." Weston continued.

Liam turned to him, "We've been at it for almost forty-five minutes and nothing— we gotta go in there."

"Are you crazy, man?" Weston jolted, "Just keep scouting the outside— we're probably just a little ways behind them. If we go in, we won't have a way to get out if it's a trap——no way to call for help."

He looked at the forest behind them and then tapped Liam's back, "We're going to bring her back, Liam."

The path along the outer rim was illuminated by the starry night sky and waxing gibbous moon. It was nearly 9 p.m. Even though they had been disconnected for twenty minutes now, Liam's determination to find Nancy kept him alert. He knew that if their roles were reversed, she would do the same for him.

Weston continued to twist the dial, listening for anything remotely resembling Jacob or Cheyenne. They lingered on their designated path outside the carnival, but with no backup plan in place, it was beginning to become more and more distressing the longer their friends were there. A sudden breeze rustled through their T-shirts, carrying the scent of charred wood.

"Liam!" a soft, cooing voice whispered, caressing his ears.

Liam looked toward Wonderland, where the voice seemed to originate, but he could only see shadows rippling along the sides of the tents. He turned back to Weston, who was now sitting and hadn't reacted to the whisper, fine-tuning his headset. When Liam looked toward the darkness again, he saw a small girl's figure peeking out from the edge of a tent about twenty feet away.

"Nancy!" he called out.

But the figure remained silent, just watching and waiting. Behind Liam, Weston thought he heard a quiet conversation and tried to identify the source. He adjusted his headset, angling the antenna for better reception. After a moment of static, Weston managed to pick up the connection and eavesdropped on the low, indistinct voices. After a pause of only static, he found the connection and listened in on the mumbles. It was too low to make out what they were saying, yet he recognized that it was a woman speaking, increasingly faster the longer he eavesdropped.

"...Mine… Is mine… Is mine… Is mine... She is mine... Mine... Is mine... She is mine," the voice murmured.

Then, there was a brief pause.

"She's mine!" A woman's deafening, raspy scream nearly shattered Weston's eardrums.

He frantically tore off his headset, watching as the battery indicator blinked red.

"Oh no, damn it!" Weston cursed.

The earpiece emitted a final wave of electrical noises before its light faded away. He pressed every button in desperation, hoping to revive the device, but it was already dead. The sheer size of Wonderland was overwhelming, even with the aid of technology. Without it, they were now relying on luck to find a way out together.

Liam hadn't moved since he spotted the girl. Seaside's cold air numbed his bare skin, causing his motor functions to slow painfully.

"Nancy, it's me, Liam," he whispered tensely.

The moonlight illuminated the girl's arm as she extended it from the shadows that enveloped her. She motioned for Liam to come closer with her slow, eerily stiff fingers. After three gestures, her hand froze in the celestial spotlight.

"Come to me, Liam," her voice floated through the air, echoing slightly.

As the sound of Nancy's words reached Liam's ears, his tense expression softened, and a faint smile appeared on his face.

"I knew you were okay," he said, moving closer to her and leaving Weston behind.

"I missed you so much," he confessed.

Weston looked up when he heard footsteps and saw Liam walking further into Wonderland.

"Liam!" Weston shouted.

As Weston attempted to get back on his feet, he found his hands covered in a muddy, adhesive-like substance. With disgust, he groaned while trying to separate his fingers. He started to take his first step in the direction Liam had gone when suddenly, the woman of Wonderland appeared behind him, constricting his skull and jugular.

The path ahead grew darker as staggered clouds moved to obstruct the gift of moonlight. Liam's backpack jangled with an arsenal of objects in the pitch-black darkness. He fumbled to find his flashlight.

"Nancy, where are you?" he called out.

A glimmer came from his flashlight when he finally turned it on after years of non-use. It illuminated his surroundings, and he spotted the silhouette of a girl walking behind another tent. He sprinted to the other side.

"Hey, wait!" Liam yelled.

Golden rays faintly pulsed from the partly open flaps of one of the tents, noticeable in the night. Intrigued, he moved closer. A glow emanated from inside, and comfort and warmth washed over him as he reached in, the light caressing his skin—anticipating a reunion with his love.

"Nancy?" Liam called out.

X

REBIRTH

Liam surveyed the grandiose tent and its spacious enclosure. No one seemed to be inside or appeared. A stillness enveloped him as he entered; the initial warmth he felt turned into a suffocating anxiety, waiting for someone to reveal themselves. His breaths were the only audible sound while the lights continued to flicker against the fabric walls from burning candles around the edges.

Liam reached into his pocket for his butterfly knife. Suddenly, a woman dressed in a nurse's outfit emerged from a crevice, walking swiftly past Liam with a bundle of towels in her hands. He jumped out of the way, barely missing her.

"She needs more towels!" Someone hollered from the other end behind him.

"I'm here!" the nurse yelled back.

Liam was puzzled as ever, swiveling his head to locate where the commotion was coming from. Cries of agony erupted from a woman as the nurses patted her wet and clammy skin. A white cover wrapped around her waist extended to the ground; the woman was in labor. Her legs were angled to alleviate the process. Liam hid behind a post to remain hidden, although the first nurse should have clearly seen him when she walked by earlier. The doctor under the cloak encouraged her to keep pushing.

"You're doing great, Wendy! Keep going!" The doctor said.

Liam started to feel disoriented; it was his mother giving birth. Her face looked much younger, with fewer wrinkles under her eyes and voluptuous hair, similar to what he remembered from old photographs at home. Liam concentrated on the man next to her now, who had the same characteristics as his father once had. John comforted Wendy through her suffering.

"We're so close, honey. Everything is going to be okay," he said.

Her wailing grew louder and took on a raspy tone, vibrating through the tent's framework. John looked at the doctor with a more serious expression and nodded his head, indicating the need to hasten the situation. They worked with little light, the apricot embers barely providing enough illumination to identify the medical tools next to them. Wendy gave another push; the veins on her neck became pronounced.

"I see the head!" the doctor exclaimed.

Wendy tried to respond verbally but resorted to short breaths guided by the nurses next to her.

"Come on, Wendy! Keep pushing!" They yelled.

Her screams synchronized with the baby's cries as the birth unfolded before everyone's eyes. Liam turned away, feeling queasy at the sight. Only the newborn's cries now filled the tent.

"It's a healthy baby girl, ma'am!" The nurse said.

The doctor cut the umbilical cord and handed the baby to the nurse for cleaning.

"My baby girl, where is my baby girl?" Wendy asked, catching her breath and attempting to push herself up to hold her.

"She's getting cleaned up, honey, it's okay," John reassured her. He continued, "You did so wonderful; I'm so proud of you."

The nurses and staff members stood in a line next to her bed while the doctor held the baby in his arms.

"What are they doing, John?" Wendy asked, growing more worried.

"Do not be afraid of those who kill the body, for the soul cannot die," the doctor said.

Wendy asserted, "Doctor, give me my baby. Why aren't they giving me my baby? John?" She began to look uneasy, nudging him.

"John! Tell him to give me my child!" she screamed.

But John, along with everyone else, only stared back at her. Liam looked over again, hearing the distress in his mother's voice.

"I said give me my fucking baby!" Wendy shrieked.

The nurses stepped aside, creating a path in front of Wendy. All but the doctor and John bowed their heads.

"I don't understand what is going on! I just want my daughter," Wendy said.

She tried to get off the bed, but before she could, the nurses and John restrained her.

"What are you doing? Get off me! Give me my fucking baby!"

Wendy struggled to break free but was already too exhausted to fight back. From the shadows came an old woman who was clothed in a white Victorian dress, limping towards her. With a face that was anemic, her unruly gray hairs would sway from every step and expose the violet-colored blood vessels blotching her cheeks. She walked carrying a sinister grin and opened her arms once she caught a glimpse of the baby.

"Honey, we talked about this; everything is going to be okay now. Please, just rest," John said to her.

"No! I won't let you do this to her! You can't do this! Please, stop! Let me go!" she begged them to free her, but the old woman now held their child in her skeletal arms.

The nurses injected Wendy with a serum that caused her to become disoriented. The doctor turned to the woman and spoke her name.

"Lilith, we bring you the offering of life to rejuvenate our own!" He said.

Lilith looked upon him with disgust and then away onto Wendy. Lilith's smile reappeared, rejoicing with Wendy's child in her arms. Wendy sobbed, "Please, take me instead." She repeated.

Lilith gazed at the baby, her yellow eyes piercing its newly exposed skin. Lilith brought her closer to her face, where she smelled her scent, and paused at her forehead. A sliver of her vile dark green tongue stroked against the baby's flesh, leaving a lustrous gleam. Wendy used her last bits of energy, attempting to grab her daughter.

John looked at Lilith, who was already looking back at him with unforgiving eyes. He shuddered and buried his face into Wendy's shoulders, keeping her from falling forward. Even with the chemicals coursing through her body, Wendy remained awake and could only watch as her daughter was taken by this evil. Lilith lifted her chin up and raised the child as though she were presenting her to the heavens; the candle's illumination fixated on her face, which was littered with wrinkles. Her baby and Lilith mirrored inside Wendy's pupils.

"Please, stop," Wendy faintly spoke.

An abrupt crack came from Lilith's fingers, and in an instant, there was no more crying echoing in the tent. John burrowed deeper into Wendy's body, trying to mute what he just heard. Wendy's jaw dropped while a cascade of tears streamed effortlessly and endlessly. The sound of skin being torn apart was followed by body tissue gushing into Lilith's mouth. Blood splattered all over the ground and smeared the walls.

She devoured the baby's feeble core maniacally, chewing faster the deeper she indulged. No one dared to make a move, even Liam, who was cemented behind the post, holding his breath. Her consumption lasted for several minutes until she ultimately finished and dropped the hollowed body. The slaughter left an uneven spread of gore on her; her hands trembled, scraping the remnants onto her tongue.

"I'm so sorry, I had to do it," John cried to Wendy, "I did it for us—I did it so we could survive and start again one day. I love you so much."

Lilith's binge was over, but everyone stood still, frozen.

But the longer he spoke, the deeper Wendy regressed into herself, muted in shock. Liam stared at the lifeless vessel that was leaking additional fluids on the floor. He rubbed his face, hoping the image would vanish, but he soon realized that what he was looking at was real. An unsettling and unnatural stoppage of time transpired; not even their clothes drifted with the force of gravity. Liam waited for something to break this eerie occult stillness, but nothing happened. After a while, with more dead air, he stepped towards them. Their skin seemed lighter when Liam came closer, and their facial features were suspended, too. The blood on Lilith's face was still wet, and Wendy's eyelids were still flushed with tears. Liam was walking around the bed when a creak came from behind. His head shot up, fearful that they would awaken from their episode, but their limbs remained unmoved.

Liam crept closer to Lilith, magnetized, enthralled by her pulsating yellow pupils. As he was lured by Nancy, he mindlessly walked to Lilith. The candles' waxes were now puddling out of its pond of beeswax, the flames slowly decaying away. Lilith's sereneness masked the ungodly murder and cannibalism. Liam was less than two feet from her and noticed the symbol of Wonderland branded in the center of her neck at the suprasternal notch; he watched the marking's outline begin to secrete a black fluid. Lilith's pupils were still moist and glistening.

There and then, Lilith blinked once but carried on staring in the same direction. Stunned, Liam's chest expanded rapidly to prevent himself from passing out. He managed to pull away from this spell-binding curse and thrust forward, sprinting away and out of the tent—not knowing where to go or what to do now.

An array of streaming fluorescent twinkles bathed his body from head to toe. The carousel of zoo animals shrilled, accompanied by horns of instruments. Astonished and perplexed by the marvel of vibrancy, Liam looked on, never having seen a carnival come to life in person.

The night dragged on much longer than they had anticipated; it was around 10:30 p.m., and they hadn't found a shred of evidence. Jacob was drained, panting in a corner after an hour of scouring in every direction.

He turned on his headset and tried calling out, “Weston? Liam?”

He continued into the microphone with a monotone mutter, but there was no response from the other end. Drowning in the drone of Wonderland’s sounds, Jacob eventually turned it off.

“Still nothing,” he sighed.

Cheyenne removed her headset, “Yeah, I’m not getting anything either. This is bad; we need to find them and get out of here.”

Posters covered the tents, advertising various freak shows. Passing by them, one in particular caught their attention. It displayed a menacing clown act, featuring a face painted powdered white with blood-orange around its mouth, contrasting with blackened eyelids. The paper showed signs of wear, with bent corners and faded colors, but the clown’s golden eyes remained strikingly vivid. Under his chin, in massive font, read the words:

BAKU IS WATCHING YOU

The clown’s image held them captive, and Cheyenne and Jacob found it hard to move past. A sequence of piano keys filled the air, drowning out the cacophony of Wonderland. These soothing chords briefly suppressed the chaos.

“It sounds so beautiful,” Cheyenne said.

“What the hell? Where is that coming from?” Jacob looked around.

The melody transitioned into an orchestration of eerie variations before a distant scream was heard. Jacob darted between the tents, following the cry.

“Come on!” He called Cheyenne.

The music grew louder as they approached Wonderland's center. From an aerial viewpoint, Jacob and Cheyenne's search was ridiculed by the increasingly vast labyrinth of huts and arrangements. Similar to mice in a maze, only the observer knew how fruitless their hopes were in evading the evil within. Their pursuit came to a halt as they turned the next corner, discovering Weston surrounded by others.

"Weston!" Jacob cried out.

Cheyenne gripped her arrow charm tightly. The music continued, but it's tempo shifted to something slower and more haunting. Weston was bound to scorched wood, fumes billowing into the air. He was suspended at least ten feet off the ground, with a shorter piece of wood nailed perpendicularly to keep his arms above his head. It stood in the middle of a pathway, marked with the symbol of Wonderland on the dried grass.

Weston's chin rested on his chest, unresponsive to the music or the light. Children encircled him, reaching out their hands to touch each other, watching Weston's will to live wane. One of the girls separated from the group and turned to face Jacob. Her complexion was ghostly, and visible gashes marred her skin, making her unsettling to look at.

She looked at Jacob impassively before opening her mouth and reciting, "Mistress Mary, quite contrary, how does your garden grow?"

Her voice dragged with every word, and suddenly, the other children dropped to their knees, touching their foreheads to the ground in submission. Jacob and Cheyenne watched in horror as the child spoke, unaware of Lilith standing several feet behind them.

The girl took several steps toward them and continued to sing emotionlessly, accompanying the subtle piano keys, "With silver bells and cockle shells, and so my garden grows."

The song ended, and an eerie silence filled the air. The girl smiled, revealing rotting teeth. She joined the other children, who all bowed in Jacob and Cheyenne's direction. Cheyenne recoiled in pain, clutching her sides.

"What's wrong?" Jacob asked.

"My insides feel like they're on fire," she grimaced.

Cheyenne collapsed, unable to bear her own weight due to the excruciating pain in her stomach. A dark shadow fell over her. Lilith, once distant, now stood behind Cheyenne. But their attention remained fixed on the children and Weston.

"We have to get him out of there. Can you stand?" Jacob whispered to Cheyenne.

She applied some pressure to her belly and winced.

"I can't. It hurts too much," she said, lifting her shirt to reveal a spreading infection across her veins.

"Cheyenne! What happened to you?" Jacob exclaimed. Cheyenne glanced at the bowing children again.

"I don't have time to explain, Jacob. Just get Weston. I'll be fine here," she said.

Although Jacob was deeply concerned, he understood that he needed to act quickly to save Weston.

"I'm fine, Jacob. Go!" she urged.

Jacob looked into her eyes, seeing his own reflection. Their lips met with a sense of nostalgia, as if they were old lovers reuniting after a lifetime apart. Cheyenne opened her eyes and gasped when she saw Weston lifting his head.

"Jacob!" she screamed, nudging him to look.

"Weston!" Jacob screamed. He scrambled to his feet and ran as fast as he could. Jacob sprinted to Weston, leaving Cheyenne alone with Lilith, who stood silently by her. Cheyenne tried standing once more but failed to get herself off the ground. Jacob skipped past the laid bodies and immediately tugged at the ropes binding Weston's wrists.

"Don't worry, Weston, I've got you," he assured him.

Weston managed to mouth the word, "Jacob."

"Almost there, just stay with me. We're going to get out of here!" Jacob said.

Cheyenne attempted to inch little by little off the ground when her hand sensed a cool dampness on the withered turf. She turned her hand over to find spots of sludge on her palm. She gently tapped the muck with her other hand and watched its adhesive strength keep form even when she pulled away from it. A low growl from behind Cheyenne trembled her bones.

Drops of warm ooze dripped against the top of her head, thumping and continuous as they drizzled down Cheyenne's forehead, then face. Lilith's repulsive and revolting claws made their way across her jawline and unforgivingly pivoted her skull. Lilith suddenly caressed Cheyenne's stained jowl, somewhat scratching into her cheekbone cavity.

Their eyes finally met; Lilith lavished a grin while Cheyenne became nauseous and winced, grabbing her stomach with both arms. Cheyenne's eyes became submerged with pallidity, and her short breaths became nonexistent. With her arms that now swayed without Cheyenne's control, she was no longer herself but rather prey that was immobilized, awaiting its predator to strike. Lilith lessened the gap between them. Her tongue ran the course of Cheyenne's temple, tasting the flavors secreted from her skin.

Weston fell to the ground once Jacob pulled the final knot loose. He was too weak to walk on his own. Indentations of red marks surfaced around his wrists and ankles. Jacob took Weston's arm over his shoulder and paused once he saw Lilith.

"Cheyenne!" Jacob blared, but his voice became silent as the musical number from the piano rejoined and roared throughout Wonderland.

Lilith ventured on torturing Cheyenne, whose eyes maintained its camouflage paste.

"You let me die, Cheyenne," Nancy's voice spilled from Lilith's lips.

"Why did you let me die?" She screamed at Cheyenne.

Weston fell back into an unconscious state, and the weight of his idle body was too heavy for Jacob to carry alone. He struggled to keep them upright, keeping his focus on Cheyenne. His skin began to burn from the inside out, causing him to let go of Weston. The horrors of Wonderland's past began to physically materialize as though Jacob awoke into a nightmare——he saw images of men, women, and children burning alive all around him.

His blurry vision flickered along with the incinerating pain. Jacob could hear the screams of the children become louder. He rubbed his eyes while teetering between two terrorizing realities. In one moment, Jacob could see the very same kids who surrounded Weston—they stoically stood in front of him as they burned alive while their flesh dripped off their bones. When Jacob blinked, the children would reappear as they did when he had first seen them——walking corpses rotting from the inside out.

He could see Cheyenne again.

"Cheyenne!" Jacob yelled.

He started for her and skipped past the children until a hand gripped Jacob's wrist with inconceivable strength to halt his momentum. He looked down at the child holding him from moving forward.

"Let go!" Jacob said.

The boy's eyes were without pupils and were rather glossed with white. His violet veins pulsated across his face, arms, and chest. Jacob continuously shouted for Cheyenne to run, but like him, she was under the mercy of the woman of Wonderland.

Lilith's fingers wrapped around Cheyenne's neck and choked her. To her delight, the traces of air that dwelled inside her lungs now croaked steadily. Smoke emerged from the crushing strength on her adolescent throat but abruptly caused Lilith to bleed from her hands. The skin around Lilith's hand disintegrated, revealing muscle and skeleton before she let go and caught a glimpse of the glimmering golden chain Cheyenne wore.

Lilith's hands were mutilated, but her face remained stagnant. They trembled the closer she brought them to Cheyenne's face and waned in a smirk of delightedness. The excruciating amount of agony should have repelled Lilith, but instead, she wiped the open wounds on her cheeks, welcoming the pain and inviting the blood.

She laid Cheyenne on the ground as though she were a newborn baby, cradling her head gently to rest while the perpetual leakage of plasma glazed her scalp and trickled down Cheyenne's skin. Lilith's hand felt against her face again.

Jacob watched as Lilith stood and turned to him. She pressed her mangled finger against her crooked lips.

"Shhhhh—" Her whisper pierced his ears, and a lull gradually overcame Jacob. Lilith walked away into the carnival.

His eyes became heavy, and his head began to languish.

"Cheyenne," he whispered.

A final remnant of energy surged in him as he tried to run to no avail. He blacked out before collapsing to the ground, reaching out as far as he could with his other hand. Tears rolled off his cheeks, knowing this might be the last time he saw Cheyenne alive.

Liam's sweat formed beads that mirrored the never-ending lights of Wonderland. He had been running and searching for what felt like an eternity. Exhaustion had seized Liam's legs, making them tremble, but his fear of dying in this place kept him going. The outside temperature was frigid, leaving his hands so numb that he couldn't bend or grasp anything properly. His backpack, laden with a multitude of weapons, continued to make a racket with each step he took.

Fog consumed Wonderland now, hugging the field and moistening Liam's face. He grabbed his head and fell to the ground as a high-pitched ring entered his ear canal. With how instantaneous its emergence was, so was its demise. Liam stood confused and startled but didn't think twice about it once he heard Weston's voice not too far away.

Echoing with no trace of what direction they were coming from, he yelled back, "Weston!"

His head gyrated like a doll, and his chest followed in a vigorous fashion. He made his way past more stationery and huts. The same posters that studied Jacob and Cheyenne now ogled at Liam; its eyes faintly followed his course. The harmonious tunes of mirth and revelry seemed to sanctify Liam's soul, soothing his troubled mind under the midnight sky. A passionate and foreign intensity surged within him as if the instruments were playing melodies meant exclusively for him. His gaze briefly caught a woman dimly visible on the horizon, walking away. It was only then that he realized his friends lay on the ground.

"Liam! Help us!" Weston howled.

He ran to their aid and lifted Jacob to his feet in one motion.

"Is he okay?" Liam asked, checking Jacob's pulse.

"I don't know, but we need to get out of here before she comes back," Weston said.

"Who?" Liam looked at him.

"Just get him up; I'm going to get Cheyenne!" Weston shouted.

He stumbled a little moving forward but was finally able to use his full force. Weston pulled her upper body over his scrawny arms and promptly shook Cheyenne. The blood was still wet on her skin, making its way onto Weston's hands.

"Wake up, Cheyenne! Wake up!" He shook.

Weston reached into his backpack and got some water to flush her face with.

"Wake up!" Weston yelled.

Cheyenne gradually gained consciousness once the water intruded into her lungs.

She coughed with eyes wide open, surveying where she was. "Where am I? What happened?"

"Give me your hand!" Weston said.

He lowered his head under her arm, and they meandered their way back to the group. Liam held Jacob and looked at Weston, who gave him a nod, directing them away from the epicenter. As they found their way out of Wonderland, the suffocating silence became a canvas upon which unspeakable fear painted itself in the shadows of their collective memory. A haunting terror began to fester within each of them, relentlessly gnawing at the edges of their sanity, like an insidious darkness biding its time to manifest in the waking hours. The harrowing memories that afflicted their families and perpetuated through generations were reborn.

XI

COVENANT

The dense oak branches immersed themselves into each other, forming a type of union. They appeared as herculean arms joining forces under the radiating atmosphere, protecting the children from the evils that lurked in the woods.

"What do we do now?" Weston quietly asked.

Chirping and cricketing shivered through in between their pauses. Jacob was still in shock, as were the rest of them—but he couldn't fight the feeling of something eluding his memories. Recollections that profusely punctuated the back of his mind, mocking him and frozen in limbo.

Since he first stepped foot in Wonderland, Jacob experienced suffocating sensations at random moments. Perceptions of what he thought were familiar quickly became foreign and then native once more. When he thought of Lilith and her presence, Jacob was constantly attuned between horror and familiarity; she was not a being he had encountered before, yet he subconsciously felt like he knew her. He remembered his forgotten drawing that Weston had shown them and tried to recall his earliest memories as a child. Jacob wondered if Lilith could corrupt their memories, too.

"I don't know," he said back to Weston.

"We're trying to save Nancy, but we have to think rationally at this point. We're going up against something we don't understand—the woman." Jacob said.

Everyone shuddered. Liam looked on into the jungle and mumbled, "She's gone, Nancy's really gone."

"Liam," Cheyenne said.

Liam looked back at them, "No, listen to me. There isn't anything we can do. Whatever happened in that place wasn't from this world," Liam's face ushered on a look of frustration, "Somehow, I saw my parents in that fucking place. It was them, I know it, but they were a lot younger. My mom was lying on a bed giving birth, and when it happened, they took the baby away from her. She cried, fuck man, she cried so loud

I thought her voice was gonna shoot. They killed the baby in front of me. They killed my sister in front of me. That woman broke her neck and started to eat into her goddamn stomach."

Liam's tears fell without him having to blink. The rest of them listened in, disturbed by the painted picture in their heads.

"It looked so real, the sounds of their voices—the smell of the fresh blood," Liam said.

He looked back in the direction of Wonderland and wiped his face, "Fuck all of this. I'm going home."

Jacob stood and blocked his way, "Hold on, Liam. We need to calm down and look at what we do know about Wonderland and the woman. Maybe we can find the pieces that explain where Nancy is and why there are so many missing kids." Jacob said.

"You didn't see what I saw in there," Liam responded.

Jacob looked at him for a while, "I know Nancy wouldn't want us to give up."

Liam forcibly slammed Jacob's body against the bricks, "I did everything I could in there; I searched alone for hours and was almost killed my damn self. Don't ever say I gave up. I loved her," Liam hissed.

They felt defeated and hopeless, but before Jacob could say anything more, an echoing of what sounded like an object tapping against the cement came from within the church.

Shocked into sobriety, they each stiffened up, not knowing what to expect at this point. The tapping became louder and lasted for minutes on end. Liam pulled a butterfly knife from his back pocket, ready to release his anger on whoever it was.

It became too unbearable to handle. Cheyenne rose and screamed, “Who’s there!” The taps halted while their breaths steamed in the brisk air. And then, there was silence. A spark flicked from a lighter that gave a dim exposure of someone just stepping away from the exit.

“God damn, and I thought I felt sorry for myself!” Vern grouched, entering the moonlight, “I thought I told you urchins to get the hell out of this town,” They looked confusedly at each other.

“What the hell is your problem, Vern? You tried to kill us the other day!” Jacob said.

Liam stepped forward, “You better get out of here before I drive this knife into your skull, old man,” Vern smiled and looked at the forest, “As much as I’d love to see that happen, you all have bigger dangers coming your way, and it involves your little friend, Nancy.”

Liam lowered his weapon, “How do you know about what happened to her?”

Vern’s face was constantly powdered with smoke from his half-finished cigar, “There’s a lot of things you morons don’t know about this town. I’ve lived here for decades and listened to the whispers that prowled the streets. Every missing person, every disappearance, every death, everything that all of you are too young to understand, I was listening.”

“You’re full of shit,” Weston replied.

Vern’s face perked up in the midst of all the smoke. He walked to Weston, steel-toed boots stomping the gravel with authority, and his thick coat brushed against itself as his arms swung. Jacob and Liam’s shoulders were hunched over, afraid of having to expel non-existing energy to save Weston from a possible attack. Vern crouched to

Weston's eye level and looked at him with great concentration. His eyes began to broaden.

"You've seen them, haven't you?" He asked Weston.

The others looked at each other with bewilderment. Weston's eyebrows danced in a fury, unable to flinch away from this agonizing staredown with Vern.

"Answer me, boy," Vern grumbled.

Something had cultivated in Weston's mind. Something he saw in Wonderland that was so traumatic it dilated into torture just thinking about it. His voice softened, and every other word Weston spoke wandered his eyes, wondering if the woman could hear him.

"It's getting harder to remember the details, but I can still feel the heat of the fires. There was so much fire. Endless, continuous, fire."

Jacob gulped; his skin quivered as he remembered the image of the burning children.

Weston went on, "It was everywhere, not just in Wonderland, though the town was burning. Every inch, from the forests to city hall, was consumed."

"What else? Did you see anyone there?" Jacob asked. Weston looked away, hesitating to answer.

"Weston, what else did you see?" Liam asked.

"The ground had melted by the time they tried to run. I saw hundreds of them, all burning alive while they sunk into the concrete like quicksand. If they didn't die from flames, they drowned below," Weston said.

The breeze acquiesced with the silence that came after until Vern stood and trudged back towards the church.

“There’s more to Wonderland than you know. And if you idiots are going to stick around, you might as well know what it is you’re up against. Follow me.” Vern said.

Jacob walked over to Weston, “You okay?”

Liam and Cheyenne joined in closer.

“I think so; I just don’t know what it all meant, though, you know? What if that was some kind of vision of the future? The future of Seaside and us?” Weston asked.

“That’s not going to happen,” Jacob said. He put his arm on Weston’s shoulder. “We were unprepared before, but it won’t happen again. Maybe Vern knows something that can help us, right? And we go back into Wonderland to save Nancy.”

Jacob looked at Liam, who nodded back.

“Only we determine our future.” Cheyenne said.

Vern yelled from inside the church, “I don’t got all night, you shitheads! Do you want to save your friend and the world or not?”

Vern’s knowledge about Wonderland enticed them enough to trail him into the darkness, brightened with a new hope and lingering fear that they were out of options.

“Hurry up!” Vern sharply shouted.

The church’s rundown infrastructure allowed for columns of moonlight to intrude on the once-sacred enclosure. They were not privy to its layout at night. During the day, it was easy to make out certain aesthetics and landmarks, but the night brought unfamiliarity at every corner. Although they spent hundreds of hours together in Impossible City, they never once dared to enter the buildings after sundown.

Shadows potently lurked the edges, each sound echoed from indistinguishable domains, and the barrier between the outside world and this man-made asylum was now synchronized. Vern led them to the church's crossing and opened the same basement entrance they had previously walked down.

"Years ago, before any of you were born, a man convened the town of Seaside here. His name was Jacy Aquene. He was the first to conjoin the idea of nature and spirituality. That everything is connected and is imperfect without one another."

Vern looked at them as they gathered around.

"What we do in life echoes throughout eternity."

He grunted, pulling the handle hidden underneath the velvet red carpet. Vern went on, "A balance must be kept. That balance is disciplined by us. And if there is an instability, nature, and the spirit world will do whatever it can to restore this balance."

"What happened to him?" Cheyenne asked. Vern reached into his coat pocket and pulled out a stainless-steel flask. The intricate details on the flask included a winding, floral filigree that encased the entirety of its body. Vines and leaves curled sinuously, forming a delicate mesh that cradled the history of a bygone era. His head clocked back, and his Adam's apple swung like a pendulum.

"He was stabbed to death where you're standing," Vern walked down the steps, leaving them gawking at the creaking wood that supported the inner dome of the church.

Cheyenne's eyes vacated left to right, her hand twirled the golden arrow necklace, "I don't know about this."

Liam and Weston were the first ones to follow Vern down the stairs. Jacob held Cheyenne's hand, "It's going to be okay," he said feebly, smiling.

Odors of aged dust perfumed the lower levels of the cathedral. The air was filled with frigid water particles numbing any exposed skin. Vern murmured to himself while he lit the wall-mounted wax candles. Groups of artifacts commenced their reveal; rustic metal objects amber in color looked to be dated hundreds of years in age.

"It smells like fucking death in here, man," Liam said as he gagged.

The motion of repelling his nose into his elbow bumped a dusty glass bottle off an adjacent shelf. Its shattering released the ancient black liquid within, momentarily spreading near their shoes before the sludge began to steam.

"Now, unless your next stop is the spirit world, I wouldn't get near that concoction! I gotta stop drinking that shit. By the way, sorry about the other day, I forgot how strong this stuff can get!" Vern laughed.

"Who killed him?" Jacob abruptly asked. He ignored the fluid—assuming it was another one of Vern's alcoholic preservatives and continued, "Jacy Aquene, who killed him?"

Vern paused; the air seemed to stand still in this dampness—an unfulfillable void.

"The woman," he said back.

Weston and Liam looked at each other and Cheyenne to Jacob, but his eyes remained fixated on Vern.

"Wonderland came to Seaside ninety-one years ago. And she was once part of the show. It was the first circus anyone had ever seen. A full line of entertainment."

Vern continued, "Acrobats, trained animals, trapeze acts, contortionists, clowns, and, of course, the freak shows. They introduced one of the first-ever sideshows in the Western Hemisphere at the time. Everyone had to see it to believe it. This town reveled in its discovery, spending hours lost in the wonders it offered. They forgot their home life and the priorities they had to divulge into what they would never fully understand. These performers were spectacles at the most to the townspeople, not human beings. The town's youth were taught to discriminate against these "freaks" for their unique features, skin color, the way they talked, and other bizarre reasons by their parents. After the first day or so, some even began abusing these carnival folk behind closed doors, torturing the pacifists and defenseless. Taking their humanity for their own selfish pleasures, these people wanted more and took it. The suffering and torment would last days, but before Wonderland departed Seaside, a group of townspeople had one last go amidst returning to the lifeless and trite lives they led."

Vern took a cigarette out of his pocket and clicked his lighter on, "Her name was Lilith, the Exquisite Extraordinair. Between her beauty and charm, her kindness was felt by nature itself. She tamed the beasts of the wild, danced with the Devil, and ceaselessly welcomed Death's arrival—seducing even him. The lines would run through the fields to watch her waltz amongst the tigers, levitate under a full moon, and rejuvenate the dried stems of a flower back to life."

"What happened?" Cheyenne asked. Vern reached into the bag and pulled out a marred children's doll. Its features were partially melted with soot stains all over.

"Her body was found burned to death in Wonderland," he replied.

Cheyenne gulped as the basement nimbly creaked. Vern went on, "She tried to stop them, but the townspeople overpowered her instantly. Groups of men bombarded the jamboree, drunken with sorrow and anger. The carnies pleaded for peace, but their prayers were only met with laughter and taunting. They all died that night in Wonderland."

Vern paused once more, his hand trembling inching towards his ear, "Their screams can be heard in the forest if you listen close enough."

The bag Vern brought out held various toys for children. Each was tarnished in its own way: chipped sportscars, ragged figurines, and punctured sports balls were brought out one by one.

"And your Nancy wasn't the first to get taken by her." Vern said.

"Taken?" Liam asked.

"Wonderland was resurrected the next day as though nothing had happened to it. Lilith sold her soul to the Devil for a new life, a life full of hatred and malice. Her only desire was to bring this town to its knees and feed off its suffering. Every thirteen years, she comes, hungry for more. She demands sacrifices to satisfy her desires, and if this goes unheeded, a family disappears one day after another," Vern said, stopping to drink more.

"Why every thirteen years?" Weston asked.

"The thirteen moons," Vern stumbled over his words, "The indigenous tribes from thousands of years ago spoke of what's called the divine feminine – the thirteen moons. It's a path a woman takes to connect with her spiritual form; it represents the natural rhythms and cycles coming into a sacred balance from within. Each moon that comes and goes represents each progression, with the thirteenth moon being the most revered. The final moon that wanes completes the woman's ascension into her true energy being."

Vern's voice grew raspy and low, "Lilith returns every thirteenth year out of spite against her native roots that gifted her extraordinary abilities. She condemned the very world that blossomed her love for humanity, for it betrayed her in the ultimate way.

After the fire, Jacy rebuked the townspeople for their actions. They immediately turned on him and offered his life to Lilith, thinking one so pure could end the spell before it was fully formed. The townspeople constrained him to the floor of this church, and while she watched, Lilith forced the townspeople to butcher Jacy's body and eat his flesh. She watched blissfully as their innocence washed away with his blood."

Vern said. He unfolded a small photograph that was torn from the bottom. Its grainy image depicted Lilith and a small boy inside Wonderland's ruins from what looked to be decades old.

"It's her!" Weston yelped.

"But her thirst was for children. She wanted the taste of youth on her tongue, and she would rampage the town into nothingness until they gave her one after another."

Vern said. Jacob delved into the picture, captivated by the woman once more. The date read 1895 on the corner, the first year a child went missing in Seaside.

"Azazel." Jacob said.

“We gotta tell the police!” Liam exclaimed.

Weston chimed in, “Did you not hear what he just said? She’s a fucking demon! Lilith will kill us before we do anything close to stopping her. And the police can’t do a damn thing to help us.”

“But she can,” Vern said, pointing at Cheyenne.

“Me?” She answered.

“Her?” Everyone else collectively said.

“This one has a different energy around her, something that is not from here. The tainted offspring that brought upon this evil cannot forgive the sins of their ancestors, but one without tarnish—one with descendants foreign from here is omitted from the curse,” Vern said.

He circled around them, “If you want to find the truth and save your friend, you must follow your own lineage and bloodline to the origins of this curse.”

Jacob looked at the picture again, “Who took this photo?”

Vern flipped the sepia film on its back – the signature “AC” caught their eyes.

“Your great grandfather,” Vern finished his flask with one final gulp.

Jacob’s dampened hoodie weighed him down as he rode through the declining road. The late night brought an onslaught of rain clouds that drizzled the town. Each raindrop that touched him went unnoticed. Jacob could only wonder how his family was connected to Wonderland.

He looked at his watch, reading almost 1:30 a.m. It didn't occur to him how much time had passed at Impossible City. Once he made it to the side of his house, he noticed the main lamp was on in his living room. The possibility that his parents found out about his night run now loomed in his already cluttered mind.

Because their front door entrance was exposed to the majority of the downstairs layout, Jacob left the kitchen door unlocked purposely before he left to make his re-entry swift and unheard. He reached towards the knob, his hand shook, trying to latch on. Adrenaline coursed his bloodstream after every heartbeat, and he soon felt lightheaded.

The door opened effortlessly, gliding against its hinges this time. His foot crept inside the vacant kitchen. It appeared to be too silent downstairs for anyone to be in the vicinity; he elongated his stride to cover more ground in less time. Jacob was able to make his way to the staircase until his attention was directed to where the incandescent light bulb radiated.

From his peripheral, he saw several guests who sat with his parents on the couch and chairs around. He couldn't recognize who they were, but he could see their faces flourishing with wrinkles. Every single person held a distinctly emotionless, unnatural expression. They sat with incredible posture, hands on their laps as though a class for etiquettes was being taught—each not making a sound. Elders, in comparison to Abraham and Martha, their silence became eerie the longer it stretched. He looked closer at one of the men sitting right under the lamp, soulless eyes gazing in one direction without a noticeable breath, humanizing this scene.

Twenty seconds had passed before Jacob retreated from this discomfort. He took a step back and felt the touch of a slender, anemic hand grip his collarbone. Petrified with fear, he turned to face a man who hadn't a red blood cell visible, "Well, now, you must be Jacob."

He smiled. The man knelt down to him and bounced from Jacob's left and right pupils. His grin dreadfully carried.

Blood poured down his lips and splattered onto their hardwood floor, "We've been waiting for you."

Jacob cowered backward and subsequently gave away his position to everyone else in the living room. His knees were locked stiff, walking in reverse; the man stayed stagnant—giggling as more blood leaked. Martha spotted him and looked to regain consciousness from her daydream, "Jacob! We've been worried sick!" She ran to him and hugged him tightly, but Jacob loosened her restraint, thinking the old man was still behind him. He screamed.

Abraham followed after Martha, trying to calm Jacob down, "Jacob, these are friends of ours."Abraham said.

Jacob looked at his father with concern. His eyes seemed stained with a dark coating glossing over his irises. Jacob twisted his head around to find the old man staring back at him, still grinning—bloodless.

"There—there was blood," Jacob deliriously stuttered.

"Son, where were you?" Abraham said, turning Jacob around, "We had no idea what happened to you. Look at the time!"

Abraham began to vent his anger as the man pricked a needle in Jacob's neck. A burning sensation came from his neck. Jacob rubbed his searing skin and felt a foreign bump. His confused state was now more prominent than ever; the fingers Jacob used to examine himself were covered in blood.

"What's going on?" Jacob groaned.

Martha padded his hair, catching Jacob as he weakened to the ground, "We're just so glad to have you back home, honey. It's going to be okay."

The others from the living room stood as one and walked towards them.

"Who are these people?" Jacob mustered with the last bit of strength he had.

The crippling of his body transitioned to numbness creeping from his feet to his neck. He could no longer move. Martha held him tightly once more, and he could feel drips of tears fall onto his face. Gibberish catapulted from Jacob's mouth now, his vision blurred heavily the more he persisted its smothering.

Less than a foot away, the strangers towered over Martha and him. He still could not focus on who they were, but it was unlikely that he would recognize them. A loud thud came from the shadows within the upper stairs.

Everyone turned their heads to the overwhelming steps that ensued, forgetting that Jacob was on the brink of passing out in front of them. He felt a queasiness combusting in his stomach and had to turn to his side to vomit. Hurls of liquid spread across the floor at a rapid pace prior to Jacob gagging out only air. Abraham and Martha did not break their concentration for a moment; the steps thundered on. Jacob's eyesight was now merely projecting shapes and colors, but he looked up to find the shadow of a figure coming from the darkness before he completely lost consciousness.

Martha held him closer to her chest and softly sang, "Mistress Mary, quite contrary, how does your garden grow?"

The blaring metal pin bashed against each side of his clock. Jacob's eyelids slung open, resuscitated into a new day. He rubbed his eyes and felt an extreme dryness plaguing his mouth. A white blanket of brightness slivered through his half-open drapes, distracting him from his peculiar state.

Seaside was consumed with an overcast of clouds. And although this was not out of the ordinary in October, its usual fragments that floated closer to the ground were nonexistent. An owl perched on their ancestral Clay tree let out a shriek that fully woke Jacob now; its yellow eyes were visible from a distance with the contrast and enormity of its black pupils. 7:17 a.m. Jacob had thirteen minutes to get to school, or he would risk getting detention. The last thing he wanted was to spend any more time at school or with Mrs. Davis.

As he scurried down the wooden stairs, he was met by their living room once again, but this time, empty. His attention was seized by this lifeless space, haunting him with remnants of memories from the night before. He tried his best to remember what happened, but he could not figure out the sequence of events leading from opening the side door to his own bed.

The floor had drips of dried liquid that noticeably was not part of its construction. He looked closer; the blobs appeared to have a unique maroon color when the light bounced off them, similar to what blood would look like poorly wiped away. With his pace of breath increasing already, the bits and pieces of what may or may not have happened the night before started to glue itself together.

A phantom sensation pierced the side of his neck as though a flame ignited, yet his hands felt nothing but his clammy skin.

"Jacob, come eat your food before it gets cold!" Martha abruptly called from the kitchen.

He straightened his back, caught off guard by the sudden voice of a human. Martha was still, holding onto a look of delight, when Jacob entered from the other room.

"Come eat with me before you leave for school."

Jacob felt unsettled looking at his mother.

"It's going to get cold. Come on!" Martha exclaimed, trotting around the kitchen.

Jacob had never seen so much food taking up so much space on their table. The spread featured an assortment of meals: stacks of fluffy buttermilk pancakes, sunnyside eggs, sausage links, toasted bread, fruit bowls, oatmeal, and the choice of drinks varied with orange juice and milk. He peered, confused.

"Looks good, huh?" Martha insisted, circulating a spoon in her cup of tea.

"There's so much, I can't eat all of this."

His mother's face sobered from the original ecstatic look she wore.

"We just wanted to make sure you had the best breakfast you could ever have," she said.

"Where's dad?" Jacob asked.

At that moment, she had broken her eye contact with Jacob and blinked several times before chuckling while stirring her coffee.

"Oh, your father had to leave this morning for his work conference in the city. You know how he gets; he's so mindful of his salesman pitch. He'll be gone for the next three days, so I wanted to start our first day alone together with a full stomach!"

Martha had not stopped mixing her cup; the steel ends scraped against the porcelain mouth, creating an uncomfortable echo inside the kitchen. Jacob looked at the food once more, feeling a distressing warmth festering in his stomach.

"Well, aren't you going to eat anything?" Martha asked, resurfacing her grin. Jacob picked a small piece out of every section of the table, hoping it would suffice her demand. Martha watched him until his first bite. After Jacob bit into the pancake, she halted her stirring.

"It's amazing, isn't it?"

Jacob nodded. Martha placed her spoon onto the empty plate in front of her and gasped.

"Oh dear, these hangnails will be the death of me!" she said.

And in an instant, Jacob's mother pinched into the skin of her left hand and peeled with such promptness that her entire finger was afflicted with blood. Jacob dropped his spoon, and the blood dripped onto her plate. She stuck her dripping finger into her mouth and closed her eyes, but not in pain, in what looked to be a euphoric state of mind. Instead of voicing her pain in groans or whimpers, Martha proceeded to exude a deep vibration from her gullet, sounding like a snarl of a tiger. Her jaw munched side to side, squeezing out more blood. She continued without a sign of slowing down.

The unwelcoming tingle in Jacob's stomach ripened into a series of twists and painful throbbings. He was frightened beyond belief—petrified as he watched this estranged woman feast on her own blood. Jacob leaned away, hoping to get to the front door and escape the house before Martha noticed.

He turned his head and made his way to the door but then realized the commotion from Martha ceased. She was already standing up, looking at him in silence—the corners of her mouth blemished with stains of crimson.

"I have to go to sch—"

Jacob started. Martha grabbed his wrist with authority using her wounded hand, smearing a combination of her plasma and saliva onto Jacob's crew neck cuff. He was frozen with fear; their hands shook from him trying to pull away and her halting his movement.

"Mom?" Jacob said in a frightened voice.

She had not the slightest depiction of emotion. Martha concentrated on him for a few seconds, ignoring his cry. The grip finally loosened, and Jacob's back collided with the chair he sat on.

A smile grew once more over his mother, "Don't be late today. Come straight home, okay?"

The clear water splashed into a murky black mixture. Cheyenne gagged one last time and spit her remnants out into the toilet bowl before staring at what was agitating inside of her. Splatters of ink covered most of the outer rim, but the inner solution that sat was paint-like. Her breaths slowed down, taking a sigh of relief. For hours overnight, her stomach ached, but she had to remain silent to avoid waking Chaska. He had left for the store earlier that morning, and Cheyenne used the time to find a way to calm her symptoms before school.

Her stomach replenished its burning sensation, and she wailed, constricting her side. The pain was so substantial she dropped to her knees and used the shower base to hold herself upright. Another urge to throw up overcame her, but she was too delirious to make herself turn to the toilet. She expelled another chunk of vile gunk all over the shower walls. Cheyenne began to cry, helpless and powerless against this sickness that was eating away at her internal organs.

"Fuck!" She said to herself, wiping her mouth. The towel she used stained immensely.

...You must follow your own lineage and bloodline to the origins of this curse.

Through Cheyenne's suffering, Vern's words repeated.

This one has a different energy around her, something that is not from here.

Cheyenne wondered what Vern meant and how she could save Nancy if she could barely stand up straight. Her fingers grazed the spew from her lips—the disgorge felt thick, sludgy. A powerful set of knocks came rumbling through her house.

Cheyenne pulled herself off the edge of the shower, hastily wiped her face, and flushed the toilet. The ticking clock in their bathroom had the time 9:33 a.m. Chaska was back sooner than she had anticipated, and he would not take kindly to her missing school. Still gripping her oblique, the flaring recommenced.

More bangs came from their front door. Cheyenne had to press against the walls of her home to keep balance. She peeked into the peephole expecting to see an impatient Chaska, but the intense white light of Seaside looked back at her instead. The door opened wide, revealing that no one was behind it knocking this whole time.

She looked on, dazed and puzzled. The hammering had happened only seconds ago, and if it was someone playing a prank, Cheyenne would have seen them run away at this angle. More pain surged, and she no longer had the patience to solve this mystery right now. The moment she moved the door to less than ajar, something caught her eye.

A tree imitating the painted one she saw in Wonderland became the focal point of the forest across the way. The noose swung from the aged branch, calling to her. Her tender intestines twisted when a spasm erupted deep inside her stomach. Cheyenne slammed the wooden door and ran to the kitchen.

With her not eating or drinking anything for the past thirteen hours, she started to realize that what she threw up was her bile. The smell of sage buried the air from a freshly burned bundle sitting on the countertop and made Cheyenne feel sicker. She instantly plunged her head into the wide stainless-steel sink. Thump after thump of mouthfuls of muck discharged from Cheyenne against the metal. When she opened her eyes, Cheyenne screamed when a creature with no legs or arms wiggled about in her vomit.

In a deranged fashion, she grabbed the closest knife in the kitchen and repeatedly stabbed the being to death. Slime sprayed across her face and shirt, and the distress screech from the varmint faded away gently. She dropped the knife into the sink and fell to the ground. Although she was still inhaling the scent of herbs, the nausea was promptly less tenacious. A moment of peace resonated with her, and then, her eyes widened as she hypothesized what could end this misery.

"The bad spirits," Cheyenne whispered, rubbing her scalp.

You dislike the smell because of the bad spirits locked in your head!

Chaska's voice spoke in her thoughts. Maybe this sickness was something Western medicine couldn't heal.

Cheyenne grabbed their ashtray and a match. Her stomach growled when she lifted her shirt. Every pump of blood that circulated her body caused the black veins to sway in various directions, like a living being reacting. She whimpered as her anxiety started to strangle her.

With a handful of sage, she laid it gently into the glass and ignited the match. The white smoke refilled the atmosphere and entered Cheyenne's nostrils. She closed her eyes. Her stomach quaked, and she could feel more discharge creeping into her mouth. Buckling to the floor again, she bawled to the point her voice altered to a deeper tone, "Get out of me!" She yelled. A splurge of dark liquid flooded onto the gray porcelain tile, accompanied by portions of blood, the most she had ever thrown up.

The kitchen bottom was slathered, but the puddle was too heavy to spread anymore. Cheyenne watched in horror but gagged when she felt something foreign lodged in her throat. It would not come out no matter how hard she gagged, so she had to use her hand to scrape it out. A silver bracelet wrapped around her fingers; she wiped the owl pendant and read Nancy’s name engraved on the back.

XII

CONVICTION

The crystal blue water drenched Liam's already sweating face. Volatile children's voices echoed in the boys' bathroom from the gymnasium next to it. He looked in the mirror and studied his face—his weary eyes stared back at him.

He was tired, more mentally than physically. And in these occasions where his solitude prevailed, it was when he could take the time to breathe. It was only the second day without Nancy, but he felt as though he had not talked to anyone in weeks. Alone, Liam stood under the row of fluorescent bulbs. After grabbing some paper towels to dry, he went into the bathroom stall.

The stream of urine that gurgled from the stall created a deafening roar. So much so that Liam did not hear someone entering the bathroom. He tried to finish quicker as the person walked into the space next to him. The shoes that could be seen from under the stall appeared too large for another student, outrageously bigger. Its rubber material and leather construct had been timeworn with much discoloration around the bulging rounded toe end.

Liam's skin crawled as slithering goosebumps perked all around his body, and his hands moistened with sweat. He laggardly finished his business and made his way to unlock the stall door while only silence came from the adjacent end where the man was. The door creaked loudly as Liam tried to walk quickly through it until the neighboring stall opened. Liam was paralyzed—staring face to face with a man in a clown costume.

His head was very long, acutely pointed. Blotchy white paint weakly covered his skin and all around his skull. The man was bald, but his temple and the top portion of his head featured a skinny white strand of hair gelled straight out.

Liam looked on in terror, "Who are you?"

Screams and loud conversations by his peers next door were now dormant. The man's shoulders accentuated up and down; the only sounds to be heard were of the clown's heavy breathing. Charcoal covered the inner corners of his eyes and spread to his eyelids.

Liam took a step away and watched whether or not the clown's stare followed. Although Liam tried to focus on his gaze, he instead fixated on Wonderland's symbol that was engraved on the man's forehead. It weakly secreted a black liquid that dripped down the man's face.

"H—hello?" Liam tried again.

The clown remained poised in his movement, unflinching. Liam moved further along towards the door until he finally latched onto the handle and felt relief. He twisted the mechanism, but the heavy wooden door did not budge when Liam pushed forward; it was locked.

Suddenly, the bulbs in the bathroom flickered before they turned off, and the bathroom went dark. Liam frantically twisted the latch, "Help!" He screamed at the top of his lungs. Sounds of electrical resurgence fluttered, and the lights flickered back on. Standing behind

Liam was Baku, the clown. Its presence hushed Liam's cries as it crouched to look into the thirteen-year-old boy's eyes.

A smile stretched over Baku's face, and his finger pressed against his own dry, scaly lips, "Shhh."

More of the dark substance oozed from his forehead.

"What do you love about Nancy?" Baku asked in his grainy and hoarse voice.

Liam could barely keep his focus on him; he was frightened beyond comprehension. Baku's enthusiastic character withered in a split-second when he did not reply fast enough.

"What do you love about her!" He barked, his body contracting at every syllable.

"S—she's my best friend," Liam whimpered.

The clown paused and let out a laugh that rhymed extensively. His ghastly breaths exhaled onto Liam. Liam frowned, repressing the urge to throw up. Stillness pierced the moment again. The man halted his chuckles and now wore a humorless look that gazed at Liam.

"You know nothing of love. To understand love is to welcome pain," Baku said. Its grimy hand brushed Liam's face, "Your blood is too fresh, too potent with hope."

Baku pulled Liam in close to whisper, "She is always watching, Liam."

He tenderly spoke, as though the words glided off his demonic tongue, "And when the time comes, she will take you to your beloved."

Liam's panting trembled throughout his body; his mouth could not form a word if he tried. The distance between them lessened as Baku leaned closer to Liam, "And I will feast on your body."

Drool dripped onto Liam's shoulder and oozed down his shirt. A static buzz rushed through the bulbs once more, and its luminosity shimmered off, then on. Baku had vanished. Liam lunged to the door and sprinted out as fast as he could.

"A five-mile radius!" Weston exclaimed, unzipping his backpack at the bike racks. The school day had finally ended, and he had been anxiously waiting to show the modifications to his walkie-talkie headsets.

"The wiring was shot when I got a chance to look at them after Wonderland. Completely burnt. And the antennas that would normally pick up frequencies in the vicinity could barely keep the signal longer than a minute before completely shutting off."

Jacob was just as confused the first time he explained all of this.

"So what does this mean? We don't have a way to talk to each other anymore?"

Weston grinned, "Yeah, until I figured out how to fix and make them stronger."

He continued, "These are the greatest inventions of the eighties. Created by yours truly. With a five-mile radius signal strength, my modified walkie-talkies are a fraction of the weight and size of traditional transceivers. It only takes one ear, and they're automated to stay on the same channel. If the signal begins to fuck up, all frequencies are changed to the next station. Long story short, these will keep us connected wherever we go in town and constantly receive transmission from each other without us having to do anything. Just turn it on."

Weston flipped the switch on the earpiece, and five white glowing bars illuminated along with five red bars next to it, "One measures battery strength. One measures signal strength."

Jacob tried on his device; he marveled at the clarity in the audio and the sturdiness around his ear.

"We need to get one to Cheyenne. She didn't come to school today," Jacob said. Weston nodded, "Liam, too. I didn't see him at his locker."

They pulled their bikes out of the rails and jumped on them, pushing towards the road leading to the less developed part of Seaside. Jacob sat on his bike, but before he was able to accelerate, he felt his chain skid off its track. He quickly parked and reinserted the cogs to align.

Weston skidded across the concrete, "What's wrong?"

Jacob looked down at a flier that was caught on his tire. He reached for it and opened the half-crumpled paper. Weston rode in next to him as his eyes expanded, reading the bold, grainy red lettering.

WONDERLAND, DREAMS OF NIGHTMARES

The date was just as apparent underneath the illustration.

FINAL ACT, OCTOBER 31

The umbrella of clouds felt like a prison ceiling. Everything dissipated in the eerie lull; ambient noise that would come from waves crashing against the bedding rocks could not be heard. And although Jacob, Liam, and Weston rode freely through the winding roads, airflow that would normally puff from the ocean into the forest and onto Seaside was now extinct. Jacob watched the rows of trees pass him.

Cheyenne's house was about a ten-minute ride and led to the part of town the city never suburbanized. It was part of the main reason

Chaska insisted on purchasing the lot a year ago, a plot of land where they would not be disturbed or need to worry about modernization. Weston and Liam were closely behind Jacob, who was growing more worrisome the longer it took to reach her home. He noticed Liam peering off into the distance.

"Liam, are you okay?" Jacob asked.

Liam eventually coiled his head, "Ever since we went inside Wonderland for the first time, it's always felt like someone was watching me. But I could never find anyone when I looked around. These things from Wonderland, they're following us, Jacob. And we'd never know if we're being led into a trap." Liam said.

Weston's eyes wavered around, scouting.

"You really saw that clown in there?" Liam asked Jacob.

"Yeah, it was exactly how you told us. Baku's face was painted on a wall inside there. He must have been one of the main acts." Jacob said.

"Maybe Baku was from Seaside, too," Weston said.

If they could trace down which families were a part of the sacrifices and those who were still carrying them out, they might be able to end the children's disappearances and save Nancy. What loomed in Jacob's mind, however, was why his great-grandfather was with Lilith years ago and took that photo. Finding the truth about Wonderland would be the missing link to the Clay family secrets.

Cheyenne's house was just ahead, and they noticed a hefty amount of smoke leaving her shed's chimney. After walking onto the porch, the boys looked around, waiting for Chaska to come out, asking why they came to his house. But his car wasn't in the driveway, and the window covers were all the way open. Jacob knocked on the door three times and took a step back.

He tried again while Liam and Weston looked inside the glass.

"Cheyenne?" Weston called and tapped.

"I don't think there's anyone inside," Liam said.

Jacob walked to the edge of the platform and watched the smoke continuously bulge from the shed's brick vent.

"Maybe she's in there," Jacob said.

It was composed of different pieces of wood that formed a generously spaced structure for all of their extra possessions. Sealed off from the outside world, she would not have been able to hear them anyway. Or see the outside light, for that matter.

"Cheyenne!" Jacob hollered, beating against the unrefined wood. They paused and waited for something to happen. Weston looked at Jacob and then opened his mouth to say something, but the sound of a locking mechanism clicked several times. The door opened, unbinding the vast smoke that was trapped inside. As the outline of a person approaching them became apparent, they each took a step back. Cheyenne fanned her face and coughed into daylight, "I think I know how to stop her." she said. There were at least two dozen candles lit around the shed, burning for hours from how much wax had dripped onto their bases. Weston gave a puzzled look, "What the fuck have you been doing in here?"

Cheyenne had squatted to her sitting position next to a large bowl of ash.

"What is that smell?" Liam asked, joining the confusion. They gathered around her and sat on wooden stumps.

"What's going on, Cheyenne?" Jacob asked. She took a deep breath and opened her eyes. The color of her irises had mutated from a dark brown to a more saturated and brighter tone.

"Nancy came to me the night she was taken by Lilith. She changed Nancy into something that wasn't human, something that wasn't from this world." she said. Their attention was undivided on Cheyenne, "Nancy was in my room and blamed me for her death, that it was all my fault. Her voice was deeper, her skin was peeling; I felt like I was looking at a complete stranger. It was Nancy's body, but it felt like someone else was controlling her."

"And then, what?" Liam asked.

Cheyenne looked to the floor, "All I could remember was this black, bile sludge that was forced down my throat. If I didn't swallow it, I would have drowned there. My stomach burned, and I couldn't stop throwing up after that night. It was like an infection. Lilith was trying to turn me into one of them—one of her own— until I found out how to stop the sickness from spreading."

Cheyenne reached into a wooden box that was next to her bowl and placed a jar on the table with one of the creatures that fed on her insides. The boys came in closer to get a better view,

"What is that?" Weston yelped.

It looked like a blob of expired jam. The creature suddenly moved and screeched when Liam lightly tapped it.

"Holy shit!" Liam exclaimed, jumping back with Jacob and Weston following suit.

"Where did you find this?" Asked Jacob.

"It was inside me," Cheyenne morbidly replied.

Jacob felt the same stomach-twisting sensation from this morning instigating.

"Inside you?" Weston asked in a frenzy.

"*Was.*" Cheyenne emphasized.

She dumped the cinders from the dish onto the ground and replaced it with a handful of herbs.

"For years, I hated when Chaska would bring more sage into the house; the smell of it always made my head spin and my insides turn."

Cheyenne carefully burned and blew on it, "And this morning, when the house was filled with the scent, the sickness became strong again. But this time, I actually threw up. More than I ever did."

She lifted the jar up, "Eventually, one of these motherfuckers came out. So, I repeated the ritual here, and I think I got it all out of me. I don't feel anything wrong inside anymore."

Cheyenne had not the slightest idea on how to successfully perform these rituals, yet she now fully affirmed that if it were not for her Native American upbringing, she would have been dead by now.

"If it worked for you, maybe it'll work for Nancy when we find her." Liam said.

"It's worth a shot," Cheyenne said.

"We have until Friday night to save her."

Jacob unfolded the paper that was in his pocket and placed it on the table, "Wonderland's finale."

They read over the advertisement and began to comprehend the pressure of it all. If they couldn't save Nancy, she would be gone forever. And the mysterious vanishings of children for the past ninety-one years would continue along with the buried truth behind Isaac's death.

Weston's ride home was the farthest of his friends. The Wednesday afternoon had hurriedly pushed the sun away and made dusk loom much sooner. He turned his bike light on, turning into the suburban neighborhoods. It never got too loud or had any commotion about it, and it was one of the reasons Weston liked living in this area. He was always left alone to work on his craft.

The inflating moon brightened, growing in prominence in the sky, as was Weston's festering anxiety. Shadows darkened around the neighborhood, welcoming the nocturnal beings that thrived in its darkness. Weston reached into his pocket and squeezed the ziplock bag of sage he took from Cheyenne to make sure it was still there. If she was able to cure whatever was inside her from the scent, then maybe they could somehow weaponize the smell for protection, too.

He looked at the houses that were a tireless repeat of architectural design, bland from the color combinations to the predictable white picket fence. It was getting close to 6 p.m. and their family's sedan was not in its usual parking space in the driveway. Adam and Mary rarely went out, but when they did, it was usually during the weekend or daytime. With the news about Nancy that was still the talk of the town, however, Weston assumed they were back at her house for whatever reason. His bike clicked rapidly as he glided to the side gate's backyard entrance.

He walked quietly once inside, still not fully convinced that both his parents were gone. Most of the windows were open, letting in a draft. Weston looked around, confused, and started to close each one by one. A staple in their household was to keep everything shut, especially and most importantly when one was going to leave the house unattended. He thought maybe they had left in a rush of some sort, but after the final window's click, Weston disregarded it and went straight to his room.

The odor of being outdoors and his body sweat became grotesque to him. Yet, he did not fancy showering and wasting more time to resume his study on Seaside's families. The earthy aroma glued to his fingertips wafted over Weston as he took his jacket off. He took a plentiful amount of sage from Chaska's garden to discreetly study tonight, but he didn't realize just how potent the smell was. His whole house must have been perfumed in its sweet scent by now. Weston rubbed what he could off his hands with this jacket and threw it on his bed. He made his way into his closet, where he shut the sliding door behind him and proceeded to enter his lair.

The inner wood frame of their house made the air damp and stale. He connected two ends of an extension cord that activated the overhead bulbs. Added to the moist environment was the stale buzz from the heated filament inside each glass. Since his commencement of detective work, Weston added more lights around to aid his eyes when reading into the night.

There were different stations in every corner, some that had biology records of Seaside and others that had newspaper pages from various years prior. A knack that Weston had that many kids his age didn't was understanding coincidences rarely happen and that finding consistency in data is the fundamental tool to solving anything. He insinuated that cases may change, but how one would approach them should be mathematical, strategic, and repeatable. He took a deep breath, looking at the mountain of books he had stacked, and grabbed an already opened and half-drunk soda can from the night before.

After taking a generous gulp of cola, Weston sat on his chair and squinted at his pinboard that had the map of Seaside. There were red dots that he placed at every recordable instance when a person went missing from town. It was a scatter plot with occurrences in arbitrary areas. Without any consistency found, he was left staring at random points on the map. He turned his attention to the pile of books next to him and grabbed the black book sitting on top.

Weston felt the spine and front cover. Because of his reputation as the only student tutor in their school, he was granted an unlimited number of items to check out. Normally, his list rotated perpetually with technology and scientific genres, but his latest insights submerged him into the realm of religion, spiritual awakening, and early-world texts about angels and demons. Weston felt uneasy reading content of this nature. His comfortability in these topics was similar to Liam's with algebra.

He laid his faith in reason and objective data. Like his father, he could not grasp the idea of an all-mighty being who determined what happened in our lives. It felt more natural to trust what humans had achieved because of the issueless fact that it was observable. But with what he saw in Wonderland, he knew he had to abort his conviction in science to understand the unexplained.

Lilith had him alone for an endless amount of time before his friends found him. The children that were sacrificed in front of him, every single one of their screams he felt echo in his mind. Their pleas for mercy—suffering without any idea why this was happening to them.

Lilith made Weston watch dozens agonize; she made him listen to children's bones crumble as she crunched them in her mouth. Skin that tore from limbs scratched Weston's eardrums, and they were accompanied by the glopping noise of blood exuding and convulsing from their mouths. Weston witnessed Hell in Wonderland. He could not sleep from these nightmares and hallucinated during the day—repetitive images of devoured bodies of children followed him all around. The feeling of being watched became inescapable; he sometimes imagined a glimpse of Lilith in the crevasses nearby watching him.

Weston's hands rubbed the embroidered finish of an owl logo that sat inside the worn leather. An odd emblem was found sutured on the back as well. A four-sided star engulfed inside a circle was noticed by Weston, but he disregarded it. He skimmed through the pages that were defiled with a combination of handwritten notes, drawings, and unidentifiable logos. The bookmarked page he was previously on illuminated under the yellow lights.

SACRIFICIAL OFFERING

The text bled into and weighed the ancient pages down. Weston read further into the preliminary paragraph introducing the chapter.

Mankind's closest relation to immortality is the gift of birth. To those who relinquish their instinctual love to sacrifice one of their own is the ultimate form of allegiance. As a tribute to a deity, the offeree is given what they desire most. However, other divine beings simply demand such a payment for sparing those involved from eternal damnation.

In the following sections of the chapter were gritty illustrations of the many ways the ritual could be made possible. Several groups from various backgrounds were shown. Each demonstrated their depiction of praise and gratitude to the deity. Tribes in indigenous lands partook with the hope that it would deliver fruits and crops before winter, women from eastern Europe during the Renaissance collated, aspiring for a deathless life, and even modern religious cults offered the lives of young women to achieve notoriety and fortune.

Weston studied the images and made similarities with his own memories. His eyes closed momentarily, the visual onslaught of death and injustice combusted in his cranium. Weston could not handle it anymore. He closed the book shut and took his glasses off.

Of the thirty-plus cases that he grazed through from the Lost Ones files, Weston retained a few of their names. It was hard enough to find death records because he could not access a public database with this sort of request. A twelve-year-old boy looking up the files of deceased children from various decades would cause too much attention. And if the townspeople were truly involved, Weston knew he had to be discreet. Weston's intuition led him to instead locate phone books from each of the thirteen-year marks and search for the last names of each person and their address. He made a list of several numbers to call, and now would be the perfect time to begin.

A fury of footsteps rumbled outside Weston's room, interrupting him out of concentration—his parents were home. Weston skipped across the floorboard and unplugged the surge. As the lights dimmed, he looked through a peephole he had made to observe anyone who intruded his space.

The room was still empty, with its door shut. But someone was walking outside with a heavy foot, sounding off the diversified creaks and cracks around their house. Weston checked the corners behind his bed and closet, his mouth pressed against the lumber, breathing deeply. His door sprung open, slamming its handle against the wall.

His father walked into his room. Adam stood upright and peered around, prudently sniffing the air.

"Weston?" He called.

Adam grabbed Weston's jacket off the bed and brought it close to his face before repelling it away in disgust. Weston's eyes widened.

"Adam? Is he in there?"

Mary called from down the hall.

"No." Adam said after regaining his composure.

"Open all the windows, god dammit! It smells like death in this house!" He yelled. Adam promptly left the room, hurling the door shut.

Weston rejoined the electrical plugs, bringing back the lights. He heard the front door open and close, followed by the weakening of his parents' voices leaving the driveway. Liberated from the pitch black, Weston hurried his way toward his puffed-out backpack and dumped its contents onto the table that had the phonebooks. The first three ziplock bags tumbled out, and the subsequent bags rolled off onto the floor. Each clear packet held freshly harvested sage. Weston grabbed one of them, brought it closer to the light bulb, and examined it from top to bottom, "Interesting."

Jacob's window overlooked the west. The candy-painted sky revealed itself once sunset arrived. Cotton skies melted into an ocean-blue sea of wonder and cherry red. His cheeks felt the flowing air brush against him. With the overcast still covering a majority of the atmosphere, the sun's orange rays—that bounced off of the dust particles from the horizon—reflected on every cloud across the heavens. And where the star could not reach, stains of sapphire made its periodical glow. Jacob experienced the benefits of being the only child, but it paired with the isolation that accompanied it.

Isaac's death was digested differently in the Clay family. Abraham and Martha were trapped in the vicious cycles of grief for thirteen years. The constant bickering amongst themselves, the wishing it was their lives taken instead of Isaac's—the deflating realization that nothing would change the present. Jacob was accustomed to this style of living now; it was the mechanism that drove him to seclude himself in nature and the wonders beyond his walls. Although, at times, it was hard to cope with his parents' distress, he always knew where he could go to find solace.

His house whispered with the winds entering and leaving. Jacob could hear noise from the kitchen bleeding into his room. He listened closer to Martha's movement around the creaking floor. He slowly locked the door but was startled by a radio frequency buzzing from Jacob's desk, "Foxtrot? Do you copy? Over."

Weston's voice blurred in between the static.

"Hey, it's me, what's going on? Over." Jacob answered.

"Do you still have your slingshot? Over."

Jacob looked at his bed rails.

"Yeah, why? Over." Jacob said.

"Bring it tomorrow night; we're going to need it. Over."

Jacob walked over to search for one of his favorite toys.

"Got it. Over," Jacob said.

"And don't forget to find your costume. If we're going to pull this off, we need to stay anonymous." Weston said.

Jacob heard the stairs croak, "Yeah, I got it. I'll see you tomorrow, man."

"Quest over and out." Weston ended.

Jacob turned the device off.

He twisted the slingshot in his single hand, reminiscing about the thousands of memories he had trying to perfect the art of slinging.

"Hi, honey," Martha said from his opened door. His mother's voice ruptured the harmony of the room, and the hairs on the back of his neck spiked. Martha stood hands-clasped together, smiling at him. An uneasiness augmented in the pause.

"What's up?" Jacob forced.

Her crooked smirk continued on, "I hope you're hungry; dinner is almost ready. I've been working on it for hours now!" she said giddily. Jacob made a face, "No, I'm okay. I think I'm going to skip dinner tonight."

Martha's face depressed into itself, and her furrowed brows made it clear she was not pleased hearing this.

"Food is very important. If you miss a meal, your body becomes weak, docile to sickness."

The unnatural widening of her lips reappeared.

"You look like you need to eat more anyway," Martha said.

She raised her hands and fluttered them, "I may even have a new bottle of red tonight."

Martha whispered loudly, "Maybe, if you're a good boy, I'll give you a sip. But don't tell your father! Now hurry down!"

She giggled and swiftly turned around and walked away. With today being Isaac's deathiversary, Jacob assumed the random gesture was warranted. The kitchen's clings and clangs resumed.

It was dim in their hallway; the only light that kindled Jacob's path was from the faint ambient sunset that was soon to conclude. Jacob never made an attempt to enter the sky parlor alone in the past because his parents constantly lectured him about the dangers that lurked.

Bacteria, dust, germs, and more await you, he was told. When he thought hard about it, Jacob could only remember a handful of times when he actually was able to go up there. But it was always with Abraham. The attic entrance had a small keychain one had to pull with a pole hook. He opened the corridor's closet door and grabbed the five-foot stick. He turned his head and walked over to the edge of the stairs to make sure Martha was still busy with the feast. After confirming the kitchenware batter, he clasped the hook onto the knob and pulled the lever down along with the staircase.

There was an abundance of debris that fell from the room above. He covered his mouth and looked in the attic and saw fading daylight breaking into the uninhabited flat. Every step squeaked louder than the last—the decades-old black walnut wood fought to support Jacob's weight. Fifty or so beige boxes flooded around him with relics from his family's past. A window with a four-sided star welcomed a dull glow.

He wandered about the loft feeling like a freed prisoner. Maneuvering between the ancient cabinets and sculptures that were blanketed with powders of dust, Jacob squinted while searching for his father's box of belongings. He knew the Freddy Krueger costume was in one of these forgotten bins. Abraham kept most of his old possessions up here instead of in the basement. The mask was a gift from an old friend, from what Abraham mentioned; nonetheless, it was a pretty penny to spend. The detailing and design of the monstrous villain from Elm Street was the work of a master craftsman—which is why his father wouldn't leave it in a plain kraft box. There was one chest that caught Jacob's eye, one that retained a hint of color through time. His eyes followed the red accents around its corners. Striking down the cobwebs and waving excess dust away, Jacob crouched to examine a way to open the box.

Scratched-off paint and dents showcased the wear and tear. In the center of the chest was a combination lock with a four-digit key. Jacob tried numerous random sets of numbers, but nothing cleared the alignment. He became frustrated and took a breath, still examining the attic and keepsakes around him. A nearby nightstand had a framed oval picture of his parents and Isaac. He stared at the photo for a while, took a deep breath before looking back at the sequence, and changed it to the day his brother died, 1029. The sound of a loud click echoed. Jacob pulled the handle, freeing the darkness that was trapped inside. His hands investigated where the mask could be. Old documents and knickknacks were overflowing from the inside, but he was able to feel his way behind everything to touch the rubber onslaught of deformities on his father's Freddy Kruger disguise.

A photo flung out onto the floorboard when he dragged his arm out. He set aside the mask and put everything back in place. When he picked the print up, however, he made a distinction. His great grandfather, Abraham Sr. as a young man, was pictured with a woman at some secluded beach. And in their arms was a baby. Jacob thought it must have been some lost family photo, but something felt peculiar. He looked closer at who the woman was. As he studied the photo, he was startled by Martha calling him from downstairs, "Jacob! I need some help down here, please!" She yelled. Jacob swiftly stuffed the picture into the mask and ran to the exit before Martha would notice his descent from the attic.

The night sky now prevailed, leaving the space full of shadows. More sprinkles of dust developed overhead, already burying Jacob's trace. In the corner of the ceiling came a glow. A particular glimmer subtly seen came from a pair of yellow eyes—the eyes of the woman of Wonderland.

XIII

WICKER MAN

It was 8:48 p.m. and the scent of meatloaf became paramount. In an unlikely turn of events, the Williams gathered at the dinner table. John sat with his fourth beer, looking at his family, taking a sip, acting as the warden overseeing his facility—with bloodshot eyes. His unbuttoned navy shirt was stained with oils and auto liquids from the last two workdays. Liam ate slowly. He couldn't stomach the food he would usually scarf down.

Wendy pushed dishes around in the background, making room in the sink for when she had to clean up. With the case being that most communication is nonverbal, the Williams household could attest to the theory. An emotional connection missed the family gene pool; the idea of togetherness was based more on discipline and conformity. Their dull kitchenware scratched and scraped against their plates under the sound of a commercial playing on their television—a household item that resonated with the power of detachment.

With this inanimate object, it had the ability to drown the silence of awkwardness and to create conversations for them as a last resort. John went back and forth observing the show and Liam. The scrutiny he faced from his father originated years ago, when every wrong behavior was met with physical punishment. It was an unbalanced rhetoric that stemmed from John's own trauma of imperfection, bestowed onto him by his father. Following this same pattern, Liam found himself emotionally distancing farther and farther away as he grew older.

His mindset pushed Liam to believe he was meant for much more than an army uniform like his ancestors. That there was some purpose to his birth, and alongside Nancy, they would find theirs together.

"Is there something wrong with the food?" John asked in a groggy voice. The already high tension in the kitchen was heightened.

"I'm just not that hungry," Liam replied.

John took another gulp of beer and chuckled, "Not that hungry. Not that hungry, he says."

John directed at Wendy.

She was at a standstill, drinking down her cup of vodka.

"He said he's not hungry, John. Let him be." Wendy said.

"Do you know how I grew up, son?" John asked.

His eyes locked onto Liam's, "We were so dirt poor that my siblings and I had to eat at different times of the day so there was enough food for everyone. For weeks on end, I had one meal to scrape off a plate. Just one. My dad would have broken my jaw if I told him I wasn't hungry."

John took a breath and went on, "You kids have no idea the kind of sacrifices that we parents make to give you the lives you have. A roof over your ungrateful heads, a bed to sleep in, every necessity that keeps you humane is at your fingertips. And you sit here disrespecting us with your bullshit 'I'm not hungry.'"

"John!" Wendy hissed, "It's just one dinner, leave him alone! He lost one of his best friends this week."

Liam sat silent. He knew there was no use in defending himself from someone who grew up in a different environment. As a person who suffered a plentiful amount of childhood trauma himself, it was always a smarter route to let the expression run its course instead of exacerbating the situation more.

"Enlisting corrected me. I learned how to become a man and repay my debts to my father, his father, and those before them. And in wartime, there was no such thing as 'not hungry.' Either you ate or died from starvation." John said.

Liam became increasingly uncomfortable as his father scooted his chair closer to him, "Thirteen years old already."

John laughed. "And you still haven't shown the guts to join the corps. You're a pathetic piece of shit that will never amount to anything."

"That's enough!" Wendy screamed.

John slammed his palm onto the table and shook the utensils off their plates, neutralizing her immediately, "I'll say whatever the fuck I want to him! He lives here without a care in the world, Wendy!" John stood and walked the tiles of the kitchen, "Our bloodline is meant for war—the cause, and fighting for freedom while he prances around with his friends doing God knows what. Thinking everything will be fine with his little girlfriend. He's wasted so much of his time already over that girl!" John said.

"Nancy has nothing to do with this! Don't talk about her like that," Liam said as his anger boiled.

John turned and kneeled next to him, "What did you say to me, boy?"

A smile slinked across John's face, studying the fight or flight instinct his son now struggled with, "Oh, I see now. It takes the death of your little girlfriend to make you a man, huh?"

A tick came behind his father's back, and without hesitation, John pressed a switchblade against Liam's cheeks.

"John, if you hurt our son, I swear to God I'll call the police right now," Wendy said, glued to her chair.

"If you so much as move from that seat without finishing your food, I'll cut your tongue out. Then you'll know what it means to not be hungry," John said.

Liam's eyes filled with tears as the blade returned to his skin.

"Why, look at this, I've never seen him so serious! Let me ask you this, son. Did you love her?"

John asked again, "Did you love her, Liam?"

John burst into laughter before he paralleled Baku's words, "You know nothing of love." John said.

His father's breathing grew louder, more congested, and deep.

"Open your mouth." John whispered.

Liam's tears fell without a whimper. His lips quivered, submitting to his father's demand. John's irises briefly sparkled a yellow sheen as though he were possessed by a demon. The knife entered Liam's back cavity, the tip of the shank dangling along his teeth-ticking every tooth.

While this sadistic scene carried on, Liam was tightly gripping his fork under the dining table. Liam's hand shook amidst this, grasping the silverware with such might that the bones on his knuckles could be seen.

"Maybe this will teach you some manners." John said, pushing the blade against his son's cheek.

"Stop it, John!" Wendy shrieked once more.

John twisted his head to Wendy and began to say something, but before he could make out his first words, Liam pierced his father's temple with the four-pointed dinner utensil.

John was reduced to a blabbering infant howling in pain with blood gushing from his skull. Without hesitating, Liam ran to his room and locked his door. The screams of pain and anger filled their house.

"Liam!" John shouted.

Liam was already preparing a getaway backpack with his essentials.

"Open this fucking door!" John repeatedly punched the wood, and cracks became apparent.

Without much knowledge of what to do in this kind of situation, Liam felt more free than he had ever been. The joyous rush of finally standing up to his childhood villain overcame him while he ran from one corner to another, grabbing miscellaneous items. He zipped his backpack as he stepped through his open window and took one last look back at his room. John's gaze connected with Liam's through the broken door. At that moment, Liam knew there was no going back. He jumped down to the dirt and sprinted into the forest, afraid of what was to come but embracing the independence he so longed for.

A loud flare sparked from the match. A release of pungent tropical scents came as the incinerating wick turned ebony. The food Martha cooked was extraordinary. All of Jacob's favorite foods and comfort indulgences were awaiting him. Every item in front of him was more desirable than the last.

"It's all so wonderful, isn't it?" Martha gallantly asked.

Jacob nodded in agreement but was still on edge because of her strange behavior. She took a deep breath and smiled.

"Well, let's pray." Martha said.

Her arm extended over the delectables, "Give me your hands."

Saying grace was a typical juncture his family engaged in and made Jacob feel a little more at ease. The moment they closed their palms, Martha's head drooped with her dried amber locks of hair strung out on the empty plate. She mumbled to herself hastily, incoherent to Jacob's ears, yet he continued to watch her, unable to recite his own prayer. After she finished, Martha released her son's hand and reached for the spoons.

Her portions were enormous, filling enough for two. Jacob looked at his minuscule plate and then at Martha's, her munching orchestra accentuated in the kitchen. Jacob could hear every chew, bite, and swallow. There was an urge to escape, but his physical limbs would not cooperate. The uninterrupted devourment lasted for twenty more minutes.

Martha suddenly cocked up from her slouch. She promptly walked to the countertop and picked out two tall glass cups from the cabinet. Jacob watched her backside as she poured a pitcher of ice-cold water into them.

Pacing back, Martha handed the beverage to him.

"Silly me, forgot the water," she said.

Jacob grabbed the glass, "Thank you."

Their eyes remained locked; a black glob contrasted at the bottom of Jacob's glass and disintegrated. Martha made her way to her chair and recommenced her dining massacre. His appetite was abysmal, but Jacob had to make a conscious effort in engaging the meal so he could leave. Jacob raised his water and took a sip large enough for a mouthful. Its crystal clear fluid was perfectly transparent when he set it onto the wooden coaster.

He looked out the window and noticed how much of the forest was illuminated by their floodlights. Jacob reminisced about when he and his father installed them years ago. Living in the uncharted forest meant they always had to know what lurked beyond their sight. The lights were so intense it bled into the kitchen—so much so that it was enough for Liam to spot over a hundred yards away.

"Did you try the meat? It's amazing!" Martha thundered.

She paused eating, yet Jacob looked on outside, not privy to her undivided attention. His eyes would transition to his cup again, only now he felt the same nauseating sensation he felt the night he came home from Wonderland.

Martha's wrinkles curved as she smiled and let out an oddly deep laugh. Jacob was having an out-of-body experience, watching his hands start to rattle and the brightness of the room altered. He pushed his chair back, and the wooden leg screeched against the tile. Jacob could not speak, and he soon began to hyperventilate while clutching his neck. It was an all-consuming and endless suffocating episode. Jacob's arms extended as he coughed violently, reaching toward the table and causing his cup to fall on the tile and shatter.

The raucous was loud enough to hear from the porch, where Liam parked his bike. He walked against the side of Jacob's house and was able to see inside the kitchen from a window above their sink.

"My Jacob, everything will be okay." Martha said.

Jacob's eyes were bloodied red before they rolled to the back of his head. The emphatic thump of Jacob's body connecting with the floor vibrated the window Liam had his face pressed against. Martha rushed to her son's side and caressed his temple.

"Always together," she whispered.

Jacob convulsed until the poison he drank mellowed his torment, and he fell unconscious.

"My babies, together forever," Martha finished.

Without a moment's rest, hooded figures rushed into the kitchen dressed in oversized velvet robes. They gathered around Jacob's unconscious vessel and picked him up. Liam watched in horror as his best friend's body was dragged away into the other room. Martha remained still on the floor with her head bowed.

Liam followed from outside, peeping through the windows, trailing where the robed strangers took Jacob. Liam hugged the outer layer of the house to prevent casting his shadow from the floodlights. Parked under the Clay's grand acacia family tree was a gray vehicle. Belted with decades of growth, its behemoth trunk was wrinkled with enormous chunks of bark. Thousands of branches intertwined, shading everything beneath the moonlight. The side door barged open, and the figures reappeared, stomping dirt into the air from their heavy steps as Jacob's legs scraped the ground.

Liam was only about ten meters from the SUV, close enough to hear the throwing of a body onto the cold, steel bottom of the truck. They were taking Jacob somewhere. A rumble ignited the pipe, with musty exhaust starting to pollute the air. Liam ran again, but this time to the opposite side of the ancestral tree. He kept his eyelids closed, preventing the influx of dust from getting into his eye. They left in haste, with the woods echoing the bumps and dips the SUV accelerated over.

The way her closed eyes swayed side to side resembled someone who was in REM sleep. Hours went by while Cheyenne and Chaska sat meditating in the grassless section of their pasture. On a hill that was several hundred feet above sea water, so high they could overlook Seaside's jungle. It was close to 10 p.m. and the relentless winds of the ocean prevailed at these heights without any natural barriers to block them.

They perched all the while from dusk into the late night. Chaska spent a great deal of time practicing ancient breathing techniques, the art of freeing chakra flows and finding a spiritual balance. Chaska said, and unapologetically repeated, the significance of cleansing the mind, body, soul, and the land you sleep on. And ever since Cheyenne cured the sickness that infested her stomach, she realized just how important these practices were. She started to listen closer and more keenly to the words Chaska spoke and engaged actively with daily customs.

Chaska awoke in a deep breath and gazed at his surroundings. The temperature outside had dropped substantially since they started. Chaska looked at Cheyenne now, who was unmoved and in deep concentration. He smiled. Chaska's voice was the first human sound to emerge after several hours, "Cheyenne," Chaska began, "It's time to go inside."

Her eyes finally opened as Chaska was making his way to a stand. She returned to reality the same way he had, without a breath to spare. Cheyenne gathered gulps of air and stood. The nearly whole yellow moon kissed her skin and guided a pathway for them to walk home. Numbness now bested her out of the meditated state. She always wondered how it was humanly possible that they could withstand the brisk night for hours and feel no discomfort. But she was typically too cold to care in the heat of the moment, and this time served no different. Cheyenne gave one last glimpse into the forest and turned away to make haste towards Chaska.

A riveting blanket of coral, teal, and jade fireworks spontaneously saturated the passing clouds in the distance behind them—without a sound to call their attention back. The brief array of spectacularness vanished before Cheyenne or Chaska would notice; the spirits of the Wonderland carnival were beckoning to Seaside.

The inside of their humble home was lukewarm—defrosting goosebumps and relaxing their muscles. Chaska grabbed two jars, one that held crushed Gordolobo flowers and another full of elderberry bits. He set a stainless-steel pot over the stove and prepared his tea water. Cheyenne gave Maka a few head scratches and checked the amount of food she had left.

They were gone for long periods of time so regularly that it was routine to check Maka's food along with closing windows and drapes, turning on lamps, leaving an incense candle fuming, and other minuscule tasks. All this was done in a hush. No words were spoken between them, just the commonality shared that these household tasks must be met before going to bed. Chaska sat waiting for the whistling from the pot to disrupt his peace. Cheyenne's sneakers squeaked about checking off the to-do items.

"Cheyenne," Chaska stopped her.

Her heartbeat pumped to a higher rhythm.

"Yes, uncle?" She replied.

"You seem much better since the other day. More energy. Your face is rejuvenated, yet you were just vomiting on your bedroom floor."

He looked more severely at her, "Is everything okay?"

Cheyenne knew she couldn't explain the events of the week without being met with repercussions for being part of it in the first place. Their relationship was a one-way street that was dictated by Chaska's mood. Even if she tried to justify her part, it was futile. He taught the culture of their people to her through such rituals and customs, but the path to an open-hearted dialogue between them was never formulated. She involuntarily swallowed, "I just had an upset stomach, that's all."

Cheyenne tried to alleviate the uncomfortableness with a chuckle, but he remained as cold as the climate outside. Chaska constantly reiterated the intentions they both shared moving to Seaside. Having Cheyenne learn through both an American schooling system and devoting her free time to their native studies would be an investment years in the making. The hope they instilled into Cheyenne was to rebuild their family name. Studying in a suburban environment away from the noise and clatter of the city would keep her head clear and focused.

Her gained knowledge, in turn, would be used to discover more sustainable and profitable ways their family could survive in this new world. Of course, this plan would come to fruition more notably after her collegiate career, but Chaska's idea was—and always would revolve around—this simple principle. Chaska began to burn the sage stick that sat on their kitchen table.

He blew on the flames and delicately careened the wad, "What we interact with in our physical form stays with us for eternity. We can adapt, alter, and abstain all we want from unwanted energy, but the connection that was made from one source to another lingers long after we leave this world. You understand this, yes?"

Cheyenne nodded. She became more anxious, suspecting Chaska knew more than she had anticipated about Nancy. She wondered just how bad she must have looked the morning after the cove. After a moment, it looked like Chaska was finished with his brief lecture; she started for her room but stopped when she heard him begin to speak again, "We are born with a sickness, Cheyenne. This sickness is embedded into us as a testament to our faith. It has the ability to consume who we are. As equal as day is to night, we cannot live in the light without suffering through the darkness."

Cheyenne looked outside their wide set windows onto the moonlit fields, "How do you keep the balance?"

Chaska replied, "The mind is incredibly powerful. It can shape our reality. To keep balance, we must learn to control our mind and not let it control us. If we can gain mastery over our thoughts and emotions, we ultimately find peace and balance within ourselves."

The night was late, 10:33 p.m.. A thick wooden infrastructure silenced all ambient noise from the outside, trying to come in. Cheyenne put away the clothes, cluttering her bed one at a time. Posters that glorified great Native American heroes mounted her walls: figures amongst her people that reminded Cheyenne of her mother. She never met her, yet Chaska spoke stories of his sister and the great warrior that Dyani was. Cheyenne's mother was held in high stature in their tribe and was well respected by neighboring factions.

Each work of art was hand-drawn to perfection and was one of a kind. As Cheyenne stared at the many faces, she opened her closet door. With every shirt she hung, her face became more and more sullen. She felt embarrassment and shamefulness from wearing these manufactured clothes.

Typically not the emotional type, Cheyenne realized just how impactful Nancy's death was now. In her stages of grief, she needed to surround herself with things that were genuine and mattered to her on a deeper level, down to the clothes on her back. The photo Nancy and she had taken at the beach one afternoon long ago rested inside her pillowcase. Cheyenne was unable to look away from Nancy's unblemished, natural face.

She wanted to always remember what it looked like before that day at the cove. Cheyenne's wall let out a noticeable thump that caught her attention. Nothing transpired for several seconds until a set of purposeful knocks followed a familiar tune to Cheyenne. She immediately shut her night lamp off and ran to her window. There was no one in sight. After sliding the glass upward and poking her head outside, she looked beneath the framework to find Liam pressed against her house.

"First Nancy, now Jacob," Cheyenne said, coming back to her bedside.

"How are we supposed to save them now if we can't even find them in Wonderland? That place is a fucking maze, and we'll only have us and Weston to search it." She said as her spirit was deflated. Cheyenne looked at her posters again—their eyes unflinching. Liam sat on her wool rug, changing his shirt and wiping the smudges of dirt around his face. Liam reached into his backpack,

"And then there's this."

He unfolded the photograph Jacob had found in his attic. After the strangers drove away with Jacob, Liam went inside the house to find any clues or details that would lead him to Jacob's captivity. Mostly, every part of the Clay household was as Liam remembered. A conventional mid-80s interior filled with pastel-colored walls, oversized furniture, and an abundance of shadows from poorly lit lamp shades.

But the moment he went into Jacob's room, he knew that his best friend was preparing for something. His backpack was next to his desk, perked straight up from the contents inside. Liam sorted through snacks, extra clothes, pocket knives, and a mask, but nothing that had anything to do with school. But what caught his attention was a photo tucked in between Jacob's earpieces.

It stood perpendicular to the ground with a special purpose for it being placed where it was. Specifically and notably of importance being next to Weston's devices, which were arguably the most vital item to the entire mission.

"Who is this?" Cheyenne asked, squinting into the grainy image.

"I don't know, I found it with Jacob's things, but it's got to be important somehow, look."

She flipped it over, revealing the initials 'AC' sketched on the bottom right-hand corner.

"AC? It's Jacob's great grandfathers?" Cheyenne said.

She furrowed her eyebrows, "Wait a minute."

She carefully examined the front image's background. Hard enough as it was to distinguish a setting that looked more than half a century old, the film also demonstrated mediocre and poor color quality.

"What is it?" Liam asked.

Cheyenne turned to him, "This was taken at the cove."

Quick steps trembled down the stairs, followed by a booming wallop. Weston opened the front door but was halted halfway through by a hand just above his head. Adam's grip was so strongly clasped onto the frame you could hear the splintering of wood. He looked at his watch, "Late for school today, Weston? That's not being responsible, now, is it? What would Mr. Matthew think of his star pupil deviating from his academic success?" Adam said.

"Yeah, I was going right now, Dad." Weston said.

Adam took a deep breath after a pause, "Coming home straight after school, right?"

"Of course." Weston replied as his grip began to slip from the door.

The passive-aggressive demeanor from his father was unusual; Adam's lurking on Weston's morning schedule was the most inquisitive he had been since Weston was in the fifth grade. His father finally calmed his clench and allowed the front door to fully open.

"Well, have a wonderful day at school today, son." He smiled.

Weston rushed outside and straddled onto his bike. He glanced back once he made it several meters away to find Adam and Mary standing unmoved, watching him. His father raised his arm and gave a sluggish wave. Weston picked up speed and glided out the cul de sac under the bright white overcast sky.

The ear-piercing bell ringing brought the chatter to a decline as the students of Mrs. Davis's class took their seats. The morning was chilly from a draft that leaked into the school and consumed every room. Cheyenne's attention was lost outside with the stillness nature had succumbed to in these conditions. She then looked over to Jacob's empty chair and then to Liam, both unsure of what was to come from a second student's disappearance in a week. Ideally, they would have skipped school to revamp their search, but doing so could lead to more suspicious eyes following them.

Mrs. Davis had not batted an eyelash in the direction of the only vacant space in the class. She presumed with attendance roll call and jotted the appropriate selection after every student responded to their name. Mrs. Davis kept her head down through this process and carried on after silence replied to her. A few more scribbles, and their teacher closed the booklet.

“Looks like we only have one absentee—maybe Mr. Smith is getting a head start on his tutoring schedule in the office!” Mrs. Davis finished.

Cheyenne looked back at Liam once more confused. She raised her hand in an instance, “Uhm, Mrs. Davis, you didn’t call Jacob’s name.”

Mrs. Davis paused from grabbing the algebra book that sat under her desk. With eyes that locked onto Cheyenne’s youthful pupils, the room felt suspended in time and appeared unnoticeable to their classmates. Only the ticking of the room’s clock could be heard; seconds that felt like hours agonizing both Cheyenne and Liam. Mrs. Davis let out a swift sigh, “Oh, my dear, you know we don’t have a Jacob in this class.”

Whispers of a madman fluttered through the air, waking Jacob. From his dazed state, he rose, blinking and acclimating to daylight from overcast skies. The mumbling emanated around him in a continuous reel. Jacob swiveled his head but could not find where the noise came from. Voices that spoke in a foreign language became more prominent and started to give him a throbbing pain in the back of his skull. Jacob pressed his ears closed.

As immediately as the unwelcoming murmurs spoke, so they ceased. Jacob blinked many times until he was finally able to focus on where he was. A terrain like no other, cultivated of blushing tangerine and amber marigold flowers, intoxicated Jacob into a nirvana. The jubilant fields surpassed the hill in a jamboree of colors. Periwinkle blossomed with clusters of cobalt perennials—Jacob was in awe at nature's grace. Scents of the ocean's salt breathed into his lungs, and seagulls squawked just over the distant highlands.

The daydream evaporated when the shriek of a young girl echoed behind Jacob at a higher altitude. He turned toward the sun's relentless shine and shaded his eyes. A colossus of a statue made up of broken branches woven together with twigs and timber locks. There must have been over a thousand pieces, small and large. With a towering height that stood more than twenty feet tall, a sickness emerged inside Jacob—who was staring into the faceless monstrosity. Even with its magnificent size, however, the small incremental spaces between made it noticeable a person was trapped inside the belly of the beast.

Her excruciating wails for freedom were unbearable to endure. A single drum beat through the land in a steady, lethargic repetition. The screams and whimpers accentuated after every thump. Appearing from the opposite side of the hill was the same coalition of strangers that lurked in Jacob's house last night. They gathered around the giant wicker man in a systematic fashion, one after another, with linked hands and encircling themselves amidst the girl's raging cries.

"Mommy! Where are you? Daddy! I'm scared! Someone, please help!" She screamed.

In their baggy wine-cloth garments, they stood unphased and unmoved by even the breeze. Each held a cold-hearted demeanor that gave a sense of something more sinister approaching. The fantasy Jacob reveled in was now a sadistic nightmare.

Dressed in all black was a man who surfaced behind the crowd holding onto a wooden torch. Flames that roared smoke into the air wafted over his beak mask; the raven disguise was topped with a hat and robe that draped over his body in the same shades of shadow.

"Who are you people? Stop! Please!" The girl cried. "I don't know what's going on! Why are you doing this!" Her exhausted yelps periodically became heavy weeping when she could no longer plead with words. The masked man looked at her with bloodshot eyes. Waves stampeded and collided hundreds of feet below them during the absent beating throb.

The man raised the sea of flames above his head, and the encompassing participants dropped to their knees and drooped their heads. Drawn under the woody idol was Wonderland's symbol in white paint.

"Wait! I won't tell anyone about this, I promise! Please, just let me go!" The girl yelled.

She punched and kicked the reinforced lumber after being ignored once again, "Help! Someone, help!" Her elongated weeps took a physical toll on her voice as a more raspy and winded outcry now resulted. When she stopped to breathe, she realized the man and everyone around was now observing her.

"What are you doing?" She questioned the man, who brought the torch closer to her feet.

Jacob could not move a muscle. He tried focusing on lifting his arms, then kicking his legs, and even wiggling a finger to no avail. The night terror had fully incapacitated him—like someone wanted him to watch what was to happen next. Jacob watched as the interior of the personified wicked fiend ignited, and the adolescent girl was slowly burned alive.

"Please! I'm begging you, stop!" She coughed.

Grey smoke clouded above—a mixture of incinerated wood and melting human flesh. Her exclaims and sobbing were now coughs and gags with the amount of toxic airborne particles submerging her. She reached out in a dying effort to be saved by someone; her arms were coated in soot and third-degree burns. The collapse of her body was the last sound she made, silenced under the fire's crackling and her blood that dripped onto Wonderland's outline underneath.

XIV

THE VOID

As Cheyenne, Liam, and Weston navigated through the neglected foliage, the razor-sharp prickles scraped against their skin with each step. In this place, the land and ocean coexisted in a way that appeared to be untouched by human influence. Even the air had a distinct quality to it—as if it held fragments of the past. Memories that were once forgotten now resurfaced, stirring up sensations that lingered in the cove. It was a timeless paradise that Nancy and Cheyenne would often immerse themselves in. Together, they would escape from the outside world, sharing anecdotes from their past and creating new ones to cherish.

But a dreamland no more. When Cheyenne looked over the lagoon, she was now consumed with a sickness. Nancy's gleaming yellow eyes, and the hoarse voice that spewed from her throat, played like a broken record in Cheyenne's mind.

"Can someone tell me why you guys chose to come here in the first place anyway? You can't walk five feet without getting whacked by these plants from the Jurassic Period!" Weston said as he slashed his pocket knife through an array of fan leaves.

"That's the point," Cheyenne said, "Nancy and I came here to be alone and away from everything. If it was easy to get inside, everyone would come."

Liam gashed a bundle of stocky vines leading the way, "How did you girls even make it past all of this?"

He exhaustively swung his arm again and continued, "There's no way you were able to clear a path without someone helping."

Commotion followed a loud snap with Liam's drowning screams coming from ten feet below. Fragments of dirt particles and fleeting insects sprayed into the air, illuminated by the day's evening glow.

"Hey!" Liam shouted and coughed.

"Holy shit! Are you okay?" Weston called looking down at him.

"No, Weston. I'm really not. Who put a fucking pit trap in a place no one goes to!" Liam grunted, padding dead leaves and bugs off his clothes.

Cheyenne poked her head into the hole and laughed at him, "I guess us girls don't really need any help, huh?"

"You and Nancy made this?" Liam asked.

She looked around him, ignoring his question—extending her neck at different angles.

"Are you bleeding?"

Liam felt his stomach, back, arms, legs, and skull, "No, why?"

"Lucky you, Nancy made this one. Mine had knives at the bottom," Cheyenne said.

Weston and Liam looked at each other in disbelief.

"Hurry up and get out of there. We're close," Cheyenne urged.

Her heart pounded in her chest as they approached the side opening just before the soil transitioned into sand. Cheyenne held Jacob's photo above one of her eyes, her hand shaking slightly as she compared the view to the picture.

“This is where the picture was taken.” she said, her voice barely above a whisper.

Liam and Weston scanned the surroundings, searching for any remnants of a trace that could lead them to something more substantial than a mere similarity. Weston kicked over a stepping stone that rolled down the steep hill while Liam overlooked the lagoon and serene aquamarine waters. The contrasting elements were a stunning display of nature’s bloom, but Cheyenne couldn’t appreciate it.

“We know Jacob’s great-grandfather is somehow tied to Wonderland, so maybe there’s a clue here that can help us. There had to be a reason why Jacob kept this photo on him.”

Cheyenne said. As she inched closer to the cliff’s edge and scouted the horizon, her eyes welled up with tears. Suddenly, she pointed towards a cave in the distance.

“That’s the last time I saw Nancy.” she said, her voice cracking with emotion as Liam perked up. The memories of that fateful day came rushing back, and Cheyenne couldn’t help but feel overwhelmed by the mix of grief, guilt, and anger.

The peach-colored sun rays caressed the millions of simple-celled algae organisms that littered the beach. As October set in, Seaside underwent a metamorphosis where the shorter days and colder nights deprived the seasonal plant life of their necessities to saturate the surroundings. A colorlessness began to flourish in the woods and everywhere else, except in the cove, where the sequence of seasons seemed to have paused, remaining eternal.

Cheyenne walked past a strip of smooth sand where she and Nancy had dozed off countless times before. The closer she got, the more apparent the fresh and subtle indentations became, as if someone had just been lying there. The three stopped in their tracks as they approached the cave's opening, "This was where it happened?" Liam asked.

"Yes," Cheyenne whispered.

The entrance to the cave emitted an ominous black aura, with no visible signs of light beyond it and no indication of how far it extended. Unnoticed by the trio, bronze stains on the ground resembled dried blood. A gust of wind blew sand over the stains, hiding yet another secret of the cove. The cave was roofed by arched rock formations, which depleted any light entering within the first dozen meters.

"Wait," Weston said, stopping in his tracks. "We won't be able to see anything inside."

He dug through his backpack, unsure of what lay ahead.

Liam scanned the area, ensuring no one else was around.

"It feels like I was just here. Nancy was standing right here, and I left her," Cheyenne said, standing frozen.

Liam tried to reassure her, "It wasn't really her, Cheyenne. Lilith was controlling her. We're going to get her and Jacob out of that place, okay?"

Weston stood up, having fashioned three makeshift devices that provided hands-free lighting. The root of these clunky devices was a pair of safety goggles with two flashlights attached to the sides. Liam and Cheyenne eyed the contraptions skeptically.

"Why couldn't we just use the flashlights on their own?" Liam asked, struggling to adjust the headset over his forehead.

Weston tinkered with his pair, glanced at the cave, then back at them, "Look, man, it's been a really long week. I was supposed to be saving up for a Nintendo from my tutoring, but instead, I'm here trying to create equipment for us on this fucking crusade. So I'm sorry if my military-grade flashlights aren't good enough for you, Liam. Here, Cheyenne, take this earpiece."

Weston checked his watch; it was 6 p.m. Cheyenne walked past them and began to blend into the abyss. With the added light, they could see how deep the cave extended, but not the end of it. The limestone walls were moist with condensation, and the nonstop drips of water created a faint reverberation. Less than ten steps in, a foul odor permeated the air.

"Jesus fucking Christ, it stinks in here!" Weston gagged.

"I don't think I've ever smelled anything this bad in my life." Liam said, plugging his nose.

Cheyenne made a face until something caught her eye on the gravel. Sticking out half-buried was a shimmering red object reflecting off her concentrated bulb beams. She dusted the sand to find that it was a DMC DeLorean children's toy car. Before she could call out to them, Liam yelled, "Hey, look at this!" The darkness enveloped them, limiting their visibility to a mere fifteen feet. They came upon a girl's white dress, crumpled and stained with maroon near the neck.

"What is that?" Weston said.

"It's blood, dried blood." Cheyenne uttered.

As they continued forward, their path grew wider, and their earpieces buzzed in the eerie silence. A faint growl could be heard in the distance. Cheyenne stopped and looked around but saw nothing—Liam and Weston's flashlight beams dimmed as they moved further ahead.

"What was that sound?" She whispered.

Soon, she realized she had been abandoned by her companions and was lost in the dark, echoing cave. Cheyenne called out for them repeatedly but received no reply, only the hissing of static from her earpiece. Her anxiousness increased as she wandered, her voice growing hoarse and her lips parched. The silence was daunting, and despair began to set in as she pondered the possibility of never escaping the cave.

"Hello?" She called out louder. The absence of Weston and Liam's complementing flashlights became alarmingly evident when her own device would only reveal what was just three feet in front of her. All that reciprocated her inquiry were hazy, distant footsteps—they were now completely out of her vicinity.

Moments evolved into minutes that gapped to hours; Cheyenne wandered for what felt like an eternity. She repeatedly spoke into the microphone, calling out to them, but the static reply hissed unceasingly back. Fatigue weighed heavier on her legs from ceaseless walking, along with looming muscle cramps. Without water since lunch, her dry lips chapped and made it more difficult to shout for help. After so long, she knew it would be best to conserve her energy.

Frustration clouded her cognition and weakened her emotionally. Cheyenne became wary of the sudden possibility of never escaping the cave. She was soaking in the pitch-black; Weston's halogen-bulbed instruments failed to pierce through the murk of anything farther than a couple inches. Instead of hearing the sporadic droplets in the background, she was now residing in total silence.

Her weary state diffused any remaining vigilance that dwelled inside. The untarnished sneakers she wore were painted with mud all over. Cheyenne stopped and sat on a nearby rock. She refrained from further straining her vocal cords. The frigid temperature inside the cave's inner cavity indicated just how underground she trailed.

Cheyenne began to experience a growing sense of anxiety as she gazed at the intimidating emptiness of the purgatory space. Her breathing became more rapid and shallow, signaling the onset of a potential manic episode. She felt her chest tightening as she struggled to inhale and exhale, and her heart pounding so forcefully that it caused her physical discomfort. She was acutely aware of every pulsation of blood coursing through her veins. As she listened to the echoes of her own breathing, they seemed to blend together with the sounds around her, making it difficult to distinguish her own breaths from those of others.

"You're so pretty." A fragile utter whisked behind her.

Cheyenne came close to fracturing a bone in her neck from pivoting so abruptly. Her flashlight made the cave's emptiness visible. She peered on.

"Who's there?" She called.

Nothing. She straightened out one arm to navigate forward and had the other clutched onto her arrow necklace.

"Hello?" She asked.

Her adrenal glands ejected the natural morphine into her bloodstream, numbing her legs from physical pain. With each subtle limp her skull rotated, she wondered if her mind was unraveling and if what she heard was formulated from her deteriorating thoughts. Her breaths became booming and more deafening—along with the breaths of others—suffocated Cheyenne's mind. This blaring orchestra of breaths perpetuated over and over, and was on the verge of bursting her eardrums, dwindling Cheyenne into the frontal fetal position, clasping the sides of her temple.

"Stop it!" She wailed.

"Shut up!" Cheyenne roared.

And just like that, the cave fell silent once again. She emerged from the cocoon of her own body, the chaos temporarily quelled. As she looked up, the intrigued gaze of a hazel-eyed child intertwined with her own eyes, reflecting a shared depth of hue.

"Hi, I'm Azazel, what's your name?"

He stood barely four feet tall and had not blinked since he introduced herself. Cheyenne felt more concerned a child was lost in this limbo alongside her than fearful of who he was or where he came from.

"What are you doing in here? Where are your parents?" Cheyenne asked.

She picked herself off the ground and looked around, assuming there was someone else with him. The boy's face had an anemic composition when his skin was kindled under Cheyenne's flashlights.

"This is where I've always been." The boy said, somewhat confused at the question,

"For as long as I can remember." His tone and physical demeanor resembled no child Cheyenne had ever encountered: candid and almost impassive.

"Azazel, do you know how to get out of here?" Cheyenne asked.

An ever so gentle hiss of air whirled passed them, with their heads following as though the invisible force could be trailed. The boy turned back to Cheyenne.

"She wants me to show you," he said.

"Where are they? Where are Nancy and Jacob?" Cheyenne asked.

The boy turned and ran into the darkness that welcomed him with open arms. Cheyenne hopped off from the dirt.

"Hey! Where are you going? Wait!" Cheyenne yelled.

The exhaustion in her legs renewed, and a severe soreness gripped Cheyenne's quadriceps with every step. Blinded by the blackness, Azazel dashed over wide crevasses and the perilous cavities. She had to make great strides to keep up with him.

"Slow down!" Cheyenne yelped.

Her hands scraped against the rock walls, pushing herself toward the direction he effortlessly barreled through. They weaved about countless pathways that resulted in a new terrain Cheyenne had not recognized whilst searching for a way out, skipping over shallow ponds, piles of gravel, and drooping vine vegetation. For a moment, however, her attention was concentrated on the color of malachite that covered the edges of the trail they ran. Finally, the boy's scampering footsteps that volleyed off the cave finally ceased.

"Where are we going?" Cheyenne asked, hunched with a huff of breath and gasping for more air.

Silence grew, and it wasn't until Cheyenne lifted her chin and realized the boy was gone.

"Azazel?" She called out.

He was nowhere to be found; Cheyenne was once again alone.

The sand under her shoes crushed and etched while she spun around looking for him.

"Where are you!" She cried.

Cheyenne reluctantly inched forward. She oscillated until a scurry of steps scrambled past her, and a stampede of goosebumps grazed across her neck.

"Azazel? Stop fucking around, kid. Come out!" She yelled.

The restlessness and fury in her words could not cloak the acute tremble in her voice. Again, the commotion skittered past her from behind, but this time, she was able to differentiate the shape of a person running on all fours when she turned—a person who was not a child, a person who was at least six feet tall that wriggled behind the distant rocks ahead. Its movements were unnatural and eerie, resembling someone who had broken bones and twisted joints. Cheyenne's heartbeat vigorously pulsated. She was paralyzed, her breaths abated, and the deep creases between her eyebrows now relaxed into an expressionless look on her face.

Her cheeks were rosied numb in the refrigerated conditions. Cheyenne crept ahead, twiddling her gold arrow pendant that lay between her chest. Passing by gargantuan stones that sat at the same height as her, she cautiously curled her head, gimping around each. The hushed murmurs of what sounded like a man filled the cave. Cheyenne edged over a nearby slab and glanced on the other side to find the man hunkered and clutching his rib cage.

Cheyenne's heart raced as she pulled herself away, grimacing and gripping her leg doing so. The drained battery of Weston's flashlight brought upon a spasm of flickers; darkness eagerly awaited. After the final twinkle, the light remained on, but it made visible that the man was perched at the top of the stone Cheyenne leaned against.

She looked up and illuminated his bleached, malnourished vessel. The man's hairless features welcomed bone—dry skin so transparent that the dull flashlight could still expose his abundance of violet veins. His only article of clothing present was a ragged cloth covering his private bodily components.

A disturbingly vocal cry surged from his throat that sprung Cheyenne into action. Her legs bicycled on autopilot, pumping with adrenaline. To her knowledge, the man followed just several feet away, within his arm's length. Cheyenne awaited his lanky, bony fingers to wrap around her neck any second, but nothing came. She collapsed, ending the torment her legs suffered. The once lukewarm sand was, in this region, turned into a cool cluster of sedimentary rock.

Following the gravel pathway introduced her to one of the ends of the cave. The wall had a charcoal composition that made it camouflage in the darkness. Cheyenne got closer and reached out to test the authenticity of this possible delusion. Its sweltering heat burned her palm when she made contact.

"Fuck!" She shrilled.

Cheyenne looked more intimately at its surface, bewildered at how something so warm could tolerate the chilled conditions. She felt the profoundly carved symbols on the rock. There were no two distinct emblems; they scattered everywhere and presented themselves in a variety of shapes and sizes. Some displayed simplistic illustrations of parabolas and merging patterns, while others held detailed depictions of the starry night sky. She continued to stalk the designs and noticed they were not only etched side-to-side but elevated upward, too.

What looked to be broken fractions of the mineral on the sides were rather mounted steps that one could climb to ascend. More was beyond the realm of what she could see, and beyond meant atop. If the artwork could make its way there, surely the artist had to find a way, too, she thought. And suddenly, it manifested in Cheyenne that the way out of here might be from above.

They lay on the frozen ground for what felt like hours since they had entered the cave. With his laid arms relaxed and crossed behind his head, Weston blankly blinked at the infinite space staring back at him.

"What happened to you in there, Weston? In Wonderland?" Liam asked while his eyes were captivated by the fire.

Weston's opaque memory was far from the truth. He did, unfortunately, remember everything under Lilith's spell—with impeccable detail. Liam went on before Weston could daze off, "I know something happened, man. Tell me what she did to you. We all saw something,"

The reminiscence made Liam uncomfortable; he adjusted himself, waiting for a response. Yet, a pause mellowed between them instead.

"Weston?" Liam said. He recoiled back into reality, sitting up and gandering at what the flames could expose.

"Her face was so pale, like she had been dead for years," Weston started. "I couldn't stop looking. The way her teeth bit into their skin and ground their flesh, I couldn't stop listening. What they felt, all those children, their torment, so could I."

What sounded like a draft whistled through the curvatures at the highest point of the cavern. He continued on, "Somehow, when she took me to that place, I could feel their agony, taste their blood on my tongue. It was like I was one of them. They were in so much pain. They each shared a regret in being born into this world and questioned what they did to deserve this."

"Jesus Christ, man," Liam responded with wrinkles of distress that valleyed on his forehead.

"When I was in there, though," Weston's piercing glare now on Liam, "She was in me. She knows who I am, where I live, who my family and friends are, my fears, everything, Liam. She showed me her memories and stole mine."

Liam ran his fingers through his hair, "And now she has Jacob. We don't even know what she's done with Nancy at this point, either. It's been four fucking days."

"And we have no idea where Cheyenne is," Weston added.

Time idly passed on; the seconds, minutes, and hours could not be dictated by any means. It could have been the next day or two for all they knew. Their radio frequencies picked up no nearby connections despite Weston's countless modifications. The only transmission they received was a static buzz that screeched back to them anytime they tried calling out to her. Weston looked fixedly back to the embers that seemed to react to the gentle gust from a moment ago. His spine perked up when he noticed just how substantial the flames were actually responding.

"Liam, give me some paper!" Weston exclaimed.

Liam glanced at the center of the pit, "Why? There are enough sheets in there to last another half hour, at least. We don't have an unlimited supply of this, you know."

"Just give me the damn paper!" He raised his voice.

With about five sheets on hand, Weston scooped the ashes that blanketed the edges. Liam made a confused face, "What are you doing with that?"

He continued to gently accumulate enough soot to cover the majority of the stack. Weston carefully raised the pile to the height of the fire and watched the particles glide off by the pinch.

"Look, there's wind coming from somewhere!" He said with an emerging grin, "Guess there's a way out of here after all."

Scrambling to their feet, Liam and Weston swiftly stuffed all their belongings back into their backpacks.

"Try Cheyenne one more time," Weston said. Liam tapped the side switch of the earpiece, discharging the low buzz hum, "Cheyenne, can you read me? Over."

The unfluctuating tone of white noise only responded back. They looked at each other dormantly. Leaving the cave without her would be murder. And the only possible way they would rescue Cheyenne would be with the aid of local law enforcement search teams. The lingering and nearly conceivable notion they, too, were privy to Wonderland's past could not be omitted from the equation.

It brewed in their preteen craniums briefly before a pounding thud vibrated their fragile rib cages and released the millions of debris fragments sent trickling to the ground. They remained still, anticipating another disturbance. The advent continued every ten seconds, rocking the subterrane's foundation each time.

Liam whispered to Weston, "What the fuck is that?"

They stayed close to one another and surveyed the darkness behind the withering fire pit.

"It came from the same direction the breeze blew. We gotta follow it."

Liam was going to object to his suggestion, but the ongoing thumps interrupted him. Weston recognized just how afraid he was but knew they had no choice if they were to have any chance at survival.

"We can either stay here—wait for our paper supply to finish and die without trying—or we can go where that noise is coming from and hope there's a way out."

Weston explained. He clicked and connected the dangling straps securing his bag, "Hope you still got that butterfly knife."

Liam agilely retrieved the pendulous blade that slid out of an aged leather holster that belonged to his father during wartime. The gambit and natural movements distilled from his fingertips rejuvenated some lost confidence. He took a breath and nodded at Weston, "Let's do this."

Ambient light glowed twenty feet out, aiding their descent back to the uncharted. Tolerable trembles soon matured to roaring booms that caused watermelon-sized stones to fall and nearly flatten them. Once outside the viewable space, Weston adjusted his ineffective headset flashlights but concentrated more on listening to where the sustaining blasts were coming from and if the wind's current was intensifying. Their pace slowed considerably while their eyes conversely enlarged.

"Can you see anything?" Weston murmured.

“No, nothing. I can barely see my hands,” Liam replied.

While their eyesight subsided, Weston became antsy and replenished of lost enthusiasm when the airflow began to blow past them.

“We’re getting closer,” he nudged.

Metallic clinks and clatter congruously sung from Liam’s balisong, the coping mechanism fidget provided a serenity to both. They paused between the sempiternal quakes. As they languidly carried on, the cavern unexpectedly narrowed where the walls depressed inward. What appeared in front of them now were lucents of azure and cerulean kissing the outline of an obstruent boulder veiling the deepest and innermost trench in the cave.

Their faces would emerge out of the obsidian—ever so gradually, like creatures of the abyssal murky depths. A furious tremor shocked through that burrowed their bodies against the stone before seeing what was on the other side. One breath after another, they exhaled their lungs. Liam and Weston dragged and abraded their backs and vulnerable skin to try looking again when the turbulence lessened. As he peeked his nose into the more prominent light source, Weston’s eyelids shut from the overwhelming sensory change and still strikingly whisking current.

With a momentary break from anything obstructing their vision, Weston and Liam gazed upon an icy tundra that stretched miles wide. The sleet ground reflected a grim sky consumed by dark blue and ash clouds. Warmth fleetingly exuded their blood vessels, refrigerating their muscle functions the second they walked in; the slightest breath appeared milky white and lingered in the atmosphere. An odorless wasteland worthy of isolated punishment, the state of being here remained and always was a place for torment.

Each step they took fractured the ground beneath them.

"Is this real?" Liam asked, mesmerized. His fascination carried him onward. The further inward they walked, the steeper it became, a cliff miraged ahead when no land materialized in the distance.

"I'm not sure," he said, stopping to retrieve his compass.

This phantasm and its reality caused a cognitive dissonance inside Weston. He struggled to find the plausibility that such a vast terrain had come about, especially since they had not descended below sea level nor elevated to such a degree during their pilgrimage that would warrant this kind of geographical phenomenon.

"I don't understand, this place shouldn't exist." Weston clicked repeatedly, hoping to find a sense of direction, but the needle continually spun.

"We walked for hours in there, and now we're in no man's land. I can't even get a reading of anything, and I think—" he paused to check his earpiece, "It's dead."

With his back turned away, Liam said nothing as he peered down over the ledge of the mountaintop. Weston raised his chin when he detected his silence seconds later, "Liam!" He shouted. He stood and made his way to him. The polished bottoms of his sneakers made it arduous to run without slipping, so the twenty or so feet amble instead became a waddle—paying caution to any false steps or hollow ice. Weston used his hands once closer to bear crawl up the snowy plateau where Liam stopped.

"What the fuck are you doing up here?" Weston grunted, still acclimating himself and adjusting his backpack straps.

An influx of air untamed by any impediment drifted across the valley. The depressed plain bottomed hundreds of feet below. Arctic humidity fogged throughout the land, but not enough to conceal the behemoth of a creature that sat halfway submerged in the frozen lake.

Weston adopted Liam's speechlessness; the two sustained a paralysis where they could not stop watching in absolute fright. Their reticent begged the other to speak, hoping one might devise a plan, suggest an alternative route, or even find a hideaway in the meantime. Yet, only the epitome of devastation and dread dwelled in their consciousness. Weston flickered minutes later and swiveled his head to calculate how far they were from the entrance.

What looked back at him was what could only be described as a result of a blizzard. The exit had been coated with abundant and ample amounts of snow blocking any exit. In a blink of an eye, the beast heaved its bulging wings to the sky, causing a gravitational implosion and drawing everything towards the center. The air vibrated like the inception of an atomic bomb; it was insurmountable for them to look away.

In the more obvious perspective, Liam was unnerved and petrified. There was nowhere to run, nowhere to hide. They had failed their friends to rescue them, and now they stood opposite a monstrosity capable of killing them both in a matter of seconds. What could not be explained or understood by Liam, however, was that he could sense a part of him that was in awe, fascinated, and nearly hypnotized by the Goliath being.

He had never seen anything of this magnitude in his life; the boundless Seaside ocean he grew up remembering lost its luster and lessened in his mind. The airspace the woods manifested—that he once admired while escaping his own reality—now felt minuscule in comparison to this unholy deity. And just as instantaneous did the claws extending from each wing soar to the ground. Each hollow web shadowed as somber skies, the bones outlined so finely it was on the verge of ripping through flesh.

A momentum like no other, it thrashed through every freely roaming particle and shook the foundations of nearby geographic formations. Their jaws dropped, observing ripples cascade, cracking into the glaciers while remaining unmoved. Weston snatched Liam to the ground several feet under, "Duck!" What sounded like dynamite detonated behind them, the mountain was bombarded ferociously with continuous surges, and snow began to spray the scenery for many minutes after.

They poked back up and continued to ogle at the being. Once the frosty vapors vanished, the visibility cleared drastically—the suppressed sound waves began to reach Weston and Liam, who were miles away. Saffron irises, bright as a setting sun staring back, waned and contrasted the fiend's ebony complexion. Mammoth horns the size of redwoods towered into the heavens, and fissures spread from its stomach, revealing its countless futile attempts to escape.

Weston nudged Liam, who wore a sodden expression and had not reacted to the fact that they were nearly obliterated moments ago.

"We gotta hide man," he said. The words seemed to elude his ears. "Liam!" Weston softly hissed.

Out of the hallucination, Liam regained command of his eyelids and fluttered them, combing the surroundings with his pupils. He pushed himself off the snow and followed Weston down the hill and into the woodland labyrinth cloaked in chalk. No walkways were palpable; their steps sunk at every imprint. Evident traces that anyone or anything had walked inside were nonexistent as well. They declined dozens of feet before land approached frozen water.

Weston and Liam paused in disbelief, both turning to each other as the vocal stimulant identified a noise that was familiar to both. What followed were the faint screams of men and women at the base of this icy Hell, numbed into the reservoir while the merciless eyes of Lucifer vigilantly watched the suffering of every damned soul.

XV

INFERNO

Remnants of chipped rock tumbled down the steep climb with each passing step. Her echoes edged on—emphasizing how distant Cheyenne was from the bottom. What started as flattened beds of many stones pushed together, forming a balanced platform, soon bound her to all fours, mounting onto anything stable enough to keep her from falling. The trail she traveled on was treacherous, with only dirt accumulating onto these loose bits and chunks for thousands of years.

The core of her body was soon cramped, and sweat streamed from her pores as the climate warmed severely. Most of what she gripped and tiptoed through was dust-coated and became spongier the higher she went. She looked up to find a gleaming apricot glimmer that came from the top; with an extension of her arm, Cheyenne groaned and scraped herself over the cliff, finally conquering the slope.

She ceased moving and breathing. The whites of her eyes were stained by the scorching flames of a thousand candles illuminating a gateway to a lurking lair. But it came secondary to what originally extinguished her rising body heat and stalled blood that had since resumed its course through her veins. Coexisting between lightlessness beyond what the fires could not reveal was the contour of a woman.

Her demented eyes shimmered subtly in and out with the dancing flames; her wrinkly grin stretched from cheek to cheek like waves welcoming Cheyenne to come closer. And then, she was no more, gone and out of sight. The flames now mingled amongst themselves in the shadows; Cheyenne stepped forward. She was astonished at the landscaping marvel that epitomized craftsmanship. Lush green herbs and flowers overflowed from the cracks on the walls, a dazzling display of pigmentations flowering at each stem.

Cheyenne was infatuated by this beauty, not a single petal withering nor malnourished without a source of sunshine. She benevolently ran her intoxicated fingers through them, feeling calm more than concern. The sound of glass breaking ended what she thought was a brief lapse in consciousness. Cheyenne looked down to see puddles of melted wax flooding the grounds, with some already drying on the sides of her shoes. The unsullied air was euphoric as oxygen plunged into her chest, coaxing her to continue into the inner cavern.

Inside elongated hundreds of feet with candles dimly lighting only portions of the tunnel. Cheyenne scoured the hallway, peering with great concentration, anticipating the silhouette of the woman to emerge and sneak into the darkness once more. Fearful of any physical threat in her immensely weakened state, she closely scaled the walls moving ahead. Swarming her ears came the sounds of the sea moments after. The arbitrary forces crashing against each other eased her mind.

Cheyenne wiped sweat beads off her forehead. The jungle's breath breathed life into the tropical foregrounds amidst Antarctic conditions just outside. Unruly vines reached from above, with virtually everything else plastered with greenery. She stopped after passing the umpteenth candle. An endless trail that led nowhere rendered her voyage to a hobble. Gravity tugged Cheyenne to the dirt, so she stared on, hoping to see any indication there was more than the unending cycle.

Before she relaxed her neck muscles in disappointment, the blackness flinched in a spasm, startling Cheyenne. A figure darted away through the shaft only several feet from her, exposing how closely they kept to her—watching and weaving Cheyenne deeper. She took a hastened huff and leaped off the soil.

"Wait!" She yelled.

The woman disappeared in a heartbeat, swinging around a corner. Her outfit had flailing loose pieces that were accustomed to what a religious ceremony would entail one to wear. It was because of this that Cheyenne could follow within a safe distance from her.

"Stop running, please!" She begged.

Her hamstring tensed up and contracted without her consent; the agonizing pain of her muscle locking reduced the chase to an escape. A final right turn brought Cheyenne to an open field of grass with a garden as its centerpiece, closed off by towering shrubs. Matured trunks that were as wide as she was tall stood side-by-side, creating an impenetrable enclosure. It extended quite a ways. One's peripheral vision was not enough to see end to end. Her eyes became lost in the contrasting, endless pitch-black that prevailed past this pasture.

She submitted to this enchantment, and her footsteps followed. It was unnaturally quiet once she was halfway through. Only the sound of grass crunching from her steps could be heard. She walked past each breathtaking flower that seeded a different color than the next. An abundance of artistry unraveled in front of her. What could only be explained as child-like wonder, Cheyenne meandered, astonished, until the voice of the woman whispered down her neck and sunk her stomach to the floor, "Mistress Mary, quite contrary, how does your garden grow?"

A putrid smell infiltrated her nasal cavity, and she began to feel a burning sensation in her sinuses. Cheyenne gyrated around, petrified. The woman was knelt down on both knees, drooping her head sharply to the point her spinal bones were visible from Cheyenne's perspective. Thick strands of damaged jet-black hair hung from her skull, concealing her facial features as she spoke incoherently under her breath. Her skin wore a darker tone—similar to Cheyenne's. A lackadaisical routine of heavy inhales and exhales moved the woman's shoulders up and down.

She sang with a raspy throat that was just as quiet, "With silver bells and cockle shells."

Slipped from her lips. Cheyenne's eyes drifted down to what lay in the woman's stained arms. Perfuming the air were odors of rancid meat that derived from the open cavity of a child lying on her thighs. Their one to two-foot-long body was completely slaughtered, leaving behind a discoloration of burgundy in the turf encircling the two. The same dark wine pigments generously painted the woman's forearms, and that also had laceration wounds. Cheyenne stopped breathing once her head lifted and their brown irises interlocked.

"And so my garden grows," she said in a more dispassionate tone.

Her pupils dilated fully once she got a longer look at Cheyenne, twin obsidian spheres glaring and enticing her to welcome the darkness. Remnants of flesh and dried blood smeared across the woman's now grinning face. Her initial haggard appearance and sullen mood transitioned into a frolic of joy, “My, oh my, and how my little girl has grown.”

Her gangly arms surged over the body and nimbly squirmed, coming to Cheyenne. She had not the time to weigh other options, behind Cheyenne opened a pathway back into the convoluting maze. The woman was already within her extended reach when a glistening of gold sparkled in Cheyenne’s eyes as she hesitated, turning to sprint away. Dangling freely off the woman’s throat was an arrow pendant.

A grip that triggered an excruciating sense of pain tugged and twisted at Cheyenne’s bicep. She screamed to let go, but the woman barbarously kneaded into her muscle tissue, shifting along the many dancing veins. With a desperation like no other, Cheyenne heaved her arm away, ripping her skin open, hoping to slip away. A final cry expelled from her soul, and she freed herself, leaving fingernail-length slashes sinking down her arm.

Into the unexplored, she eluded, making swift swings here and there until goosebumps ridden across the top of her spinal cord settled. Drops of blood trickled on the grass, making it difficult to conceal the route she traveled; Cheyenne used the jacket tied to her waist to wrap her wounds. Her ensuing gnawing footsteps were accompanied by repressed asthmatic breathing.

Nature thrived under what mimicked fluorescent lighting—a soft radiance exposing every course like the everlasting sun. The visual disharmony turned her stomach; an ersatz environment swayed her—toying with what could be a dream, nightmare, or something much worse, real. The leaves were dense in composition, and their thicker vines intertwined with each other the way coiling boa constrictors suffocate their prey. She calmed her panting to a steady rhythm now that only silence escorted her.

Her fatigue was so overwhelming that Cheyenne had not noticed she had been walking a straight line for a prolonged period of time. She waddled down an extensive line, becoming more and more delusional from the blood loss. What occupied her attention now consisted of only primitive visual and touch stimulations rather than the whereabouts of the woman, who crawled somewhere behind Cheyenne unknowingly.

Humming past her ears came a low-frequency buzz vibrating through the air. Her eyes broadened. Upon facing where the noise came from, she watched the woman sluggishly twisting and wriggling toward her. Cheyenne checked corner to corner, locating a nearby turn. There was an opening some ways onward that she limped toward, her attention still fixating on the woman whose head tensely rose in contrast to her spine. With a smile only a mother could love, the woman gazed with delectation at Cheyenne. The sight was unsettling to digest; a deficiency in joints or the removal of many limbs still would not explain how she was able to move as she did. When Cheyenne finally spun her head in the new direction, she found the woman once more. Creeping closer than before, wearing the same sinister stare.

Cheyenne blinked several times before retreating out the way she came. Whimpering back upon the mile-long walkway, the woman's dragging body became more audible, yet the sounds echoed behind her. Cheyenne abruptly looked back to find the woman closing in on her. In a panic, she hobbled straight on the endless trail again.

Nothing but a green wall glared back at her while she stumbled forward. With every other step, her neck would warp behind to eyeball how far the woman was, hoping the distance between them blurred beyond sight. Yet, the woman was projected no farther, no matter Cheyenne's efforts. She looked forward and gasped. The woman cackled, approaching from ahead, slithering inch by inch.

A total impairment of sensation numbed her once adrenaline fully diluted throughout her bloodstream. She tried pushing through the stiff shrubbery by her side, but it's deeply rooted base and ancient branches were too formidable against human flesh. Cheyenne's last hope came by crying into Weston's earpiece.

"Liam! Weston! Answer me, please!" She manically pressed every button on the device. The woman was only several feet away at both angles, "Guys, say something!" She begged sobbingly.

Words barely uttered and incoherent babbling developed from her berserk weeping. Cheyenne closed her eyes as the woman converged near enough to taste her skin. There was no sense of urgency or necessity in rushing; the built-up anticipation actualized the woman's sadistic pleasures. She latched onto Cheyenne's shoulders, dragging them both to the ground. Stretching her skeletal fingers against her jugular, the woman coddled and caressed her way about the collar bones. A strikingly noticeable deep tan fulgent from Cheyenne's neck made the woman's hand appear evermore lifeless.

The handcrafted arrow clinked against her uncut nails, "Please, stop."

Cheyenne bawled. Her hands hovered higher until they stopped at her temples. The woman cogitated over her twelve-year-old facial structure with her bulging eyes—these gigantic optical organs that twitched simultaneously at every curvature of Cheyenne's face, violating any sense of individuality she had left. A resounding croaking laughter cloaked the two inside what indistinguishably tethered between reality and imagination. The perception of trauma became nonexistent, and Cheyenne's bodily response to affliction disappeared just as emphatically as her emotional well-being.

"One by one, they're going to die," The woman softly spoke into her ears. Her eyes were unmoved with a tongue that sang an angelic, hushed voice, "The sins of your elders will be paid with your blood."

All but the expelling roars that were pressurized in Cheyenne's lungs could be heard. Pressure relentlessly built along the outer rims of each eyeball until she was unable to keep awake. She lost muscle control and passed out while the woman dug deeper and deeper.

The air was colored with a surfeit of voices orchestrating from the ice. Torment troubled their lips, and agony impelled their pleas to God for forgiveness. Liam and Weston camouflaged themselves some fifty feet inside the forest where snow piled. A dimmed depiction of the heavens befell this continent over their time spent.

Dusk wavered twilight and cosseted fragments of what daylight remained. A windless winter waned their spirits as the beast glommed oxygen and breathed out a steady stream of fog. Its posture leaned to the side more heavily, displacing titan-sized slabs of frozen sheets now. Liam and Weston had not said a word since settling into their hideaway. While Weston internally checked their earpieces for any wiring errors or debris,

Liam's trenchant and tractable attention left him standing unblinking, forever observing the creature.

Condensed in the coal-colored epicenters that were his pupils, which resonated the reflection of the underworld they were lost in. And Liam's once radiant indigo irises synchronized with the darkened landscape. This barren wasteland's personality intertwined with his sense of urgency and enthusiasm mellowed away as the day turned into night.

A mechanical twirl softly played behind him, breaking the silence. Liam turned around to see Weston meddling with Adam's camera. A malleable device that was custom-built, adjusted itself to any sized lens, and was constructed of pure steel. It was physically and engineeringly more advanced than anything in the current market. The perfected shape of its sleek body, smooth button maneuvers, and array of versatile functionalities made this contraption a catalyst for Weston's creative mind. It was one of the few items he left in his father's original structure, preserving the novelty of their family jewel until now. The alignment was disrupted in a way where the shutter would not open and burn an image onto the film. If he could tailor the trigger to open on his command, they would be able to photograph everything within the parameters of a thirty-five-millimeter lens.

Weston looked up, "How did you know she was your sister?"

His faint voice vaporized in the air. A shiver wavered down Liam's abdominal cavity, causing a compulsion of contractions to sicken his stomach. The sensations of anguish, animosity, and sorrow he suffered lingered so heavily on his psyche that his physical state was affected just as substantially. His lips quivered while slightly stuttering, "What are you talking about?"

Liam asked, hoping the question would be dropped. Weston snapped the backing of the camera in place after checking the unused roll of film.

"You said you saw Lilith kill your sister in Wonderland. But you've never mentioned anything about having another sibling besides Dalton. So how did you know? Did your parents ever mention her?"

Liam had no words to explain what it was he felt in Wonderland. His mind wandered back and forth, trying to recall memories of his sister, whom he had never met before. Low rumbles of an owl's hoot pulsated through the lofty trees.

"I—I don't know how," Liam started, "When I was in that tent, I couldn't remember anything outside of it."

He tensed up, "It was like I woke up in the middle of a dream. Without any idea where I was, how I got there, or who I was even with. It became more and more real the longer I stayed. And seeing my parents sort of made it seem normal, even though I knew something was different about them, too. My parents looked so much younger; they looked much happier."

Liam's face became flushed with unease.

"I could feel the same fear she did. It coursed through my veins. And when she started to cry, I knew who it was. I knew what was going to happen. It suddenly felt like I always knew."

He restlessly twiddled his butterfly knife.

"But the weird part is, and the part that I can't get out of my head, is that it didn't stop me from leaving, you know? My body wouldn't move, no matter how loud I screamed in my head to run. I don't know why I was there or how I was able to see all of it, Weston."

Liam scratched his head, "But I think she wanted me to see for a reason."

Weston glanced around their perimeter. It seemed any noise traveled great distances here; their self-muffled voices were no exception. The beast's snake eyes sauntered aimlessly, yet the feeling of being watched was constant and menacing. He crept back down.

"Do you remember that file I took from school?"

Liam nodded; he noticed how strangely, stagnantly, the time passed.

"I studied how they died. For hours. I couldn't stop reading. Their names etched into my brain, their personalities too."

He continued, "These were kids, man. Our age and younger. Most died from blood loss, and some killed themselves. How does shit like that happen? I thought I was going crazy reading this, until after Wonderland."

Weston spoke with more enthusiasm, "I started to see them. One by one, their deaths replayed in front of me. And one by one, she came to collect their bodies."

Weston's words pierced through the tundra, "I felt their sorrow and hopelessness. She wanted me to feel the suffering with them."

His eyes widened at Liam, "It gets harder to breathe every passing day; I can feel her around me everywhere I go. I can't help the feeling of her grip choking me."

Weston picked the camera back up and meddled with its base. Liam tried to comprehend just how much his friend had endured since Wonderland, how much they all had. He thought about all the gruesome images he held in his head and all the memories that would never be shared. He then thought about how each of them would do the same, living the same trauma, hiding different wounds.

The heaviness in its breathing incrementally became louder. And although they were hundreds of feet away, Weston and Liam could feel the creature's presence immediately behind them.

"No one's going to believe us if we try to explain what's been happening," Weston said.

"And even if we make it out of this place, we don't know who we can trust in Seaside anymore."

Adam's camera made a distinct tick, "Our only shot is to get help from the city. It's three hours away, but we can take a bus—the four of us."

Liam stood from his previously sitting stance. His brows creased, squinting into the grainy scenery.

"How are we supposed to get out of *here*, Weston? There's a monster the size of a fucking skyscraper out there."

Weston proceeded to work on the camera. Without lifting his head, he told Liam to look closer at where the ice met the beast's stomach. The faint shades from earlier now darkened, turning the landscape fuzzy to the human eye. A once minute glow now beamed from the sizeable fissures around its waist. It leaned away into mountain tops, huddling deeply where its head rested on the pallid powdery plateaus.

The obscurity instantly became less daunting, and sunlight punctured through radiantly and overwhelmingly. Rays that resembled the intensity of a clear midday forecast melted the illusion.

"Sunlight," Liam whispered. Weston matched his hushed tone, "Could be a way out, could be where we die."

"I'll take those odds," Liam said. Another tick set off by Weston was followed by the camera's flash. They looked at each other in astonishment.

"And now we can get proof," Weston smirked.

A soundless descent from their refuge agitated their paranoia. Only the rhythm of their steps meeting the snow vibrated their eardrums, and nothingness filled in between.

They had a distant walk ahead before reaching the start of the ice-covered lake. The lowly glare painted just under the horizon softly illuminated their path once free of the congested branches. An overcast amassed of cherry red gradients and contours of amethyst mixed, conveying a tangerine concoction.

This had been the longest Weston and Liam had spent together. They were only introduced when Jacob invited Weston to test the flammability of pinecones with everyone else one summer afternoon. He was impressed with their rebellious spirit but scolded their lack of imagination. It was not until Weston joined the group that they created Molotov cocktails using a cone, a drill, a rag, and Martha's vodka. Impossible City's already disintegrated infrastructure burned for several hours that night.

Virtually everyone in Seaside knew each other or at least knew of one another, and their parents were no exception. John and Wendy felt resentment in the way life unfolded for them; most of their acquaintances had a formal education and jobs that paid well as the years progressed. They, however, were frontline blue-collar workers who barely earned enough to survive. While John's hourly wage at the auto shop and

Wendy's tips at the diner stayed unchanged, folks like Weston's received raises and bonuses rewarding them for their hard work for the year.

This built-up bitterness was concealed and unnoticed by all but Liam. He was the bridge between what Seaside saw and their private life. The reality of his home spoke only through the thin walls Liam pressed his ears into daily, listening in on his parent's screams and shouts that would poorly disguise themselves when they were all together.

Liam had less worry about possessions and money defining a person's social status. Weston's ideology on judging a person was based on what they could create with their brain instead of what they could buy. Their friendship surpassed such superficial qualities to meet, yet what always lingered in the backs of their minds was how much they differed from the generation before them.

They made their way down where the arctic forest ended and where they would have to continue forward without concealment. There was just enough light glazing the base to distinguish ice from flesh. With a collective gasp, Weston and Liam beheld hundreds upon hundreds of bodies that were now frozen halfway in the water. Nonstop wails that were gyrating during the day were hushed once the beast rested and the ice hardened all over. Their bodies were morphed, mended in excruciating positions, with their jaws unhinged.

At ground level, the light spewing from the beast's waistline became more prominent. Liam's eyes, however, wandered. With a fortitude that was all but depleted, the involuntary gaze stirred an unsettling feeling brewing in his stomach. Weston tapped him, "Hey, you okay?"

Liam rubbed the back of his head. Weston could easily see the fear in his eyes.

"Yeah. I'm good," he murmured.

"We got to do this now, let's go."

Liam took a breath and nodded. Adam's camera was the key to proving their story to outsiders. Without concrete evidence, Jacob and Nancy were as good as dead. And the lost cases of all the missing children would remain lost. Weston had one chance at snapping an in-focused shot, but the less-than-ideal lighting here made it virtually impossible. There was also no way to predict how the film would develop in this realm after a bright flash of light of this sort.

Ice cleaved and crackled as their weight met against the sleet. Liam and Weston stood a dozen or so meters away from where the bodies began to accumulate. They moved with great hesitation and halted every several steps, watching the lake blossom into a bay of condemned souls. After the third or fourth pit stop, Weston turned back to Liam.

"I gotta get closer; I can't zoom with this lens." He said, peeking in and out of the viewfinder while adjusting its focus.

With a tight grasp of his knife, Liam followed him. Murky indigo depths plagued the foundation beneath them. The concern of collapsing through the ice and drowning in freezing water was a constant thought as they unknowingly trudged onward.

Weston's lighter build allowed him to adeptly maneuver around, while Liam had to develop a more conservative approach, testing each step until he was confident enough that it could support him. A brief pulsating ringing subtly wheedled his attention—straying him off his route behind Weston. Liam turned to his side to find a massive open cavity with flowing water rippling about. The phenomena would have gone unnoticed had it not been for the boy across the way looking back at Liam.

With stealth as their main priority, communicating with words from their lengths proved unwise. But before Liam could raise his arm to extend his greeting, the boy rapidly stood from the ground, matching his stance. The puzzled look on Liam's face caused his head to involuntarily follow; tilting at this odd behavior—the boy mimicked his movement once more. Liam kneaded his eyes, unsure if what he saw was real.

A sudden whirl of warmth fevered his internal temperature; adrenaline catalyzed his blood pressure. Liam's sweat steamed away from his skin as he stood stalemated in this staredown. The boy measured the same height as him, mirroring the exact position as Liam did without error. Liam straightened his posture and released his blade from his palm, and like clockwork, the boy fluidly shadowed him.

There was, however, no object in the boy's hand. He held a closed fist to continue on the charade. Liam lowered his wield and paused. He squinted, flexing every muscle responsible for making far-away images momentarily vivid. The boy wore an inherited sooty coat that reached his knees and hid his face behind strands of ebony locks that stuck adhesively onto his forehead as though he had just been in the water.

Liam's eyes broke contact when a speck of blackness in the distance began to manifest near the boy. Their eyes grew in unison, but Liam was the only one witnessing the being growing taller as it approached. He waved like a madman trying to get the boy to turn around, yet his hands only imitated Liam's desperation. Liam stopped again, lowering his arm. The speck evolved more human-like curvatures and carried an unnatural limp.

Faltering at every step, the creature disgorged blood by the pint. Its bottom jaw was absent as its tongue dangled and was cascaded with bits of flesh and other fluids. The boy, however, didn't stop waving once Liam rested his arm. A smile caricatured from cheek to cheek—the creature hovered over him now.

Dark droplets drizzled down the boy's skull; his everlasting welcoming gesture sent Liam chills. The creature's face lifted and a woman unveiled, glossed with black marble pupils and translucent skin. She acknowledged Liam's presence with a raise of her hand, her waves synchronized with the boy's. His lips tightened, attempting to utter the first syllable of Weston's name.

But before anything could be voiced, the woman's hands abruptly migrated and positioned across opposite ends of the boy's neck. She moved with grace, and her hips thrust with enough momentum to fracture the young bones out of alignment—three unnerving clicks echoed over the lake.

A gasp of air was ingested through Liam's esophagus. He awoke from the hallucination to Weston ogling at him with his pocket knife, ready to defend himself.

"Liam, what the fuck are you doing, man?" Weston trembled, asking.

The side of Liam's head was throbbing in pain, and his kneecaps were frostbitten by what felt like a prolonged exposure to ice. His arms were raised high above his head in a worshiping pose. His devotion left both limbs numb. He looked back in the direction where the boy was executed. Bronze and hickory wick stood only inches from Liam's face. He momentarily gazed inside the darkness within.

He began to sob, "Wha—"

He stammered as drool splattered under his chin. His body didn't react in time with his mind. His motor functions delayed the physical response, yet his thoughts raced at an incredible speed, piecing together what was happening. With much discomfort, Liam raised his jawbone to the soaring structure he knelt to.

He bowed before what looked to be the anatomy of a being composed of both man and animal characteristics. It stood tall, taller than a grizzly bear on its hind legs, and balanced on eight hooves the size of tires. Wooden arms like tentacles sprouted from all over its vessel, portraying the ability to grab anything within a six-foot radius. Dried gore and decaying remains of a woman's face rested beneath broad branches woven together that formed antlers.

The daunting extravagance of what this world could conceive reminded Liam of how meaningless and worthless his own being really was.

"What—what am I doing here, Weston?" He cried.

An uncontrollable release of emotions submerged his ability to fully communicate. Even with the quiver in his tone, Weston leaped into action after coherent words finally surfaced from Liam's lips. He had been trying to wake Liam out of this trance for almost an hour.

"It's going to be okay," Weston consoled. He had no idea what Liam had experienced, and Liam had no words to describe it out loud.

"Come on, we gotta keep moving," Weston tugged him to his feet, and they carried on towards the beast.

An aroma of rotting meat startled her nose. Inhaling cold and salt-infused oxygen for hours desensitized her ability to distinguish scents, but this putrid odor was unbearable to go unnoticed. Cheyenne uncoiled from her slumber and winced in pain as she stretched her spine and neck. The thousands of candles that formerly illuminated the cave's entrance were now nonexistent in her awakening.

She lightly grazed the corners of her eyes, itching away compiled dander and dust. Pale and flat linear blemishes descended her arms. Scars that were unfamiliar to Cheyenne appeared healed through months of repairing and tending to. She looked at the hollow cavity, but only darkness grinned back. Moments passed until she was ready to move.

Flashbacks of escaping the woman hazily recollected in her head. However, she couldn't remember how she got away or ended up here. A warm, golden luster expelled out of the cave, distracting her contemplations. She haltingly drifted near the opening and peered inside. Cheyenne looked upon the never-ending tunnel.

The divine light originated from deep within the corridor of the cave. She didn't have a choice of whether or not to engage this enigma; all that waited behind her was an empty void leading to oblivion. But she also couldn't withstand another encounter with the woman; her body ached, and she was dying of thirst. It had been hours, even a day, since she had spoken to Liam or Weston. Time moved at a rate unknown and unidentifiable to human senses without the aid of electronics. She sat on the dirt, rummaging in her pockets.

The only possessions Cheyenne had on her were two photographs and an inconspicuous dagger that clutched the side of her hip. Multi-colored tones gorgeously scaled the homemade sheath despite the years of wear and dirt it accumulated. She pressed the blade against her forearm with enough pressure to puncture her skin. Cheyenne grimaced. The only reliable source of time was her own physical body. If she were to fall unconscious or asleep again, she would be able to generalize the amount of time that went by based on the healing state of her new cut. Cheyenne chuckled to herself; she wouldn't have guessed she'd be utilizing ancient Native American survival tactics at twelve years old. She wiped the blood and confined the weapon. It was one of the few belongings that Cheyenne had to remember her mother by. She found it in one of the untouched moving boxes when they first came to Seaside prior to it being weighed in with the dozens of other boxes that would never be opened.

Chaska's stories about Dyani personified the keepsakes Cheyenne kept of hers. A child with no parents at such an early age influences their ability to comprehend why certain things happen the way they do. In Cheyenne's case, the missing mother and father components she longed for turned into an admiration of the items they left behind. Idolizing their legacy was easier than the reality of their tragic death when Cheyenne was born. It even bled into her own perception of herself—she assumed she was brave and courageous because of her parents, believing those attributes would never be associated with her name alone.

Cheyenne meditated in times she couldn't think straight, a breathing technique Chaska taught her that he learned from Dyani. It calmed her anxieties, and she imagined her parents watching over her when she did it. The memories she vicariously experienced through her uncle's words brought ease and a sense of familiarity. She knew she had the strength to go on; she just had to find where it was hiding. A faint noise funneled from the cave's depths, and Cheyenne's eyes opened.

The split second was long enough for Cheyenne to audibly recognize the sound of waves crashing against the shore. She eagerly stood up and sprinted towards the beacon. There was nothing spared in each step she took; the shine brightened with acceleration. The walls were inscribed with the same kinds of illustrations Cheyenne found previously at the lower level of the den.

She slowed her pace once the Tuscany yellow rays kindled her out of the darkness. Its intensity grew a thousandfold after. Cheyenne tried to peek inside while still somewhat distant, but its construction angled in a way where one had to reveal themselves when looking in. She leered at her surroundings from all orientations, making sure this time that she was alone. Cheyenne entered the lair.

The blinding lights she anticipated were generated by a mere candle that centered in the middle of a room. Hundreds of artifacts filled the space while cobwebs and globs of dirt infested the rest. There were jars that held liquids spoiled through decades of rot, rustic metal objects appealing to Victorian Era torture devices, and a grand display of books without any titles or covers. She looked up and read the name carved on the ceiling, "The Exquisite Extraordinair."

Cheyenne roamed the spacious chamber, yielding to every item. She picked up an odd handheld steel contraption that had three pointed rods like a chicken claw. Its oxidized surface felt rough and unwelcoming; two plates fit on opposite ends of the rods that tightened with a twist of a screw in the middle. It seemed its only purpose was to clamp and squeeze something in between. She put it back down and traveled further inward.

Her curiosity kept her alertness tamed. She hadn't looked behind her since coming into the lair. An aura of hostile energy exuded from every corner, as though each relic were screaming at Cheyenne to get out while she still could. Her eyes were as intrigued as her hands. Posted all over the walls were posters of men and women exemplifying superhuman abilities and oddities unbeknown to mankind today. A nine-foot man illustrated lifting as many as six children sitting across his wingspan, Igor Stravinsky was the first human giant in modern history to travel with the Wonderland circus.

There were dozens of individual posters saturated with acts that could only be seen once the sun went down. Siamese twins, the missing specimen between man and ape, live captive mermaids, a four-legged woman, the half-man, half-wolf being, and more came alive in the twilight. The freak show and its marvels performed at high capacity every night for a week before getting back on the road. Its eerie slogan,

You only need to come once to stay forever

She unexpectedly skidded to a stop, her eyes looking at another pair. The chalky-white face paint was impossible to ignore, his shiny scarlet red shades whisked all around his smirk. The same fright Cheyenne felt in Wonderland rejuvenated her with fear and sorrow. Baku's watchful stare from the printed ink soared twenty feet tall and was just as nerve-wracking to look at for a second time.

Dyani's knife made its way out again, and she anxiously crept deeper. The dancing shadows from the flames of the candle created the illusion of lurking figures. Beyond the artwork and piles of scraps was a grand walnut vanity difficult to see without fully submerging inside. Its immaculate and uncommon features were articulated in every carving that represented a cloud, wave, or flower.

An oval mirror outlined with the same pattern hung above the desk. Cheyenne looked at her murky reflection cloaked with powders of dust particles. She turned around for a second but came back to the piles of papers scattered along the table. There were clippings of local newspaper articles documenting every stop the traveling jamboree took across the country. Coffee-stained pages published with bold typeface titles condescendingly praised Wonderland's public display. From every show they would perform to every photo that was taken of them, the same things transpired in every town. Their livelihoods were constantly ridiculed by the townspeople; their hurtful remarks, taunting, and the customary refusal to allow carnies into their shops for vital resources followed suit.

But with as many columns and editorials as there were, a myriad of handwritten letters surmounted the aged wood. Cheyenne picked one up and squinted at each scribble, decoding what the cursive writing conveyed,

July 13th, 1895

Your love is with me even in times apart. I think of you always. I think of your touch that caresses my scars and wounds, your touch that holds me close and sincere through the night. I think of the happiness you give that eradicates my dark thoughts—the joy that renders me a fool blinded by love and fearless of death.

The illegible sentences following were smeared and faded with time until the last bits of the letter,

The date of my final acts is soon to come. This business is that of a parasite from which it takes everything from you that keeps you who you are. Bearing each day is becoming harder and burdensome without you. The unwelcoming New World has exhausted me of all the kindness I have to give—yet all these animals can do is take. They look upon us as devils of the night, wicked in our ways and malice spewing from our hearts. Their inebriated eyes spoke the truth of their souls—they looked down upon the unintelligent and primitive beings. I bear a sickness that contrives in the innermost pits of my stomach, which has no cure without submitting to their suspicions.

My family here is all I know, and for what they have done, I cannot ever repay them. I love them with all my heart. But you, Abraham, are the only person that truly understands me. You are my heart and soul.

The dull signature at the bottom spoke through Cheyenne's lips, "Lilith."

She put the crinkly paper down in disbelief and grabbed another—reading every word. Then another. The endless barrage of misery in each of her letters to Jacob's great-grandfather was troubling to read. The dates read back to the early part of the 1895 year, and several from 1894, but none came after the first letter she read. Cheyenne rummaged through the extra sheets that were inside the drawers and came across a photo lodged in between the sides. The same "AC" signature was infamously inscribed on the back.

Her muscles became rigid, and her skin tingled. She reached into her pocket and pulled out the photo Liam retrieved from Jacob's house earlier. Cheyenne's stomach became heavy, and a sense of coldness shivered through her as her focus went back and forth between images.

The same man stood beside the woman who had been torturing them for the past week.

A short-lived hum passed Cheyenne, ceasing her scouring. The cave maintained its soundless composure as though knowing someone was now watching. She felt nausea churn her insides and contort her intestines. The cut on her arm was still dripping with blood, but Cheyenne forced herself to continue.

The lost sanctuary of forbidden love was littered with bottles of complexion creams, soft bristle brushes, and containers of milky white face powder. Countless vials of raven lipstick accentuated the dark depiction Lilith carried as her self-image. Cheyenne followed the trail and bits of glass remnants that twinkled in between the narrow spaces of her cosmetics. She came to where the cluster of shards met under a brass hand mirror laid over an envelope. The weight of its composition was a true testament to its time. Crafted copper and zinc rustically intertwined the shape of the mirror and was almost intimidating to hold.

Jacob's great grandfather's name reemerged in the same handwriting—she looked over her shoulder before quickly stashing it along with other letters in the knot that held her jacket around her waist. With this novel evidence, they were a step closer to understanding how Wonderland's origin came to be. Cheyenne started for the exit, but the glimpse of her reflection from the piece of glass still intact to the mirror's backing caught her attention.

Subtle and diluted variations of violet and red wine daintily inflamed the corners of her eyes. The crust of shriveled blood latched like dried tears down her cheekbones; she padded the inflictions only to feel nothing. Cheyenne fixated on the wounds and their hastened healed state; she had somehow come back from the dead.

Life breathed into this abandoned lair through the cave's fluctuating air pressure. A gust of wind exhaled in the room from a crevice ahead. Cheyenne surveyed where the breeze flowed. A single poster weakly glued against the corner wall came undone. Its thick material bent with the draft and echoed loudly.

Her chest accumulated more and more weight as she cautiously approached the product of lithography. Wrinkles could be seen worn on the paper, authenticating its ancient inception. Cheyenne glanced about without focusing; her elevated state made it virtually impossible to concentrate on anything but the noise of the turning page inviting her nearer. She lunged to cease the racketing. Her hands and arms remained locked in place—Cheyenne allowed the silence to bleed back in.

The candle's glow revealed a medley of dazzling colors and pigmentations stained on the canvas. Her palms made a distinctly gooey sound when she took a step back. The artwork's paint was still fresh. Cheyenne's shadow slowly retreated off the poster. Her gaze glistened with tears; she read the name of the latest show debuting in Wonderland.

Unveiling October 31st, 1986—The World's First & Only Human Puppet Show: The Nancy Doll

Her exact features were illustrated by the mixture of oil and water without the slightest hint of inconsistency. Heavily contoured lines defined Nancy's laugh grooves. Her flesh appeared rock-solid, forever holding onto a flexed expression of contentment. Makeup chalked her skin while overapplied red blush scavenged the apples of her face. A disturbing smile was manufactured, but Cheyenne only saw the stare of a lifeless puppet.

Painted behind Nancy was the silhouette of a person traced in coats of charcoal. The dilated obsidian pupils of the being were enclosed with golden irises—the wet paint sluggishly melted and mixed with each other. The violently drawn shades of gloom fascinated Cheyenne. As the absence of light prevailed, it consumed everything Nancy was and controlled her every movement.

She had to be dreaming again, Cheyenne thought. But before she had a moment to collect herself, she was swooned by the sound of a voice she thought she would never hear again.

"Do you miss me, Cheyenne?"

An eruption of emotions internalized in Cheyenne, but she couldn't physically coil to where the question came from. The clinging terror acted like venom in her blood, paralyzing any muscle movements. The voice seamlessly parroted Nancy's. However, it was evident something was distinctly odd about the question.

The candle's luminosity burned on. Cheyenne's stomach sputtered with gulps of air at irregular intervals and tears streaming uncontrollably. She finally turned around when the spine-tingling sensation of being watched was too uncomfortable to handle. Upon facing each other, they stared into each other's eyes as the lull grew once more.

Sitting on the opposite end, where the darkness hoarded the chamber, was Nancy. The flame of the fire twinkled while the drifting and shifting shadows amassed the walls.

"Because I missed you," Nancy's jaw mouthed.

"Nancy, I—" Cheyenne couldn't utter a full sentence.

When she tried to speak, she noticed that Nancy wasn't alone. Someone was casting a larger obscurity behind. Someone who was using Nancy's four-day-old corpse as a puppet.

Her body swayed like a pendulum, weightlessly moving with each word she mouthed. The makeup she wore could only do so much to conceal Nancy's decomposing body and blood-containing foam leaking out of her mouth and nose.

With a steady pace, she whispered, "Never leave me again, my love. And you will live lusciously."

Her throat and skull bobbed as the darkness spoke from Nancy's lips. The entity's lunar eyes moved not once or blinked.

Cheyenne quivered under her breath, "This isn't real; you aren't real."

She pinched her eyelids together and repeatedly told herself to wake up. Nancy's voice began to sound like several people talking at the same time—both youthful and elderly tones.

"A mother cannot live without her child."

The words from its sly tongue spoke in cursive. Cheyenne used her dagger to slit the softer flesh of her thigh. She winced and bore the pulsating throbs, hoping it would be enough to wake her from this nightmare. Cheyenne carved another incision and screamed. Yet, time cruelly carried on.

Nancy's cadaver was silenced; it was the darkness speaking to Cheyenne now. The voice lightened and annunciated each letter of a word as though a serpent, "Would you like to meet Dyani?"

Cheyenne froze immediately. She looked back into Nancy's hollow eyes; the choir's swarming murmurs were more discordant, "Come to me, my child, and I will show you where she is."

Cheyenne glimpsed at the blade dipped in her own blood, her three self-inflicted wounds leaking, and then at the vertical scars whose regeneration was still a mystery. The wafting current had suffocated minutes ago, and the dead air thrived.

And then, in a fraction of a second, Nancy's ghoulish mannequin plunged to the ground and slithered toward Cheyenne. Her rotting, lanky hands that oozed decaying substances grasped the entire outline of Cheyenne's skull. But before Nancy could pry open her flesh and devour her insides, Cheyenne's legs gave out, and her full weight rested in Nancy's palms.

Endless amounts of blood gushed into her arms from Cheyenne's neck, where Dyani's blade was fully lodged.

XVI

AWAKENING

Each adjustment lasted about ten seconds until another modification had to be made. The lens rotated left, then right, then again to the right, and eventually angrily spinning left. It became stinging cold by the time Liam and Weston grew closer to the center of the lake. Air frosted their flesh and pierced through the thin cotton fabric of their clothes.

The starlight beneath the beast fluctuated in intensity the same way sunlight sparkles in moving water. They were standing hundreds of feet from land where the ice-covered graveyard commenced.

“What’s taking so long?” Liam impatiently asked.

Not much time had passed since the apparitions beckoned to him. They found themselves in a near frenzy as Weston desperately tried to bring this inferno into focus.

“We only got one chance at this photo, and one turn of the lens means everything. If the camera doesn’t focus absolutely perfectly, all that’ll develop on film is a blurry picture of the bodies and a fat smudge behind them. And then all we have is our word against theirs.”

Weston sniffled and compared his poor vision of the scenery to what he was able to see through the fogged viewfinder.

Liam wondered how a place like this could exist, the horrors infested within, and what evils they had yet to surface. Frail men and women beset every step moving forward; their frostbitten bodies seemed to still react to the extreme brisk, yet they did not freeze to death. The mold of ice held them in place, and the coldness coagulated their insides, constraining any movement. There had to be thousands in the lake with Liam and Weston. They differed in many visible aspects—their age, weight, what they wore, and other minute details were evident—but they shared one commonality.

The sky was where their arms reached. Where every condemned mortal pointed to from whatever deformed position they were in—the sky was where they yearned to be taken to. They soon, too, realized that individual bodies didn't just freeze in the lake; there were piles of human remains all around the interior closest to the beast. If Weston and Liam were to escape through where the sun peeked, they would have to climb and crawl over the bodies of the damned.

The creature's breathing fumed beyond the hilltops, and the skies reflected an absence of God in the valley of abandoned hope. Particles embellished in a wave of blond perpetually disintegrating when shined into this world.

"That's the best I can get it," Weston exhaled deeply.

"There's still a chance the film doesn't capture the image well, or it comes out a little blurry, but with the amount of light I got to work with, it's that or nothing."

They glanced at each other before looking upon the slumbering cemetery. Their pupils were broadened while slivers of rich lemon and amber hues veered the murkiness within themselves.

“Do you think there might’ve been a way to prevent all this?” Liam asked, his focus remained ahead.

Weston looked at him, then at the resting beast. He took another sigh and had difficulty wording out his response, “I mean, this all began when you failed algebra, man.”

Liam laughed and started to consolidate his pocket items into his backpack; Weston followed suit. Adam’s camera had malfunctioned earlier where the trigger button wouldn’t initiate the shutter’s opening—allowing an image to burn onto the film. Weston’s handy Swiss army knife allowed him to manipulate the internal mechanics, but that meant he had to control every aspect of the camera that went into making a vivid picture now. The focus, flash, aperture, and shutter all rested in Weston’s hands.

They would need more than just a photo of what they saw, however. One of them had to be present in the frame to prevent anyone from discrediting their case as a simple light manipulation or edit. About two hundred meters stood between them and their supposed entry back home. They didn’t have the slightest idea as to what would occur after the flash, but being light on their feet seemed most logical. Their zippers concluded.

“I still think this is the only way we have a realistic chance at stopping this. We’ll be able to show the cops in every town and mail copies to every newspaper company we can find. And we’re going to keep sending them until someone listens to us.” Weston said. The reality of their plan coming to fruition was settling in.

“I got this,” replied Liam. He cautiously took several steps out.

"Don't go too far; just enough so you're in the picture," Weston continued.

The ice sheet cracked more noticeably, and puddles emerged the deeper Liam trudged. Rancid metallic odors pungently fumed while a drowning humidity lofted. He could feel the surveillance of an army watching. He kept walking until he saw Weston silently waving him down.

"On the count of three."

Weston mouthed and gestured with his hands. Liam nodded and kept a tight stance. Weston placed two fingers on opposite sides of the camera that would distinctively discharge the flash and shutter. He lifted his left hand once in position.

"One," He mimed.

Liam closed his eyes.

"Two."

Maybe he'll wake up in his bed tomorrow morning, and this would have all been a dream, Liam thought. He opened his eyes after wavering about when to look again. The luminous flare powered by lithium-ion batteries briefly blinded his vision. Liam instantly sunk three feet into the water by the hands of someone clutching his ankles underneath the ice.

"Get off of me!" He shouted. Their scaley touch slipped and scraped his calves without relent. Weston grabbed Liam's shirt collar and pulled him out of the restraint of four or five severely malnourished beings that oozed onto the ice floor. They were skinless creatures that dwelled in the frozen lake and feasted on the bodies of those who relinquished their will to go on. A deathless land offered its inhabitants the only exit—through the gnawing teeth and gorging appetite of Satan's slaves. Weston yanked Liam again, "Come on!" Their shoes slipped constantly, and there wasn't much regard to the amount of noise they were now making, escaping to the belly of the beast. Their pathway was abnormally staggered for the first fifty meters, with human hurdles along the way, and they almost lost each other because of it. After tirelessly swaying in several directions, they found a straightaway. It led to a steep slope where they would have to climb the rest of the way into the radiating waistline. Liam turned his head right before they met the ascend. He was relieved to see they weren't being chased.

He heard a sudden shriek from Weston coming from the opposite direction of him, "Liam!" Liam felt the foundation he stepped on vanish and an exhilarating rush of cold. The arctic lake swallowed him whole into its lightless depths. The ice wedge splashed open with slabs of sheets floating about. Liam's gagging was the only thing audible. Moments later, he heard a voice call out, "Grab my hand!" He was immediately propelled out of the water when the arm gripped his. Liam gasped to breathe while glacial fluids spewed out of his lungs. He leaned against the chest of a much bulkier person than Weston. He profoundly scrubbed his face to clear his vision. When Liam attempted to stand, he was met with an overwhelming squeeze, detaining him in place, "I'm so sick and tired of you always disobeying me, boy."

The man said in his ear; his hug became tighter.

"Every single thing you have ever needed in your fucking life, I gave you."

His musty stench was unique and reeked strongly—a mixture of machine and mechanical fumes that abruptly became familiar to Liam.

"And you still don't show any respect."

He went on. Liam screamed for Weston and jerked about, yet his father's strength overpowered him.

"Liam! Get up!" Weston exclaimed from afar. He was hoisted at the beast's stomach.

John compressed his restraint even more, "I see her face in yours all the time. Not a day goes by that I wish it was me instead of her. My sweet girl. One day, you'll understand what it means to truly love your child."

His voice trembled, "She never lets me forget. It's an ache that's tormented me since that day. And she always wants more."

Weston's wails echoed in again, "Liam! Get up!" He chanted in a rhythm.

"This must be done for our family, Liam."

John said. It became increasingly difficult for Liam to inhale. He coughed the last bits of oxygen he had left and winced at the bone-crushing power constricting his organs. His father dragged him away from the waterhole's opening as his legs spasmed.

And then, just after the first gush of blood sloshed on Liam's stomach, the clamor ceased. John gave a tremendous thrust and vigorously misaligned his son's spinal cord. He was numb to the affliction at first; all he could feel were the sudden snaps that internally vibrated. Liam faded in and out of consciousness. He feared the last sonance he would hear before dying would be the shattering of his back—or so he thought.

"Mistress Mary, quite contrary, how does your garden grow?" John sang.

He unbound Liam after the severe fracture and breaking of the bones in his vertebrae left him immobile. His eyes never once shifted nor blinked after dropping him. He seemed to be looking, waiting for something. He went on, "With silver bells and cockle shells—"

A droning buzz rang like springtime hummingbirds rejuvenating nature's eternal cycle of life after death. Liam could barely keep his head from drooping. Heaps of plasma drooled off his lips as he lay on his side, wheezing with a possible punctured lung. The figure of a woman emerged from the ground in the reflection of John's eyes.

His ecstatic smile welcomed an old friend. She weightlessly roamed the ice bare without shoes. The color of a starless sky stained the marvelous ball dress she was adorned in. Her hand gently raised Liam's chin up. The woman's soft words spoke in a hush, "And so my garden grows."

Liam looked at the woman, and she onto him. Her beauty was transcendent and eclipsed the physical aspect of allure. She looked into your heart as though she would nourish, replenish, and love you for who you were—forever.

Lush blackened locks of hair volumized and swept past her shoulders. The warmth of daylight beamed from her sunny irises. She was a fallen angel gifted with a flawless facial structure and moved with impeccable grace. The woman's fingers stroked and embraced Liam's warm-blooded skin. Her raven-polished lips moistened, and the slightest unhinging of her jaw flashed a mouth full of fangs.

Her rosy cheeks were a result of the blood vessels that dilated and burst from the frigid temperatures. She studied Liam longer; her ever-twisting and convulsing sly tongue slipped out before quickly retreating back in. It was a mesmerizing as well as a gut-wrenching sensation that Liam had only experienced one other time before—in Wonderland.

"Liam! Get up!" Weston emphatically called.

Liam's eyes shuffled, looking for him. He tried to spit out a shout, but it was too painful. Lilith lurched her skull next to his, Liam's neck braced by her palm. Again, her words ferried a lullaby, "Find me, and I will take you to Nancy."

Her angelic accent was the anesthesia swooning Liam into a relaxed, lethargic state. He could hear Weston right by his ear now, but he became too drowsy to move, "Liam! Get up!" A sudden rush of heat scorched one side of his neck, lugging him back into the night terror. He felt his flesh loosen and tear off, and a hefty mass of blood funneled out of his laceration. Lilith looked on, malevolently grinning as her teeth flushed with gore and she basked in the glory of the undivine nirvana.

The shining rays of the afternoon sun awoke Liam. He was sprawled over the toasted sand beach, parched with a thirst insatiable by water. Standing above him were Weston and Cheyenne, staring at him.

His clothes felt peculiar, a stranger's outfit. The inseams that dictated where the pants would crease, how much leeway he had to rotate his arms without stretching the shirt, and how fast he'd have to run before escaping its confines circulated in Jacob's discombobulated head.

His eyesight was still acclimating to the dreary architecture and dullness of the massive room. Jacob saw not three feet in front of him, and he became queasy trying to visually digest everything at once. The material of the garments he wore and the blanket covering him chafed his sensitive skin—every slight movement was mentally trying and physically demanding. An irritation singed the back of his legs, and his forearms pulsated with trapped blood cells, leaving a tender bruise the size of a sweat wristband.

A continuous throbbing thumped with his heartbeat from his inner left elbow. He used the torque in his waist to pull off the dingy rag. Jacob jolted once his eyes met the IV pricking his vein, feeding a dark, murky liquid mixture. His eyes followed the tubing to a clear sac just above and behind him that consisted of floating substances of both fluid and chunks.

"What—What is this?"

Jacob peered closer at the hunks of glob resting at the bottom of the bag. There was a stew of stringy pieces and other oddly morphed shapes. He'd been to the hospital on a number of occasions for his own routine checkups and was even present during his grandfather's bedridden weeks at Seaside General. But Jacob had never seen something like this before. Oxygen gasped into his lungs, and the bag twitched.

"Shit!" Jacob said, scooting higher in the infirmary bed he lay in.

He started to hyperventilate, and sweat beads bubbled across his forehead. Twirling particles in the clouded concoction rapidly sipped in the ports and chambers of the medical instrument and into his arm.

He became squeamish, which brought upon a feebleness in his grip as he hesitantly tried to pluck out the needle. A better-sized bit caught his attention, vacuuming sluggishly through the clogged channel. He watched in despair as it entered his bloodstream and could feel the pressure the IV stressed forcing itself in.

His muscular system violently convulsed, and he saw a clementine-sized bump rise in his skin that began to scurry. Jacob screamed with all his might, hoping to wake up from this nightmare, but he couldn't. The critter crawled and cleaved at Jacob's vein, causing irreversible damage. It glided down the full diameter of his arm several times while a symphony of stridulations orchestrated from its rubbing wings. The chirps were menacingly endless until Jacob ripped the IV out and witnessed the black ink surge onto his bedside. He uncontrollably whimpered and sobbed, pressing on the open wound before spotting the wandering parasite again.

Jacob slid his palm over the bulge and pinched his skin with as much power as his adrenaline allowed. Cracks and pops became audible, crushing the menacing vermin, yet Jacob kept his fingers clamped for an extended amount of time, leaving a bluish-red contusion. His head plummeted to the back of his pillow, and it took a while before Jacob's breathing regulated. The bleeding sludge coagulated at the point of entry, stopping the flow.

Some relief came after he let go of his clasp but was soon replaced with another worry. He stared at the lifeless and stagnant tumor. An untreated gash like this would mean risking getting an infection. There had to be something here he could use to get it out with, he thought.

His ability to see was rejuvenated once Jacob's fight or flight response unloaded a fury of hormones priming his physical body for any imminent threat. The sheen from atop a bedside stand grabbed his focus about an arm's length away. Several stainless-steel instruments were laid out on a white towel, and one of the tools was a scalpel. Without any time to think himself out of it, Jacob lunged for the knife and pressed it against his skin—carving around the lump's sides.

He shrieked as he parted his flesh. His blood blended with the murky liquid into an amaranthine red and poured out like spoiled milk staining the wool blanket. He dropped the cutting blade and wiped the sweat off his upper lip with his shoulder. Jacob's skin loosely hung while the blob gravitated towards the opening. His heart pumped ounces of blood that unsparingly leaked once Jacob squeezed his bicep and dragged his grip forcibly down, pushing the cluster into daylight.

His teeth clenched as the lifeless insect legs exuded the narrow cut—but too narrow for its entirety to come out at once. Jacob's incision tore wider, and his screams echoed throughout the entire wing of the building. A final push propelled the head and abdomen of the beetle out of his arm. Jacob bounced himself off the bed, landing on the cold, dusty floor.

Shivers clung to his neck, and the phantom sensation of those six legs crawling inside him perpetuated. His hemorrhaging seeped faster and showed no signs of slowing down now that the obstruction was removed. It was evident no one was coming to his aid. Jacob needed to find a way to wrap his arm in the next couple of minutes, or else he'd blackout and possibly wake up somewhere new.

The pillowcase covering was enough to hinder the spillage with a couple of binds. The room Jacob woke in was more of a hall and had obnoxiously outdated decor with an even more outlandish, musty odor. Vintage maroon drapes showered the eight vertically dominant glass windows the sun bled in through. A dozen beds totaled two rows facing each other on opposite ends of the cobwebbed-infested beige brick walls. Each breath Jacob took was filled with dust dampened by the humidity of an aging mold that was older than himself.

The back wall was reserved for the religious and spiritual that Jacob drifted towards. He walked past the beds covered in raggedy blankets and avoided stepping on the scattered alphabet building blocks beside them.

Shrined with a multitude of votive candles and sacred portraits of biblical figures, the embodiment of Christ was overlooked by none other than the Son of God himself. His brass figure had tarnished in the midst of father time, yet the handcrafted details from each hair follicle to the definition shadowed between every muscle were flawless.

Three industrial-sized bolts drilled the wall, holding in place the life-sized Savior. The idea of church was a staple in the Clay household; the importance of creating and maintaining a relationship with God made its way into the conversations between Jacob and his parents quite often. And what followed was the over-explained, well-rehearsed repercussions of what happened to those who disobeyed God's commandments. Or questioned their faith in Him.

Jacob looked into the eyes of his Messiah and wondered if this was all a punishment that they had brought upon themselves. Maybe their devotion had and was not to the standards of what good Christians demonstrated.

"What did I ever do to you? What have I done to deserve this?" Jacob muttered. The inanimate product of manmade alloy was silent. The light reflected off the alternating black and white tiles, illuminating the metal's green and pinkish corrosion.

"I know you can hear me. Say something!" Tears began to accumulate, and his voice broke down. Jacob grabbed the crucifix lying amidst the array of candles and other religious novelties. It was made of the same rustic material and weighed as much as a clay brick.

"Say something!"

He pushed the cross in and through his chest—Jacob gasped and staggered backward. He expected the collision to leave a dent at the most by his twelve-year-old hands, not actually pierce through it. Only the sound of ringing metal was orchestrated in the room.

Jacob's eyebrows furrowed, and his almost resting heartbeat again accelerated. His pupils followed the dark tar substance that spewed from His rib cage. The thick muck traveled at a lethargic pace and leaked as though pressure from the inside forced it out.

The presence of someone watching Jacob from behind could be felt burning into the back of his neck. He quickly turned to the door.

An overwhelming surge of goosebumps froze him in place as he saw a girl hastily turn away and run down the hallway. She couldn't have been older than seven, but the fact that she was here in this rundown building with Jacob meant she knew something.

"Hey! Wait!" He started for her. Her lightweight footsteps grew more distant when he entered the hallway. The slim corridor highlighted the rickety walls with its cement foundation peeking through the mossy paint.

Room after room spaced less than three feet apart from each other housed this floor of the building. She looked back at Jacob from the far end before making another turn—vanishing into another section. It was as though she hinted for him to follow. He saw her golden blonde hair shine under the sun and her white school dress rippling against a breeze.

Fearful of who or what else was in this abandoned place with them, Jacob abstained from calling the girl again. His strides crushed and crunched the accrued debris on the ground. He noticed the child-like artwork hand painted on the walls and the many different toys that scoured about. The lost vibrancy in the seven-colored rainbows made the solitary layout more distressing to ponder over. As he passed the staple designs composed from premature imaginations, Jacob grew uncomfortable, wondering about the purpose of this facility that housed dozens of children.

The end of the hallway opened to an inner courtyard. And much like the interior, this area also depicted the aftermath of nature's rehabilitation of the land. The complex was encompassed by the profound forest and now suffocated from its vegetation. Its untamed vines perforated from within the foundation and camouflaged the brick walls.

He followed the fractured pavement to the edge, and the open patio ascended acres of untouched land. Jacob watched as the soaring birds disappeared into the evergreen mountaintops and the gusty winds brushed against his face. Wherever he was, it was somewhere no one would ever look to find. He optimistically had two hours at the most until dusk, which meant he had less than two hours to escape.

There appeared to be a number of levels—one or two above the current one Jacob was investigating and several below him. A bell tower with a clock indicating the time 6 p.m. caught his eye. He remembered having dinner with Martha the night before, but not much after that. Jacob was distraught that nearly a whole day had passed, and he hadn't the slightest idea of who took him, where he was, or why.

His forearm grew increasingly sore in the midst of looking all over for the girl. Jacob's stomach began to ache—but not from hunger. He came across a statue of an owl sitting atop a slab of concrete with a phrase spelled out underneath.

Only In The Darkness Can One See The Light

A booming crash of metal pots and pans emanated out of the higher levels. It startled Jacob, but he assumed it could have been from the breeze entering the windowless and gaping infrastructure—until it happened again in irregular instances.

Jacob made his way to the other end of the court. The noise softened, but his alertness remained vigilant as he reentered the building. There were many other rooms in this quadrant, but catered to different activities. Elongated wooden tables like the ones in his school's cafeteria filled what might have been a mess hall. The roofing had collapsed in on itself, leaving the story above visible. Jacob could hear the scurrying rats go about their business and was confident there was a dwelling insect sanctuary by which his naked eyes couldn't see.

Another room held twenty or so student desks aligned in uniform with each other. It reminded him of his own homeroom class with Mrs. Davis and her particular need for the desks to be perfectly straight. That kind of persistence was tiresome for both the students and her, but it served a purpose. She made it abundantly clear from the first day that her authority superseded anyone else's—including Mr. Matthew.

The map of Seaside was also pulled down, yet notable landmarks weren't showcased in this outdated edition. Jacob stared into the unmarked terrain in the illustrations. If he could escape the confines of this building, he could study this map to distinguish some general mapping directions. He knew all he had to do was follow the scenic route out of Seaside, and that would take him to the closest city, but he had to figure out which way that was.

Of all the desks, there was one with a sheet of paper lying upside down. Jacob went closer, glancing behind at the doorway and around the teacher's desk. He flipped over the centered white stationary and analyzed the cartoon drawing of the same building he was in. There was a girl in a massive castle high above a sea of trees. The atmosphere was filled with wildlife, and bursts of colors at the base detailed the springtime perennials. His eyes drifted to the name signed at the bottom.

Emily, Seaside Asylum

A faint clink brought his attention back, and he hesitantly moved on.

There was a stairway towards the end where the noise increased. The termite-infested lumber creaked and scratched every step of the way up. Jacob cautiously maneuvered around the piles of sawdust and prickles of standing wood. He followed the treacherous U-shaped staircase all the way up.

There was an unusual scent he picked once the air on this level settled in his nostrils. It was a smell not of deterioration in the physical structure he was somewhat acquainted with now, and it wasn't the microorganisms that infected this environment. It was the smell of sweat and fuming body odor.

Jacob read the yellow-stained sign that featured three-digit room numbers listed on them. Beside them were the names of the doctors who used to be stationed there.

Victor Bohmer, Joseph Melbourne, Carl Cline, George Davis

The walls spoke in a metallic mutter as the resounding commotion brought Jacob in further. He ambled through the slender hallway, passing by the closed doors and their fogged glass. The last office at the end was opened ever so slightly.

The abundance of holes in the roofing gave way for the setting sun to kindle Jacob's pathway. His throbbing heartbeat thumped every muscle in his body. He looked at his puffed arm and feared his kidnapper was waiting for him on the other side. His sweaty fingers slipped before fully grasping the copper door handle—Jacob was about to set foot inside when he realized the noise had stopped.

The screeching hinges eventually swayed the door open, revealing a ransacked office. Lackluster wallpaper peeled off every corner, and the file cabinets were completely emptied out. The floor felt less stable going in, its spongy base depressed in on itself as he tiptoed around. Jacob was relieved to see there was no one in there with him. There was a window behind the desk that surveyed the other end of the building. When he looked out of it, he saw a gray car parked within the facility's gate fencing.

An immediate thud banged from the closed closet next to him. The impact was so strong that dust sprinkled off its door frame. Jacob's head spun, looking for something he could use for self-defense. He found a broken piece of glass twice the size of his hand and stumbled to get a sturdy handle on it. Jacob noticed the door was locked and tried to listen in on the other side. Not a single sound emerged—not a breath nor any indication a person was there, but he knew someone was.

Jacob was counting the seconds it took in between the pauses. He reached down to unlock the door and instinctually recoiled when the door was bashed again. A portion of the top corner broke off, allowing the darkness within to peek through. Jacob knew the aged wood could only resist one more blow until it was completely obliterated. He thought to run away, but there was nowhere to run. And if he escaped, he'd die of starvation out in the wilderness. Jacob's sole hope for survival was to confront and kill his abductor.

He firmly yanked the door open. The handle slammed through the weakened walls and screeched, rotating back. His palms were pale from the pressure in his grip. All that was in the space were cobwebs oscillating with the breeze and an interior that extended several feet deeper. Jacob was again left with silence.

His eyes widened when he detected a shift in the shadows, and the ground jingled with the same metal clanging. The unnaturally elongated wingspan of the black owl glided past Jacob. He fell and frantically scooted away to the edge of the room like a cockroach. The horned bird landed on the desk and leered at Jacob. Its eyes were frightening and watched him as though it understood his terror. The owl stood monumental in size, consuming half the height of the room. It towered over Jacob before gusting its wings and flew through the broken window.

Jacob could breathe again. He tossed the shard and relaxed his neck. The fatigue his body hid from him finally exposed itself. He rubbed his eyes and succumbed to this lazed state. He almost fell asleep right there when the starting of an engine blared outside. Jacob saw the car drive off down the winding pavement. The license plate was momentarily visible, and he tried to memorize the arbitrary sequence,

W7R—

His back flattened to the ground, and an unevenly sharpened knife weighed against his jugular.

"Who the fuck are you? What are you doing here!" The stranger said, agitating the blade and slicing it into the upper layer of Jacob's skin.

Jacob saw that the person holding him at knifepoint was a boy around the same age as him. He had scars marred across his face, and the clothes he wore reeked tremendously. The boy looked into Jacob's eyes, bouncing from left to right, then right to left. His gnashing teeth slowly receded, and the dark expression he wore melted away.

Jacob didn't say a word. He was still looking at the boy's physical features, but his focus went on his brown irises. The golden shimmer he saw in him reminded Jacob of his own. The boy dropped his weapon,

"Jacob?"

"Who are you?" Jacob's voice trembled.

"I'm your brother, Isaac."

Weston looked at the digital pixels of his wristwatch flashing 7 p.m. Less than an hour had gone by since they had last remembered entering the cave. The road to Impossible City quietly dragged on. Weston lowered the volume on his earpiece that picked up the freely swinging bike chains.

"Are we, uh…" Weston started.

"Are we gonna talk about what just happened?"

They all struggled to fully submerge back into this reality. No one had spoken since leaving the cove—each still digesting their own traumatic episode. Neither Liam nor Cheyenne wanted to answer him, but the windless forest made Weston's question all the more resounding in the silence that followed.

"You saw what happened in there, Weston. You were with me." Liam said.

Weston gave him a perplexed look. Seaside's two-way highway swung with hills and depressions going near sea level. Cheyenne rode ahead, standing up to peer over the incoming slope.

"What are you talking about?" Weston asked.

"What do you mean what am I talking about? How did you wake up before me?"

"Liam, I was never in there with you."

They rode with their heads side-by-side, not paying attention to Cheyenne, who had stopped moments ago. Weston went on, "I was never asleep, I—"

"Guys!" Cheyenne interjected.

Their brakes skidded to make the choppy stop. The three of them parked just before the roadway declined. Gray clouds from the burning oil took the saturation out of their eyes. A pickup truck driven halfway into an oak tree bled with liquids and appeared to be deserted. Liam instantly recognized the crashed vehicle that almost killed him and Jacob days prior. They looked about, but no one was in sight. It wasn't until movement came from inside the rear window that the truck swayed back and forth.

Liam dove forward, "We gotta help them, come on!"

It took less than ten seconds for him to get there, with gravity accelerating him to dangerous speeds. Liam hobbled off his bike, letting it joyride into the concrete. He froze when he looked inside the cracked glass.

The driver's head leaned against the window, and the car was in shambles from the collision. Automobile odors fumed into Liam's breaths, reminiscent of his childhood. Weston and Cheyenne caught up.

"Holy shit," Cheyenne said, letting her bike fall.

Weston examined the surroundings, unsure if there was someone watching them. Liam tugged on the driver-side door, but it was jammed, "Weston, come here!" They met at the handle and pried the dented metal open. A man in his late forties tumbled to the gravel without any resistance when the door no longer supported his weight. Cheyenne screamed, and the boys jumped back. The corpse's limbs contorted in awkward angles on its way to the ground.

Blood painted the fabric and inner windows, but not only from the alleged impact. The man's hands smeared art of his own. A canvas of hopelessness and the physical rendering of someone who begged to be freed. The outline of his body swelled with blood.

Liam studied his face, "That's Timmy's dad."

Weston crouched beside him.

"That's odd," Weston observed the profound inflictions along Mr. Anderson's temple and the back of his skull.

"How does he have marks going around his head from hitting a tree straight-on?"

Liam and Cheyenne silently stared until the back seat rattled. Liam ran and opened the rear door. Mrs. Anderson lay against the opposite end of the truck, her head utterly bashed in as well. Her eyes rested as though her passing soul caused the commotion.

Liam turned to Weston and Cheyenne, "We saw them—me and Jacob saw them leaving town on Monday. They looked like they were in a rush."

Weston looked at the front seats and the sides where Mrs. Anderson rested, "I don't see Timmy."

The three of them made eye contact. The oil's burning ignited short flames peeking out of the engine's hood and made an emphatic pop, jolting the vehicle.

"We gotta move!" Weston yelled.

Liam spotted a folded piece of paper in Mrs. Anderson's hand. He hurried into the combusting wagon and stretched as far as he could reach.

"What are you doing!" Cheyenne exclaimed.

As soon as Liam felt the smoothness of the paper, Mrs. Anderson clutched his wrist, "Get out."

Her voice croaked with remnants of what life she had left in her. Her strength, however, was undoubtedly preserved. She looked at all of them, then back to Liam with a more focused expression.

"You have no idea what's going on here. They're going to come for you all."

She began to speak with less assertion. Liam listened closely, "And they won't stop until each and every last one of you kids are dead."

Her life force faded with the pumps of blood trickling out of her lacerations. Weston and Cheyenne couldn't hear what she said after this point.

"Where is Timmy, Mrs. Anderson?" Liam asked—his wrist still held. Her head involuntarily bobbled, gazing around. She began to sob, looking at the vacant passenger seat smeared with more blood.

"They took him," she said.

"They took my baby."

Liam felt his skin crawl.

Mrs. Anderson pulled him in, "Nothing but pure evil has or can exist here. Everything in this town is tainted, condemned by God himself. Hell's passing sits under Seaside. And that woman, that woman. She comes for the children every thirteen years."

Mrs. Anderson peered at Weston and Cheyenne, "And the demons are awaiting a feast. Get out, or they will kill you."

"Who are they?" Liam asked.

An inferno erupted out of the hood. The truck was moments away from its engine, detonating and incinerating anyone within a ten-foot radius.

Liam squeezed her hand, "Mrs. Anderson, who is trying to kill us?"

"Liam, get out of there!" Weston yelled.

He jerked Liam's shirt, and Cheyenne came to his aid, dragging him out. Mrs. Anderson smiled at Liam.

"Tell me who!" Liam demanded in the midst of resisting and holding himself up against their attempt to pull him.

"Everyone," she said.

Mrs. Anderson let go of the note and his wrist. She laughed in the midst of the fire permeating into the interior and sizzling her skin to a crisp.

"Let's go!" Cheyenne yelled.

The engine heaped chunks of engine parts in the air while they straddled onto their bikes and pedaled vigorously to pick up momentum.

Liam looked behind and saw the pickup truck jump three feet off the ground and burst into a hellfire of flames.

He swerved onto the verge of the road with the others following. The black smoke was so thick the air's current couldn't ripple through the forming mushroom clouds. They heard the roaring crackles arise from the mixture of motor oils and human flesh. Mrs. Anderson's note was pressed between Liam's hand and the handlebar.

"We gotta get out of here before someone spots us," Liam said, jumping back on and continuing to where the pavement ended and the dirt road began—where the entrance of Impossible City awaited them.

The hour before dusk subtly captivated the lost city in a vintage sepia overlay. An enormous gathering of the trees and surrounding vegetation gently coaxed by Mother Nature into their inevitable death. The withering scarlet and wine leaves favored the amber petals rather than the evergreen that once controlled the season. In this humanless accord was a place where man failed to control the natural forces in life—where the balance rested in the imbalance of it all.

The church's garden was cultivated just beside a cliff such that it could easily take a person's life if they slipped over. It was always a place of privacy and less needed precaution; the extended peak made it ineffective for anyone to eavesdrop on them without first exposing themselves. Cheyenne ran her fingers against the outer brick wall until she brushed over a faded crescent moon etching the size of her fingernail. She used her mother's dagger to loosen the lining and joggle the brick out. The stache box Nancy and she hid was, in actuality, a Marlboro pack cloaking their herbal essentials.

Liam sat with the thoughts of a dying man weighing his chin into his chest. His hand fiddled with the gloss print while Weston paced between the crumbling benches. Cheyenne joined them and flicked the flimsy match while she sat. She inhaled enough smoke to burn through a third of the joint before passing it to Weston. Her stained lungs were comforted by the euphoric influx of dopamine.

"What did Mrs. Anderson tell you?" Weston asked.

Cheyenne gazed over at Liam when the luster of the paper grabbed her attention.

"She kept telling me that we had to get out of Seaside and that they were coming for us."

"Who?"

"I'm guessing the same people who took Timmy. What's that? You haven't let go of it since we got here." Cheyenne asked.

"It was in her hand," Liam paused briefly.

He unfolded the crinkly ends. A look of bewilderment settled on his face. The page itself manifested in many colors, attracting his eyes to every pointillistic stroke.

Weston impatiently waited for his laggard narration, "What is it?"

A whisper replayed in Liam's head,

Find me, and I will take you to Nancy.

Her soft-spoken tongue gave Liam shivers down his back even as he recalled the sound.

"It's Nancy," he said with a tense face.

He showed Weston and Cheyenne the poster of *The Nancy Doll.* Cheyenne was stifled. Her heart thumped in quick and rapid intervals, nearly causing her to lose consciousness. The blackness that lurked behind Nancy glared back at Cheyenne; the last atrocious memory of her best friend was now flawlessly depicted before her.

"It wasn't a dream," Cheyenne mumbled.

The perception of what reality was contrasted with her imagination, and now the two were indistinguishable. She had believed that what she had dreamt was only in her head, but the more she wanted to believe that fallacy, the more Cheyenne realized how real everything was.

Weston recognized the terror his friends felt and how the short period of time they had laid asleep at the entrance of the cave troubled their thoughts. Their carcinogenic breaths diluted the tension enough for Liam to break the silence and regurgitate bits of what he could remember. And as he recalled the fragmented memories, he accounted for Weston alongside him in everyone. Liam explained the journey through and about the findings of an entirely new world, unlike anything he'd ever seen.

They had eluded death on more than one occasion. Yet, Liam's recollections were ultimately obscured by those hundreds of wailing souls trapped in the frozen lake—and the watchful beast. The only flashback that he could vividly recall was the way he died in this dream. His ribs breaking, one by one, and immense pressure crushing his intestines until all he could hear was Weston's voice screaming for him to wake up. His story was far-fetched and downright unbelievable to Weston's ears. But as unreal as it sounded, Weston was more sure that Liam couldn't fabricate a tale like this even if he wanted to.

"You were with me, Weston. The whole time. And it wasn't just that. I could feel Lilith watching us while we were there—following us wherever we went. She made us see those things for a reason."

Cheyenne rubbed her arm as though blood still leaked from it. The memory of being mauled by the woman who skulked the inner cave ravished her mind. Her memories differed from Liam's because she could remember it all.

"What happened in your dream, Cheyenne?" Weston asked with a dry and coarse throat. She stood and let go of her arm, "They were in love."

Their eyes grew in unison. Cheyenne took out the photograph Liam found at Jacob's the night he was taken.

"What do you mean? What did you find?" Liam asked.

"Love letters. Piles and piles of them from Lilith to Jacob's great-grandfather. They were written while she was traveling with the carnival and had them mailed here to Jacob's address. There were dozens she wrote. Her words, the way she talked about him—I just can't imagine how things must have ended. What turned her into what she is now."

"What were in the letters?" Liam continued, his inquiry pressed on.

"She talked about how she wanted to leave the freakshow business and marry him. The show life was lonely, and the places they'd stay were always very unkind to them—using them for their own selfish and sadistic dark pleasures. The letters went on for at least a year and stopped just around the time when the missing children cases started in Seaside."

Weston and Liam had no words; the forest had a breathless and static ambiance that listened in on their conversation. The lower level of the wood shingle roofing over the garden's entrance gave way to decades of deterioration, demolishing into splinters once meeting the Earth. The church had neighboring structures awaiting a similar fate, but what grabbed their attention after the debris cleared was the figure of a man watching from a distance.

He was draped in a long, faded coat with matching tattered bottoms that also deviated from its original color. The man walked a wobbly line from twenty or so feet away toward them. They sighed in relief after recognizing the familiar drunkard stumble. His footsteps chomping through the grass became louder the closer he came.

"You kids look like you've seen a ghost," Vern said.

"Jesus Christ, Vern. We really need to work on your people skills after all this. You can't just stare at people in the middle of the fucking forest!" Weston said.

He sat on the bench next to them and unscrewed the flask hidden in his coat pocket. The engraving, now slightly worn, hinted at the hands that once held it and the stories whispered into its metallic embrace. His gluttonous gulps were resounding in the quiet.

"Missing another one, aren't you?"

Vern turned his head, searching for Jacob.

"We saw where she hid in Seaside," Cheyenne said.

"It was inside the cove, a cave full of posters and memories of Wonderland. Where she and Abraham escaped. I read all the letters between them. They were in love."

"They were?" Vern hissed. He drank another mouthful. "Tell me, what did Abraham write in these letters?"

Cheyenne copiously blinked at the fact that there was not one letter addressed to Lilith; it was always from her.

A grin caught his face, "They weren't in love; she was."

Vern stood and walked to the ledge.

"Abraham was a man with unimaginable secrets that he kept from her and the entire town. He came to Seaside as a young man eager to make a name for himself as an aspiring photographer. But he was heavily engaged in the black arts behind closed doors—performing rituals and animal sacrifices in hopes of a life provided by a deity. And when he laid his eyes upon Lilith for the first time, he knew she could manifest the darkness needed to summon Satan herself. He spent the first nights alone in Seaside, where the forest met the ocean. He heard a serpent's tongue speak sinister things in his head; it convinced Abraham he had to kill dozens of innocent lives to prove his relentless devotion."

Vern's words echoed Impossible City. Cheyenne, Weston, and Liam hadn't moved from their original positions.

"The night Wonderland was reduced to ashes was the night Abraham got his wish to meet the devil, but Lilith was the one who harvested the unholy powers from him. And she accepted them with pleasure. Her curse would be lifted upon the rekindling of her physical body, yet it was never found after the rampage. Abraham made sure of it. And as long as Lilith is apart from her mortal bones, she is bound by Wonderland's bloodthirst every thirteen years—and the townspeople reap its unholy pleasures."

The violet skies beckoned to the emerging twinkling stars.

"Her death was repaid in the flesh of their children, and their children's children—from the blood that courses through your veins now. Wonderland's anniversary falls tomorrow night."

Vern's words bore weight on their shoulders, suffocating their thoughts with a helplessness that they wouldn't be able to save Nancy and Jacob.

"Can't we just burn it to the ground?" Liam asked. They heard the low, accentuated rumble of an owl's hoot far away.

"What is born from the fires cannot perish by it, and Lilith will not stop until her body is laid to rest."

"She wasn't buried?" Asked Cheyenne.

"No one knows where her body is. It was never found after the site was investigated. Some tried to locate Lilith's whereabouts, but they had no success scavenging the hundreds of secluded spots Seaside was known to hide."

"Where does this lead us now? Like he said, hundreds of areas. And we still don't have any evidence for the police even if we do make it out of town!" Weston said.

"Hundreds of areas," Liam muttered to himself.

"That's it!" He exclaimed to them. Liam leaped over the fallen branches and leaves. He nearly slipped turning around, "I know where Abraham hid her body." He quickly said.

Cheyenne and Weston looked at each other in astonishment before hopping in his direction.

"Where are we going, Liam?"

"Into town, we gotta get to the library before it closes."

The boys kicked off, picking up the decline pull. Cheyenne made it halfway onto her bike when the handlebars were locked in place the moment she tried turning them. Vern held the steel frame in place, gawking at her.

"I knew you'd come back. I just knew it," he said. His face lightened, "Everyone said I was crazy. But I always knew I just had to be patient."

"Vern, what are you talking about?"

Cheyenne nudged her bike away from him, but he held on, continuing to beam a jovial expression she'd never seen out of him—she became uncomfortable.

He wanted to say more, but he stopped himself, "This time it'll be different, won't it?"

"Cheyenne! Come on!" Weston shouted.

She swiftly steered through Vern's grasp and zoomed away. Cheyenne did a double take at him, unsure if he would chase her—but he didn't. Her heart was already pounding by the time she reached Weston and Liam.

Vern watched as she rode, snickering to himself and rubbing his head.

XVII

BLACK MOON

Seaside Asylum was a three-story construct with a ground floor, basement, and one additional level above where Jacob and Isaac had been introduced to each other. The crumbling clock tower peaked two stories on top of the offices and labs. It was here in this aloft, secluded area that Isaac had built his hideaway. The base, however, had deteriorated a great deal over the years and caused the inner structure to collapse in on itself. Jacob and Isaac were able to pass through the entrance with ease because of their smaller physical makeup. Isaac's trusty lantern flickered up the winding cement steps that hugged the walls of the steeple.

"We're almost there. Careful, this area is dangerous for kids," Isaac said, attempting his first joke.

An exposed belfry allowed dirt and grime to immensely accumulate inside, yet it was a place that felt safer than anywhere else there. It was a fraction of space that Isaac could call his own. The lair he designed was an almost replica of the room Jacob had woken into. Stacks of dusty comforters formed a bed in the corner, while magazines and books littered the rest of the base. A soft hiss came from atop a small wooden desk at the opposite end. Jacob walked closer to the sound of static as the pillars exposed the dense jungle. There was a foliage of papers that had graphite etchings of subjects that could be seen from this altitude—birds flying under the skies, a sea of trees in a never-ending wave of shades, and the midnight glow under the moonlight that kindled the mountaintops.

The radio's crackle screeched when Isaac turned the knob and jumped through different stations, "Found it in one of the offices. Pretty neat, right? Solar-powered."

"These are amazing!" Jacob's attention was still on the sketches.

"Yeah, well. I guess everybody's gotta get good at something eventually, right?"

He crouched on a stubby stool and pointed to the pile of sheets.

"You can sit there if you want."

They held similar awkward postures; their eyes blinked in unison, contemplating whether or not the other was really there right now.

"So, this is where you've been?" Jacob asked.

"For all of thirteen years," he replied.

"Martha and Abraham said that you died a little while after you were born. Some birthing defect or something that the doctors couldn't figure out."

"You believe everything your parents tell you?" He smiled weakly.

Jacob didn't say anything back. The tower had a panoramic view of the miles of woods that separated their hometown from the rest of the world. Jacob's eyes trailed the single road where he had to squint to see the main road junction.

Isaac grabbed a water bottle and handed it to him, "It's too far, trust me."

The free-falling temperature stabilized around the fifty-degree mark once the sun faded away, but at their altitude, the conditions were severely more frigid and ruthless. Isaac set fire to the wick of several other candles that were already diminished in wax—the shadows began to frolic around the interior dome.

"Abraham brought you here for a reason. It's where he knows the others won't look to find you." Isaac said.

Jacob's spine stiffened, "The townspeople?"

He nodded back to him.

"All of Seaside knows about Wonderland and what is supposed to happen when it returns."

Jacob's head spun with a walloping force, "But why didn't he bring you back when the carnival left? This place is a ruin!"

"If anyone saw me or knew I was here, they'd burn our entire family alive and erase our names from existence. Medical records, driver's licenses, birth certificates, everything—gone. No one would ever know. A while back, Abraham said he built me a treehouse not too far from where you guys live—in the forest close by so I could be somewhat a part of the family. But he never brought it back up since then."

Isaac strolled the edges, observing what could be seen under the glistening moon.

"And this is the only place he can inject you with that black shit," he pointed at Jacob's still very swollen arm.

"Lucky for you, there is a shit ton of first-aid kits and manuals available in a mental institution."

Isaac rummaged through a clear container abundant with surgical equipment: cotton gauges, bottles of solutions, sterilized packaged instruments, and other tools that would otherwise only be found in an operating room. He lifted his long sleeve and showed Jacob the numerous self-inflicted cuts that spread up and down his arm.

"Lotta time to practice, too."

He popped the top of a plastic bottle, "Alright, let's see how bad it is."

The torn fabric Jacob used to stop the bleeding was now embedded with his dried gash. He winced, ripping away and reopening the cut. It was mostly coagulated under an ebony, sickly coloration and was a testament to how desperately he needed to get cleaned. The sting of the ethanol and hydrogen peroxide sank inward and dispersed into the depths of Jacob's flesh where the vermin had crawled. The solution fizzled immediately, killing off the growing bacteria. However, Jacob's throat became raw as he cried out in pain until his lungs became exhausted. His brother wrapped the wound with a clean towel after Jacob's dried bits and remains were flushed out.

"What was in the IV?" Jacob asked, sniffling his nose.

"It keeps the woman away. When you're injected with it, it contaminates your blood, so she can't find you."

"But what is it exactly?"

"Abraham's blood."

Jacob found himself speechless yet again.

"Our family has a pretty fucked up history, Jacob."

He listened to Isaac continue on, yet it was his father's voice that he heard. He went into greater detail about the torture many children suffered once they went missing and how easy it was to manipulate any leading evidence in a police investigation. Jacob soon realized there was a member of this cult present in every significant position across Seaside—a complex cobweb of connections under a single agenda.

There is a chemical reaction that happens within an adolescent who experiences severe trauma, and it's this emotional response that makes their blood irresistible. This intoxicating convocation was the equivalent of the fountain of youth—an undivine gift from Satan that could only be manifested by the cruelest abuse. The feeding was euphoric, with sensations that were unparalleled to anything humans had ever perceived before. The woman would feast on the offerings while the rest finished what was left. Their gluttonous appetite reamed a new life and thirteen years of peace until everything had to be repeated. And it was the youngest in each of the families who would be mutilated and sacrificed upon Wonderland's return.

Generations of families that were alongside theirs performed these sadistic satanic rituals behind closed doors. These weren't anonymous individuals or groups that were foreign to the natives of Seaside. These were the grandfathers and grandmothers of his friends and kids who grew up here. They were going up against the grain, Cheyenne, Liam, and Weston included. However, it was Jacob and Isaac who had the most to fear. Their grandfather's blood coursed through their veins, and it was for that sole reason that Lilith desired their blood the most.

"Sometimes I wonder about all the relatives we never had a chance to meet and how big our family could really be. But it's sort of like that with any family, right? People live, and then they die; the only difference is that we never get to hear the stories about them."

Isaac took some moments to gather his breath; the whistling woods embraced the open iron moldings shaping the circular clock structure.

"What do you eat when you get hungry? Or thirsty?" Jacob asked.

"I don't have much of an appetite after Abraham finishes the blood transfer. You kinda just forget after so long, you know?"

They talked for a great deal until Jacob's eyelids grew too burdensome to keep open. He heard Isaac say something before falling asleep, but he only caught the last sentence, "Get some rest."

His neck relaxed, and Jacob snoozed into a short-lived, intoxicating slumber.

The unwelcoming pulsations reeled Jacob out of his fleeting nap. A car alarm followed that beeped twice. Jacob was startling to a more woke state.

"He's back," Isaac said, pulling him to his feet.

"Hurry up! We gotta get you back in that room before he notices."

Each step was a guess for Jacob; his unrested legs lugged the weight of his body down the pitch-black stone stairs.

"Okay, you're just gonna pretend you're asleep. And make it look like the needle's still in your arm."

"What's he going to do?"

They stopped in the hallway leading into the room. Isaac checked the window next to them when he saw the glimmering LED light wave by. Abraham was unloading a box from the trunk.

"Come on!" Isaac rushed them past the doorless opening. Jacob flipped the bloodstained sheets, renewing their aged oatmeal appearance. Isaac did a number of takes behind, anticipating the creaking hinges from the front entrance. Jacob's body tingled with adrenaline that ramped his breathing and pumped every muscle he had. He tried to compose himself through his nostrils—inhaling slowly and deeply.

The sharp-tuning tinnitus overwhelmed Isaac's senses and rang him into a light-headed state.

"Isaac," Jacob's voice disarmed the drone.

"I don't know if I can do this. I can't stay here forever, I just can't."

Isaac knew Jacob wasn't physically or mentally ready for a life of solitude and conditioning himself to a whole new way of living. But Jacob would need to do more than just adapt; he would have to learn to leave the world as he knew it.

A creak loudly sang and was followed by a slamming door that vibrated the wary ground-level walls. There was a pause that filled the void. They looked at each other.

"Just stay quiet and don't open your eyes until I tell you, promise?"

Isaac blew the lantern's candle as a surge of electricity twitched the fluorescent lights on. Isaac stuck his palm out, "You need to trust me, Jacob."

He briefly looked at his older brother, and then at the doorway, Abraham's steps echoed closer and closer.

Jacob grabbed his hand, "Okay, I trust you."

Isaac swooped to the tile and crawled under the bed next to his. Jacob took one last gaze at the room and noticed that the Christ figure he attacked earlier was undamaged and stainless. He closed his eyes once his father's shadow intruded the infirmary.

Grunts routinely came after the squeaks of rubber boots. Jacob couldn't breathe fast enough to keep up with his speeding heart. A thud boomed next to him—he felt his father's glare tracing his body. Abraham rested his hand over Jacob's chest, unable to notice each pulse of blood pounding inside his rib cage. Isaac emerged from under the bed, watching them—terrified.

The empty IV bag needed to be replaced. Abraham crouched and opened the hefty box he carried in. Its contents were a scattered bunch of clothes, books, and blank notebooks that came from Jacob's room. He grabbed a sealed bag of murky liquid that was hazy to look through. The same inconsistent material floated around—Isaac stared without a shiver in his spine.

A softly spoken sentence came next to Isaac that only he could hear.

"You won't get another chance," Emily said.

He turned to her, unstartled. She held an unclenched expression, almost a daze. Her pale skin darkened around the crevasses of her skin.

She kept her focus on Jacob and then toward him, "It's time, Isaac."

When Isaac looked at Abraham again, he stood and nimbly pulled a sleek, snake-like wire from his pocket. The strand stretched about a foot end to end and had a shimmer under the artificial tube lights. Abraham gathered some more medical equipment out of the box to replace the IV. His six-foot posture knelt short enough for Isaac's own to tower over him. With both arms raising the wire, Isaac lunged at him but stopped immediately—just inches away.

An obnoxiously rapid pinging came from his father's back pocket. Isaac froze in place. He retrieved his mobile phone from his pocket, which resembled a TV remote.

"Yeah?" Abraham answered.

Isaac tried to listen in on the caller, but all that resounded outside Abraham's ears was gibberish.

"It's fine, he's still here. The bag is completely used up."

Jacob's stomach twisted. He was but a specimen to them, awaiting what would happen next, and what Isaac would respond with.

The conversation shifted to a different topic after another series of chirps came from the earpiece, "Martha, you need to stay hidden until I get back to the house. Don't open any doors or answer any calls unless it's from this phone."

Isaac smelled Abraham's cologne, desperately trying to mask his pungent sweat stench.

There came a long pause until he ended the call, "I'll be home in an hour or so. Lock the windows."

He had to gather himself to say the next words, "I love you."

Those three words unknowingly severed any emotional connection Isaac had left with his parents. It was the first time he heard the phrase out of his father's lips. He was nothing more than a reject in his parents' eyes—an abomination spewed out by greed and selfishness. Keeping their children hidden wasn't to protect them; it was to save themselves. Abraham and Martha's conscience stayed clean while reaping the rewards of what these rituals entailed. Isaac wondered how many children had died, kids who would never see their hopes and dreams manifest into reality. He observed Jacob's lying, vulnerable to all this darkness—a perpetual cycle that would begin anew with him.

At that very moment, Isaac hardened. His once trembling hands were now serene and stable. And it was upon seeing this that he realized he was free all along. He couldn't expel the darkness that rotted in him throughout the years. No one could. But sometimes, seeing the bigger picture was enough.

As his fluttering eyes swayed in REM sleep, the silence tormented Jacob. Tears cascaded Abraham's face.

He sobbed, mumbling to himself, "It wasn't supposed to be like this, son. I'm sorry, Jacob. I'm so so—"

His voice ceased mid-breath. In those several voiceless seconds counting in Jacob's mind, the gripping sound of leather stretching and twisting consumed the room. The blinding bulb above dilated his pupils as they opened and trailed the peculiar noise.

Jacob saw his father's lanky figure convulse on the monochrome tile—flopping and squirming about kicking the facility's equipment around him. The cable ran above and across his Adam's apple, constricting the flow of air into Abraham's lungs—Isaac tugged harder. He reached out to Jacob in desperation.

"Ja—" Only partial annunciations came from his mouth.

Abraham's distressed veins protruded from his skin, and his complexion became blotched with burgundy and blue spots. The moment lasted a lifetime.

"I can't hold him for long!" Isaac shouted at him.

Abraham's upchucks and gasping arose from the loosening of the wire's clench. He pried his fingers between the choke; they had ten or so seconds until he was freed. Jacob became hysterical, looking for something to constrain Abraham. He dug into the box assortment, bolting through the random items inside.

"Jacob!" Isaac yelled again.

The heavy hammer hidden underneath begged his attention and was clutched by Jacob's sweaty palms the moment he made contact. Without hesitation, he stepped on his father's chest amidst his attempt to sit up. Isaac closed his eyes as the tool dropped from above.

Thump.

The first blow heaved Abraham's momentum back on Isaac. He was disorientated and submitted immediately by the face of the tool.

Thump.

Their father's ribs imploded with parts of the hammerhead pulverizing into his flesh.

The never-ending pounds vibrated Isaac simultaneously as heaps of blood splattered on his face.

Thump.

The relinquishing of life and the struggle to survive eased in. The sound of the steel and the shattered bones carried on even after Abraham passed.

Thump.

Jacob heaved oxygen like a madman and backpedaled into the bed—looking at the hammer, then at his father's dead body.

Isaac started to pull himself away underneath two hundred and fifty pounds of weight until he felt the car keys bulging from Abraham's back pocket. Isaac's shoes squeaked along and around the puddles of blood as he made his way towards Jacob. Their breathing became synchronized while staring at the dead body. Jacob nor Isaac spoke; they allowed the ringing fluorescents to carry the conversation instead. Isaac stood up after almost ten minutes of reticence.

"Let's go," he said, extending his hand out to Jacob.

They made their way to the family car.

The radio played as soon as Jacob started the ignition. He recognized the same station frequency that was on Isaac's. The music was deafening, but they didn't adjust the volume,

'Outside in the cold distance, A wildcat did growl.'

Jacob shifted the gear to drive how he remembered Abraham did and looked at Isaac one last time before they rolled down the hill—escaping Seaside Asylum together.

'Two riders were approaching, And the wind began to howl, hey!'

XVIII

SHADOWS OF THE PAST

Their spinning bike chains whirled against the wind. Blooming saffron street lights could be seen from the rural parts of Seaside. Weston turned his head against the gust, “Why are we going to the library, Liam?”

“If Jacob’s great grandpa hid Lilith’s body, there’s gotta be a clue in his book.”

“He literally photographed a hundred different locations around the town and forest. How are we going to check all of them before tomorrow night?” Weston asked.

“Because only one location wasn’t photographed. He called it *The Seed.*”

Weston and Cheyenne listened on, “I don’t remember it entirely, but I knew it wasn’t a picture. It was just a small drawing of a seed around some dirt sketches. I think that’s where he hid the body.”

They rolled down a curvy dip.

“I can’t go back home to get my copy, but I know the library has a bunch,” Liam finished.

Weston glanced at his watch, 8:37 p.m.

“Who would have thought we’d be relying on Liam’s brain to end a cult? We have about fifteen minutes till it closes.”

They hastened their cycling. Cheyenne was distracted, still thinking about what Vern said to her—everything had a repetitive feel, like she was reliving the same nightmarish experience again.

Liam, Weston, and Cheyenne glided past the town's welcome sign just before the road widened into avenues and boulevards,

Seaside: Nature's Canvas, 1882.

An eerie buzz radiated from each light post they rode through.

"What the hell is going on?" Weston said in a hush.

It was so quiet that the clicks of their pedals echoed off the building complexes and small business shops. All but townspeople filled the sidewalks, and all but cars drove on the streets. There had never been a time that downtown Seaside was vacant, yet it was now a ghost town.

Neon colors continued to beam and advertise as though customers were wandering around. Wide-set windows revealed the still operational insides of clothing boutiques and cafes. Even the movie theater had an extravagant parade of colors showcasing the latest Hollywood releases.

"It's like everyone just stopped what they were doing and left," Liam said.

"We're not that far from the library. Let's get the book and get the fuck out of here," Weston said, picking up the pace.

They cut through the town's square, where a stretch of grass was used for events and gatherings. And where the one-hundred-four-year-old grand oak tree of Seaside was rooted.

As they sailed the main intersection, a figure wisped behind the nineteenth-century wooden behemoth, barely catching Cheyenne's peripheral vision. She reversed her pedaling and skidded her rubber tires several inches while Liam and Weston stopped ahead.

“What’s wrong?” Liam called.

“The tree!” She pointed at the oak’s smooth, shadowed silhouette that became irregular by a hanging object from one of its branches.

They lethargically approached, watching the darkness materialize into something else.

The tension in the noose croaked as it swung; they came close enough to detail the body of a child hanging at the neck.

“It’s, it’s—” Weston stammered.

The boy’s eyes had been gouged out of their sockets, leaving a smear of blood over the white garments he was dressed in. A sign had been stapled to his chest written in the same stains of scarlet,

Now I can see. Now I can fly

“Timmy,” Liam muttered.

They were horrified, one of their own slain in such a way. Cheyenne looked under his feet, where blood was still dripping.

“Someone did this not too long ago. He’s still bleeding.”

They collectively stared at their reflections from the murky puddle. The fluctuating bell chimes sang in the new hour, and nine dongs came at a high then low octave. They made their way towards the library.

Cheyenne, Liam, and Weston hid along the shrubs that outlined the independently standing structure. Not a soul appeared through the grand entrance despite every bulb turned on—from the ceiling and wall fixtures to the lamps on the tables.

“We’re in and out, okay?” Liam assured.

A myriad of steps elevated up the concrete stairs. Cheyenne turned around once at the top. She surveyed dozens of surrounding shops around them and felt the watchful presence of a hundred eyes following them.

"Hey," Weston tapped her arm.

Liam had the door halfway opened, waiting for them, "Let's get that book."

Cheyenne nodded, and they ran into the library where Seaside's past forever lived on. Parallel rows and columns of nonfiction publications composed the first floor, while the open second level featured fictional works. They saw their breaths extinguish the air.

"You two keep lookout."

Liam rushed past the rounded desk piece that sat in the middle where the librarian's station was.

The library's lights exuded a sickly green moss overcast. Electrical hums droned out his thoughts and became more profound as Liam approached the east-end wall. He was in a blind spot that Weston and Cheyenne couldn't see now. The photography section was far less potent in volume form. He had, quite frequently, funneled through many of these photobooks imagining the various places around the world he'd hope to physically see one day with a camera of his own.

He caressed his fingers over their spines but instantly stopped when all but one empty space was left where his favorite book had always been placed.

"What? No, no, no!" He pulled out several neighboring titles and let them tumble to the ground.

Liam reached his arm inside, but all he felt was the cold concrete wall. He tried to steady himself and scanned the rest of the shelf, but his heart sank when he saw a pair of arms slither to the row behind him.

Its crackling, unsettling bones and lowly groans vanished as soon as Liam's eyes focused. He gingerly pressed his feet approaching the corner. The emphatic chews of mush swishing in its mouth agonized Liam's eardrums with each pulse of its tongue moving the contents around. With the body of an adult man, he was gowned in a raggedy white cloth that also covered his face.

The man was hunched on all fours with the posture of a goat feeding on a field of grass. Liam could hear his chews magnify—his mouth met the library's broadloom carpet where a pile of severed limbs lay. Only the man's head turned to Liam, his mouth opened, drizzling with gore.

Liam stumbled backward into another bookshelf. The man stared at him through the cloth with eyes that were hollowed cavities of blackness. He desperately wished to vanish into the books behind him, but the man kept his attention locked—still gnawing at his meal. Liam's sweat chilled in the freezing temperature.

He tried to turn and run back to Cheyenne and Weston, but he felt his shirt tug as though caught on the shelf's corner. Before Liam had the chance to react, he was immersed by dozens of hands that cropped up from the gaps and spaces within the bookshelf.

He was buried in a matter of seconds. Their grotesque fingers crawled over every part of him, binding him in place. The hysterical hands muffled Liam's lips, and his throat wailed with a vain resonance. He forced his head down and saw his legs were completely wrapped. Liam was immobilized and started to sink into the shelf.

The once-feeding man was not alone anymore; several beings stood just inches away from Liam. Their stillness was disturbing, and their gaze violating—they crept closer.

Liam wriggled and writhed enough to free a sliver of his face, "Help!" His voice surged the building until he was silenced and swallowed by the hands again. The tube fluorescents flickered on and off until Liam found himself on the ground with no one else around him.

"Liam!" Weston shouted as he and Cheyenne came bursting through the lane.

"What happened? Are you okay?" Liam stuttered incoherently as he squirmed away from the wall. He brushed himself off and regained his composure,

"It's gone. The—the book is gone. It's not there anymore! They know we're here." He repeated. They fled the corner as Weston led them towards the staircase.

"They might keep extra copies in the backroom. Maybe there's one in there!"

He snatched the lanyard attached to a single key that sat at the front desk.

"I'm getting a bad feeling about this place," Cheyenne said.

The doorway to the underground storage was hidden to the naked eye. Only until you were through the low ceiling and swiveled a sharp corner did one see the entrance.

Weston fiddled the brass key in the lock and let the flimsy wood glide open. They entered and descended several feet. A wafting odor reeked of rot—stale air circulating mold and mildew that thrived in this abandoned cellar.

Ten rows lengthened wall-to-wall under the dilapidated lights. It replicated the layout above, but the furniture was riddled with dirt and age on the verge of collapsing. Weston vanished into an aisle at the farthest end where the numbered titles started. Liam trailed him while Cheyenne's attention was captured by the still-dripping hand-painted sign that only she saw.

Native Americans

She found herself in a trance as her legs propelled ahead. A vast collection presented itself, encompassing every inch of the twelve-foot towering bookcases. Cheyenne aimlessly glanced at the stories associated in this archived section: massacres of indigenous tribes, Native women who were abducted, raped, and slain by these colonizing groups; poisoned water wells killing thousands, treaties preluding night ambushes—these unimaginable and horrendous crimes of genocide were inscribed in the pages here.

The dull assortment of monotone colored book covers distinguished the rosy red book, which slightly peeked out. Cheyenne ruminated in the eerie silence within the empty row. She grabbed its spine and felt the weight of its contents, bringing her to the ground. A set of photographs revealed itself in the first pages that appeared to be Seaside from years ago.

The images were initially of the town and of its building developments before she came across photos of the uninhabited and fascinating locations nature surrounded them with. Although Seaside boasted its growing construction, the photos mainly portrayed the landscape's untarnished beauty only possible without the intrusion of man.

One of which was oddly familiar to her. She studied this particular image for a while until she realized what she was staring at. It seemed to be of the cove from a different perspective—at a higher altitude and hundreds of feet away. Her curiosity ceased with a turn to the following photograph—extinguishing Cheyenne's intrigued facial expression.

Its colossal tents swirled with candy cane patterns. Her pupils reflected the film's vibrancy—the neon lights broadcasted showtimes and the carny games that dominated the frame. The subject and focus were centered on a pregnant woman standing in front, her belly extending past her toes, seemingly ready to deliver at any moment. Her complexion mimicked Cheyenne's, and the tailored outfit the woman wore featured tribal patterns not usually found in common department shops. Cheyenne's eyes read the text written at the bottom.

Wonderland, 1973

She began to hyperventilate and frantically flip more pages, becoming more familiar with what these pictures were and of whom. Tears rolled down her cheeks, and Cheyenne sobbed in disbelief as she unraveled the memories captured of her mother and father in Seaside thirteen years ago.

The presence of another made her look toward the end of the row.

The woman browsed with an uncanny peacefulness—her hand moved in a searching motion, but she picked nothing. Cheyenne only saw a fraction of her face, just enough to recognize the physical likeness they shared. The decorations in her clothes followed the colors of fall—earth tones that almost concealed her in the shadows.

"M—Mom?" Cheyenne mumbled.

She gracefully spun to the call, and Cheyenne saw her mother for the very first time.

"Cheyenne?"

Dyani's voice was soft, calming, as though not a malicious word could spring from her lips. It only took a moment for the two to fully register the other's existence. Her mother joyfully exclaimed, and Cheyenne leaped into her open arms.

"Is it really you, mom?" she cried.

Dyani's warmth and snug hug was soothing and mellowed the anxiety Cheyenne had.

"Of course it's me, my love. You've finally found where I've been all along."

They unhinged but kept latched at the waist.

"How are you here right now?" Cheyenne asked.

Dyani rubbed her daughter's temple. She smiled, and her eyes began to water.

"My beautiful baby, I'm just so happy I thought I would never see you again."

Dyani brought Cheyenne in close once more—the hold this time was much stronger. Cheyenne was bewitched by the loving touch of her mother and hoped the moment would never end.

"I love you, Cheyenne," Dyani whispered in her ear.

"I love you too, Mom," she exhaled back.

"Cheyenne?" Liam's deepened voice shocked her out of the dream.

"Just please put it down, okay?" He said with a stern and serious tone.

Cheyenne's eyes opened to where Liam and Weston stood at the end of the row until she noticed a great deal of pressure coming from her forearm.

When she looked down, she found herself holding her mother's dagger against her veins, partially piercing into her wrist already.

"What's going on?" She demanded louder.

"What's the fuck is going on!" Cheyenne screamed, lifting the blade as blood leaked to her fingertips.

A door slammed from above, "Someone's here!"

Weston jolted to the stairs, pulling Cheyenne with her as Liam followed them, holding the elusive *One Hundred Locations* copy tucked to his side. They ran up the steps back to the corner, hiding them from what was happening at the front.

Multiple footsteps could be heard scraping the carpet before something heavier dragged against it—ceaselessly echoing in the library's dome. Plain-clothed men and women populated the center, most of whom were doused with blood splattered all over their garments. The massive library windows were painted black by the night sky, and condensation bled against the interior glass. Cheyenne, Liam, and Weston watched Timmy's body hauled by his hands and heaved onto the librarian's table.

Thread ripped along the scissor's edges, exposing Timmy's torso. Dried mud and clots of blood were spread all over, and violet bruises contrasted with great vibrancy against his pale skin under the luminous lights. The men and women moved in a practiced procedure—meticulously preparing Timmy's corpse. The absence of any vocal communication among them was evident, as though this was something all too routine.

Weston counted two men and two women circling Timmy. The library's second exit rested on the west end of the building, only about fifteen meters from where they hid.

"They'll see us the second we turn the corner," Weston said.

"Crawl," Liam replied.

The men and women murmured amongst one another—all symmetrically aligned in a clockwise fashion. The study tables obstructed the view of the kids, giving them enough coverage. Liam crouched to the carpet, then Weston, and lastly Cheyenne—but she paused at floor level when the glimpse of a man entering through the front door startled everyone. His footsteps were stout enough to hear even on the rugged surface. Weston's eyes glimmered as Mr. Matthew approached one of his deceased students.

His arms opened as he stopped at the top of their pentagram.

"Brothers, sisters, I am most gracious for your presence here tonight. Our generation's calling has been bestowed upon us—an indisputable oath bound by the blood of our ancestors before us."

Mr. Matthew's hands moved with his words, and at random moments, his hand would rest on Timmy's chest like he was nothing more than his podium. Liam, Cheyenne, and Weston were frozen—restlessly anticipating what would happen next.

"We are all one and the same, yes. We share the glory that is to come!" He smiled, "And consequently, the filth condensed in our souls. Let us not forget. What was once a seed shrouded in darkness is now an everlasting tree that watches over you and me."

The women hummed an unsettling pitch—it resembled a moan that was almost a painful weeping that bulged the veins of their necks.

"Come on!" Liam waved at Weston and Cheyenne.

The vocal onslaught made for a needed distraction for their scurrying until they collectively halted at the sound of a thunderous cracking. The library's chandelier vignetted Mr. Matthew's blood-sprayed face and the ominous silence that followed. In his right hand was a stone the size of a cantaloupe that left a visible depression in Timmy's skull.

He breathed deeply through his nostrils while his fingers brushed over the uneven ridges of the bone cavity. The others moved in and hovered their palms over Timmy—their mouths salivating and their pupils dilated with excitement. Weston looked ahead at Liam and then to Cheyenne behind him—the adults began to menacingly feast on their former classmate.

"I fucking hate this town so much, man," Weston said.

Cheyenne briefly studied the sick gleam on their faces that depicted a true internal bliss—a euphoria unlike any other. They yelped with joy, chuckled upon the sight of another, all while chewing on the dead carcass of a child without remorse. All for the sake of what they believed was righteous and holy. It was masked, instead, with torture and murder.

Weston tapped Cheyenne on her arm to follow; they were almost halfway there. Her backpack screeched a static frequency that sounded throughout every corner of the library.

His words were broken up by a weak connection, "Do you copy? I said I'm downtown, it's Jacob!" Cheyenne panicked, trying to turn her earpiece off, but the technical imbalance of inputs and outputs created an unpleasant blaring squeal.

"Let's go!" Weston tugged Cheyenne to her feet. Mr Matthew and the others watched them with mouths full. Liam, Weston, and Cheyenne rushed through the exit doors and toward their bikes. They saw an SUV rolling down Main Street.

"It's Jacob!" She shouted.

The library's front doors slamming against the concrete walls yielded their attention as the men and women ran straight at them. Jacob honked the horn, yelling out the window. By the time they were twenty meters away, Jacob floored the gas pedal—the men were right on their tail. Cheyenne could feel fingertips scantily skim her neck while biking through the grass. The asphalt accelerated their speeds and created enough distance for Jacob to stop the car for them. They jumped into the trunk and ditched their bikes on the road.

The pursuants still had pieces of flesh bloating from their cheeks; the man who nearly grabbed Cheyenne waved at them as they drove away—his face wore a smile while he flapped an arm, Timmy's severed arm.

XIX

DARKNESS CALLS

The engine's churn roared through the van's open windows, and the frosty air blew colder by the minute. Streetlights started to wane and appear at distant lengths as they drove along Seaside's outskirts. They each occupied a seat while Liam sat in the back, constantly checking if anyone was following. It was nearly 10 p.m. and they were two miles from Cheyenne's house; the whooshing trees passed by, welcoming them back to the forest.

"Isaac, right? How's Seaside treating you? I mean, the actual town, not our hidden asylum in the woods," Weston asked Isaac.

"So far, I'm having a killer time," he said.

Weston paused, "Oh yeah, I forgot to tell you guys.

We have a test tomorrow at school."

"What class?" Jacob replied; his eyes were glued on the road, and he seemingly hadn't blinked for a while.

"Algebra," Liam said.

The rocky driveway crunched and popped as Jacob jerkingly brought the car to a park. Cheyenne noticed the chimney smoke clouding under the moonlight—its radiance in the sky left a celestial glow on the earth without the need for flashlights. The living room's light bled around the outline of the blinds.

"Chaska's still up," Cheyenne said.

They came to the porch, where she unlocked the front door and led Jacob, Liam, Weston, and Isaac into her house. The scent inside came across as foreign, bludgeoned by an intruding smell of another that lingered. She thought it could have been in her head, but the stench only strengthened the further inward they went.

The flames from the fireplace kindled their grungy adolescent faces. There wasn't a single bulb turned on, and it left the figure that sat in front of the fire devoured in shadows.

"Chaska?" Cheyenne weakly called, unsure if it was really him.

She gripped her dagger, and the others reacted to her hostility by grabbing their own weapons. Cheyenne tried calling him again to no avail. They kept close to the wall and inched closer until they were able to see Chaska's mutilated face. His teeth were exposed on one side of his jaw as a piece of flesh looked to have been bitten off.

"Oh my god! Chaska!" Cheyenne cried.

He was barely conscious. She dropped Dyani's blade and fell to her knees, grabbing both his hands. His eyes wearily opened, and he breathed at a fast pace but couldn't muster a word.

"What happened to you?" She exclaimed.

Chaska's movements were sluggish and shaky. His wounds were coagulated and bruised. He couldn't shift his weight or adjust himself with the probability of a bone break in his ribs.

"Chaska, who did this?" Cheyenne whimpered.

Isaac peeked out the curtains, "It's not safe; we gotta get outta here before whoever did this comes back."

"Where's the first aid?" Weston asked.

"The kitchen!" Cheyenne was neurotic.

Jacob helped Weston retrieve the kit while Liam and Isaac tried to get Chaska to his feet. He screamed and sank back into the chair.

"Chaska, tell me who did this!" She demanded.

Her hands clenched his with tears falling down her cheeks. After several moments, he looked at her and opened his mouth.

"I'm sorry to have lied to you for all these years, Cheyenne." He sounded broken, but not only of the body—his willpower was perishing, too. The toughness he once exemplified was now dwindling.

"This town is a timeless cesspool that spreads from poisoning the mind and soul of a person. Spirits come here; they are attracted to the darkness and tragedy—they lurk all around us, waiting patiently until it is time to feast once again."

He leaned away and coughed blood on their wooden flooring.

"Chaska," Cheyenne's voice was broken.

The man she had looked up to since she was a child was dying right before her. The boys stood behind, anxious about what to do to help, but they remained where they were.

"We didn't come here to live in Seaside, Cheyenne. We came here to avenge the murder of our parents."

"Our? What do you mean by our? Chaska!" Her stomach became queasy, and she nearly vomited on the ground next to the splatter of blood.

Chaska's head turned to Jacob, and he gave a stare until he finally spoke again.

"She's still inside you,"

"And you,"Chaska eyeballed Isaac.

Chaska glared at all of them. He coughed violently at their feet with a hunched back.

"Chaska!" She tried to prop him up.

"Help me!" Cheyenne screamed.

They tried to lift his chest, but Chaska pushed them off. He wheezed with a forceful gasp as fluids drained into his lungs—every inhale was a splintering sensation of knives stabbing his organs that he couldn't stop. Chaska clutched his chest when blood oozed through his fingers.

Cheyenne moved his hand and opened his flannel shirt that concealed a laceration that was cut into his entire chest. She shrieked at the reveal of Wonderland's symbol carved into her uncle's skin.

The tall grass curled with the weight of the dew glistening their blades. Jacob closed the sliding door and rejoined everyone in the pasture out back. Weston checked his green-lit watch; it was 12:13 a.m.

"Here," Jacob said to Cheyenne.

But his voice instantly drowned out of Cheyenne's head, and she was instead consumed with that continual ringing that suffocated her other senses. Her eyes rested on Chaska's decorated corpse.

"Cheyenne," Jacob called again, handing the can of gasoline to her. Chaska had died from internal bleeding hours earlier, and they had since then moved him to a dirt patch right outside Cheyenne's backyard.

Cremation of the body was a customary ritual for the people in her tribe—the dead were clothed in sacred outfits and shrined with jewelry, an excess of food, and weapons for their journey into the afterlife. Cheyenne had prepped her uncle as thoroughly as she could, desperately remembering each detail of the process that Chaska had once explained to her. They covered him with a winter blanket. Once she finished, she soaked the fabric with the lighter fluid Jacob gave her.

She was normalized to the concept of death. Her culture emphasized the importance for the soul to be guided and protected once relinquished from the physical body, yet all Cheyenne could understand now was the pain and suffering of losing a loved one. She had been left with more questions than answers.

The scraping match combusted and hissed loudly until its flame calmed. Cheyenne let go and watched the blanket catch fire. Four incense candles were placed on the opposite side where Jacob, Isaac, Liam, and Weston stood.

"Light them up," she told them.

They flicked their pocket lighters at the same time. As the body burned, it was important to keep the surroundings clean of bad spirits and thoughts—from the north to the south and east to west, this ancient ritual would transition Chaska's physical being into the spiritual realm.

Cheyenne wanted to cry. She tried to cry, but she couldn't bring a single tear to drop. All that resonated was anger and confusion—how anyone would be heartless enough to kill an innocent man in cold blood.

“Chaska,” Cheyenne mumbled under her breath.

The crackling continued until Jacob and Isaac dropped to their knees and cried out, clutching their stomach.

“What’s happening!” Weston reacted, jumping back.

Their veins expunged from their throats, and they squirmed on the ground like earthworms dug from underneath the soil. Their cries were loud enough to echo from the forest’s barrier that enclosed the pasture.

“What the fuck!” Liam yelled when Isaac threw up a vile, murky substance that was riddled with writhing maggots.

Jacob looked at Cheyenne with tearful eyes and sweat bubbling across his face—his pupils were entirely black now.

Mouthfuls of vomit gushed on the dirt around him and began to steam in the cold night when a swarm of scurrying beetles began to escape from the discharged puddle. The scent of sage drew Cheyenne’s attention before Weston saw a blinking twinkle coming from the forest’s entrance behind.

“Guys, what is that?” Weston pointed.

Cheyenne and Liam caught a glimpse of a flickering flashlight held by a tall figure standing next to the trees. Liam peered closer and closer—only able to momentarily focus on the face before the light vanished. Its face was changing expressions from a smile to a frown on pace with the flicker. Liam gasped at the ghastly leather-painted face. Several more blinks went by until Baku locked eyes with Liam and kept the flashlight on him. His discolored teeth glistened with saliva and dripped off his lips. Blood smeared Baku’s chin and neck—his hollow gaze never let up on Liam.

Isaac and Jacob hadn't stopped disgorging their intestinal fluids and insects. The light suddenly vanished.

"We need to get inside, now!" Liam yelled.

As soon as she ended her last word, the entire edge of the woods that lurked outside the property lines was kindled with a magnificent glow of hundreds of flashlights held by the hundreds of cloaked townspeople with bloodied bags covering their skulls.

Cheyenne grabbed Jacob by the collar and shouted at Liam and Weston, "Let's go!" Liam and Weston helped her drag them into the house. Cheyenne closed the sliding door and curtains.

"We need more sage!" She said.

Jacob and Isaac's wails were dwindling to whimpers, words into mumbled agony like their lives were fading away.

Weston rushed to his backpack and poked around inside before tossing a pinecone at Cheyenne, "Burn the tip!" A white string protruded from one end, and it felt much lighter to the touch. She confusedly stared at him before the string ignited and intensified as it led into its core.

"Now what?" She quickly asked.

Jacob and Isaac collapsed to the floor, moaning out for help.

"Put it next to them and stand back!" The fire burning inside the pinecone caused a gentle smoke to expel from its opening but gradually became thicker and released at a faster rate. Cheyenne turned to Weston, "I said we needed sage. What the hell is this thing?"

"Look!" Shouted Liam.

An unusual combination of internal noises ruptured from within both Isaac and Jacob. The smoke made the house hazy, but they could see the two begin to dry heave upon breathing in the fumes.

"It's sage," Weston said as the smell of the smoke reached them.

Isaac held his neck and choked at the regurgitating object bulging out of his esophagus. Cheyenne, Liam, and Weston were stunned. All they could do was watch—there was nothing they could do at this point. The heaving eventually released globs of blood from Isaac's mouth as he finally spit out a tennis ball-sized piece of flesh. He looked at his hands and saw the blackness in his veins that were spread across his arms like tree branches beginning to relinquish their color.

"What is that!" Liam exclaimed.

The blob pulsated as though it carried a heartbeat; each throbbing motion spewed a dark fluid from within itself. Isaac panted heavily in relief while Jacob gagged as he reached into his own mouth and pulled out a string of flesh that was connected to an object lodged in his throat, too. More blood spilled when it made its way into his mouth now, and it splashed, hitting the small pond of Isaac and Jacob's blood.

The sage smoke settled from Weston's pinecone and left the house with only the sound of Isaac's and Jacob's breathing. The color rejuvenated in their faces almost instantaneously.

Creak.

A noise came from the wooden base of the patio just behind the curtains. Cheyenne gave out a small cry before Liam muffled her, "Shh!" Baku's enormous silhouette was outlined by the outside light that was left on. Baku remained still.

They tip-toed across the way while a soft squeak emitted every now and again from lumber loosened with time. The photo of Chaska and Cheyenne caught her glance by the kitchen entrance as she passed by. It was one of the first memories she had when they moved to Seaside.

Look to the moon, as we always have, Cheyenne. Her spirit watches over the beings on this land forever and always. Search for the moonlight in the darkness, and she will guide you.

Weston grabbed the keys from Jacob when they all huddled by the front door. Baku's presence prominently lurked in the same spot. Liam nodded at Weston, and they each gingerly walked to the car as the front door was ajar. When everyone else made it out, Liam looked at Baku's shadow one last time before closing the front door and saw another person next to the clown.

Her lush curls blossomed behind the curtain's covering.

"Nancy," Liam uttered.

Her arm suddenly rose in an unsettling motion as though her joints had rusted. The car's engine turned over, causing Liam to twist his head. When he looked toward the sliding door again, he found no one there.

He kept his gaze fixed there until a scratching noise caught his attention from the shadows of the hallway next to him. A nail against the oak walls dragged faintly. Baku's eyes appeared from the darkness, wide as ever before—looking at him, smiling at him. Liam ran out of the house and slammed the car door shut. The flesh remnants on the floor that had been inside Jacob and Isaac gave another pulse.

Time mercilessly continued on, 1:33 a.m. Their body heat fogged the windshield as they drove down the windy road. Cheyenne's attention was elsewhere—her eyes roamed unfocused about the faintly moonlit vegetation that reached out from the forest.

"Where are we supposed to go?" Weston asked. His hands were awkwardly clenching on the steering wheel while he unevenly accelerated the car, "Everyone's trying to kill us!" Jacob was restless since they fled Cheyenne's house; his stomach throbbed ever so often and woke him if he drifted too close to sleep.

Liam did a double-take at the dashboard, "Weston, we're on E!" The fuel gauge was nearly touching the end of the meter.

"That's impossible," he rebutted, "We had a half-tank when we left. I checked it!" Jacob remembered it being full when he drove it from the asylum, too.

"Fuck, man. We need to find a place to hide for the night," Liam said, picking up the photobook.

"My treehouse!" Isaac called from the back.

He startled everyone with his sudden exclamation. The last they had heard from Isaac came by the sound of him spitting out the creature dwelling inside him.

"It's behind our house, a little off into the woods. We can stay there."

They all looked at one another.

"How would we know where to go?" Cheyenne asked.

"Abraham said it's 300 steps north of the family tree."

Weston pressed the gas and propelled them as fast as he could to Jacob's house. They were only about a mile or so away, and since there were hardly any stop signs out there, Weston was able to let the car cruise to save gas.

The V4 engine coughed out, turning onto Crestwood, the insufficient fuel signaled by sputtering and intermittent surges of power propelling them uncontrollably.

"Park in the woods; we don't know who's there already."

Liam kept a sharp sight on the empty driveway a hundred yards. The SUV made it just off the pavement and into the dirt before completely dying out.

The light post next to the house provided a dim glow while they walked through the timbers. Branches by the thousands stretched over them under the twilight—their footsteps were concealed ever so often by the hooting owl that sat on the Clay's family tree.

Jacob pointed, "There it is."

"Which way is north?" Liam whispered.

Weston's compass spun in full revolutions, searching until it landed in the direction away from the house, opposite to where they stood.

"300 steps, let's go," Weston said.

Jacob's bedroom window reflected the streetlight. He stared into the elongated frame that overlooked the oceanside. As they walked away, the ambient moonlight illuminated a person standing behind the glass—watching them with a grin where all 32 of their teeth glimmered.

Liam counted the steps in his head,

88.

"So, how does it feel being free on the outside now? I mean, besides all the sacrifices and rituals." Weston asked Isaac.

There were several dips that brought them out of sight from Seaside's ground level. Liam clicked his flashlight on.

"It doesn't feel that much different, honestly."

The cold was exhilarating yet brutal as time went on—numbness kissed any piece of flesh uncovered, and their sense of smell was unable to distinguish the various scents inside the deep woods.

"I used to dream of leaving this place, exploring a whole other country or something—find out why I'm even supposed to be here. There's gotta be a reason, you know? For everyone."

No one responded. Liam hopped over a fallen oak,

163.

"But it isn't like that, not even close. The world's an even worse place when you aren't locked up away from everything and all its bullshit. It's all run by the same kinds of sick fucks here. All they care about is themselves, and they'll do whatever it takes to keep things the way they are," Isaac said.

Scraggly vines contorted out of their usual growing patterns and curved the straight-lined path. This unrefined inner realm was a natural deterrent against human innovation—where nature breathed without interruption.

231.

Liam trudged forward, eager to settle somewhere safe. But Isaac's words lingered in his head and were impossible to ignore.

"The shit they're doing to kids here, it's everywhere," Isaac said.

"What do you mean?" Jacob asked.

"A big family, that's what Abraham called it."

Isaac sneered, "One big happy fucking family."

"Man, this just gets creepier and creepier, doesn't it?" Weston groaned.

"There are thousands, maybe millions of them all over the world. Sometimes, a small town might have a couple members or something, but the major cities are usually controlled by them."

"Are you saying there's more than one Wonderland?" Cheyenne asked.

Liam clicked his light off as fast as he could—a whisper hissed across the land. Everyone froze in place. There were sounds of leaves crunching in the distance that had a delayed stop—maybe realizing there were no other noises to cloak its steps.

Liam softly said to them,

"293."

He pointed at an almost unnoticeable object lodged at the top of the tree a couple feet ahead. They heedfully tapped the ground to avoid breaking branches and withered leaves; the unknown footsteps were still muted. The moonlight provided enough sight for Liam to examine a way for them to climb up the trunk.

His hands chafed against the bark until he felt several depressions chipped in. Liam poked his hands in and was able to hold his weight by grabbing a handle that was inside each hollowed rectangle—Abraham had crafted a built-in ladder.

He looked back at them, "There are holes in the tree. We can use them to climb."

Cheyenne went first, then Jacob, Weston, Isaac, and then Liam last. It became brighter as they ascended. The night sky welcomed their emerging faces free of obstructions. Cheyenne pushed on the wood barrier under the treehouse, and it swung open, cascading a spray of dust and small insects over their heads. She coughed while pulling herself up.

There were heaps of rubble and mounds of dirt that had accumulated from the past thirteen years of vacancy.

The treehouse's foundation was fortified through the main branches of the tree that held it in place—the structure molded to the tree as it grew around it rather than being cut into to fit the space. Once everyone was inside, Liam slowly shut the gate, and they each proceeded to peek at the forest floor through the small windows and gaps.

They waited for a resurgence of footsteps from the person following them.

"I don't see anyone," Weston said.

"Shh," Isaac hushed.

A disturbance yielded ten or so meters from the treehouse—an outline of a person calmly walking into the moonlight from the darkness without saying a word.

"There," Liam barely voiced.

A man stoically roamed about without a flashlight, having no apparent discomfort from the brisk temperatures, even with only a pair of shorts and a tee shirt. His head was fixed forward as he strolled through at the same pace as he passed the treehouse and went further into the woods. When they could no longer hear the man, they sat and felt the sudden relief of letting their whole body finally rest.

"We'll hide out here until the morning," Liam said.

Whether it was the fresh air they could consciously now breathe or the safety they felt at this altitude, it didn't take long for their eyelids to droop and their muscles to spasm into sleep.

A few moments had gone by—or many; Jacob couldn't tell anymore in this drowsy state. He heard Liam and Weston snore quietly.

"Isaac?" Jacob called.

He was surprised his brother responded so quickly, "Yeah? What are you doing up?"

"I was just thinking. If there's more of them out there, does that mean there's more of us, too? Survivors?" Jacob asked.

Isaac adjusted himself and stared at the beaming twilight trickling through the cracks in the ceiling.

"Yeah, I think there are."

Cheyenne listened on, unable to fall asleep. Isaac continued, "Only one way to find out, right?"

XX

COME HOME

The early morning birds sang with a choir of species that could be heard far and wide. But it was accompanied by something else that woke Jacob out of his sleep—something not produced from the nature around them. His neck was stiff, and his arm deprived of circulating blood; a cool breeze whisked his curly hair.

The noise came again, a crackle as though firewood were being burnt. This time, it was much closer. It came from behind, where Cheyenne slept.

"Cheyenne?" He called.

Jacob rolled over to look at her and saw someone much larger sitting over her.

"Cheyenne?" He called again, trembling in his voice.

The man turned his head to Jacob. His hands were in her stomach—his mouth gnawing on a raw organ chunk. Jacob's throat muscles clenched like he was being choked; he couldn't generate a sound to wake everyone up. The man continued to chew, his head remaining focused on the open body cavity buffet.

Cheyenne's eyes were opened wide, looking at him.

"Jacob," She weakly said.

He was paralyzed in place, unable to move in any direction.

"Jacob!" Cheyenne began to scream.

The sensation of her intestines moving from the man's giddy fingers. Jacob closed his eyes.

"Jacob! Jacob! Jacob!" She shrieked over and over again.

He felt a hand touch him on his shoulder, and he flinched, looking up.

"Jacob?" Cheyenne asked.

He awoke this time to her standing over his sweating body and to everyone else looking at them.

"Are you okay?"

He felt his heartbeat pound and move his chest up and down. He had to catch his breath, "Yeah, sorry. Just had a bad dream."

They were all groggy, waking up. The sun was barely surfacing the early morning horizon, and the day felt odd, as though they awoke in an entirely new season. A glassless window sniffled their noses, and their heads ached with headaches. The foundation squeaked as Weston stuck his head outside.

"That can't be right!" He exclaimed. Weston tapped his watch repeatedly.

"What's going on?" Liam asked.

"The time!" Weston ran to his backpack and grabbed another wristwatch. He looked at it and paused.

"It's 6 p.m.!" They slept for nearly sixteen hours without interruption. Liam opened Abraham's book for the first time since they were at the library.

One Hundred Locations, by Abraham Clay Sr.

"We need to find Lilith's body before the show," Liam said.

"What are you talking about? Whose body?" Jacob asked.

Cheyenne showed him The Nancy Doll flier that Mrs. Anderson had in her hand.

"Vern told us, 'What is born from the fires cannot perish by it, and Lilith will not stop until her body is laid to rest.'"

He looked at the illustration and shivered at the eerie depiction of Nancy as a puppet. Jacob continued to study the artwork and each grueling detail—the need to vomit nearly came back.

"Are you crazy? She'll kill all of us the second we step foot in there. It's a trap. We shouldn't risk going in there."

Isaac continued, "We're the only kids who know what's going on. We gotta get out of this town and find someone who can help us."

"Nancys still in there. We can't just leave her behind," Liam said, "We're the only hope in ending Wonderland."

He flipped through the pages of the photobook until he landed on the page they were looking for. The painting was that of a sketched seed with broad roots that spread in every direction on the page.

Liam read aloud the page for Abraham Sr.'s *The Seea,*

"We nurture under the sun and lay to rest in darkness until the seed blooms from its branches—for it will watch over us always and forever. We are but seeds to the sky and poachers of the soil."

"The hell does this even mean?"

Weston exclaimed after Liam finished reading.

"Under the sun and lay to rest in darkness. Is he talking about the cove?" Cheyenne suggested.

"He said it watches over us. Maybe it's something that overlooks the town?" Liam said.

Isaac's eyes widened as he looked at his hands, which were once consumed with the same black branching roots that appeared in his great-grandfather's etching.

"No," he hesitated, "That's our family tree."

They wavered as the leaves shuddered against the wind.

"Her body is in the tree."

A day's long slumber wasn't enough to alleviate the restlessness throbbing in their bones. They keenly retracted their steps back to the house under the radiating amber-setting sun. No one was following them this time, daylight exposed the gaps between the trees and made it easier to locate where an irregular sound came from.

Jacob walked beside Cheyenne, "I can't believe this is really happening," he said.

"Neither can I. There's so many things going on, I can hardly remember them in order anymore."

She continued more worriedly, "How's your stomach?"

Isaac was leading the way, with Liam and Weston a couple feet ahead.

"Way better than before. Ever since we left the asylum, it felt like something was getting heavier and heavier in me. And once I smelled the sage, everything went black, and all I could do was throw up."

Jacob looked at Weston, "What was that anyways?"

Weston grabbed a small pinecone from his pocket and tossed it to him.

"I took the sage Cheyenne had and stuffed them in a hollowed pinecone mixed with gunpowder. Glued a strong, rubber top to the opening and voila—sage grenade."

They stared at him in awe of his casual explanation of a homemade spiritual weapon.

Weston turned around when he noticed their silence, "Yeah, we would've been a whole feast for those motherfuckers if it wasn't for these."

Weston unzipped his bag and handed each of them one.

"Use it for emergencies," He gave the last one to Isaac.

Isaac's thumb pressed against the cone's ridges, and he thought about the thirteen years of his life that he had lived with a parasite in him. He could breathe and fill his lungs entirely for the first time—he felt lighter and more fluid in his physical movements, too.

The ocean blue skies contrasted the leafy green bushes that bundled upon every branch of the lush Clay family tree. The colossal oak, whose arms reach was twice the length of Jacob's house, watched them appear from the depths of the forest and into the refined space. The air was still stagnant without flow, which welcomed a rotten taste on their taste buds.

"What is that smell?" Weston said. They surveyed the area, and there was still no car in the driveway.

"Is there something we can use to cut into the tree?" Liam asked Jacob.

"The barrel over there should have a machete inside if it's not too rusted." He pointed at the drum container against the house. The foul stench became stronger over the mulch covering the tree's exuding roots. Cheyenne crouched to look closer at them.

"You really think the body is in there?" Jacob asked Isaac.

He touched the bark that was surprisingly soft and moist, as though it had rained not too long ago.

"Our great-grandfather wasn't drawing roots in that book; he was drawing veins."

He circled the tree, "Last night, when we were throwing up, I saw my veins turn black—they looked exactly like the drawing in the book."

"It will watch over us always and forever," Jacob said quietly.

Liam came back with an old machete that showed rust along its steel edge. He looked at them, "Alright, you guys ready?"

They stepped away and braced for the first swing. Liam struck the trunk near its base and had to use his legs to retrieve the blade caught in the woods. The machete slipped out of his hands when it made contact on the second strike—he looked at his hands and saw blood sprayed on both palms.

Liam's face was splattered with more blood that ejected from the tree. He wiped his face with his shirt and paused before starting up again. The deeper he pierced, the heavier the flow of blood drizzled from within.

"Wait!" Jacob shouted after several blows.

He reached into the newly formed cavity and pulled out the chipped wood in the way.

As he tore at the layer still connected to the tree, globs of maroon liquid flooded out at their shoes.

"Jesus Christ!" Weston jumped.

Once the pressure had settled, Isaac pointed at something a few inches deeper, "What is that in there?"

"Stand back," Liam said.

He chopped around to create a bigger opening. He could feel heat escape from within—steaming over his bloodied face. Liam was drenched, yet the more disturbing detail was the fact that the fluids were warm, too.

"It's her," Isaac said.

Cheyenne felt a chill—Lilith's body was wrapped in a cloth bag, left to rot for all of eternity in the Clay tree. The air became dense, a pressure built with each inhale as though someone was constricting their throats tighter and tighter.

Liam stuck the machete inside and tried to reel her out. She was a weightless collection of bones flung to the outside world once more. The wooly material used to conceal her was discolored with a sickly brown. Isaac used his razor to tear a hole in the bag. The fibers tore away until it was widened enough for them to see Lilith's skull staring back at them.

Jacob broke the silence, "I—I got a backpack inside we can use to carry her."

The words rambled from his lips in haste, his mind racing, thinking about how this dead woman's body was buried right outside his bedroom for all these years.

Cheyenne peered into the forest where the sun descended, "It's getting late, guys."

They had less than three hours until Wonderland's finale.

"Weston, go with Liam and bring her to the kitchen, and we'll get the backpack in the downstairs closet," Jacob said.

He looked at Isaac and Cheyenne, "We keep a spare key on the side. Let's check if anyone's home."

They made their way and left them as Weston called, "Why do I gotta help with the body!" Liam glanced at his blood-doused clothes, "On the bright side, this is already half my costume for Halloween."

Weston glared at him momentarily, "Well, can't deny that. Maybe Jacob's got a hockey mask you can use." They grabbed opposite ends of the bag and walked to the back door.

Cheyenne fluttered down the stairs, "No one here."

The lights were kept off in the shady kitchen. Jacob looked at his dinner plate, which still had his food from last night. Martha's entire feast had been decaying for the past two days and was riddled with colonies of ants and clusters of flying insects.

Liam and Weston laid the bag on the tile. The dense skull clinked on the hard surface.

“Did Vern say anything else about this plan? What do we do when we see Lilith? Chaska said we can’t let her get to the body.” Jacob said, gesturing to Cheyenne.

“We have to reunite her bones to where Lilith was when she died, inside Wonderland. If we run into trouble, we use the sage bomb for protection.” Cheyenne said.

“And then we find Nancy and—” Liam started.

“Incinerate that shit show to the depths of hell.” Weston interrupted him.

Isaac walked to the window and looked around,

“That sounds like a great plan; it really does, but there’s just one problem.”

The moment he opened his mouth, the sound of a thud came from above their heads. Their eyes quickly shifted up at the ceiling as the floorboards creaked as though lethargic footsteps crept across. They looked at Cheyenne—she had a frightened, still face.

“No one was up there.”

The stairs were anything but conspicuous, with a wail of squeaks crying out at every step. All the doors upstairs were opened except the master bedroom. Ambient daylight bled under the small gap between the floor and the door frame. Jacob reached out to grab the handle, but before he could swivel the steel knob, someone walked across the room—disrupting the light at their feet.

Their eyes became wide, and their hearts beat with anxiousness. Jacob’s hand paused until Isaac forcefully turned the handle and kicked the door in. The emphatic collision vibrated the house’s foundation, and in the silent seconds that followed, their breaths were heavy. One of the windows was opened with the screen unhinged.

They inched inside to find no one in sight and no sign of someone fleeing into the woods when Weston looked outside the window. Abraham and Martha's room was a mess, as though someone had broken in and rummaged through their belongings. Isaac peered into one of the boxes that was near the bed's mantle that was filled with Halloween masks.

Jacob started, "Who was—"

"Jacob," Cheyenne stopped him.

The lights that came from the fluorescents in the bathroom flickered, catching their attention. Liam gripped his butterfly knife, and Isaac did the same with his unshielded razor blade. Jacob took several steps closer and then realized there was someone sitting in the bathtub behind the blurry curtains.

Weston hadn't glanced away from the window—he watched a perched owl sitting on the other side of the field, where the woods began. A deep and frightening tone vibrated through the owl's throat.

Jacob smelled an undesirable and pungent metal scent once he touched the half-shut door. His parents' bathroom featured a pearly white clawfoot tub that sat at an angle away from plain sight. The dripping shower head splashed ever so often into a fully filled bath.

"Mom?" Jacob called.

The head above the water remained unmoved. Isaac and Liam were right behind Jacob, and Cheyenne stood where Weston was. He extended his shaky hand over the curtain.

Jacob pulled with all his might—the metal cling of the curtain rings came to a halt. And what was left was a pool of blood with Martha lying in the broth with milky eyes.

Jacob recoiled back slowly; the writing on the wall above her dripped freshly and ran down the turquoise ceramic tile. The light twinkled again over each letter,

COME HOME

XXI

HOUSE OF MIRRORS

An involuntary psychological transformation happens between adolescent siblings when both parents are suddenly gone. A state of shock is experienced in unique ways until a new behavior and mentality is sown into their psyche. One may mimic the protector persona—watching over the other as a father would his son. By contrast, one could regress into oneself, shutting out the outside world or entirely repress and carry the burden the experience bears. Isaac looked up at the forest's ceiling where a flock of birds escaped into the atmosphere—flying to their next destination with only the weight of themselves.

Without their bikes or another car to steal, they had to resort to walking through the woods to get to Wonderland. Time carried on, 7:13 p.m. Cheyenne shivered at the clatter of bones in her backpack when she hopped over a fallen branch or turned too quickly. A steep hill was a climb away until they'd be able to see the circus.

"It's just over here," Liam muttered.

Jacob attentively hiked the tall dead grass—each step, crunching louder than the last. There was a subtle voice of a girl heard when they reached the halfway point. Their faces were afflicted with concern when the voice turned into frantic screams that became louder and louder.

"Nancy!" Liam shouted.

“Liam! Wait!” Jacob called.

Isaac, Cheyenne, and Weston rushed to the top, chasing the two.

“Liam, stop!” Cheyenne yelled.

The higher they went, the more ambient noises they heard. Mechanical gears shifted, and engines roared on, yet what was most noticeably heard were the dozens, if not hundreds, of voices that saturated the girl’s sole-sounding screams. Liam pulled himself over the hill.

He was immediately petrified, gazing over the horizon. When Jacob caught up to him and realized what Liam was startled by, his own movement froze. Isaac, Weston, and Cheyenne came up from behind and looked over the hill, too.

“You gotta be fucking kidding me,” Weston said, shaking his head.

They held their breaths, ogling over the living and breathing Wonderland filled to capacity with everyone from Seaside.

“That’s what I was trying to tell you guys earlier,” Isaac said.

They collectively turned to him.

“Abraham told me that on the last night of Wonderland, everyone in town has to come—no matter what.”

“Then we’re fucked! How are we supposed to get in without getting caught? Our whole town is looking for us!” Weston exclaimed.

Jacob furrowed his eyebrows and squinted at the group of people by the entrance. They each wore masks that concealed their faces and were dressed in costumes covering every inch of uncovered skin. Jacob turned to Isaac, but before he could say a word, Isaac had his backpack open with several masks inside.

"Well, it is Halloween, isn't it?"

Wonderland's neon glowing sign radiated from the arching gates and reflected in their adolescent pupils. At least thirty or forty people were walking inside, adults and children alike, dressed to a tee. It was seamless to settle amongst the crowd with these disguises and gave them the notion they wouldn't be seen or recognized.

A man in a pinstripe suit hollered as the guests walked through the gate. His voice was blaring, and he spoke nonstop, "Welcome! One and all, to the spectacular, extraordinary, and grandest carnival across the land! Trust not what you see from your eyes—tis but a dream of your imagination—tis but a nightmare of your imagination."

The man's face was consumed with black paint and shades of white smeared unevenly. His mouth would open with murky pink gums and yellow tarnished teeth glistening with saliva.

They walked past the man—their lungs ached as they held their breaths. Once he was out of their sight and behind them, he silently turned as they entered the jamboree. He spoke slowly, "Wonderland, dreams of nightmares."

He chuckled. The extravagance of the carnival's atmosphere overwhelmed their senses. Hundreds of people packed within the confines—they laughed, screamed out of joy, and reveled in the countless carny games as far as the eye could see.

The vast flow of guests funneled them into a current that unconsciously pushed them deeper inside Wonderland. As the night sky enveloped the dwindling dusk, the vibrancy and luminosity in every bulb and lighting fixture intensified.

The gleam and glamor of the gyrating Ferris wheel towered over them. Cheyenne squinted at the top, where the ride halted. She became terrified when she saw someone staring back at her—unmoved and concentrating on her and her alone. The person began to wave at Cheyenne, but before she could say anything, the screech of the rollercoaster whirled near them. When she looked back, the seat of the ride was vacant.

It was difficult enough to communicate with one another with the noise, but the masks pressing onto their faces caused their sweat to stick their skin against the rubber interior. Liam continuously peered around for a sign of Nancy yet saw nothing but a myriad of costumes. A stampede of kids ran past them, bumping Liam as they playfully screamed.

"Hey! Watch it!" He huffed.

Liam's anger was swiftly extinguished when he realized who they were running from. Heavily weighted steps puffed small dust clouds from the dirt fields—they turned to Baku, the clown, sprinting toward them. With his hips rotating at every step, each stride he took was long, and his lanky arms stretched out, trying to grab the fleeing children.

A raspy and hoarse voice came out of his throat when he spoke, "Run, children! Run!" Baku came mere inches from Liam and the others until he paused as though he could hear their throbbing heartbeat. He crouched to Liam's eye level and maintained an expressionless face under the ounces of greasy paint. Although they were encompassed by hundreds of bystanders, Liam felt just as he did in the school's bathroom, where Baku had him all to himself. No one uttered a word—Wonderland's infamous clown grinned as blood appeared from behind his teeth and oozed through the slim gaps between each tooth and dripped on the ground. Liam couldn't move a muscle, and the rest maintained their paralyzed stance to avoid drawing any more attention to them.

Baku went into his pocket and held a frayed teddy bear in front of Liam's face—Isaac's childhood toy.

"Baku is watching you," he said as the blood slipped from his lips. He set the bear at Liam's feet, turned to the direction where the children ran, and continued on his way.

Isaac grabbed the stuffed animal, "We need to keep moving. Put this with her bones."

He gave the bear to Cheyenne, "Come on."

The circus broadened the further in they went, showcasing nearly a dozen unique freak show acts illustrated through the posters plastered across the tents and game stations. Many of these performers were mixed in with the walking crowds. Guests clustered around and gasped at the woman who crawled at their feet with legs that bent backward as she galloped about. Whispers and gossip ferried amongst the townspeople when she finally stood from her two hooves.

Chords of a banjo strung behind her by a man whose skull elongated at his crown so severely and sharply that his bone bulged from his skin like a horn. The woman danced to the tune, entertaining her audience. Cheyenne looked on, as did Jacob and Isaac. Weston and Liam, however, were preoccupied with something else.

A small stage was propped in the center of the carnival. On a four-legged stool sat the two boys—twins who were conjoined at the torso. Flash photos were taken in awe of such a creature. Their autonomy was hindered at the shared oblique and hip joint—however their eyes were free to wander the crowd's look of disgust upon them.

Wonderland's central tent was nearing. Cheyenne was mesmerized by the coral and white swirls that left her feeling disoriented the longer she stared.

"Guys, up ahead," she said.

They soon scraped shoulder to shoulder with an influx of people who swarmed around the main path to get inside. It became suffocating as they shoved their way closer. Liam pivoted his shoulders, slipping off adults and kids one after another. He reached his arm back to help Jacob and the others keep up. A single-filed line was the only way to advance.

A hand grabbed Liam's before disappearing into the plethora of bodies. He just caught a glimpse of blonde hair that brightened his pupils, and a sweet scent of perfume left a residue of memories that he promptly recognized.

"Nancy!" He shouted.

Liam let Jacob's arm go and frantically maneuvered to where the girl vanished.

"Liam! Stop!" Jacob screamed.

The girl's lemon curls subtly peeked in the mix of visitors ahead. Liam hadn't looked back for his friends. He had to get Nancy before it was too late.

"Nancy! Slow down! It's me, Liam!" He begged.

The crowd lessened at the edge, leading to another end of Wonderland. The girl sprinted toward one of the stationary rides that was oddly the only one vacant. She stopped at the entrance once Liam made it out of the horde.

"Wait!" He called.

Nancy turned her head and smiled at him. Liam was hypnotized.

"Come on, Liam!" She ran inside the open door with only darkness visible from the outside. Liam blindly followed and ignored the shouts from Jacob, Isaac, Weston, and Cheyenne as they emerged. Isaac ran up the stairs with the others behind. The standing building they were on was separate from everything else in the circus, and not a single soul there seemed to notice it but them.

Jacob was last running up the steps. He glanced around before diving into a sea of darkness that awaited him and his friends inside the *House of Mirrors.*

With each step she took, Cheyenne heard less and less. She felt something in front of her amidst the lightlessness—a door with a freezing handle. She came through into a room bright with sun and warmth. The door's latch clicked behind her and emitted a slight echo. There were large windows against one end of the room, with one that was pushed out, letting in the chirping birds' tune and slivers of sunset.

It was a plain space that housed a person of few belongings. A nearly made bed, a study table, a pair of slacks, and a mirror furnished the room. A sudden chime from a bell strung and vibrated the walls and her chest. The dings alternated back and forth—she ran to the opened window and gazed upon the lost paradise that was Impossible City.

Ruins no more, the city flourished with vibrantly painted buildings edge to edge and freely roaming animals basking in the neighboring pastures. Cheyenne looked above where the church's bell struck nine times total. When she turned around, she saw someone slip into the hallway from the opposite end door. Their stocky physique and neutral-toned clothes resembled her uncles.

"Chaska!" She ran after him, but he was gone by the time she got to the door.

Cheyenne walked towards the church's worship center, where distant footsteps faded. Cheyenne had never seen a place so exquisitely made by man—she saw colors so divine, artwork so flawlessly sculpted and contoured on the ceramic foundation.

The stained glass illuminated the great chapel and the man who sat in the front row with his head bowed. He wore a different outfit than the man who Cheyenne thought was her uncle—yet she felt a subtle familiarity with him anyway. She approached the man; the velvet carpet was colorful in its youth, she noticed. As she crept closer, Cheyenne smelled the ocean. She squinted onward into the beaming sunlight that came in—Impossible City was at an altitude that could allow one to admire the ocean if the trees were regularly maintained.

Cheyenne sat next to him. The man's head remained down—concentrating in a trance-like state. His lips moved intermittently, and incoherent words came out at random.

"Hello?" she asked.

Nothing but his praying thoughts slipped out. The heavy chamber doors opened behind them. Cheyenne thought to pounce to the floor and hide, but the man walked in too rapidly. He was of a tall, slender build with thick brown hair sprawling from his head and face. Cheyenne saw the man before, but only in photos. She looked into Abraham Clay Sr.'s eyes. However, he saw only the seated praying man.

"My, my, Father."

Abraham smirked at him and studied the cathedral's extravagance.

"Surely one who devotes their entire life to the divine is allowed some time for recreation?"

He sat next to him, "Jacy!" Cheyenne stood nearby, still unnoticed by the two. Jacy opened his eyes.

"Is there something I can help you with, Abraham? I'd prefer my time in solitude before the day's end."

He walked to the podium, closing a book in his hand—his eyes avoiding Abraham's. When Jacy noticed the entrance doors, he softly gasped at how dark it had become—as if hours had passed without his knowing. The stained glass windows were now painted black by the night.

Abraham appeared next to him, flicked his zippo lighter, and lit a cigarette. Jacy quickly gave him his undivided attention.

"What is this?" Jacy asked.

Abraham puffed smoke, fully lighting the stick, "You know, that's the funny thing about solitude, Father."

Abraham inhaled and let the burning of the tobacco fill the reticence. His eyes drooped with Jacy's following his, and they focused on the paper sticking out from the book Jacy had placed on the podium. Abraham pushed it aside to reveal it was one of Wonderland's flyers—a flier of *Lilith, The Exquisite Extraordinaii*.

He chuckled, "We always seem to find someone in that loneliness, don't we?"

He ashed his butt on Lilith's illustrated face and violently struck Jacy on the temple with enough force to bring him to his knees. Abraham grabbed him by his throat, "I hope whatever God you fancy shows mercy on your soul—because I, Father, will not."

He whispered in his ear, "Maybe she'll be waiting for you with open arms, just as you had been praying for all along."

He pricked his dagger gradually bit by bit into Jacy's stomach, piercing several organs before twisting the blade. Jacy's screams only made the pain more agonizing as he had to choke for air as the knife dug further in.

"What did you do to her, Abraham!" He shrieked, holding the dagger's handle.

Abraham wandered around the stage, and the eyes of the archangels on the glass followed him.

"Life, death. Do you know what these are, Jacy? These are the concepts by man that only hinder and constrain what is beyond our understanding of what's around us. But you, as a man of spiritual awakening, know that. You and I are not so very different, Father. The only contrast between us is our devotion to what we believe in once our physical bodies decay and all we have left is our spirit to guide us into the beyond."

The behemoth entrance doors welcomed in several more guests cloaked in white robes and bags over their faces, hiding their identities.

"And I choose to side with an eternity of riches and glory, Father."

Abraham smiled at him as Jacy winced, "You son of a bitch! What did you do to her? If you hurt her, Abraham, I'll kill you myself."

He tried to sit up but couldn't with the foreign object still lodged. The uninvited surrounded him, eerily silent like mindless beings unable to feel compassion for a man bleeding to death in front of them. Jacy looked into the pupils of their eyes hidden behind the cloth—golden brown, blue, and green irises stared back at him.

"No, Father," Abraham said. "Death does not fancy me tonight."

He turned toward the door once more, as did the masked mutes; the final guest had arrived—Lilith.

"Go in peace, Father," he whispered.

She lethargically walked the aisle with ash remnants blackening and tarnishing the carpeted floor with each passing step. Before Jacy could speak another word, a second, third, fourth, fifth, and sixth stab came from the others. Cheyenne watched on in horror and listened to the sounds of a man being murdered.

She moved away, inching towards the back hallway. Lilith stood over Jacy's lifeless body now, allowing his blood to puddle around them. Cheyenne's heart beat so viciously she thought they would hear it. The masks were taken off, one by one, and the men and women who were plastered in Jacy's blood began to feast on his flesh. Their chews and bites echoed the church's inner dome.

When Cheyenne made it to the hallway, she froze. When she glanced back, everyone was staring back at her. Jacy's bodily fluids dripped from the men's and women's mouths. Lilith's joyous expression from seeing Cheyenne was met with a gentle wave of her hand that had severe burn wounds.

"Well, now," Abraham said, "Leaving so soon, aren't we, love?"

Cheyenne stood paralyzed—as did everyone in the church—until Lilith lunged at her in a psychotic frenzy. She sprinted through the murky hallway with each step Cheyenne took weighing her down heavier and heavier like she had been running through quicksand. Lilith trailed, crawling on the ceiling within touching distance. Cheyenne saw the door of the room she came out of and burst through—slamming and locking it behind. She heard and could feel Lilith's monstrous pounding, trying to get in. The closet space she came from was opened, displaying the same dark void with no indication of what was beyond.

The banging ceased. Cheyenne turned around and saw Lilith glaring at her with the door broken off its hinges. She turned and escaped into oblivion once more—leaving behind this nightmare and awakening to another.

The resonating abyss that consumed Jacob's pupils dilated against Seaside's bleeding sun. He awoke in a field of grass that had several hills and depressions as far as the eye could see. His attention, however, focused on the dozens, if not hundreds, of tombstones that immersed the town's only cemetery.

The burial ground was a forbidden place Abraham and Martha warned Jacob to never wander off into—to show respect. It was the first time he was inside. The deceased overlooked the ocean as the site sat on a mountain's edge. Jacob walked onward, keeping a keen sight if anyone was there with him.

He read the names of those laid to rest as death festered in his mind. To let go, to not have to be responsible for anything but one's soul moving on. He wanted nothing more than to forget and disintegrate every gruesome, agonizing, and cruel memory circulating in his head.

The temperature dropped with each step Jacob took that brought him higher in altitude. He thought it was a coincidence, consecutively finding that the dead he came across were younger than ten years old, until he noticed the row behind, adjacent, and over in an entirely other section had one thing in common—they were all the graves of children. When he tilted his chin all the way up so that his eyes were parallel to the heavens, Jacob realized the once-gray skies were no more.

It was a suffocating darkness that grew larger as dusk ushered in. It almost began to envelop him when her raspy voice brought Jacob back into the nightmare.

A woman crouched before him—extending her hand out, offering Jacob a single picked ebony rose. The woman's complexion was golden, and her presence gave Jacob a warmth of familiarity—he was not afraid of Lilith anymore. Instead, he was rather relieved he wasn't alone anymore.

A child of the sun, Lilith radiated even with the rain sprinkling over them—she was flesh and more, as Jacob was.

"Without death, there is no peace. Only through one's own will can they truly be," She paused, moving the flower closer to Jacob, "Free."

He grabbed the flower at the stem.

"Be free, my child," Lilith murmured in his ear.

Jacob gazed into her hazel irises, "Will I still remember everything?"

Her hand caressed his cheek as a mother's did when consoling her child, "Only the good memories."

She smiled, turning his head to the four open graves next to him. Jacob walked the aisle now alone. Lilith's apparition had disappeared.

The six-foot-deep ditches were filled with mutilated bodies—ripped open as their organs and flesh were riddled with rot. Jacob's expressionless demeanor hadn't changed while he passed over Isaac, Liam, Weston, and Cheyenne. He barely recognized them; remnants of their faces gave subtle hints, but they reeked of a rancid odor that Jacob was overwhelmed with.

He saw them as free, and that's what he yearned for in this reality.

"I'm going to be there soon, guys," he uttered, continuing forward.

Lilith could be seen far behind him—a standing corpse that now watched Jacob near the end of the graveyard—and the mountain's edge. The rain prominently poured, drowning the dead and any conscious thought he had left.

"Mistress Mary, quite contrary, how does your garden grow?" The rose in his hand wilted as though Jacob had been holding it for hours.

"With silver bells and cockle shells," Jacob's skull locked in place, eyes on the dark gargantuan ocean revealing itself as land diminished with each step. A dozen or so children stood alongside Lilith, wide-eyed and waiting—anticipating a new friend to play with.

The waves bashed against the shallow shore, and the white water foamed over the sharp rocks teething through the water's surface hundreds of feet below. Jacob shivered, but the words slipped soothingly off his tongue, "And so my garden grows."

Jacob was again as he awoke in this place, alone. And while the weight of his twelve-year-old body plummeted to his death, he had never felt more free.

The kiss of death came and ceased. The excruciating pain of his bones shattering against the earth vanished instantly. He felt the cold, dirty tile floor and looked around at reflections of himself inside the *House oi Mirrors*.

His friends were nowhere to be found, and the attraction was as silent as the grave he had come from. It was a decayed architecture, and debris contaminated every corner. Pieces of demolished mirrors scavenged and crumbled beneath Jacob's shoes. He was in a hallway, walking in the direction where a herd of whispers came from.

The mirrors by his side had slivers of space one could squeeze through. A number of slim alleyways appeared as Jacob moved on that stretched a fair distance.

Stomp.

The abrupt force tingled the floor he walked on. Jacob squinted down one of the alleys where he thought the noise came from. A shadow of a figure arose.

Stomp.

This unbearable anxiousness sunk into his stomach when a tall, suited man walked across the other side of the alley. His hands held the skulls of two unconscious children—whose bodies dragged against the reflective glass flooring.

Stomp.

Their skin screeched, following his footsteps. Jacob didn't dare to blink until he was gone. But the man's steps only became strident and more assertive as the seconds passed. Jacob turned his head behind and saw the towering man creeping towards him within arm's length from him.

Jacob darted away, stumbling and bumping off his reflections. It seemed no matter how fast he tried to run or however many turns he made inside the ride, the man appeared no farther away every time he looked back. A hand reached from the darkness and grabbed him, pulling him into one of the alleys.

As soon as he was reeled in, another hand covered his mouth.

"Shhh," Cheyenne whispered.

Jacob tried to calm down and nodded his head when he saw Isaac, Liam, and Weston on the opposite end without their masks.

Stomp.

The man strolled by without hesitation—the loosely swinging limbs of the two children lugged by with him. They tried to see who the two unfortunate kids were, but the man's palms were so massive they covered their entire faces. The footsteps echoed softer until the man was no longer in sight. Liam poked his head out to confirm and nodded at Cheyenne. She leaped out on the main path and led them the opposite way Jacob came from. A gush of wind cooled their sweaty foreheads.

"The exit's up here, come on!" Cheyenne said.

The path became increasingly compact before their shoulders rubbed the glass.

"Fuck!" Liam said.

Jacob could hear the sounds of the circus bleeding through the gaps. Another several turns congested them side by side. The burning sensation of their flesh was an accepted suffering if it meant escaping the *House ot Mirrors*. They inhaled their organs and held them inside their rib cage, nudging through the end of the mirrored maze. Cheyenne grunted, pulling the other half of her body through the glass. She helped Jacob out, and after came Isaac, Liam, and Weston.

"Whoa," Isaac froze.

"What the fuck is this?" Weston murmured.

They looked around Wonderland, where the hundreds of costumed guests now lay on the dirt ground under the flashing neon lights. Before anyone else could say anything, the loudspeaker crackled on and screeched, "Come one, come all! Wonderland's grand finale is now finally underway! See with your own two eyes—the bizarre, the phenomenal, the mystical! The eighth wonder of the world, The Nancy Doll!"

XXII

THE NANCY DOLL

They gingerly threaded through the flood of bodies, an unburied cemetery that lay at their feet as they trudged. Each carcass had just enough space for Jacob, Cheyenne, Liam, Isaac, and Weston to maneuver forward—leading them toward Wonderland's main tent.

The fallen sun escorted the low temperatures in, biting into their skin amidst the incoming twilight. A blaring array of circus music played out of the speakers, but it couldn't fight off the constant static. Their journey inside the stomach of the carnival halted once they were at the grand tent's open slit entrance.

Not a single word surfaced on their lips as Jacob walked inside, followed by Cheyenne and the rest. Weston didn't immediately go in; however, he peered around and retrieved one of the sage grenades in his pocket. He broke the head of the glued tip and began to slowly proceed inside.

A spotlight channeled onto the empty center stage and ever so gently illuminated the darkness cast over the sitting audience. The music faded behind them, and the eerie lull accentuated from the dozens in attendance. Their heads remained fixed ahead; not a single pair of eyes shifted toward the children or acknowledged their presence.

Familiar faces filled the crowd. Priests, teachers, city council members, business owners, doctors, and others of Seaside's community sat idly by as Jacob led his friends farther in. Weston looked at his watch as he conspicuously spilled powder next to him. It was almost show time. They stopped once the stage met them at the end of the walkway—six empty seats were placed at the front row with their names written on each.

Their eyes grew upon the sight of those who sat behind them.

"Mom?" Jacob muttered.

Not a muscle in their bodies twitched. Martha and Abraham continued their deadened stare at the stage's spotlight. Liam, Weston, and Nancy's parents all sat behind the seats with their children's names. Isaac was petrified by his father's bludgeoned appearance. Jacob could still feel the sensation of the swinging hammer that connected over and over again to Abraham's skull.

The last seat furthest from them had Cheyenne's name—where a shady figure sat obscured even with the ambient stage light. Cheyenne moved past Jacob to get a better look; the soundless ambiance emphasized her footsteps—the audience remained still.

Cheyenne gasped and ran to the man.

"Chaska! What are you doing here?" She exclaimed.

His attention didn't divert as Cheyenne shook and struck him repeatedly.

"You can't be here! You aren't supposed to be here! Chaska!" Her voice cracked, "Say something!" But like the rest, Chaska was unresponsive and solidified in his stance. Jacob and the others made their way to their seats. Liam and Isaac hesitantly sat down while Weston led his trail of powder that kissed the fabric edges of the stage's bottom to his chair.

"Cheyenne," Jacob tapped her shoulder.

"I think they're waiting for us to start."

Hard bottoms clinked on the stage the moment Cheyenne let herself down. The ringmaster tapped on the standing microphone before speaking, "Ladies and gentlemen. Children and infants. We welcome you to a realm of imagination. Where wonder consumes the very fabric of logic and rationality. Your consciousness will roam bewitched by your very own dreams and nightmares."

Weston kept his hand clutched on the last clot of powder in his palm.

"In this place, in this time, look not with your eyes, for what you choose to see may be but a figment of your own manipulation. A sight unlike anything you have ever seen before! For the very first time in its existence—I bring to you!" He paused as the tension bred.

"The Nancy Doll, the world's first human puppet!" His last words echoed through the microphone until it ceased, along with the spotlight. The beam re-casted onto center stage, where Nancy's golden locks shimmered under its intense luminosity.

Their jaws dropped as Nancy's head rose into the light. Weston's grip on the remaining powder slipped. Liam's spine tensed up.

"Nancy!" A smile almost escaped onto his face.

She's here, she's still alive!

He thought.

The girl he was in love with was only several feet away. The tailored raven dress contoured to Nancy's figure, the softness in her skin wrinkled by an ecstatic grin; a reunion of twinkling irises was shared between Nancy and Liam.

Paralyzed in their seats, Cheyenne and the others were horrified and nauseous, watching an entirely different spectacle than Liam. With eyes burning with accumulating tears, Cheyenne looked on at Nancy's decomposed body that sat lifelessly on Lilith's lap. Nancy's corpse bounced up and down, turned in various fashions, imitating the bodily mechanics of speaking. She was bound to Lilith's movements as a puppeteer controlled its puppet.

The vile liquids from within Nancy's insides contrasted in the light. A discolored pattern of blotches stained by cherry red blush cracked through every crevice on her face. Nancy was beautified with touches of sapphire and dark yellow around two hollow cavities where her eyes once were.

Liam smiled at Nancy's mirage. She took a breath, "You guys came!" Lilith's voice spoke behind Nancy's body after several moments of quiet. The shrill words came out in awkward gaps, and as though no breaths were taken, "Of course they came. It's your special night, my love."

There was more silence, and a draft brought in the outside cold. The tent was frigid, freezing Jacob's fresh blood as his heart frantically beat.

"How about you tell your friends about that poem of yours?"

The darkness continued, "The one you wrote for them."

Nancy nodded.

"Fly away," She began.

"Fly away, fly away—sapphire skies so plentiful, Ashes of dreams glow embers in a spectacle.

Gone are the youth, vanished without a sound, A yearning desire to be free and found.

Angel's tears rain ceaselessly; a fancy in Hell was more divine,

But even in death, love consumes me with ever so gentle time.

The home I have longed for, her arms welcomed me in, For her eyes were once like mine—innocent and free of sin.

So I say, who's next? Who will come fly with me?

In this paradise, we can be together and rewrite our own story."

The buzzing limelight emanated as Nancy stopped speaking. Liam was at the edge of his seat, giddy and nearly smiling. His short-lived excitement dissolved when he saw Cheyenne, Jacob, Isaac, and Weston weren't sharing the same enthusiasm seeing their friend. Their eyes instead followed Nancy's carcass as it was propped up and moved about the stage by her puppeteer, who no longer hid in the shallow shadows of the spotlight.

Lilith's arm was delved into Nancy's rotting back, maneuvering her weightless body to the words spewing from her own lips. Cheyenne's best friend suffered several days of decay since she died at the cove. The unrelenting and unforgiving cycle of life was put on as a performance, mocking the very delicacy and fragility that human life was.

The audible drought suddenly replenished when Nancy collapsed to the floor like she had been thrown.

Liam ran to her, "Nancy!"

"Liam, no!" Jacob said.

He tried to stand up but promptly felt a hefty set of hands pushing him back down. Isaac, Weston, and Cheyenne froze along with him—their calls to Liam hushed by the cold grips of their parents holding them still. Isaac stared at the ghastly fingers on his shoulder and followed it to Abraham's scaly, mauled face.

"Shhh," he whispered to his son.

Liam squinted under the spotlight, "Nancy, are you okay?"

Her forehead had several bruises and sprinkles of blood trickling down her forehead.

"I'm sorry I couldn't give you the perfect show."

She began to sniffle, "It was supposed to be special."

Liam moved closer to her, "No, Nancy. It was perfect. It was beautiful—you're beautiful."

She touched his cheek, "I can't tell you how much I've missed you, Liam."

In the shadows of the audience, Jacob, Cheyenne, Isaac, and Weston watched on as Liam held Nancy's cold, dead body and spoke to her, but it was only his own echo on that stage.

"We came to get you out of this place,"

Their temples beaded with perspiration, Jacob looked at Isaac and then to Weston—their parents' clench on them hadn't weakened. A droplet of sweat trickled down Weston's clammy hands. His fingers grazed over the smooth stainless steel edges of his zippo lighter—ready to ignite the extended path of gunpowder and sage beneath them.

"There isn't much time, Liam," Nancy said.

She turned behind, where the darkness lurked with no one in sight.

"Wherever Wonderland goes, I have to go with it."

He shook his head, “We can run away like we always wanted to, remember? They’ll never find us again. Not the circus or your parents. Nancy, we need to leave now before it’s too late.”

“Liam, my love, it’s already too late for me.”

She held out his butterfly knife, “But not for you.”

The handle slid into the familiar grove between his thumb and index finger. It was cleaned with a sheen that reflected Liam’s drowsy eyes. Her voice lingered in his head and soon drowned out any other background noise, “In this place, we can be together forever. We don’t need to run anymore, Liam.”

Without anything left to spare in his lungs, Jacob screamed for his best friend to run. The gravity from Abraham pressing his body into the earth now constricted around his neck, bringing his voice to a croak. Cheyenne, Weston, and Isaac soon felt the same crushing choke, squeezing remnants of spit and phlegm from their mouths—while the lighter Weston held had slipped his grip.

Cheyenne tried to pry Chaska’s hands off, but they were clenched so firmly. The adults all shared this dry and unrelenting grasp. Weston scraped at the dirt over and over, trying to scoop the lighter, but his arms were too short to reach where it had fallen.

“Will you come with me, Liam?” Nancy asked.

His eyes were entranced on his knife while the question curated in his mind.

We could be together forever.

“We could be together forever.” She said.

No one will come between us now.

“No one will come between us now.”

Her words coaxed Liam to bring the blade closer to himself. After their breaths were extinguished, the only sounds heard were the desperate stomps and scraps of their rubber soles against the dirt. Martha's chokehold shrunk Jacob's throat by almost half its diameter. Cheyenne scratched at Chaska's arms, leaving sizable gashes. Her fingernails were filled with her uncle's skin. Isaac was nearing a complete loss of consciousness; his once valiant legs were slowly straightening and going limp.

Weston's vision became hazy, and he knew he would soon follow Isaac in the next several moments if he didn't break free. He closed his eyes and let his jaw snap up—the minimal gap he created around his neck was just enough for him to lower his fingers to the ground as his chair snapped at the abrupt force.

Her voice came again, this time more stern, "Liam."

The unevenly sharpened trim that strung the length of Liam's childhood toy grazed his jugular. Waves of goosebumps rose along his back, but he couldn't mentally feel the fear that was physically distressing him. He shut his eyes as a welcoming warmth surged through his veins like morphine rushing through the bloodstream.

Liam smelled pungent, sweet scents. Sweet scents that reminded him of Saturday morning pancakes glazed with globs of maple syrup. A resurgence of Nancy's words came in as a lullaby, "Mistress Mary, quite contrary, how does your garden grow?"

The song rang familiar, but Liam was far from able to make any recognition during his delusion. Sweat dripped, and his hands dampened. Nancy went on, "With silver bells and cockle shells, and so my garden grows."

Streams of salty tears stung Liam's eyes open, and his first nudge back into reality came with a tickle he felt within his throat as though a nerve were pinched. A stiffness overcame his neck that locked Liam's chin in place. He could hardly contain the twitching muscles in his hand as he reached for his neck.

His fingers ascended and descended along the all too familiar alloy casting of his butterfly knife's handle. The warmth now spewed onto his hands—ounces, if not pints, of blood—poured out from his slit throat into a growing pool around him and Nancy's corpse. She lay submerged in his blood, looking back at him with two decayed hollow cavities. His blue irises were tarnished with the dark red oasis, and the heat he felt now cooled rapidly throughout his body.

Weston's eyes bolded at the touch of his Zippo lighter.

A weak snap of the ignitor flared several sparks, but not enough to start a fire. Weston flicked a dozen attempts until the sparing butane finally burned and let out a massive flame as it fell from his hand. Weston's head drooped, yet the fire moved consciously, without his aid—as though it were attracted to the malevolent beings inside the tent.

The familiar buzzing that continuously rang in Jacob's ear ceased when he felt his mother's chokehold release. Their screams filled the tent, the one thing about their parents they recognized. Jacob lunged out of his chair in time to turn and watch the fire consume Martha. Not a goosebump nor a shiver escaped him—not even pity or remorse succumbed as his mother burned.

The demeanor of each and every guest had aged to a collective pain. Grabbing their stomach and scrunching their belly fat were those still not engulfed by the blooming fire. Yet, it was the myriad of moans and shrieks from the charred and incinerated that stole the spotlight.

Isaac and Weston squirmed amidst the clouds of dirt, trying to regain their footing and awareness while Jacob's eyes remained fixated on his mother's, then his father's lifeless corpses exuding a strong metallic odor he could taste.

Cheyenne struggled to pry off Chaska's hands even with the fire creeping—searing up his legs. She loosened enough of a gap to let out an emphatic gasp.

Jacob snapped out of his trance, "Cheyenne!" He gouged his fingers between Chaska's hand and Cheyenne's neck.

"J—J—Ja!" She sputtered.

"Hold on!" Chaska's strength was no match for him. The scorching flames singed away at Chaska's oversized flannel, leaving his torso peppered with third-degree wounds. Jacob's fingers discolored, as did Cheyenne's neck, while the unforgiving flames reached Chaska's arms.

The agony Jacob endured by the flames' first kiss was unimaginable. Milliseconds dragged into minutes as long as the fire imprisoned him. Cheyenne blinked erratically in a spasm under Chaska's power.

Jacob wailed, "Let her go!" A sudden force pushed against Jacob's back, propelling him and Cheyenne out of Chaska's grip. They looked up through the dust particles and saw Weston facing Chaska now—his hands gripped tightly around a broken piece of wood that he drove into Chaska's heart.

His body fell forward without a buckle in his knees or bend at either elbow. Chaska landed in a thump beside Cheyenne—his dying gaze reflected in her still disoriented eyes as she came to.

"Chaska," She barely muttered—her voice trembling through the syllables in his name. He closed his eyes almost in relief, allowing the fire to devour him entirely.

Look to the moon, as we always have, Cheyenne. Her spirit watches over the beings on this land forever and always. Search for the moonlight in the darkness, and she will guide you.

Cheyenne barely heard the roaring wails of the townspeople or Weston screaming at her. It took him all three attempts to get her to acknowledge him, "Cheyenne! Get the fucking backpack!" The backpack coiled upon the high temperatures, melting the material before she yanked it away and extinguished the lingering embers. Watching her, Weston, Jacob, and Isaac, was Lilith across the way. Crouched and beside Liam, Cheyenne saw his dwindling life fading away in a pool of his own cold blood.

Her jaw frantically moved, whispering words into his ears in psychosis as saliva drooled off her lips. They felt the ground shake.

Thump.

The screams lulled ever so gently. Cheyenne's concentration on Lilith relinquished, and she instead joined her friends, looking around at where the gargantuan force came from.

Thump.

Cheyenne went closer to Jacob. Isaac stood and closed in next to Weston.

Thump.

Liam raised his chin towards the tent's entrance, where the slits bled in the colorful fluorescents and where Baku emerged.

"You can end this, Cheyenne—all of it," Jacob said to her, "For Nancy, for Chaska, for all the kids that died because of her, and all the lies our parents told us."

She stared at him and tried to think of what might have been her last word, but all she could do was kiss him.

Thump.

"Go, we'll hold Baku off!"

She looked back at the stage and saw Lilith smiling back at her, her hand weakly shielding vast amounts of blood from spilling out of Liam's self-puncture. Her lips remained still, yet the soft chill in her voice materialized in Cheyenne's thoughts and shivered her skin,

Follow me, my love.

Gravity dragged Liam as though Hell opened beneath, and its demons yearned for his departing soul. Lilith backed away until she slipped through the tent's exit slit behind. Her eyes still on Cheyenne,

Come, Cheyenne.

"Cheyenne, go!" Weston screamed.

Cheyenne ran to Liam, "Liam!" She helped him sit up, his blood gushing into the pond around them.

"Cheyenne?"

She wrapped her jacket around his neck, "Here, put some pressure on this. We're going to get out of here, Liam. You hear me?"

"I was always so jealous of you, Cheyenne. Ever since you came to Seaside and the two of you became best friends."

He chuckled and then coughed as more blood made its way up his esophagus with every completed sentence.

"But I knew you really cared about her. A true friend."

"Liam," Cheyenne said. He was wasting away irreplaceable energy.

"If you see her in there, the real Nancy—our Nancy. Tell her that I love her, will ya?"

Cheyenne watched Liam breathe slower and more deeply until he exhaled for the last time in her arms. She reached behind her neck while tears trickled down one after another and roped Nancy's necklace around him. His eyes were already closed as the owls' sapphire jewels twinkled under the spotlight.

"I'll tell her."

She gave Liam a kiss on the forehead and laid him gently on the ground next to Nancy's corpse. Cheyenne sprinted towards the exit, wiping away her face and fully shouldering the backpack.

A true friend.

Liam's last words echoed in her mind.

This *is* going to end tonight, she thought. And she would burn alongside Wonderland to make sure of it.

XXIII

OCTOBER 31, 1895

The screaming and commotion behind her died off. Any lingering sound that vibrated through the air at that moment withered, and all Cheyenne could acclimate to was the blissful calm that silence brings. Wonderland's mechanical orchestra of rides and stationeries were mute. They appeared only momentarily from a sea of shadows when the alternating fluorescent lights flashed.

Cheyenne walked and peered about, pupils dilating at every burst from every corner. Her solidarity felt odd; however, like someone was watching her from afar.

"Hello?" She called out.

Not a soul in sight in any direction. It wasn't until after she started again that the pricks of hair on the back of her neck elevated. She whirled around and looked down at the little boy staring back at her as an old friend did another.

"Hi, I'm Azazel, what's your name?"

Cheyenne's mouth opened, but words failed to materialize. Azazel's face was saturated with color, his light brown hair shined with the oils of an unwashed scalp.

"Azazel, do you remember who I am?" Cheyenne asked.

He giggled and ran past her, turning into an alley riddled in shadows when the carny lights went dark.

"Hey! Wait!" His steps leaped in meters, distancing himself from Cheyenne while her legs heavily swung, trying to keep up. Azazel waited for Cheyenne, baiting her on his trail. The climate shivered her skin the farther she ran.

"Azazel!" She called out again. The childish game of cat and mouse ended with Azazel facing the opening of a beige tent housing what could only be seen as darkness within. Cheyenne made her way closer to him, lurking and watching him as Lilith would watch her. She muttered his name several times, but he was rooted at what beckoned to him inside the tent. He ran through the slit, leaving Cheyenne alone once more.

The continued reign of neon rays glimmered off her face. Her unblinking eyes floated about. She looked into the tent where he had vanished, "Azazel?"

Her heart sank. His limp arm reached out from within, a relaxed palm that gently curved with subtle twitches in each finger. One by one, Azazel's fingers curled, inviting Cheyenne to come in before disappearing inside again.

A chilling breath quivered in her lungs. She gazed around the silent circus as the lambent forged on. There was a lingering glow resonating in the tent that brought her closer to its entrance. The full moon watched over her, and a warming sensation glided through Cheyenne before she went in.

Two figures at the tent's end outlined as one before Cheyenne made the distinction in their awkward positions. The man's head was buried in the woman's ear, whispering, twitching Cheyenne's eardrums after certain syllables were enunciated. A beautiful vanity stood behind them, its wooden stain lush with sheen conjoined to a dazzling mirror. The intricate oakwood craftsmanship bordered the pentagram frame and continued on by its base counterpart.

She remembered the man in a dream not too long ago, Jacy's brutal death that she witnessed with her own eyes. And as exquisite as the posters illustrated the woman, Lilith was considerably the most beautiful being she had ever witnessed.

Cheyenne flinched.

"Where is she!" A man called afar. The voice trembled the tent and diminished the sense of stillness inside. He went on, "Lilith! Answer me!" Jacy looked at Lilith and then at the tent's exit, where the shouting and commotion became louder. She grabbed his face with both hands and kissed him while the man continued to shout.

"You need to leave from here before he sees you, Jacy."

A breeze mellowed in from the outside, cooling their nervous sweat and curling the paper in Lilith's hand. He put his hand over hers and widened his gaze, "Let's leave."

He grabbed the paper that illustrated her extraordinary persona and otherworldly talents, "After your finale tonight, we'll run away and hide at the cove."

"Jacy, I—"

The clamor was too loud now to ignore, and Jacy ran to the other end of the tent. The man's blaring voice became recognizable to Cheyenne—it was Abraham's.

"Lilith! Where are you!" The front and back slits wavered as Jacy fled and Abraham entered. He paused as an unusual whiff gyrated his glare around the tent. Cheyenne ducked behind stacks of suitcases and moving equipment.

"So, is this how you treat the love of your life? You hide like a frightened child as I shout like a madman out there?"

He walked and stood parallel to her, his attention on the various photo prints and newspaper articles Lilith propped up with her makeup anywhere Wonderland visited.

"Do you remember where we first met?"

Only the resounding reticent at that moment responded to his question. She sat petrified while the cold sweat dried on her face.

"You were a sight to wonder about. There was no one else who could come close to your savory mysteriousness. Especially on that stage."

He went on grabbing an earlier dated photo of them some odd years ago before the countless tents surrounded the central giant. When the circus was but a coalition of freaks that were humiliated everywhere they went.

"You came from absolutely nothing. And I saved you; I saved you all—beyond what your feeble minds could comprehend. Now you're thriving off my relations and people I knew to bring you your audience, special guests, and, of course, all the money they brought in."

He slammed his palms on the dense lumber top of the vanity, "And you sit here and believe I am to be made a fool of!" Lilith's breathing accelerated, and her eyes locked on his shoes, unable to look directly at him. He knelt under her chin where her exposed jugular throbbed, "You reek of him, even with all your fabricated scents and oils."

"Abraham, I—"

A stunning bang boomed in the tent. His massive knuckles connected where her sweat beads had crusted. And from this inharmonious blow, Lilith's body followed his hand's momentum and plunged against the earth with her skin skinning to stop the continued drag.

Howling dogs wailed far off; Abraham waited to see if anyone would come in. No one did. Cheyenne blinked for the first time in a while and nearly forgot she still had to consciously move and stay hidden in this nightmare. Abraham wielded a machete with a blade's width the size of his forearm. Lilith's skull rested in Abraham's hand, tilted back to reveal her most vulnerable point.

The steel blade then settled on her flesh.

"You will be sorry," he said, catching his breath and adamantly gawking at her like a madman, "You all will, every last one of you freaks."

Her epidermis, then dermis, effortlessly ripped against the manmade alloy with the slightest pressure. Lilith winced yet suppressed the scream brewing inside. Her blood ran, drizzling to her clavicle bones, then between her breasts.

"Abraham," She uttered.

His nostrils flared with oxygen as she prepared for death to come for her at any moment. Her eyes closed, waiting—but again, no one came. He let her go and stormed out of the tent without another word.

Lilith stumbled to get a hold of herself upright and ran after him, "Abraham! Come back!" Cheyenne came out of the corner as Lilith went through the slit. She grazed over the same photographs that had been camouflaged with dust and grime at the cove; they were labeled with the locations at the bottom borders of each image: New Jersey, Louisiana, Oregon, Texas, and Washington. Wonderland had been recognized by not only the local newspaper at those stops but, at some points in time, had mayors and elected officials pay visits as well.

Elegantly crafted bottles with unusual groves and indentations stood side by side, each filled with spectrums of the color wheel. It was, however, the smaller framed photographs that veered off between the jar mixtures that attracted her attention. Their happiness plagued each image as the mountains behind them, the oceans, and the forests depicted a point in time where Lilith and Abraham were in love.

Candid portraits, too, were turned away to prevent the seated from relieving the deadened memories. Her stomach quaked. The third and final time Azazel would appear before Cheyenne came by his sepia-printed face in the arms of Abraham and Lilith.

Abraham, Lilith, Azazel—1895

Cheyenne excitedly grabbed the photos around her and realized he was in all of them at various ages. She brought one of the photos closer. Azazel stood in front of Wonderland's grandiose tent—clutching a teddy bear in his chest. Weston's words spoke in her head.

"Seaside was founded in 1882, and the first recorded death came thirteen years later in 1895. Azazel, he died by fire."

If it wasn't for the ruckus outside, Cheyenne would have studied through all of Lilith's life history along the desk's length. A sudden shatter came from outside and startled her out of memory lane. Voices began to argue louder while Cheyenne tiptoed to the exit slit, anxiously peeking out before reentering the carnival grounds.

The smoke fumes irritated her lungs, and the sensation of heat was unbearable. Screams Cheyenne thought came from a dozen or so individuals now begged hundreds. In every direction she turned, chaos reigned across Wonderland. The skies were painted with strokes of gray clouds that birthed from the burning tents. An inferno surrounded Cheyenne, and she soon suffocated at the squeezing pressure as the guests and workers of the circus all attempted to escape its confines.

Carnies escaped their smaller teepees, adding to the calamity, "Please, stop! This is our home!" Cheyenne followed the crying man's voice. The once jolly clown begged on his knees. His belongings, like the others, were all they had to their names—thrown to the ground by bands of burly men who towered over the performers and entourage.

"Do it!" One man yelled to another. Gasoline poured, and matches flicked, scorching the dirt into flames that lingered above gas puddles.

"Everything burns, boys!" Abraham howled. The circus lights dwindled under the rising smoke and golden orange blaze—coloring the night sky along with the moon. A loud snap and subsequent cracking came, turning Cheyenne towards the northern end of Wonderland. One of the tents began collapsing in on itself by the fire weakening its structure inside. However, something else caught her attention.

Standing by this coming demolition and watching amidst the panic of it all was a small boy, paralyzed in terror. Another crack tipped the tent's top, where a dozen lumber poles roped together slipped. Cheyenne darted at the boy when the dense wood fell from twenty or so feet above him.

The ground erupted with dirt, and pieces of split wood ejected into the air as Cheyenne's entire side chafed to break the fall with the boy in her arms. The scene attracted no attention to them. A fiery torching through the circus left many in their own attention bubbles; Cheyenne and the boy were no exception.

"Are you okay?" She asked.

He was unusually calm, breathing slowly with stomachful breaths. His brown eyes were like hers but couldn't conceal the worry worn into his face.

"Are you lost?" He nodded.

She stared at the unique patterns repeating on the ends of his tee shirt.

"Where are your parents?"

"Inside." He pointed to the caved-in tent that still retained a standing portion without its top, as though the Grim Reaper sat on stubs looking back at them. The boy ran into death's open arms.

"Hey, wait!" Cheyenne followed closely behind until the drooping interior drapes and coverings weighed her down to a walk. Wonderland's demise extinguished the further in she went, intimate and isolated enough for her thoughts to freely roam again. The boy's lingering scent lured Cheyenne and her curiosity. She kept both arms extended and swinging about. The fabric maze led to the tent's spacious center, where several men and women were gathered. Coated in enormous velvet robes, their heads bowed to the ground and stayed drooping while Cheyenne entered.

Dim lamps burned wicks of unscented wax, and their shadows danced while Cheyenne realized no one spoke—characters in intermission awaiting its audience to settle in for the final act. The boy's odor came back, hauling her attention towards the barricade of cases that held stage equipment and other miscellaneous material. She followed the aroma until she found him creeping next to a suitcase twice his size, spying on the two women sharing each other's intimate space on the other side. Their sun-kissed amber skin glowed against the tasteless candles.

Cheyenne tried to say something to the boy, "Hey, y—"

A woman's piercing cry came so intensely it squinched her eyes, and the residual echo of her scream remained in Cheyenne's head until she somehow recognized who it was—a voice that mimicked her own but with a deeper tone and raspiness. She turned where the boy looked and saw a woman clutching her stomach as blood poured from it. Lilith's hand was entrenched inside of her—the silhouettes around the two remained bowed in reticence.

Pressure built over Cheyenne's temples, and a numbness swayed from her legs to every muscle in her body. Lilith's spine poised upright, gouging thoroughly into the woman's intestines as blood spilled around them. The woman's neck soon went limp, and the weight of her skull snapped her head back.

"Mom!" The boy shrieked and lunged out from their hiding spot.

Cheyenne tried to grab him, but it was too late, "No! Wait!" Her hand was gripless, weakly scratching the boy's arm as he ran into Dyani's withering arms. Lilith retracted her hand from within her, letting gravity have its way with her.

"Mom, wake up!" He cried.

The saffron in Lilith's irises followed the boy's movement, but nothing else on her body moved or so much as pulsated. Dyani's blood dripped from her straightened fingers. Her disciples were one and the same, motionless and now kissing their foreheads onto the ground.

"Please, Mom," His voice cracked.

She was barely conscious but had enough adrenaline coursing her veins to see the boy and painfully smile back at him, "Chaska, my baby. I love you."

The sun left a radiating sensation on his arms and neck as he sat in the shade. Nature's perfume wafted over newly birthed flowers that boomed in the humid breeze. Jacob remembered this day and moments when time seemed to stop. The sounding bell caused an overwhelming flow of students rushing to leave Woodland Crest Academy, but not all were so eager to depart. Weston's candy wrapper crinkled while he took another bite, "It's a dumb question in the first place. I mean, what are we actually learning from this?"

"I dunno, but we need to get an A on this presentation, or I'm grounded for the whole fucking summer," Liam said.

The sugar-coated snack mushed in Weston's mouth while its plastic joined the wind and stopped at Cheyenne's boot. Jacob smiled at her. They hid under the metal bleachers across the school's football field where no one would see them.

"There's something more to this question, guys. Mrs. Davis wouldn't make it that easy." Jacob said.

"What's the question, again?" Nancy asked behind him.

Jacob gulped at the sight of everyone staring at him—waiting to continue the scene. Although the climate was warm, goosebumps drifted down his back. Jacob stumbled over his words, trying to remember their group project. His hand held a paper that he hadn't noticed before.

His friends waited for his answer, and so did the spring breeze. He read slowly, "The question was—if a tree falls in a forest and no one is around to hear it, does it make a sound?"

The normality returned as a pulse from a heartbeat.

"Well, it's a yes or no answer, right? What else do we say? Does she want a poem about it?" Weston said.

Nancy laughed, and Liam joined. Cheyenne grabbed the binder paper out of Jacob's hand.

"I don't think she wants a yes or no. I think the question doesn't even have a right answer. The tree falling happens either way, and so does the noise. Maybe it's just realizing things will happen whether or not we're here to listen to it." Jacob finished as their unusual blank stares resurfaced like actors concluding their roles' dialogues while a stillness unfolded—one that could only be felt amidst a dream.

Thump.

The bulky step came from the bleachers above, squeaking decades of age at every step.

Thump.

Dust and particles of sand washed over them. Jacob closed his eyes.

"Jacob! What are you doing? Jacob!" He could hear Weston yell.

But in the darkness was where Jacob recoiled, hoping to continue this pleasant memory with all of his friends. Crow's feet wrinkled across his temples as the glorious sunlight vanished.

Jacob eventually pried his eyes open. Weston and Isaac looked back at him, pressing their index fingers on their lips. The space they were in was confined with abysmal space for three.

Thump.

Jacob felt debris drift down on his head. Gaps between the wood blackened by Baku's footsteps. His breath fastened.

"Shh," Isaac whispered to Jacob.

The stage's flooring shook in its foundation. They hid beneath because they had nowhere left to run. Jacob hadn't been able to remember how they had gotten there in the first place but before he had a moment to think, Weston screamed,

"Now!" He and Isaac kicked the prop legs that held up the stage's trapdoor. Crashing to their lower level was Baku, who let out a grisly wail that sounded like several voices crying out from inside him. Confused at first, Jacob then realized that Isaac and Weston weren't hiding from Wonderland's terrorizing clown—they were waiting for him.

His sense of fear dwindled as the two circled Baku. The apricot radiance from the fire still ravaging the tent left a shining bronze on their smoke-kissed skin. Their clothes were battered, and the wounds they had were coagulated. Jacob had similar features. His time spent daydreaming felt brief, yet time bled in an ooze in this reality.

Isaac took the unrefined wood block he had in his hand and bashed it against Baku's skull—the bone-crushing sounds reminded Jacob of his father being beaten to death. The onslaught continued.

Weston caught his breath and stretched his lower back, letting out a groaning relief, "So, it turns out the sage bombs bring these motherfuckers into a kind of physical form here where they can actually feel pain."

Thwack!

"Hey, Jacob, you okay? You look like you're gonna throw up." Weston asked in a calm tone.

Jacob couldn't stop staring at the amount of flesh and bits that became airborne after Isaac's swings.

"Anyways, that physical form is very susceptible to these wooden rods."

Thwack!

"Very susceptible!" Isaac reiterated.

"How long was I out for?" Jacob asked.

"A good thirty minutes. You sure you're okay?"

"Yeah, I'll be fine. Have you seen Cheyenne yet?"

A final thwack retired Isaac, and he joined the two.

"No, we haven't been able to leave this tent. Baku was the last of them." Isaac said, scraping the clown off his wooden weapon.

"Last of them?"

Isaac glanced at Weston and came closer to his brother to offer his hand, "Come on, we aren't out of the woods yet."

They emerged from the stage's ruins to a bounty of rotting bodies around them. An overwhelming musk of metal scents met them—the resonating heat of the fire left some bodies scorched, leaving only the putrid and rancid odor to breathe. The once sold-out showroom was left decimated, "Like I said, very susceptible," Weston said.

They made their way over to the front row, where Jacob saw his mother looking back at him with stale eyes. Weston tried to make out what remnants of his father were left and of Chaska. Isaac kept watch for anyone still moving.

Jacob looked at Weston, "You guys killed everyone?"

"I mean, technically, Lilith killed them all, right?" He glanced at Isaac, "But yeah, everyone. We had to unless you prefer sticking around here for all eternity."

Weston moved closer to the tent's center, stopping where Liam's pool of blood began. His slain corpse crookedly lay next to Nancy's, their fingers separated by an inch or so.

"Maybe this is a dream too." Jacob said, "And we'll all wake up any second now."

He fought back aching tears amidst the sullenness and the soulless eyes that Liam looked back at him with, "I'm sorry we couldn't save you, Liam. I'm sorry, Nancy."

"We did everything we could, Jacob," Weston said.

Isaac's attention, however, fixated on the fire spreading outside of the tent. He squinted through the burned drapers where shadows of the flames moved. Faint screams and cries followed. He gasped as it grew louder, "There's people outside."

Their eardrums beat with the tune of the frightened voices. Jacob turned to them, "Cheyenne."

Isaac gripped his stake and walked closer to them. The wood was stained wine, and hunks of flesh were caught in the hundreds of splints in the lumber, "We need to get you something to fight with," he said.

Susceptible.

Jacob thought.

The steady breaths of sage brought him to a more lucid state where he started to comprehend the vast amount of deaths surrounding them. A fury of emotions stirred inside him like a vortex, yet it was only anger that resonated in his consciousness. This fathomless grudge brewing, welcoming any violence he could release onto this damned place.

"How many grenades do you guys have left?" Weston asked. "One," Jacob said.

"I got one, too," Isaac followed.

"Okay, we each have one left. Put them in your top zip."

Weston took his backpack off and moved his last sage bomb to the small compartment just below the backpack's handle. Jacob and Isaac did the same until a skittish movement came about in the mutilated audience a few feet in front of them. Amongst the ashes, debris, and bodies, the flux continued.

Weston and Isaac spread out around the clatter, dirt kicked up following a weak, gasping breath. Jacob kneeled to grab the remnants of a stool and carried it over his shoulders. His anxious hands danced up and down the smoldered edges, finding the best end to wield. Isaac stood opposite Weston, both peering into the smoke with ferocious eyes that were as focused as a starving man's glimpse of food.

The gasps grew more profound, anxious to escape the rubble. Isaac and Weston's faces drew a hysterical look that Jacob noticed before anything else transpired. He saw they, too, had digested any fear they had left being in Wonderland. And the everlasting ache in their bellies subsided into a dying desire to kill everything in the circus.

Jacob looked at his new weapon and then back at them. His sweating palms dampened the wood.

Are we just as evil as our parents? What are we? Humans? Or animals? Or savages?

He thought. A hand reached out from the pile of corpses, coated in soot that stuck against open wounds. The man's slurred words materialized and echoed what was left in the tent's structure.

"Ch—Ch—Ch—Ch," he stuttered.

The man was powdered in ash while he lethargically crept towards Jacob like a cockroach nearing death. Isaac came closer, arching his spine back to gather as much torque, before bashing the man's head into smithereens.

"Ch—Ch—Chey—Chey," Drool spilled over his trembling lips.

"Just do it already," Weston said, losing interest.

"Cheye—" With a sharp inhale, Isaac descended the baton of death from above, ignoring the man's last slurring words.

"Wait!" Jacob leaped at his brother and tackled him to the ground.

"What the fuck are you doing!" Weston cried, now keeping his bat ready to swing at the man.

"It's Chaska! Look, the real one!" They all looked down at him as he rolled over on his back, revealing the stake that Weston drove into his chest.

"Chey—Cheyenne, where is Cheyenne?" He finally said.

Jacob stood up and met Chaska's gaze, "She's out there, Chaska. She went after Lilith."

He roared in disbelief; the puncture wound hushed his anger to a babbling whimper, "No, no!" Chaska's belly gingerly expanded and released, "She can't face her alone!"

The excitement outside grew louder.

Weston kneeled next to him, "We brought Lilith's bones back here to lay it to rest. That's what will stop all of this, right?"

"You fools!" Chaska grabbed him by his shirt's collar for a brief moment until he felt the wood stab deeper into his already pulverized organs.

"Get off of me!" Weston yelled.

Isaac and Jacob pulled him away from Chaska.

"You mustn't—you mustn't let Lilith wield her bones."

"Why? What will happen?" Jacob asked.

The tent's open slit flashed person after person running in all directions as the fire raged onward.

"Tell us!" Weston demanded.

"The curse shall be lifted, and Lilith will no longer be bound to the thirteen year cycle or within Seaside—she will bring chaos and suffering onto this world, tormenting all of mankind until the end of time."

His diminishing glare fell onto each of them, "Your blood and that of your children, your children's children, hereafter will only quench its thirst, and generations forward will suffer as did your ancestors."

They were speechless at the burden weighing on their shoulders.

"There has to be a way to break the chain," Jacob said.

Moonlight cast through the open roof and settled in Chaska's irises.

His demeanor became calm, accepting his dwindling mortality. He reached for Jacob's hand and held them between his—placing a dense object small enough to conceal within his palm. Chaska tightened his grasp, "A balance is kept within each of us, a battle between good and evil—the sun, the moon. Without this, we are weak and vulnerable to the forces of nature. Lilith's power comes only from the moon, this dark void without light to keep the harmony. And as the moon waxes and wanes, so can her strength."

The charred infrastructure fractured against its own weight above them. Chaska coughed words back to Jacob as black fluids expelled his lips and trickled onto his chest where the stake was embedded. He pulled Jacob in, "In the eyes, through the skull,"

A final crack echoed over their heads. Chaska's hand went limp, and before Jacob could say anything, Isaac yanked him in the opposite direction.

"Watch out!" The silent sounds of weightlessness followed before it brought down hundreds of pounds of wood, crushing Chaska moments later. The influx of screams was all they could hear now; a horizon on fire was all they could see—illuminated by the nearing full moon. Weston and Isaac looked about. Hundreds, if not thousands, of guests scattered about.

The fires had extended far into the distance, wide enough to circle Wonderland's perimeter and trap everyone within. Jacob's hand unclenched, and the shimmering from Chaska's quartz dagger sparkled in his eyes. He looked at the moon and the passing clouds smudging its celestial beam.

Wonderland's grand tent was decimated to oblivion, and the hysterical guests began to permeate its perimeter. It was too late to run from them. The mob closed in on Jacob, Isaac, and Weston, but as they came closer to them, Jacob noticed their eyes focused on everything except them.

Weston grabbed his grenade, "Jacob, you ready?"

Isaac swung his weapon over his shoulders, "Hurry! Light it up, Weston!" Isaac said, "Wait! Don't do it; they can't see us!" Jacob yelled at the two. In the span of three seconds, the mob swallowed them. The countless shrieks were deafening, yet the only physical sensation they felt came from their shoulders brushing against theirs.

"Get out of my way!" A man shoved Jacob aside, and he tumbled onto the dirt like a ragdoll. He tried to stand before getting trampled until his right hand crumpled a paper as he pushed himself up. He smoothed out the old and filthy flier. The colorless print read from his lips, "Lilith The Exquisite Extraordinair."

Her petite body was centered and reminded him of Nancy's before he saw the date bolded on top.

October 31st, 1895

He was afflicted with confusion and disbelief. Jacob stood to the passing crowd. He studied their features, their facial expressions, joint movements, their skin tone—they weren't dead, this wasn't a dream. His eyes widened.

"Excuse me, excuse me!" He yelled at passersby. Not a breath was lost as they continued on, ignoring him. A boy, who was about a hair shorter than Jacob, looked away from him when they made eye contact.

"Hey! Stop!" Jacob grabbed his arm, "Can you see me? What is this? What's going on? Answer me!" He cried.

The boy was dressed in hand-me-downs several sizes too large for him. He flinched at Jacob's interrogation questions until his mouth opened, and he rambled soft words Jacob could barely hear. The crowd lessened around them, with enough room for Weston and Isaac to see the two, "Night after night, these fires chase us, stopping only once the last of our bones have melted onto this land."

The three of them listened keenly to the boy, "We live and relive tonight for all eternity. This nightmare that feeds on our suffering and pain."

He stopped, "All I want is to die, to be free from all this."

The boy's face brightened when the sudden wrinkles across his face formed a smile, and he emphatically clutched Jacob's arm, "But you're here to save us, right, Jacob?"

The boy's fading grin curled to a frown as his skin's crevasses were more defined now like he had aged a decade at that moment.

"Tonight..Tonight is…," The boy's arm rotted to a yellow-brown color that spread throughout his body. The disease then blistered his skin to flakey bits that flew away into the air. Death had kissed a milky white wax over his pupils, "Tonight is the night when the bad men hurt Wonderland." He crumbled away with his last words to Jacob. An explosion detonated with enough force to level several tents in their vicinity.

"Jacob, get up!" Isaac pulled him.

They joined what was left of the fleeing horde until the unsettling noise of a beast roared from the mouth of a man—and that man was Jacob's great-grandfather.

"Upon my last breath, this damned circus will burn! Every structure and soul that remains shall be welcomed in the loving arms of our beloved Father."

The hellfire rained down on them and colored the moon red as though the rapture had begun.

"What is this guy's fucking problem, man!" Weston shrieked.

Jacob turned to them, "It makes sense now. He hid Lilith's bones to keep her under the curse!" "As long as they were able to make the sacrifices, they'd have another thirteen years of peace," Isaac added.

The howl of a woman drilled their ears, stopping them in their tracks, "Cheyenne!" Jacob turned to the only standing tent that stood about fifty yards away. He led his brother and Weston, firmly clutching Chaska's quartz dagger that began to glow under the blood moonlight.

XXIV

DREAMS OF NIGHTMARES

Dyani's soulless eyes stared back at Chaska with a discolored gaze, "Mom, wake up! Say something!" He wept.

Dyani's skull hung off her shoulders, and her arms released to her sides, revealing the carnivorous incision left by Lilith's gaunt fingers.

Chaska's scratchy adolescent cry came from Lilith clenching his temples. She sat atop him, and her claws walked about Chaska, face—squeezing and kneading his flesh like dough.

"Let me go! Get off me!" He yelled.

Lilith finally showcased an emotion that embellished her face, and it was that of nirvana. The fresh and young blood throbbed Chaska's veins. Her rotten teeth gleamed with saliva, and in a nimble motion that brought his begs to hysterical screams, she crept the edge of her finger down Chaska's forehead to his eyebrow, to his eye—tearing his skin.

Idle no more, Cheyenne dashed at the two from the shadows. She ran past the cloaked men and women whose heads never so much as lifted an inch from the ground. Goosebumps riddled Cheyenne, and an almost aching sensation grew the closer she came to Lilith. She closed her eyes and barreled between them with all her weight—sensing, only Chaska's bony body brushing hers as though the woman had let go just before.

She scrambled to her knees and picked her brother up, “Chaska, run!” Cheyenne forced him towards the tent’s open slit. Blood had blended in with his tears as he applied pressure to stop the bleeding. He looked back at Cheyenne, perplexed, wondering who this stranger girl was. She screamed at him again until an agonizing sting mounted on her right calf.

The fingers that were inside her mother’s torso, which was just slicing her brother’s face, had now found their way digging into Cheyenne’s leg. Her cries brought Chaska’s focus back on her while he was halfway out of the tent—and thunderous enough for Jacob to hear in the distance.

“Come on, she’s somewhere here!” He said to Isaac and Weston.

Cheyenne flipped over and used her untouched leg to push away from Lilith. Each finger gradually retracted out of her calf while Lilith retained the same maniac smile. She hovered over Cheyenne, stagnantly and breathless. Lilith allowed her to squirm away as her hand slipped out.

Cheyenne hobbled to the exit without stopping or looking back. The woman of Wonderland raised her hand above her head, letting Cheyenne’s blood rain down onto her. Her ridged nails scraped with friction against her tongue, slicing herself as her hand descended.

The heavy fabric tunneled ahead until Cheyenne was finally through. Her pupils shrunk against the bright fluorescents shining from above and saturated by the peculiar green grass at her feet. The open field was no more. Cheyenne paused as the artificial lights only illuminated the straight-lined path of grass in front of her. What strayed off the beams and rays appeared as pure darkness—empty spaces in an endless void looking back at her.

Where am I?

She touched the blades, twirling and bending them at their stems, feeling their natural fluidity. Cheyenne stood when footsteps shuffled on the grass ahead. The once lost color in the boy's skin had returned now, and his clothes seemed new; his vibrant white collared shirt belted inside iron-creased slacks that planted into two shiny dress shoes reflecting the lights.

"You're here," Azazel said. The ends of his words lingered, echoing in the endless space surrounding them.

"We've been waiting for you. Come with me," He extended his hand to Cheyenne. The air she breathed brought a thirst for more. With each cycle, Cheyenne's tension was released from her muscles, and this calming sensation blurred her lucid state. An unbalanced balance between the two soothed her as she trailed Azazel's momentum. They stayed in the light, turning corners where walls of shrubs would eventually direct them through a maze.

The grass crunched on, and Azazel's hand was ice cold, but Cheyenne could focus only on the marvelous vegetation that sprawled the farther in they went. Exotic crops grew rich in dazzling luminous colors that she had never seen before. Roots and branches thickened with age in peculiar angles while their flowers bloomed in a spectacular rainbow.

Although the hint of a breeze was not present, Cheyenne watched the pedals waver side to side, coil inward and out-flowing with the garden's flow. She let go of Azazel's hand and approached a plant the same height as her. Blue specks glowed on the flowers' magenta pedals and emitted a low buzzing sound. The particular pattern of the flowers entranced Cheyenne with its uncanny allure.

She reached her hand to touch the bulb but stopped as her palm opened. The unique pattern Cheyenne recognized on the pedals was identical to the creases on her palm. The size and shapes of the neighboring plants now resembled parts of the human body to her. Bones stood as their foundations—limbs were curled vines and branches she saw. A horrifying and surreal depiction of the cycle of life was before her.

Azazel's voice startled her, "She's waiting for us." She held his hand once again, and they moved along the labyrinth. It was a sound that would attract Cheyenne next. The subtle drips beaded on soil and drummed on leaves. A pause ensued before it rained on again. Azazel turned one last corner, and they entered a magnificently vast space after being confined to the narrow pathways.

The droplets spilled from the other end by a person standing with their back towards them.

Cheyenne's lips trembled, "Nancy?"

Azazel crossed the grass field as the lamp atop hummed on and glistened the girl's curly yellow hair. The endless herbage pulsated, and the grass wiggled before several strands began to curl onto Cheyenne's shoes—gripping them in place. They sprouted from the soil, flopping and squirming about like they were suffocating underneath.

Cheyenne reacted in a series of gasps,

I'm dreaming, I have to be dreaming!

Cheyenne's voice delayed in her own head. The grass clotted in on itself, clumping together mimicking fingers—then hands that tugged her lower.

"It's time," Azazel said, shifting Cheyenne's attention back onto him.

She looked down again. Her shoes were freed of any restraints, and the grass appeared as it was before, fluctuating with the garden's rhythm.

"In the absence of darkness, only can the light free us," he smiled, "I'm glad we had a chance to meet, Cheyenne. Go to her." as he looked at Nancy, who continued to pour water out of the everlasting spout—unattentive to their presence. In no time at all, Azazel walked back towards the opening they came through.

"Azazel, wait," Cheyenne shrugged her backpack off and unzipped the main zipper. She held his teddy bear, smiling back at him.

"I think this belongs to you."

His cheeks turned red, and he was overwhelmed with joy, "Teddy!" Azazel ran and hugged the plush toy that was ripe with decades of age—dust clouding over its mohair strands.

"Thank you, Cheyenne."

That elation never left his face. A grin from cheek to cheek, child-like and pure. It continued even as he made his way out of the garden and into the maze, lost once more.

The dribbling droplets beat on. Cheyenne gathered herself and lifted one shoe off the grass before stepping forward. The garden exhaled in a wave that ran through the plants and field as she strolled to Nancy.

The watering can wavered in Nancy's arm, sprinkling over the magnificent magenta and emerald bulbs that were enormous in size—retaining their bodily similarities. Their vines reached where thousands of petite flowers bloomed in clusters. A twinkling sheen glazed Cheyenne's irises as Eden blossomed before her, yet a stench wreaked of rotten meat in the air.

When just a few inches separated the two, Cheyenne stopped. Nancy was wearing the same clothes she was killed in. Turquoise streaks permeated through her stainless white top and matching nylon shorts.

Her face eluded Cheyenne, however. The water spilled on where a bush of roses bloomed away from the garden.

You left me, Cheyenne.

She saw Nancy's corpse under Seaside's blissful sunset, piercing her thoughts in a series of flashbacks.

Her voice came again, this time more profound.

"Aren't they beautiful?" She asked, smirking at Cheyenne.

"Nancy, you—" Cheyenne stuttered.

Nancy was without lacerations, and her once-gouged eyes that haunted Cheyenne now stared back at her. Nancy's flawless skin softened under the fluorescents like she was lathered in a cloud of flour.

Nancy crouched to meet the isolated roses, "On and on, forever, these roses will grow their little hearts out. Rooted in eternity, they're fooled by the freedom that comes from what their petals can only touch."

She looked at Cheyenne, "Never to see the entire garden. Until—"

She pulled a stem closer and coddled the flower's head in her hand, caressing each delicate leaf, "They're freed."

Her fingers twitched, and a bone-chilling snap left the rose decapitated. Murky slime spilled onto Nancy's hand from the split ends, and the rose slowly lost its vibrancy.

"You see, Cheyenne? Only in death are we truly free."

A blue aurora hazed above the dying flower.

"Eternal souls without bounds, before its time to return home."

She made her way to the garden's center, where a congested concentration of plants was cultivated. Cheyenne remained but a watching spectator following her best friend before she knelt again where a patch of soil was without any growth. She dug a shallow grave and rested the rose inside.

A pair of pruning shears laid by her side. Nancy grabbed them while keeping her eyes on the freshly transplanted flower, "And the cycle continues on."

The sharpened blades that were used for precise cuts and were strong enough to tear through branches tickled the creases in Nancy's palm. Her skin peeled open, gliding apart with ease as the sound of the carving filled the silence.

Nancy made a fist over the rose, "Do you think God stays in Heaven because he lives in fear of what He created?"

The rose rejuvenated with color, absorbing her blood and sprouting a stem several inches high.

Cheyenne finally spoke, "I think in the end, our universe unfolds how it will; no one has a voice. No one can run from it."

Nancy stood rubbing blood between her fingers, "Except here. In here, even death is inescapable—hidden. No, stolen from all of us. Lilith trapped our souls here; every single man, woman, or child who died by her doing will never leave this place until someone takes hers."

"Her soul?" Cheyenne asked.

Nancy wore an indifferent expression, "Give me your hands."

She extended hers to meet Cheyenne's. Their hands repelled from each other the moment they touched

"You're not dead! How did you get here?" Nancy asked.

Cheyenne took a step back to examine herself, "No, I don't think so." She tried to recall where she was before here, "I don't remember dying."

Nancy smiled, "Because it's not your time yet. It's really you, isn't it?"

Cheyenne couldn't contain her unbound happiness in seeing Nancy again, "And it's really you."

They embraced each other in a hug. Cheyenne slightly recoiled again from how frigid Nancy's body felt while Nancy envied the warmth Cheyenne still clung to.

"You're going to free us, Cheyenne."

"How?"

Nancy's eyes drifted behind Cheyenne. She followed her sight. The garden echoed her weeps, cries that came familiar to Cheyenne.

"Please," A coat of ash gowned the woman as she knelt over another body, a smaller vessel no more than three feet tall.

"It's—" Cheyenne started. "Lilith," Nancy said.

"Go to her, and she will show you everything you need to know."

Burnt flesh contaminated Cheyenne's nostrils the closer she came. The weeping continued rhythmically.

"It's not my fault," Lilith whispered.

"Shh—shh—shhh, my baby, it's okay."

She carried the weight of her dead son, Azazel. His corpse swayed lifelessly in her arms, smeared with third-degree burns, and scorched black skin. Cheyenne sat next to her, now seeing her face that was dried by the flames, charred where her bones defined.

"He did this. He caused this—bringing this evil into the world. My baby. My sweet boy," she strayed off, rambling off incoherently, and then reverted back to words of hatred.

"Who did this?" Cheyenne spoke.

"A filth of a man, the scum so selfish, blinded by his own arrogance. The devil's slave—Abraham." She bawled more. "He made me do it, I had to, I had to do something. I couldn't let my baby boy die!" Cheyenne recoiled and bumped into Nancy.

"The demon promised she'd be with her son again. And that they would remain in each other's arms for all of eternity. Away from the world's suffering and pain." Nancy said.

Lilith stood, leaving Azazel on the grass. Cheyenne remembered the boy's smile moments ago but now only saw his rotting carcass looking back.

"But it was a lie, all of it. I was left here to rot in this never-ending chain of my dreadful memories. Then, one by one, more children came. And with each new addition in this lost world, the garden grew wider and wider."

The garden's many exits around them bolded its ceaselessness.

"How do I stop the demon?" Cheyenne asked.

Lilith's eyes lit up, her chestnut irises saturated with color as her pupils dilated.

"The soul," she hissed.

"One must ingest all the memories it carries. The deaths, the despair, and the agony it feeds on—all will converge to wallow in your mind forever."

She opened her arms to Cheyenne and spoke comforting words, "Oh, my dear. There is nothing to fear in this world or the next."

And then, Cheyenne heard Chaska's voice speak through Lilith's lips, "As equal is day is to night, the balance we maintain is solely determined by each of us. We cannot live in the light without suffering through the darkness."

Cheyenne swiveled to Nancy; behind her were the children who made their home in this purgatory. They watched Cheyenne in a way where she realized it wasn't of malignant intentions but of hopefulness.

"It looks like our time is running out," Nancy pointed at the grass where elongated leaves vigorously sprouted in bunches. Cheyenne sniffed the air upon detecting a potent smell that made Nancy chuckle.

"What is this?" Cheyenne asked.

The earthly odor dwelled over their heads, and the grass soon elevated with pungent white smoke. Memories flooded Cheyenne's head. The afternoons spent snuck away at Impossible City with all her friends, where they were free from their worries and problems.

"Just like the old days, huh? It's Jacob. He's trying to bring you back, Cheyenne," Nancy said.

"What's going to happen to all the lost souls if the demon goes away?" Cheyenne paused, "Where will they go—where will you?"

Nancy grabbed her hand, and Cheyenne felt another chill, "The same place we go to when we dream. Wherever we want. Goodbye, Cheyenne." she said. The smoke beneath them steamed into dense clouds, Cheyenne's eyes teared up as the sage filled her lungs. A numbness crept over her, and she soon lost sensation of everything.

"Goodbye, Nancy." She whispered back.

Lilith came between them and guided Cheyenne through the smoke, "Demons are not natural to our world; they can only exist in a host's body. And if the vessel is damaged, not viable—they'll find another to latch onto."

The fumes cleared the field, and several children stood watching them. An engraving was etched into the soil, Wonderland's crescent cross. A shiver slithered down Cheyenne's back. The children were immaculately dressed in traditional school outfits, yet their hands were sullied with dirt and mud from clawing in the symbol.

"The mind and body represent a duality that can be separated at our will. Unbalance the balance, and it is from this split that will beckon the demon to you."

Lilith centered Cheyenne over the symbol.

"End this nightmare," she said.

The children looked on wearily with eyes begging for rest. Cheyenne looked back to Lilith and the unforgiving past that vilified her. She was once the most beautiful spectacle in all of mankind. Divine in nature and acquaintance of the darkness. But here, Lilith was but a mere product, manufactured in this hell—left to rot forever.

"I will," Cheyenne said.

Lilith stepped closer to Cheyenne until they shared the same air space. Lilith settled her palm on Cheyenne's stomach and gripped her skull with the other hand—Lilith's thumb rested over Cheyenne's third eye chakra point.

"Breathe."

The landscape rumbled in a low growl beneath them, and a current discharged from where Cheyenne stood as though water rushed through the garden. Her eyes drooped, and the sensation of sleep swept in until they finally closed. Sage inhaled into her lungs at every mouthful and left a residual amount of heat that developed where Lilith's hands were.

When Lilith spoke again, it was with words unbeknownst to Cheyenne, an ancient dialect beating to her heart's throbbing. The darkness Cheyenne visualized in her mind as she remained paralyzed morphed the flat plane into a motioning kaleidoscope of geometric shapes. They reigned in various colors, reappearing and vanishing.

The intricate patterns stretched larger as a force dragged Cheyenne closer to them. Her physical senses were overwhelmed with an immense fluctuation of colors and vibrations until, in a single moment, everything went black, and the color spectrum bled only a bright white light.

It was mother nature's aroma that Cheyenne recognized first before the blistering heat or her cold sweat soaking her clothes.

Move.

Cheyenne's brain understood the command, yet she couldn't muster a physical reaction. She opened her eyes with a series of blinks, still dazed. The demon knelt over her, wearing Lilith's existence. It sculpted the essence of the original woman of Wonderland. However, the drifting fires encircling them kindled imperfections across the demon's face.

Where joints bulged, so did flesh, stretching beyond their means. Sew marks that kept the rotting skin tight were vivid to Cheyenne now.

Move!

Cheyenne's eyes rolled down to her chin as she became increasingly claustrophobic in this incapacitated position. The length running her chest to her lower naval sat Lilith's bones. Her skull sat on top of Cheyenne's stomach, looking back at her with hollowed, aged cavities.

She saw her backpack ripped to shreds next to her before the ground throbbed, and a subtle orange glow emitted below them. The demon opened its eyes with a snarl. As Cheyenne screamed in her head, the demon's mouth opened, looking at her with a smile that exposed hundreds of teeth. Her heartbeat magnificently thumped with every beat pulsating her up and down, accelerating as it crawled over her. A rancid odor overwhelmed the sage and smoke concoction, leaving Cheyenne to breathe in the fumes exuding the demon.

The blood moon bled onto Wonderland. The celestial rays faintly kissed Cheyenne, then came a stinging rush of sensations agitating her joints and coursing her veins. The demon's shriek drilled her ears, but she was now able to turn her head and finally shout for Jacob.

There came a hesitancy in the demon's pounce; its glaring yellow eyes focused in on Cheyenne's throbbing neck—on the shimmering necklace Cheyenne wore. The arrow pendant that was once Dyani's seared the demon's hands upon touching its sacred metals as it did when she first encountered the fiend in Wonderland. The moonlight faded amidst scattering clouds, as did Cheyenne's vision. She blinked and furrowed her brows, awaiting death.

The demon's vicious snarl repelled any nearby smoke, and it plunged where Cheyenne's throat was exposed, where the most blood would spill when bitten.

A thunderous bash deadens any ambient noise. Cold sprinkling droplets splashed Cheyenne's face, sending shivers rattling her spine, yet she felt her heart continuously beat. She was still alive.

Her eyelids weakened with eagerness, and when she opened them, the demon was frozen in place. Its unhinged jaws that were wide enough to swallow Cheyenne whole had relaxed to a slight ajar. Jacob stood over the demon, pressing Chaska's quartz dagger deeper into its skull. He let go and stepped back, panting wildly in the stillness.

The liquid that splattered on Cheyenne melted over the demon's—a cascading gooey black paste branched to its chin as it fell to the ground and convulsed. Weston and Isaac came running to them from behind Jacob, "Holy shit! Are you guys okay?" Weston said. Jacob helped Cheyenne up, "I think so," The demon squirmed some more.

Isaac kept his weapon ready to swing, "Is it dead?"

There was a warmth flaring inside Cheyenne, a fever that radiated all over. It was staggering, suffocating, and it distracted her from realizing she was walking toward the demon.

"Cheyenne, what are you doing?"

Jacob exclaimed. The demon gestured weakly, swinging at the lodged crystal, and moaned in agony with each fading breath.

"I know how to end this," They looked at her dumbfounded.

"I saw everything. The night Wonderland was attacked, Abraham's rage, Lilith's curse, the townspeople part of it all. Nancy and the lost souls in all of those records are trapped inside of this demon."

She paused.

"They killed my parents here. In Wonderland, my family was once here years ago. And they were slain in cold blood."

“Cheyenne,” Jacob started.

“I have to do this; otherwise, this curse will go on and on, and this carnival will keep coming back no matter how many times we burn it. I just need to find the beginning—when the demon possessed Lilith.”

The circus grounds were vacated, with only the endless flames emanating around the perimeter, never protruding into the outer forest as though a force kept them confined. Cheyenne pressed her right palm onto the demon’s stomach and looked at Jacob, Isaac, and Weston, “Hold the body down.”

In the absence of darkness, only can the light free us.

Her full weight sat on the demon’s chest, hands and fingers gripped identical to how she remembered in her hazy dream. Each breath brought a tranquility that allowed her mind to escape the physical world. The boys struggled to constrict the demon’s convulsions. Jacob cradled its head with both arms, keeping it as still as possible for Cheyenne to maintain her thumb against the demon’s forehead.

She wondered if her dream could have been a hallucination after all when nothing began to happen until a sharp pressure mounted her third eye chakra point. The blackness Cheyenne perceived with closed eyes dissolved into a frozen wasteland shrouded with fog. An unforgiving Hell.

She floated above an ice-covered lake that filled a basin in the middle of a great forest. The water under Cheyenne darkened with corpses trapped beneath. Flashbacks rang into her head relentlessly; their faces, their names, she somehow remembered them. More and more bodies sailed by, each that Cheyenne could recount for.

Then she recalled their screams. The delusions became sinister in nature, and Cheyenne visualized torturing them with her own two hands. They were mauled, ripped open, and eaten alive without the luxury of death to release them—left to suffer over and over again until reincarnating back here. Cheyenne mutilated them not once or twice, but thousands of times without end. These cruel memories weren't of her own doing, she thought. They were the demon's poisoning hers.

The fleeting thoughts were so intense and all-consuming that Cheyenne hadn't noticed her body changing. Black feathers ruffled through her skin, and her bones elongated several feet. Cheyenne's face dramatically protruded outward, and a beak developed into place.

Her peripheral vision expanded beyond human capabilities, and she perceived everything around her, including the gigantic smoke clouds fuming out of the forest, causing half the sky to hemorrhage red.

"I see it," Cheyenne said aloud, where Jacob, Weston, and Isaac could hear her from the outside, "The beginning."

She flew there instinctually and found herself looking over Wonderland. The desolate tents and stationery smoldering, all but one person lay in the center of the flames. The woman, Lilith, who was burned half to death, held her hand stretched out with the circus's mark cut into her flesh.

Cheyenne closed the distance between them until she saw Azazel burned to death, cradled in her arms. She begged the dark skies for another chance to live, offering her soul in return. Lilith cried repetitive phrases in another language as she opened and closed her fist—leaking blood to the ground.

The demon within guided Cheyenne's wing towards Lilith—to the memory of the moment it was summoned and freed from Hell and welcomed into our world.

"Cheyenne," Jacob said with worry in his tone after seeing the struggle Isaac and Weston were having holding the demon.

It was becoming lucid to Cheyenne's intrusion in its mind. The ground shook, and fissures parted through the soil around them.

"I'm almost there," She whispered. Her wing unhinged, reaching closer as Lilith's prayers grew louder. Weston grunted, "I can't hold on much longer!" And then, the demon's eyes opened and glared at Jacob.

"Cheyenne!" He yelled. Cheyenne grabbed Lilith with her monstrous talons, and upon their touch in this underworld, she was fed a feast of atrocious recollections.

The children's salty blood tasted on Cheyenne's tongue, their murmured last words heard by her ears. What the demon lived, Cheyenne felt as though from her own recollection. Ninety-one years of terror reigned through Seaside, the decades digesting into her psyche within seconds.

Jacob peered at Isaac, who stared at Weston, looking back at them, "What's happening?" Weston asked.

As still as statues in a thunderstorm, the demon and Cheyenne were motionless in their physical union. Scarlet skies above reflected the moon's red brilliance; the shadows around them marveled in the dimness.

The demon's memories decelerated as it brought Cheyenne closer to the present day. She regained, for a moment, the autonomy of her human body and saw that her hand was back to normal without feathers. Her brain ached with a resounding throb while she stood in Seaside's town center next to the treasured oak tree and its whistling leaves. There was no one but her here, not a sign of life anywhere to be heard.

Her first step forward scraped a paper that was one of hundreds scattered around. The thick card stock suggested it was a flier of some sort, and when she flipped the white end over, she was not only correct, but the ad was for a missing child—Cheyenne. Her monochrome photo was a splitting image of herself, yet she didn't recognize where this picture was taken.

A breeze curled several fliers by her shoes, and Cheyenne snagged them to find they were all copies. When she raised her chin, the compound city buildings and their shades of bland gray were gone. The sunset over the horizon wavered in the ocean's waves as they crashed against the shore.

Seagulls shrieked by and vanished in the blue sky. The sand glittered with golden minerals, and the air breathed unpolluted. The cove remained a glorious and marvelous hideaway, beautified by nonhuman intervention. But Cheyenne only saw the daunting hollow cave looking back at her.

She squinted when the smoothness in the shadows within disrupted. A figure lurked with the sun scarcely brushing over their brown skin. The figure vanished before Cheyenne blinked. An immediate weight followed that rested over her shoulders; this sensation was so excessively burdensome it forced her to heave oxygen to breathe.

She could sense the presence of something behind her. Glittered in golden trinkets and hatted with the skull of a ram, the creature towered three feet over Cheyenne. Its face wore a woman's cinnamon complexion that soaked in the daylight. Its torso was that of a human, and limbs fostered from the flying beast of an ancient era. The wind ceased to flow, the mirage halting in the silence.

"Such a treacherous path for one so young," Its voice was dainty—a snake's linguistics, unnaturally elongating every syllable.

"Tell me, little girl, why dost thou seek death so willfully?" Cheyenne's lips quivered.

The vast sea beside them hadn't a single ripple over its surface, "The life I once had was stolen from me. It breathes only in ruins and scattered memories now. My loved ones, friends, and the innocent were tortured by you, demon—until they were no more, forever lost in their own nightmares."

The demon spoke again, "In desperation does one's blood bleed deliciously. Wouldst thou wish to see them again and forever?"

"Yes, I do."

The eternal sun pinned in the sky shined on.

"Wouldst thou give anything for this gift?"

"I would," Cheyenne said. Her pupils expanded, and she could feel her heart beat again.

"Face me, child." She did as she was told and gradually turned around.

The mind and body represent a duality that can be separated at our will. Unbalance the balance, and it is from this separation that will attract the demon to you.

As the beast ogled from above, Cheyenne was in awe below. Beauty was accentuated in its physical impossibilities; perfection riddled its symmetrical jawline that defined so very tightly, lush lips full of blood, and eyes immense like a toy doll. A disproportion levied from the woman's petite cranium and the rest of its body—one so disturbing, Cheyenne grew nauseous the longer she looked.

It spoke more, "Submit thyself to me, and all your desires will come to fruition, my child."

You need to get closer to its head.

"I submit, demon," Cheyenne said.

The whites in the demon's eye tarnished black, and its lips opened, revealing a graveyard of teeth decomposing from its black gums. It descended to meet Cheyenne, close enough to smell her.

The final words said by the beast slithered out, and a chill shivered Cheyenne, "Death is only the beginning."

Tears glossed over Cheyenne until they cascaded in streams. Her vision became blurry, and she had to peer through the fluids. Sunlight shifted to moonlight and back again as the celestial pair oscillated the sky from day to night. Gravity subsided without Cheyenne's notice, and her heels lifted off the sand. She could feel her heart sing once more, yet each pulse that came thumped from her stomach instead of her chest—robustly after each contraction.

It was neither her detachment of comprehending time and day nor the demon's asphyxiated cackle that maintained Cheyenne's attention. Her stomach beat again.

Thump. Thump.

Then twice as fast.

Thump—thump. Thump—thump.

And then the sequence went on in an erratic manner while the demon laughed harder. The ground was nearly ten feet away when

Cheyenne looked down at her dangling shoes above the pool of blood that dripped from her soles, bleeding onto the soft sand.

It trickled from Cheyenne's stomach, where the demon's hand pierced her fresh—where it remained encapsulated within her internal organs.

Thump—thump.

With an open palm inside her, the beast clasped its claw and caused a vibration to quake throughout Cheyenne's body—imitating her heartbeat. The pain settled in and sang from Cheyenne's mouth as billions of nerve cells relayed distressing signals to her spinal cord, to her brain—the sensations became insufferable.

Nirvana possessed the demon, and a look of pure bliss came about the woman's face as Cheyenne's delicious cries echoed the cove. Her cries rippled waves across the stagnant ocean.

Closer. Cheyenne, closer!

She dug her nails into the beast's feathered arm, pushing deep enough to wield a tight grip. The laughter ceased, and the relishing demon was stunned and expressionless as Cheyenne pulled herself into its wing—dredging the stab inch by inch. Her legs soon lost sensation, and she could sense the numbness creeping through her arms.

The demon raised Cheyenne closer to its salivating mouth.

Almost, just a little closer.

Nothing supported her dangling neck from swaying about. The demon's breath tickled Cheyenne's nose, "And so my garden grows."

Now!

Cheyenne's spine erected in a fierce jolt, and before the beast could react, Cheyenne clutched its skull with both hands. The horrific memories she had relived before in the dream with Nancy had returned. Of the damned who once walked this earth under God's grace only to be cheated in death and tortured for all time's end. Of the malicious beings that were cast out from His kingdom—these memories lingered longer and longer until she realized they were not floating thoughts anymore. They were her own and now trapped in her mind.

The ground around them ruptured, and the fires jittered as though the soil exhaled. They exchanged looks, "What's happening, Jacob?" Isaac asked.

"I don't know."

He grabbed some loose dirt and twiddled a small clump between his fingers. Instead of crumbling and falling back down, the bits and clods floated before him. And soon thereafter, the entire field vibrated until it brought levity to any lightweight objects that were not bound.

"Guys, Cheyenne!" Weston cried.

An outline flared over her forehead under the crimson moonlight—the tormenting crescent cross branded Cheyenne's skin. The tension gripped in her hands showed no sign of fatigue.

From Cheyenne's knuckles through her arms and body, a sudden flood of toxins blackened her veins.

"What do we do?" Weston shouted.

Isaac tapped his pockets, "No grenades."

They were shrouded with shock, unable to do anything but watch.

"Jacob!" Weston repeated. "I don't know!" He yelled back. An owl's hoot waned Wonderland along with a faint breeze that caught Jacob's attention.

As equal as day is to night, the balance we maintain is solely determined by each of us. We cannot live in the light without suffering through the darkness.

This was the moment Cheyenne had long awaited. The memories of the Lost Ones spurred in her mind, bearing the weight of their hopelessness, despair, and misery—their regrets, secrets, and last words spoken. She suffocated to find her own thoughts amongst the dead. She took a breath; the demon remained tranced under her grip while its wing rested in her stomach.

That breath exhaled from Cheyenne's lips into their reality, where Jacob noticed.

"Cheyenne? Are you there?"

She continued to take stomach-full inhales until a powerful vibration concentrated at her chakra point. Each cycle brought Cheyenne lucidity, and her mind wandered no more. All but her eyes felt detached from her body, and the everlasting energy prominently resonated through Cheyenne's cranium. As she furrowed her brows with eyes wide shut, a peculiar muscle flexed aside her temples, and she experienced a remarkable sensation, like her soul shifted from her physical body.

The clouds had dissipated in the heavenly sky, but its moon still bled feverish rays. Neither a blink nor word was shared between Jacob, Isaac, and Weston—only the haunting buzzing in the background along with the suspended objects floating about. The contaminant poisoning Cheyenne's veins spread past her arms and surged through her body like the roots of a tree. It painted her face so much so that Cheyenne became nearly unrecognizable to them.

Each breath now waned softer and softer until a hush rippled Wonderland and the cove. The ringing ceased, leaving them halted in this soundless purgatory. Cheyenne's eyelids rapidly fluttered to the rhythm of a waking nightmare. Jacob leaped and skidded on his knees, bringing him next to her and Lilith's body.

"Cheyenne! Can you hear me? Wake up! Ch—"

"Jacob, the moon!" Weston said.

The scarlet atmosphere above dissolved and revived the twinkling starry night behind. Creatures lurking within the woods could be heard again in an echoing symphony, along with the freezing Seaside wind. The pearl moon beamed over Cheyenne whilst casting a hazy fog upon the carnival.

Gravity returned the moment Cheyenne opened her eyes.

She spoke weakly, "J—Jacob?"

She wiped away the tears, blurring her ability to see, and saw the horror on his face. A nauseating spin sickened her stomach. Isaac and Weston came closer to them, "Cheyenne, your eyes," Jacob said.

Her fingers rubbed together like an adhesive stuck in between them. Under the bright moonlight, she saw her hands stained with blood. As more tears bled down her cheeks, she looked up to the moon, and the blackness in her veins gradually retraced, as did the blood's saturation in her eyes. The nausea lingered inside; however, the memories of the Lost Ones were inert—buried distant within Cheyenne's subconscious. Their deaths and suffering weighed on her, but their souls were imprisoned no longer.

They're free—you're free now, Nancy.

Cheyenne exhaled, "It's over."

Lilith's body lay lifeless, her rotten flesh deteriorating, bones liquefying to a paste spilling onto the dirt—as it should have done so nearly one hundred years ago.

Jacob helped Cheyenne up.

She turned her head around, "Where's Liam?"

They all hesitated. But it wasn't because of the guilt that detained their tongues or the realization that Liam was Wonderland's final victim. The earth again quaked, shaking them off balance, and fissures ripped the earth open, broad enough to see lava flowing to the surface.

Cheyenne cautiously took a step back before flinching further away when a hand reached out from beneath and wrapped over Lilith. Incoherent whispers hissed words that came from the lips of hundreds, maybe thousands. A second, third, then too many to count, sprouted through the soil and dragged the decaying corpse below.

The crevices had displaced enough to swallow them whole, yet they stayed to watch as the woman of Wonderland drowned down the depths of Hell. There came a subtle calmness after she vanished—a moment of clarity in a nightmare just before waking. A gut-wrenching cry deafened their ears.

"Isaac!" Jacob yelled. The undead arose, latching onto his brother's ankle with a vice grip while magma scorched Isaac.

The three rallied together to pull Isaac away. His screams enticed an awakening, a graveway, an army of death—unearthing beneath them.

"Pull harder!" Weston said. Its grip loosened only when Isaac's skin ripped away, peeling from the severe heat. They stumbled backward once he was freed, and Cheyenne fell to the ground. The seismic activity rumbled the forest's floor like a waterbed.

The tents, stationary games, and rides shook before they, too, began to sink.

Jacob picked Cheyenne up, "Come on!" They bolted through Wonderland, searching for its exit—the neon lights twinkled a gorgeous rainbow of synthetic colors from any remaining fixtures amidst the ashes. The landscape combusted at the rising lava, and it was nearly impossible to hear what Weston was shouting at them. Cheyenne looked back to where he pointed and saw figures rise from the soil—bodies covered in black sludge as featureless mannequins.

Their ghastly voices painfully shrieked. They moved almost with the purpose of escaping the depths below rather than chase them—decades, maybe hundreds of years under Satan's bounds, freed to roam God's world again. Jacob, Cheyenne, Weston, and Isaac, nonetheless, veered past and hopped anything moving on the ground. Each step they took barely grazed the creatures' reach as they infested the land.

Their paths skewed and separated them a considerable amount of times until they sided next to one another, shoulder to shoulder again. The circus was abandoned, and not a single guest remained as they escaped Wonderland's ruins.

Wooden stilts anchoring one of the gigantic tents collapsed and tumbled toward Jacob, "Watch out!" Isaac pushed him out of the way before its impact could demolish him. Smoke and dirt clouded them in a massive engulfing, yet the exit's blinking arch lights were lustrously calling their names. They ignored the particles caught in their eyes or the fragments irritating their lungs after every gasp.

"We're almost there!" Weston coughed.

Jacob made it out of the milky clouds and slid over loose rock bits that propelled his heel toward the back of his head. The pain was nonexistent until the sizeable gash in Jacob's forehead seized his sense of balance. He started back up, wiping his drenched face, but fell once more when something held his leg in place.

A distorted voice moaned his name, "Jacob, Jacob, Jacob."

As he was laid on his back, Jacob burrowed his nails into the warm earth to twist himself around. He shivered when their eyes met again. The muck only partially covered the creature's face and revealed most of its beaten, skinless flesh amongst the black vile—enough to paralyze Jacob from crawling away.

"Dad?" The opaque haze hid Jacob from everyone's sight.

"Where is he? I can't see him anywhere!" Cheyenne panicked.

A fog marooned above Wonderland after its decimation. The larger structures were nearly consumed, while anything under twenty feet was already submerged. The outskirts of the carnival where the lush forest reigned was a placid lull, motionless and seemingly hindered any noise coming from within the jamboree's reach. Cheyenne, Weston, and Isaac were hardly amiss to the calmness that came in the nocturnal night; the rejuvenating fresh pine air flowing through the tree also brought in the untainted taste of the ocean.

The sludge spread to Jacob's thigh like an ever-growing leech. It consciously separated from Abraham's arm, and every inch of Jacob the disease touched incinerated his skin.

"Everything my family has built in this town—you've ruined, Jacob," Abraham said.

Jacob tried scooting away with his other foot but immediately felt the third-degree singe immobilizing both his legs.

"Killing you will be worth the eternity spent in hell, my son."

Jacob sunk halfway into the ground, screaming for his friends as only the moon gazed down upon him now. The ooze reached Jacob's collarbone, and he raised his chin until his neck strenuously bent backward—he cried in agony. Abraham laughed, dragging his son lower, "Death will welcome you with open arms, but I won't."

Jacob, at that moment, wondered if his fate would be no different than the hundreds of children massacred over the decades, and his soul would be one imprisoned for all eternity with his father, never to experience life by his own will, journey the world autonomously—to be liberated from his family's stalking shadow.

The slime had infiltrated his mouth and caused him to uncontrollably gag as he sank with only his hands above ground. His eyes closed for the last time, and he welcomed death's swooning darkness. Abraham's laugh was hushed while the dirt buried his son's eardrums. It wasn't before Jacob saw a white light and sensed his body refrained from descending when he felt someone clutch his hands.

Jacob rose from below, resurrected in an unholy baptism, able to breathe the air again. His frantic coughs were dry, producing, but the phlegm lodged in his throat and the rancid sludge taste no longer on Jacob's tongue. He was unbound from his father's grasp, and once he brushed the dirt impeding his ability to see, Jacob saw a familiar pair of battered sneakers by his side where the fissures sealed, trapping Abraham beneath.

“Maybe, next time, we just go to the movies instead of a carnival,” Liam said with his hand reaching out to Jacob.

The moon had cast an angelic glow that gave him a soft paleness in his complexion. Jacob was reeled to his feet as the diminishing tremors battered on. Abraham was gone without a trace of him left around them.

“Are you really here, Liam? I saw you die back there.”

Liam smiled at his best friend and stared off where the stationery *House of Mirrors* had erupted, fading into the underworld.

“Who says you can’t live after dying?” He asked.

“You need to get out of here before it’s too late, Jacob. They’re waiting for you on the other side.”

He reached into his pocket and sprung open his trustee butterfly knife, “A whole world is waiting for you out there,” Liam closed the blades and put it in Jacob’s hand, “For your future son.”

“Liam, I—”

But as soon as Jacob looked up from the shiny metal, Liam had vanished. Jacob wallowed in the reticence and lonely ambiance—his lifelong friend was gone before he could say one last goodbye. The inferno bled onto the surface, and a series of explosions stunned him back in the exit’s direction. He climbed over the cratered landscape and was able to see Cheyenne, Weston, and Isaac just outside the gate.

Mother nature embraced the return of one of Her own as Jacob crossed under the daunting fluorescents humming above his head.

Wonderland, Dreams Of Nightmares

Cheyenne hugged him with all her might, “Jacob! Where did you go? We thought we lost you.”

A sense of relief was voiced in his words, a steady breath where time could not be felt nor rushed—a sereness quilting them outside Wonderland's demise.

"Liam saved me."

They looked at him, stunned.

Jacob looked at Cheyenne as though their memories were somehow synchronized.

"How did you do it?" He asked her.

"Lilith showed me how to break the demon's curse. Without their memories and souls to keep, there is no Wonderland. All of them, the ones that died since 1895, they're all free now,"

Weston turned to the desolate field behind them where the last earthly structures melted away.

"And now, time has come back to reclaim what should have perished a century ago,"

Twilight emerged, painting the navy atmosphere a gory violet as the sun birthed upon Seaside. Ash whisked in the winds above a muzzled cemetery; Hell had sealed its lips, bringing the damned back into its inescapable depths.

"Come one, let's get out of here."

Jacob said. He inched closer to the towering redwood embraced by daylight at their peaks.

"Where are we gonna go?" Weston asked.

"Anywhere we want. There's a whole world outside of this town waiting for us; let's go explore it."

They followed Jacob into the condensing woods until Cheyenne stopped just before entering and took one last glance at Wonderland.

Amidst the ashes were the Lost Ones looking back at her—prisoners no longer. A smile creased across Cheyenne's face; she hoped she'd never forget this moment.

Chaska waved at her in the distance as he stood next to Dyani. Liam, Nancy, Jacy, and Azazel soon appeared—freed from the nightmarish depths of Wonderland. The sight of Jacy raising a flask, its curling grooves and floral filigree mirrored Vern's precisely, as if they were two sides of the same coin all along. The revelation hovered in the air as dozens of children gathered behind them. The clues, hidden in plain sight, suddenly coalesced into a realization that Vern and Jacy were, in fact, one and the same.

Lilith emerged last among them, enveloped in a warm embrace from Jacy—the man who had, and would forever, love her unconditionally—transcending the confines of time and space. As Lilith reunited with Azazel, she cast a glance at Cheyenne and waved. The relentless torment of reliving their deaths lost its grip as Lilith embraced the consoling warmth of their shared reunion, a balm to soothe the wounds of the past.

Cheyenne waved back with tearful eyes, knowing their souls would finally be at peace. And as she saw the dawning sunlight wane the full moon away, they, too, vanished from Wonderland.

Wonderland

DREAMS OF NIGHTMARES

Intertextual Echoes of Salvation and Judgement

A Literary Analysis of Wonderland

By: Joseph Fredrickson

Abstract

In examining the novel *Wonderland*, a masterful narrative is unveiled that intricately weaves together motifs from seminal religious and literary works such as the Bible/Torah and Dante Alighieri's *Inferno*. This analysis uncovers the careful alignment of *Wonderland*'s characters and plot to the core narratives found within these texts, exploring themes of judgment, redemption, and divine intervention that run parallel to the tales of Abraham, Isaac, Lot, and esoteric figures like Azazel/Lilith. The paper aims to present a nuanced understanding of *Wonderland* beyond its surface narrative, viewing its characters as not merely protagonists within a fictional setting but as representations of a greater metaphysical journey treading the paths of eschatology and biblical ancestry.

I. Introduction

Wonderland emerges as a nuanced literary odyssey, wherein the characters entangle in a complex dance with biblical history and mythological prophecy. Providing an intricate tapestry of sacrificial lore, escapist admonition, and spiritual guidepost narratives, this paper unfolds an intertextual analysis, exploring the depths of *Wonderland*'s allusions to the Bible/Torah and Dante's *Inferno*. Through the critical lens of religion and classical literature, this analysis reveals the novel's allegorical framework, rendering its narrative a contemporary echo of ancient tales of salvation and judgment. Beyond the immediate text, the novel murmurs tales of Babelian overreach and Sodom's sin – a dualistic haunt reminiscent of moral decay and divine wrath. The thesis for this paper is that through its interwoven allusions, *Wonderlana* serves as a modern canvas of redemption, reconstructing timeless narratives of sacrifice and spiritual ordeal to evoke a sense of universal human struggle and the quest for existential meaning.

II. Allegorical Setting and Atmosphere

The haunting cesspool the protagonists navigate through in *Wonderlana* is no mere settlement; it is laid out as a stage mirroring the Circles of Hell as described in the *Inferno*, and a modern-day Babel riddled with despair. This setting, somberly painted as "a cesspool reflecting biblical depictions of Hell," is meaningful far beyond a mere habitation—it is the crucible of the characters' moral fortitude. In this Dantean playground, residents teeter on the brink of perdition, with Weston's outcry, "Everyone's trying to kill us!" piercing the text as a visceral echo of this ceaseless combat within. Here, the reader is presented with a meticulously crafted journey of symbolic darkness, wherein each twist unveils a deeper layer of allegorical depth engaging the inhabitants and land in a spiritual gambit that refracts across multitudes of damning and deliverance narratives.

III. Character Analysis and Biblical Parallels

In *Wonderland*, the characters' journeying is not merely physical but metaphysical, as they grapple with the same existential burdens that weighed upon their biblical counterparts. Cheyenne's Christ-like attributes unfold through a thread of self-sacrifice, drawing a line of parallels from Calvary's cross to her own. Jacob's narrative is a modern reincarnation of Abraham's trials, his defiance against his slaughter preempting a generational upheaval and a defining introspection into a spectacle reminiscent of Sodom's fiery fall. In his quest, Weston embodies the numinous essence of the Holy Ghost, his radios resonating as divine whispers guiding the assembly of the chosen, his solitudes stark against reciprocal loyalties of the other characters. Here, *Wonderland* transforms into a stage where individual characters embody archetypal lore, religious narratives, and cosmic battles between established heritage and individual destiny.

IV. Themes of Sacrifice, Redemption, and Moral Dilemma

Winding around the bend of sacrifice and redemption, *Wonderland* augments its narrative with subtexts rich in ethical crossroads and salvific aspirations. Cheyenne's sanctified conundrums ring with messianic prowess, her fate intertwined with the parables of redemption stretching over millennia. As the manuscript unfolds, the catastrophic ruins forewarned to Lot - with Nancy obliviously succumbing to the saline fate of Lot's wife – evoke a grim alternative to the biblical narrative: Liam's lineage arrests, and his saga concludes in enigmatic silence. Delving into the liminal spaces between sacred scriptures and *Inferno*'s tiers, the tension of divine mercy against human hubris plays out through agonizing choices and ethereal trials woven into *Wonderland*'s fabric.

V. Conclusion

Wonderland reveals its intertextual dimensions as a crucible of ancient and existential contemplations. Each chapter, motif, and character traverses paths laid out in seminal religious works, renegotiating terms of morality, redemption, and divine salvation. This paper has articulated the profundity of *Wonderland*'s biblical and Dantean correlations, elevating the narrative to a canonical dialogue spanning between antiquity and modern literary expanse. Concluding, *Wonderland* champions the enduring relevance of spiritual odysseys, affirming the power of literary works to revivify perennial themes and engage readers with the moral tapestries that unravel within human consciousness and legacy.

www.talesbysk.com

@sham00t

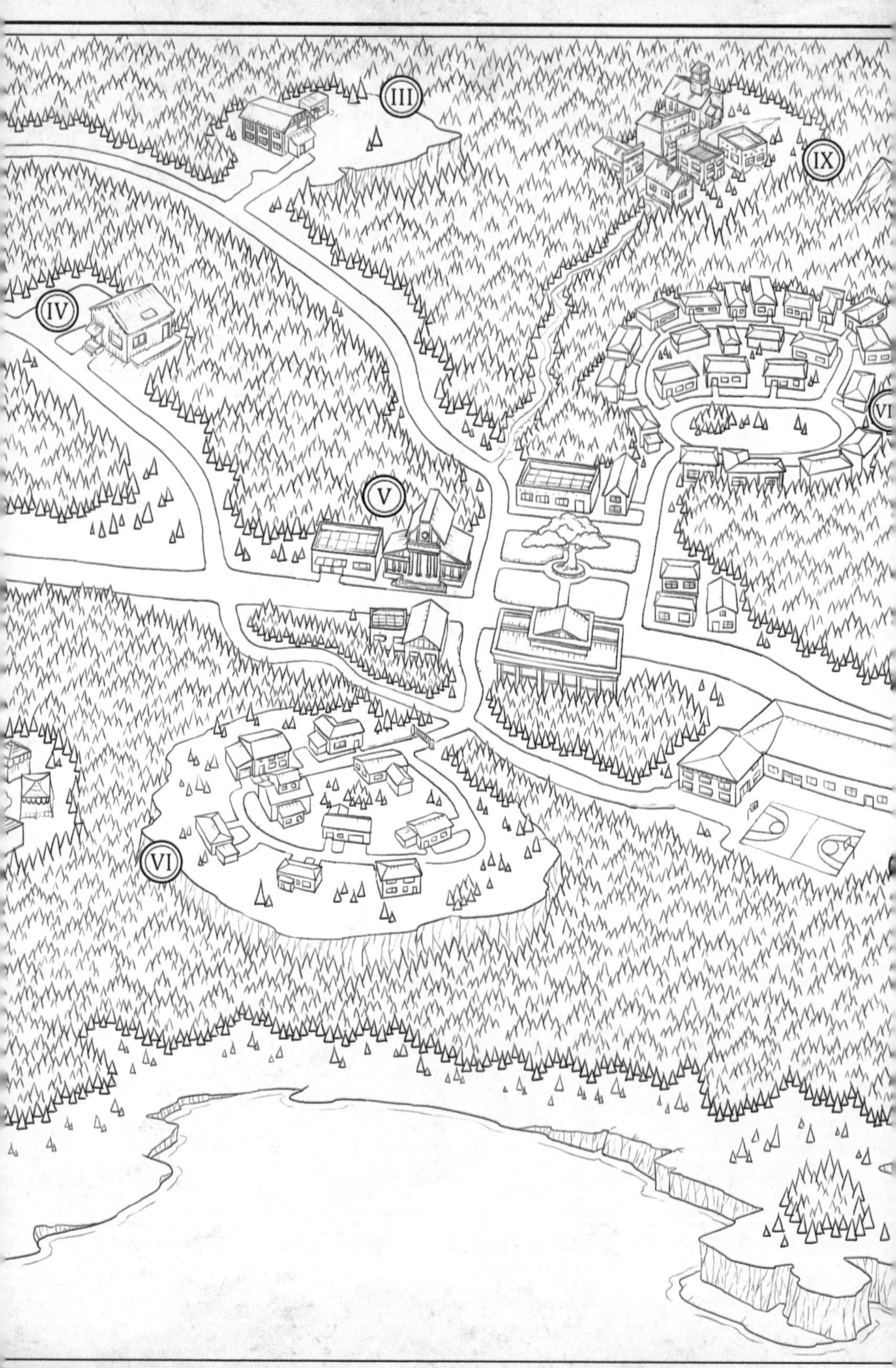

III
IX
IV
V
VI

www.ingramcontent.com/pod-product-compliance
Lightning Source LLC
Chambersburg PA
CBHW020304030826
48979CB00027B/2088/J

* 9 7 9 8 2 1 8 5 7 0 6 5 1 *